The Archetypal Antihero in Postmodern Fiction

Rita Gurung

Published by

7/22, Ansari Road, Darya Ganj,
New Delhi-110002
Phones : +91-11-40775252, 23273880, 23275880, 23280451
Fax : +91-11-23285873
Web : www.atlanticbooks.com
E-mail : orders@atlanticbooks.com

Branch Office
5, Nallathambi Street, Wallajah Road,
Chennai-600002
Phones : +91-44-64611085, 32413319
E-mail : chennai@atlanticbooks.com

ISBN 978-81-269-1356-5

Printed in India at Nice Printing Press, A-33/3A, Site-IV, Industrial Area, Sahibabad, Ghaziabad, U.P.

For my parents

Shri Dhruba Gurung and Smt. Bharati Gurung

Acknowledgements

My sincere and heartfelt thanks to Prof. E.N. Lall, without whose help and guidance, this work would not have been possible. Indeed, I have been very fortunate to have him as my guide and mentor.

I express my gratitude to Dr. Sukalpa Bhattacharjee, Dr. Utpala Sewa, and Prof. Esther Syiem for their kind and timely advice. I would also like to thank Dr. Pandey of CIELF, Shillong Centre and Dr. Nath of Dibrugarh University for allowing me access to valuable books. I acknowledge my thanks to the British Council Library, Kolkata for help in this regard.

I am also very grateful to Dr. N.N. Bora, Rita Namairekpam, Debasish Bora, my friends Deepanjali, Kaveri, and Anupama, my cousin Anju, Krishna and my colleagues in B.B.S. College for their motivation and tremendous support.

This work would not have been a reality without the trust and faith that my family and Amarish, my husband reposed in me. I will never be able to repay their kindness of being with me at times when the completion of this work seemed a distant and unrealisable dream.

And finally, though, there will never be enough words to do so, I bow my head in gratitude to the one who, though invisible, always remained with me, opened windows of opportunity and hope when all doors seemed closed and for giving me the best of guides, the best family and the best of friends. I thank God for letting me keep my faith in Him.

Rita Gurung

Preface

Antihero can be defined as a principal character who lacks noble qualities and whose experiences are without tragic dignity, or a protagonist who lacks the characteristics that would make him a hero. The term archetype denotes a primordial image, character or pattern of circumstances that recur throughout literature, history and thought consistently enough to be considered universal. Postmodern means of or relating to any of the several artistic movements that have challenged the philosophy and practices of modern art, or has amounted to reaction against an order view of the world.

For centuries, heroes and heroic characters have been the focal point of literature and culture. A hero is one who represents honesty, integrity and bravery; one who leads his people away from crisis, is a saviour and a leader. However, with the passage of time, the character of the main protagonist in literature has undergone a radical change—from that of a hero to that of an antihero. This study is an attempt to understand the concept of antiheroism, dismantling the myth of the hero. It also tries to explore the relationship between antiheroism and postmodernism, and explain who is an antihero, why and how does the failure to act in a prescribed and socially accepted manner make one an antihero.

Archetypes have always existed in life as well as in literature. The archetype of the antihero can be found in several cultures and different timeframes throughout the world beginning with Lucifer. In the past, instances of the main protagonist being an antihero were few and far between. The concept of the antihero emerged early in literature but began to gain prominence when the central character began to lose the trappings traditionally associated with heroism. Here, one can cite the example of not only Lucifer but also the Wandering

Jew, Don Quixote, Orestes, Dr. Faustus and many more, down to the very characters discussed in this study. With the antihero, there is an inversion of the heroic codes and values. This study tries to find out as to why there is a proliferation of antiheroic characters in the post-war and postmodern world. This it does by discussing six antiheroes by six different novelists—Jack Merridew by Golding, Seaton by Sillitoe, Mr. Biswas by Naipaul, Mugo by Ngugi, Scoobie by Graham Greene and Molloy by Becket. Though some of these novels are conventional in tone without the extreme use of postmodern narrative and stylistic strategies, their authors' visions of the posthumanist man and the contents are of novelistic defiance. The world has developed technologically but there has been a massive breakdown of religious, social and moral values and securities. At the same time there is a rise of alienation, hedonism, inhumanity, despair, and authoritarianism.

Does God exist? If He does, why does He not interfere at the injustices committed throughout the world? What is freedom? At what price comes freedom? Does living from day-to-day carry the same meaning as being alive? Who or what is a man? Is language capable of coping and expressing the trauma that mankind has to undergo, especially in the last two centuries? Does having knowledge and power free a man from all his responsibilities? These characters try to find answers to these questions and frequently failing to find it, come face to face with the chaos and the void.

Postmodernism has always been a slippery term, being both definite and indefinable, and being contested on several levels. For some it is the rejection of modernism, yet for others it is the taking of modernist strategies to an extreme point. However, it speaks, in all, of the "end of grand narratives of reason, progress and universal emancipation."

The antihero illustrates the concept of *corruptio optimi est pessima* which means the corruption of the best is usually the worst. The postmodern post-war world is no longer an assured place, and it no longer lends itself to an assured definition. The major common ground where antiheroism meets postmodernism is the questioning of the tenet of enlightenment, that man is by nature heroic, reasonable and prone to goodness.

The novels and the characters offer a concise iconography of contemporary and postmodern corruption and disorder in one way or the other. The antihero emerges as a fragmented man deprived of his identity. The parallel evolution of postmodernism and antiheroism seems to announce the end of rational enquiry into truth and the impossibility of an absolute truth. The only way left to the antihero to survive is both to defy and accept the ironic, chaotic and problematic condition that is life today. Thus, the archetypal figure of the postmodern antihero represents our contemporary confusion, despair and the anguish of time, space and destiny.

The book will prove extremely useful to the students and teachers of English literature and researchers in the field of postmodern fiction.

Rita Gurung

Contents

1
Introduction

Archetypes have always existed in literature and in life. An archetype can be defined as a pattern from which all other things of similar nature are made. Archetype/Myth critics are literary critics strongly influenced by the belief that primitive man is yet within us and that myth, ritual, and poetry found in the beginning of every culture have the power to make us aware of the collective experience of the race. Myth provides an important avenue for readers to see beneath the surface of the story. The archetype critic is concerned with these enduring patterns and how these are reflected in works of art.[1]

Carl Jung stated that archetypes are primitive, preconscious, instinctual expressions that are universal and that they derive from the fact that men always undergo common and essential experiences.[2] It is, thus, an expression of our hidden, unconscious life. Freud, who was deeply entrenched in the study of the unconscious, directed his attention primarily to the artist rather than to the art; art, for him, was the working out of the artist's psychic problem. Jung, by contrast, was primarily concerned with the work of art, for the work expressed an archetype, a typical manifestation of the human race.

Archetype[3] is Jung's term for the ever-recurrent road marker of human experience, images, forms, and patterns, symbols, and *rites de passage* that transcend any particular culture. Man is, like other creatures, coded with the experiences of his past, necessary for his survival. Animals have been observed to pass on acquired habits such as mating, territorial aggressiveness, and leadership prerogatives; these experiences are available to each species as unlearned, coded pattern. The code is the archetype, what Jung describes as the "psychic residue of numberless experiences of the same type",[4] experiences which have happened not to an individual but to his ancestors, and of which the results are inherited in the structures of the brain, *a priori* determinants of individual experiences.

Turning away from the speculation of the origin of archetypes and focusing on myth, folklore and literature, one observes that almost all cultures seem to share a pattern, basic system of symbols. In order to systemize these symbols, anthropologists have developed two "monomyths", large overall patterns that contain diverse myths and symbols. These two "monomyths"[5] are the Seasonal Myth and the Myth of the Hero. "Hero" is the high name that we give to those to whom we turn for strength in an effort to find ourselves a motive or in the worse an effort to create in ourselves a conscience.[6] It is the latter myth that mainly concerns us, for the hero is the opposite and mirror image of the antihero. Postwar and postmodern literature seems to be obsessed with the shattering of the second myth.

This study is undertaken to analyze six protagonists of six different novels with an attempt to see them as antiheroes. They are Jack Merridew (Golding, *Lord of the Flies*, 1954), Arthur Seaton (Alan Sillitoe, *Saturday Night and Sunday Morning*, 1958), Mugo (Ngugi, *A Grain of Wheat*, 1968), Mohun Biswas (V.S. Naipaul, *A House for Mr. Biswas*, 1961), Henry Scobie (Graham Greene, *Heart of the Matter*, 1948) and the eponymous Molloy (Samuel Beckett, *Molloy*, 1951). Mention of these characters has been made here to facilitate the identification of the protagonists in the latter part of the study.

The condition of the common man is quite relevant to our study of the antihero. Contemporary man's abject condition and the regressive nature of his humane qualities are mentioned in detail because it is the common man that the antihero reflects, and has come more and more to represent. It will also be helpful for us to remember that traditional heroes were representations of the ideal; the opposite might as well be true for the antiheroes. Societies, institutions, and literature change, but human condition remains the same. The archetypal approach, which tries to understand these changes, is interdisciplinary linking anthropology, psychology, sociology and religion *inter alia*. Leslie Fiedler[7] also states that the archetypal critic is delivered from the temporal bondage, speaking of 'confluences rather than influences' and finding the explication of a given work in things written later as well as earlier than the original piece.

Archetypes repeatedly appear in the cycle of life, exhibiting consistent traits, intentions, functions, and relationships with other characters. Archetypal themes as enumerated by Joseph Campbell and also by Shawcross *et al.* include among others initiation, fall from innocence to experience, the task and the quest. Among the characters in a work of art, the most important and indispensable to the plot is the hero; but today it is the antihero, the antithesis of the hero who holds centre stage in postwar and postmodern literature as more and more authors are dispensing with the hero and also with the conventional plots.

Since this study is concerned with the antihero, as situated in postmodern fiction it would be pertinent to shift the focus to this character. The antihero is described as "a principal character who lacks noble qualities and whose experiences are without tragic dignity".[8] He is also "the non-hero or the antithesis of the old fashioned kind who were capable of heroic deeds, who were dashing, strong, resourceful...he is the person who is given the vocation of failure, a type who is incompetent, unlucky, tactless, clumsy, backhanded and buffoonish".[9] He lacks the qualities of nobility and magnanimity expected of traditional heroes and heroines. A loser, the antihero is an example of "antiheroic ordinariness and inadequacy".[10] However, Baldick also cautions that though the antihero is an ineffectual failure who succumbs to the pressure of circumstances, he should not be confused with the antagonist or the villain. Consequently, one wonders why the antihero appeals to so many people particularly in the modern and the postmodern world. M.H. Abrams[11] contributes to this definition by describing the antihero as a person who "instead of manifesting largeness, dignity and heroism in the face of fate, is petty, ignominious, ineffectual and passive". Does such a character deserve to be the focal point in any work of art, and if so why?

There is usually a disjunction between the perceptual, outside world without and the spirit within. Defining man's nature in terms of fundamental contradiction originating in what he calls the biological dichotomy between missing instincts and self-awareness, one can quote Erich Fromm's statement about man's existential predicament:

> Man is the only animal who does not feel at home in nature, who can feel evicted from paradise, the only animal for whom his own existence is a problem that he has got to solve and from what he cannot escape. He cannot go back to the pre-human state of harmony with nature, and he does not know where he will arrive if he goes forward. Man's existential contradiction results in a state of constant disequilibrium.[12]

The actions and recoils of the contemporary selfengage that dense area of reality where our epochal consciousness and our literary forms meet. Ever since *Don Quixote* (1605), the novel's primary objective has been to show the movement of the self-suggesting regions of tensions and repose in our cultural life. Ever since Cervantes brought Quixote to literary life, the Western novel has subjected idealistic heroism and chivalry to parody.

Corresponding to Fromm's idea and also in a sense, corroborating with it, Ihab Hassan makes the following statement regarding the modern protagonist as the antihero in his *Radical Innocence* (1961):

> ...because part of the mental make-up of the hero of (American) fiction of the past was his ability to mediate between the world and the self, the restlessness and the rebellion of the heroic soul remained quiescent and the

> heroic struggle affirmed the harmony of the inner life of man and the eternal world of God, nature and society. Today, however, the harmony is rapidly disappearing.

Moreover he writes:

> The world at our times seems to have vanished, or become a rigid, intractable mass; the anarchy of nihilism and the terror of staticism delimit the extremes between which there seems to be no viable means. Mediation between the world and the self appears no longer possible; there is only surrender and recoil. In his recoil, the hero has become the antihero.[13]

The concept of the antihero emerged early in literary art but began to take root and gain prominence when the hero conspicuously began to lose the trappings of the traditional heroism and the heroic ideal—the conventional values, the urge for quest and even for new discoveries. According to Lionel Trilling,[14] the particular concern for literature for the last two centuries has been to show that the self has been in a quarrel with culture. Hassan further adds, "the image of the self in its standing, and embittered quarrel with culture—comes into focus in the picture of the antihero".

To understand the antihero in a better light, let us first concentrate on the then indispensable—now dispensable Archetypal Hero. What are the characteristics that bestow upon him the exalted position?

The Hero is an Archetypal figure recorded in works of art throughout history and cultures from all around the world. Traditionally, he represents the old values such as honesty, integrity, courage and bravery. Campbell brings out the several faces of the hero: he cites the hero as a warrior, as a lover, as an emperor, as a leader, as a world redeemer, and as a saint.[15] Naturally, when one comes across the antihero, there will be a total inversion of the aforesaid roles.

A hero means self-sacrifice, even of itself, for the sake of others. Some of these figures undertake fantastic journeys that test their strength, endurance and worth. Some like Christ undergo tremendous suffering for some great heroic purpose.

The hero may be a god-man exemplifying the course of action needed to achieve the task and make the journey successful. Often they reach a level of heroic transcendence in a victory over adversity and their own limitations. The nature of the heroic figure may receive a different emphasis in different periods/eras and in different cultures.

Joseph Campbell demonstrated the universal path of a hero against time and culture. Every society has and needs heroes. They reflect the values we revere, the accomplishments we respect and the hopes that give our lives meaning. By celebrating our heroes, we honour our past, energize our present and shape our future. In studying several known cultures, Campbell discovered that though the details of heroic action change with time, the typical path of a hero could be traced in almost all cultures through three main stages.

I. **Initiation:** into the unknown; beginning of the hero's adventure;

II. **Encounter:** with hardship, rise, failure, loss and discovery; and

III. **Return:** into the fold with something new or better than it was before.

When one comes across the antihero one frequently finds that though they encounter these three stages, their reactions differ starkly from that of the heroes. It is their reaction to these crises and its ironic consequences that reveals their antiheroic nature.

Moreover, in the same book Campbell declares that the cosmogonic cycle is now carried forward not by the gods, who have become invisible, but by the heroes more or less human in character, through whom the world destiny is realized. "The archetypal figures became less and less fabulous, until at last in the final stages of the various local traditions, legend opens into the common daylight of recorded time."[16] This passage apparently delineates a parallel movement in literature, which attests the fact that fiction, both European and non-European, during the last fifteen centuries, has gradually and steadily moved down from the centre of gravity to the low mimetic mode abounding in irony and contradictions. Changing times have created new literary figures. Often heroism seems impossible at certain times, as in the contemporary period, thus, the creation of a contemporary less idealized character has been established. The type of unheroic and ordinary characters that one comes across today may be an announcement that the antihero as a dominant archetype has come to stay.

Heroes classified as Messiah, Saviour or the Christ figure fall under the Prophetic role under the high-mimetic mode protagonists. Literary heroes can be classified as those represented by Achilles in *Iliad* (Homer); Aeneas in *Aeneas* (Virgil), Hamlet and similar literary protagonists who lead their constituents successfully out of danger even though they may themselves die in the process.[17] He, as such, is the hero of tragedy and the epics, the kind of hero Aristotle had in mind. Northrop Frye also categorizes a list wherein he places the ironic hero in the lowest scale. In his *Anatomy of Criticism* (1957), Frye[18] classifies the hero into the following categories:

- If superior in kind both to other men and to the environment of other men, the hero is a divine being.
- If superior in degree to other men and to his environment, he is a typical hero of the romance.
- If superior in degree to other men but not to his natural environment, the hero is a leader.
- If superior neither to other men nor to his environment, the hero is one of us. This is the hero of the low mimetic mode, of most comedies and realistic fiction.
- If inferior in power or intelligence to ourselves, so that we have a sense of looking down on a scene of bondage, frustration and absurdity, the hero belongs to the ironic mode.

This list shows the slide from idealized heroism to ironic antiheroism. It is the last two mentioned categories that concern this study. Mention may be made here that the characteristics of Frye's ironic hero and the hero of the low mimetic mode are similar to our antihero. Thus, from here on the two titles of the ironic hero and the antihero will be used interchangeably.

Not many thinkers have found hope in such conceived messiahs or leaders of men, seeing the rather pessimistic injustices of life. For Nietzsche, Dostoevsky, and Beckett, man is but a pawn in the hands of unseen forces, and thus cannot hope to achieve improvement of his life either through moral or physical action. Here, the protagonist rejects the concept of task, journey and quest and even the possibility of attainment of the soul image and salvation. He thus, often, becomes a demonic figure driven by libido only. Such antiheroes are perhaps best defined in Dostoevsky's *Notes from Underground* (1864).

In earlier times, heroes were religious or God directed, i.e. Moses, later, they became secular and military as Beowulf.[19] With the advent of realism, they became typical representations of their society; however in almost all cultures, heroes remain brave, generous, and socially harmonious. We have no common basis any longer for a heroic ideal and thus the role of those we elevate to be our heroes are constantly changing, and people from the world of science, society, politics as well as show business appeal to the individual requirements of the individual persons today.

In the mythical sphere, the hero was often the repository of power and knowledge, both human and divine, which enabled him to conquer evil and free his people from bondage, destruction, and death. Thus, he was seen as a saviour. However, in the postmodern world of exhaustion, the protagonists rather than being heroes are *schlemiels*,[20] ironic antiheroes who are the apt representatives of the society of failures. In a society where success is measured in monetary terms or that of external affluence, the protagonist often exists in a static state, either unwilling to move ahead or wreaking chaos around himself. Rather than being the centre which binds all the loose threads of society together, the postmodern antihero is himself a victim of alienation, cultural and spiritual sterility, seeking solace and refuge in alcohol, self-deception, power, social withdrawal and anonymity.

Campbell is of the idea that since tribal rites and mysteries have lost their force, their symbols no longer interest us. The notion of a cosmic law, which all existence serves and to which man himself must bend, is now simply accepted in mechanical terms as a matter of course. The shifting of interest throughout the centuries in Occidental sciences from 17th century astronomy to 19th century biology and their concentration on man himself, illustrated by psychology and anthropology in the 20th century, traces the transfer of the focal point of human wonder. Man himself is now the crucial mystery. "Man is that alien presence with whom the forces of egoism must come to terms, through whom the ego is to be crucified and resurrected, and in whose image society is to be reformed".[21] But a failure in faith and hope brings about the transference of the heroic to the antiheroic and of the eternal to the mundane.

The reluctant hero, one upon whom the task of heroism is thrust, may also typify as an antihero. He apparently has no way out except to go by the expectations of the people. One such protagonist can be seen in David Wagoner's ironically titled poem "The Hero with One Face".[22] In this poem, the protagonist is given several tasks which he, as hero is supposed to perform. But these are thrust upon him not because of his heroic qualities but because of the fact that he was born. In the context of the failure of the task by the antihero, Shawcross says, "achievement of the task makes one worthy of the quest and the journey or actually the quest or the journey". Today, in the postmodern times, "when literature often presents not heroes but antiheroes, protagonists may ruin the task they are to perform so as to oppose the mythically heroic."[23] One of the antiheroes, Mugo, in this study is one such reluctant hero. In Ngugi's *A Grain of Wheat* (1963), Mugo is the reluctant hero. The task to lead the people is thrust upon him. He is burdened by the expectations of the people upon him. However, the guilt and the realization of his self-delusion finally lead him to reject the role of the hero-leader.

The gradual process of atrophy of the hero perhaps began with Don Quixote or even before him with Job, and Orestes. The genesis of the archetype, the seeds can be traced back to the biblical character of Satan, the arch-antihero, and Cain, the social outcast, the Old Testament counterpart of the Wandering Jew. Antiheroes have emerged early in the history of literature. As far back as the 16th century, Christopher Marlowe's Dr. Faustus, the overreacher held centrestage. A more famous and comic instance can be found in Don Quixote, the eponymous hero who raises difficult questions regarding appearance and reality, the ineffectual knight who attempts to do his best to save the world but commits folly whenever he acts. Henry Fielding's *Tom Jones* (1749) set the trend rolling in the picaresque tradition, where the picaroon undergoes several mollifying experiences before he identifies his true vocation or discovers his true identity.

A critical phase emerged in the late 18th century. Goethe's Werther (*The Sorrows of Young Werther*, 1774) introduced the tragic romantic hero, who in his inordinate conception of himself severs the traditional bond between himself/the hero and the society and who points the way to such extreme instances of alienation which later found expression in the Byronic and the Sadean heroes. A similar sense of alienation is also felt by Ngugi's Mugo, who sees himself as Moses, bringing about a break-up from the very community he dreams of leading. Later the heroes of Stendhal, Balzac, and Flaubert often seem, as Raymond Giraud has recognized as "'heroes of ironies', whose ideals of desires and feeling are in disharmony with their adult conception of reality".[24]

Even Victorian fiction was disposing off the heroic protagonist with the signs perhaps appearing with Thackeray's *Vanity Fair*, curiously subtitled *The Novel Without a Hero* (1847-48). The ambivalence of a bourgeois hero in a middle class society raises for the character, serious problems of estrangement and communion, sincerity and simulation, ambition and acquiescence, which we recognize as the patent themes of the 19th century. Victim to immitigable cosmic laws with little control over his own fate in the world, man turns inward again. Mario Praz[25] in *The Hero in Eclipse in Victorian Fiction* (1956) concludes "Disillusioned observations of life as it really was, led to the eclipse of the hero and the disclosure of man's swarming internal world made up of disparate and contradictory things."

The antihero embodies deviations from the heroic standards of the day. He may be an oaf, boorish (Mr. Biswas, or even Arthur Seaton) in an age doting on politeness, or he may be the degenerate Lovelace in Richardson's *Clarissa* (1747). With more flexibility permitting proper heroes, authors had to go further afield in search of striking antiheroes. An *avant-garde* self-destructive antihero of the 20th century can be seen in Conrad's *Lord Jim* (1900). From Joyce's dubious Leopold Bloom, we have fallen or risen with Camus' effect free stranger, Genet's homosexual pickpockets, Celine's psychopaths, Herman Hesse's hallucination ridden Henry Haller to Saul Bellow's Herzog.[26]

The change in the depiction of the hero to an antihero led D.H. Lawrence to write to Edward Garnett "you must not look in my novel for the stable old ego of the character. There is another ego, according to whose action the individual is unrecognizable, and passes through, as it were, allotropic states".[27] This was in reference to the new kind of character, more commensurate with the unreliable, but real human nature. A new shifty ego, the new concept of man emerges; the history of the antihero is nothing more than the history of man's changing awareness of himself.

With the retrenchment of the individual, the drama of good and evil, objectified by the hero and villain, becomes blurred. The traditional forms of moral conflict are so internalized that victory or defeat can claim to be more than pyrrhic. The passionate, bitter concern of the modern antihero remains to become someone, to know what one is, to reach another human being with love. Antiheroism emerges with the encounter of the new ego with the destructive element of experience. The antihero represents the dominance of the libido. He may manifest the "wisdom of Silenus".[28] Frequently, the antihero rejects the structure of the life cycle, the concept of task, quest, and journey, and the belief in the attainment of the soul image.

In his *Anatomy of Criticism* (1957), Northrop Frye depicts the antihero in the ironic mode, generally inferior in power or intelligence, so that one often has the sense of looking down on a scene of bondage, frustration and absurdity. This mood rings true when the reader feels that he might be in the same situation as it is being judged by the norms of greater freedom. The central character no longer retains the exalted idealism—rather he becomes one of us—*homme moyen sensual.*

The characteristics and qualifications of the antihero, apparently the opposite to that of the hero features spiritual aridity, mundane lives, failure, attraction towards evil and chaos; thus we have indecisive and bumbling, ineffectual and clumsy protagonist in literature today, illustrated by the characters here, be it Biswas, Molloy, Scobie, Mugo, or Seaton. Life and the world for him are *de trop,* which however exacts more energy than he has in his personality.

> No one can define for sure what the new protagonist exactly stands for. He is not exactly the liberal's idea of the victim, nor the conservative's idea of the pariah, nor the radical's idea of the rebel. A victim of angst and existentialism, perhaps he is all of these and none in particular. Suffering from dread and anxiety, he encounters the void and often fails to find justification for the choices he/she makes. His capacity for pain seems saintly and his passion for heresy almost criminal. But flawed in his sainthood and grotesque in his criminality, he appears as an expression of man's quenchless desire to affirm, despite the void and vicissitudes of our age, the human sense of life.[29]

The antiheroic figure, according to Ihab Hassan, refers to an assembly of victims—the fool, the failure, the clown, the hipster, the poor and the freak, the outsider, the scapegoat, the rebel without a cause, the 'hero' in the ashcan, the 'hero' in the leash, etc.[30] If the antihero nowadays seems to hold us in his spell, it is because the deep and disquieting insights revealed to us by modern literature often require that we project ourselves into the predicament of the victims. The major writers of the 20th century, Kafka, Sartre, Camus, Beckett *et al.* as well as that of the latter part of the preceding century felt that the idea of man's alienation is axiomatic and for them the ontological problem of man's being—the encounter with nothingness—is the cardinal question. In this particular sense, our awareness of the modern experience is supremely existential. Not only that, but the antihero also suffers from a split in his personality—the split of a man into fragmented mind and body, with the two divisions often moving in opposite directions.

For Shawcross, the antihero is one who does not accept the ambivalences of life,[31] but more often than not who does not often seek to assert his self and even often attempts to counter or thwart the task of the hero. Contradictorily there are some antiheroes who try to assert themselves too forcefully. The latter espouses the demonic and may become the Satan—devil figure, streaks of which are present in Golding's Jack Merridew. In fact, Merridew identifies himself with pride, evil and the destructive instinct. Merridew, the dark god and Dionysus incarnate, thrives on chaos. In one of the most visual scenes, one finds that Jack likes hunting, not as much for food or for survival but for the pure thrill of being a hunter. In another of Golding's novel, *Pincher Martin,*[32] Martin's pride, time and again leads him to assert that it is his will which keeps him alive and gives him an identity. The rejection of salvation and of God's presence, even when he is given a second chance, makes Martin too a satanic antihero.

The archetypal characters represent man in his journey through life. The various forms of mythic patterns that play in and out of literature help us to comprehend the intricacies of man's archetypal and mythic mind. It is thus but natural that in this postmodern age, the antihero should represent exhaustion and chaos. He is one who is deeply afflicted by existential concerns and nihilism. He, the representative contemporary man knows that there is no way out of life, since his reach, the horizon of his awareness so often exceeds his grasp. The antihero has thus become a dominant archetypal character in the contemporary world. His condition is symbolic of the universal human condition. Frye's characterization of the antihero in the ironic mode gains in concreteness as he becomes identified, on the one hand, with the ritual alazon, eiron and the pharmakos[33] and on the other, with the existential hero.

The antiheroes studied here are more or less steeped in existential philosophy. Existentially speaking, each man is what he chooses to make himself, he cannot escape responsibilities for his character or deeds by claiming that they are pre-determined consequences of factors beyond his power to control or resist, nor can he justify that what he does in terms of external or objective standards are imposed from without. If both Fredrick Nietzsche in the 19th century and John Paul Sartre in the 20th century declared the "Death of God",[34] the antihero emphasizes the theme in modern European and American literature. In a universe where life is meaningless and anxiety the only reasonable mood in the face of ultimate oblivion, the heroic themes that have existed till now begin to dissipate. The Socratic advocacy of the 'virtuous life' becomes obscure in the ambiguities of relative 'good' and 'evil'. Individual relativism, the proper posture for the modern period, justifies only personal commitment and self-motivated action. That 'existence' precedes 'essence', the theme of existentialism dismisses as meaningless all the comforting absolutes of both science and religion that have come before and isolates the individual in a 'community of one', i.e. nothing can be more lonely than the person who must confront his death in a universe that does not care. In such a modern temper where does the hero stand?

The modern temper admits that men are mortal. Paradoxically on the one hand, despair and destruction characterize the artist, on the other, this destructive element is put to constructive use. Both elements emerge in the new figure of the contemporary, ironic hero. The concept of the antihero becomes anti-logocentric.

The main problem of the antihero is essentially one of identity. His search is for existential fulfilment, both of freedom and of self-definition. Society may often modulate his awareness, but only existence determines his stand, the recoil is a way of taking a stand. The retreat weakens his involvement in the living world leading one to a life of violence and alienation, augmenting his sense of guilt and absurdity. In the succeeding chapters one can observe the point to which the antiheroes will stretch in order to assert their identities and gain acknowledgement, as in the case of Biswas, Mugo, Merridew, and Seaton; and the limit to which one can reach in order to nullify one's identity in search of anonymity and solitude, exemplified by the characters of Molloy and Scobie.

In its recoil, the modern self has once more discovered that all truths must be bloody and personal truths, one experienced in anguish, pain and action. Hassan quotes Nathan A. Scott, Jr.'s observation: "What every reporter on the present condition has to take into account is the sense that men have today of being into the nudity of their own isolated existence."[35]

The antiheroes' inability to mediate between the external society and the internal world and between the outer and the inner real self leads to the splitting of their personalities. Often the significance of the act of fragmentation reaches far beyond pathological behaviour: it confronts us with the unspeakable fact of pain in the world. Schizophrenia entails the withdrawal of libido from real objects and its reversion back to the ego. Indeed, reversion has become the postmodern attitude towards history. The social and political experiences of the 20th century reveal two contradictory tendencies at work: the unrelenting organization as society and the unleashing of vast destructive energies against civilization.

Schizophrenia usually results in madness, as one can see in the condition of the paranoid Mugo who time and again reverts to fantasy as a method of trying to cover the bitter truth of betrayal from himself. The conflict that arises between pain and pleasure, between self and reality, and between power and love receives full recognition in Freud's *Civilization and Its Discontents* (1930). He reaches the conclusion that:

> ...the price of progress in civilization is paid in projecting happiness through the heightening of the

> sense of guilt. Conscience becomes more intolerant, repression stronger, guilt harsher. Guilt produces aggression towards the self.[36]
>
> .... Every impulse of aggression, which we omit to gratify, is taken over by the Superego and goes to heighten the aggressiveness.[37]

Aggression breaks when guilt is swollen to an intolerable degree. Freud also supports the idea that the sense of guilt is an expression of the conflict due to ambivalence, the eternal struggle between Eros and Thanatos, the life and the death instinct. Mugo's guilt in *A Grain of Wheat* arises from this tension, with the conflict that begins as soon as men are faced with the task of living together. In certain situations forcing an individual to live a communal life and abide by the communal ethos may have unwanted consequences. Along with Mugo, instances may be cited of Mr. Biswas and Merridew.

Freud's idea of the death instinct suggests that the self is not only opposed to the world but is divided within itself. Man in this pessimistic view is as much his own victim as he is a victim of society. In this context, Hassan quotes Theodore Reik's argument, "machoism, that malady of the modern man compounds fantasy with rebellion".[38] When there is the undifferentiated consciousness, man is at home in his universe. Later awareness and gradual emergence of self-consciousness leads to the fragmentation bringing about the loss of innocence, of wholeness, and spontaneity, leading to infected will, a terrible sense of responsibility and the onset of guilt. An attenuation of senses and a deprivation of the inner harmony leads to the descent from essential harmony to essential chaos.

Man's rise to consciousness has ensured his survival and contributed to his evolution but it comes with a price. He has become alienated both from the true self and the universe moving steadily further from his true self. On the one hand, Darwin saw this movement anthropologically as a successful form of evolution. On the other hand, a writer like Golding viewed it metaphysically, as a failure. Thus, the 'Descent of Man' as propounded by Darwin is inverted and interpreted in Golding's works not only literally, but also in the theological sense of the Fall. With reference to his discussion of Golding's works V.V. Subbarao[39] brings forward Gabriel Josiporici's observation that the new world is an illustration of the observations of such thinkers as Freud and Nietzsche that greed, envy, and lust are the inevitable concomitants of civilization.

But here the question that needs to be asked is: What makes the modern man, the true antihero, the victim of the world? Ihab Hassan has assigned the role of the rebel-victim to the antihero. In *Radical Innocence* (1961) he brings out the fact that:

> ...man seems to have overcome contradictions of his experience in destructive or demonic element, by assuming the role of the antihero, the rebel-victim. The rebel denies without saying No to life, the victim succumbs without saying Yes to oppression. Both acts are, in a sense, identical; they affirm the human against the non-human. The figure of the modern man, when he chooses to assert his full manhood, always bears the brave indissoluble aspect of Prometheus and Sisyphus, the eternal rebel and the eternal victim.[40]

Hassan's approach towards the antihero is uncompromising. In a critique of Hassan's idea, C.C. Walcutt[41] says that the *Radical Innocence* represents the quality of the passion of the antihero. This Radical Innocence is the property of every anarchic self. It is the innocence of a self that refuses to accept the immitigable rule of reality, including death, an aboriginal self the radical imperatives of whose freedom cannot be stifled. However, one can ask, how can a victim gather enough strength to rebel?

The acceptance of the situation, of the punishment, by the victim becomes, as it were a stoic challenge to the punishing authority. Acceptance of the suffering Prometheus-Sisyphus like situations shows his defiant stance against freedom and authority. It shows his stoicism in accepting his hopeless position as if it were to turn defeat into a kind of moral victory. However, the rebel-victim represents a single embodiment of the eternal dialectic between the Primary Yes and the Primary No. Hassan's view of the ironic hero as a rebel-victim is supported by the fact that the contemporary world presents a continued affront to man, and thus his response as a rebel or a victim, living as he is under the shadow of death is inevitable. The contemporary postmodern world reveals that escape is not possible and that nothing really exists beyond the invisible prison walls. The contemporary self recoils from the world having discovered the absurdity of life. The destructive element in the life of the antihero reflects the harsh reality in our own age. The quality of his passion, like that of his awareness is radical and extreme, troubled with vision. Furthermore, the disparity between the innocence of the hero and the destructive nature of his experiences defines his concrete, existential situation.

The imperative of suffering and rebellion constitutes the modern response to some grim and strange developments in the 20th century. History, philosophy, and psychology have inquired seriously, time and again, into the cause of the modern distemper and the answers are not far to seek. Man's awareness of his history has caused him much shame. Imperialism, urbanization, and mechanization of elemental life are often the precursors of such dissolution. The idea that man must always work against nature and in a recurring process is the one that defines his predicament in radical terms.

The modern self oscillates between sainthood and absolute nihilism. Hassan states that the modern antihero does not have the privileges of the traditional heroes.

> In the encounter with absurdity, with death, with chaotic anarchy and nothingness, it tries to discourage ways of affirmation that the earlier traditional heroes did not envision.[42]

One can see clearly that the modern antihero stands between the creations of Blake and Marquis de Sade, both of whom prefigure as the two sides of the coin—the saint and the criminal sides of man. Awareness of one's paradoxical condition brings consciousness and guilt together. The burden of freedom becomes too heavy for the ironic hero to carry. His world is characterized by the ironic affinity between consciousness and guilt. Consciousness brings man individual freedom and responsibility—both a blessing and a curse. Sartre saw man as a creature condemned to be free, with a kind of freedom where he is allowed with no choices except to accept it or to fight against it, he is accountable for all his acts, because of which there is a tragic friction in his soul.

Joseph Conrad also envisions the fate of man as a solitary being who must suffer and endure his trails and tribulations alone. The only way to compromise with this absurd situation is to submit oneself to the chaos.

> A man that is born falls into a dream like a man falls into a sea. If he tries to climb out into the air as inexperienced people often endeavor to do so he drowns. The only way is to the destructive element submit yourself....[43]

This submission to the destructive element is true both in the case of the artist and the contemporary protagonist-man. The unintelligible/unintelligent brutality of existence leaves man with no choice. Alan Sillitoe feels that this perhaps is the best way to exist. Arthur Seaton, the antihero in Sillitoe's *Saturday Night and Sunday Morning* (1958), submits to the incomprehensible chaos around him. Any attempt to understand this chaos results in further confusion. According to Seaton, man is just like a fish bound to be baited one day. The freedom enjoyed by the victim is just an illusion making his fate cheerless. In our age man seems to have become aware that his humanity rests precisely on the fact that he is an unredeemed and unredeemable creature. To his condition in the universe he must always cry 'No' even while yielding to its inevitability.

Unlike his classic predecessors, the ironic antihero is not created in the social image. It is now the altered apprehension of the self, the changed position of the society that defines the character of the new hero. This generic hero fulfills his destiny by mediating between the contradictions to which we are heir, and mediates between them in the process of his initiation, his discovery, which often leads him to the brink of defeat. Here one may point out the relation that exists between the creation of the antihero as a dominant archetype and the postmodern condition in which he is sustained. The antiheroes that one comes across in these novels are alienated and asocial by nature and in certain cases like that of Mugo and Merridew are in fear of being overshadowed by the other. In this context, mention may be made of the fact that in modernism, man was seen as being unable to enter into social relationships with others. Since these antiheroes are viewed in the postmodern perspective of estrangement, it may be mentioned that in the postmodern context, as exemplified by these antiheroes, this alienation and separation becomes the central, inescapable fact of existence. The paradigm of form in contemporary fiction may be the pattern of encounter; the shifting, straining encounter of the rebel-victim with the destructive experience. The radical innocence of the 'antihero', his deep awareness of life, makes him a throwback to a pre-social condition of the mythic struggles.[44] It is not surprising that the ironic antihero should discover some archaic and regressive qualities which remained in disguise while the novel enjoyed the loyalties of bourgeois society especially during the placid Victorian era.

Unlike the ancient hero who is somewhere below the gods and above the common run of men, the antihero is a religious symbol without religion, a mythic figure without the benefits of myth. In him, the essence of the world and the essence of the self are not one and the same; the broken pattern of all his action recalls the futile courage of a Sisyphus toiling to unite one pole of experience with the other. He is no longer the representative of all the divine powers that men want to propitiate; he is now merely the mediator of forces that torment their existence. Insulted and injured, his strategy is more often sub-human than super-human.[45] Yet if the antihero seems mythic in the sacrificial quality of his passion his actions have the concrete self-definition of an existential encounter.

The existential pattern implies a view of life that may be traced back to Job, but it is neither less distinctive for that nor does its historical reach diminish its peculiar relevance to our experience. Major writers of the contemporary period have often placed the existential pattern of the experience at the centre of their work. And this is perhaps where the lines of existentialism and postmodernism converge, for while having a tremendous impact on postmodernism, existentialists also placed the centrality of the individual narrative as being the source of one's values, morals and understanding. The character of the antihero, and the insolence and contradictions of his life can be understood if his life is seen in the context of the existential pattern.

The new type of hero is both a child of doom and opposition; his character is defined by the ironic tension between the ageless mythical function and the modern spirit of skepticism. There are certain functions that an individual is expected to perform, this is especially true when he holds a central position, it may include leading the community and bringing hope and renewal to it. But the alienation of the antihero generally brings about a failure of these expectations. The traditional rites of initiation and quest and the existential ordeal culminate either in the isolation of the hero or in his defeat. This existential pattern is the language of experience, a different mould of expression.

Along with the search for identity, another existential question is one of freedom. Freedom is known to the hero of Dostoevsky's *Notes* only as a caprice, he understands that men must seek freedom and must be repelled and horrified by it. Seaton finds the concept of freedom meaningless and ambivalent; it exists in his world only as an idealized word. Freedom for Golding's Merridew means destruction of anyone who obstructs his path while he seeks for meaning to justify his stand. For Scobie, it means choosing to end his life over living it. Freedom consists of revolt against morality, against the social order, against history, but it demands a blood-curdling price that only heroes and superheroes can afford to pay. Arthur Seaton, for instance, finds shocking behaviour the only way of asserting his individuality. Though Sillitoe's sympathy is strongly with him, yet he, socially seen, is not the substance heroes are made up of, unless one sees his drinking, puking and seducing spree as a form of heroism.

The antihero, more often than not, fails to rise to idealized expectations. Both Biswas and Mugo fail to rise to their expectations and dreams. The latter fails in his quest for peace and security; utterly isolated, Mugo realizes that "the last person to claim him is dead". Similarly, Naipaul undermines Biswas's achievement repeatedly. Even though he finally succeeds in getting a house, Naipaul reminds us time and again that it is a squat sentry box, which is heavily mortgaged. Thus, it is his defeat, more than his achievement, which is frequently emphasized.

Unlike the heroes of classical tragedy, the antiheroic protagonists act in the full knowledge of their fatality. There is never any reconciliation. Thus, Sartre's Roquentin (*The Nausea*, 1938) suffering from metaphysical disgust comes to believe that existence itself is superfluous. Nothing happens in his life, nothing begins or ends, and everything simply exists in a limbo, rooted in the Absurd, the irreducible condition of all reality. Man becomes not only a clown or a transit compromise, he becomes for one, an eventuality of existence.

The victim, like the hero, has a thousand faces, and this is because human response in culture manifests itself in a thousand levels and he attempts to reconcile these layers of perception. The victim, the fool, the rebel and the holy gull are the representative heroes of our time. His condition is the test case of our moral and aesthetic life.

The figure of the archetypal antihero can be identified in the Biblical figure of Satan, the archangel of God. He is probably the first antihero because the heroic in him yields to the perverted. This view is strongly supported by Milton's identification with Lucifer in *Paradise Lost*. Satan anticipates the figure of the antihero in a peculiar way. Taking Hassan's yardstick of the 'rebel-victim' one can put forward the view that in several ways Satan himself is a rebel-victim. Firstly he acknowledges God, the Creator, to be supreme who has evicted him from Heaven. He admits that God is omnipotent and that his own revolt is unjustified. His pride makes him reject the very thought of submission. His position is a *la Sisyphus*. He attempts to thwart all good but also has the knowledge that it will all come to naught. Secondly, his pride stops him from seeking forgiveness, his gateway back to Heaven, all he has to do is to ask and God will forgive him. But for him, it is better to rule in Hell than be a servant in Heaven. If one believes in destiny, then perhaps to suffer like Lucifer is also destined. Perhaps, he is the first true existentialist, for an outcast from God's Heaven; he has the awareness that he is an isolated being, cast into an alien universe which possesses no inherent truth, value or meaning. His life, moving thus from nothingness to void defines an existence which comes across as both anguished and absurd. It is the anguish of one who has the foreknowledge that all his actions will be meaningless but yet has to act. He is one in whom evil is mixed with good but who is doomed to destruction by the flaw of self-love. He embodies the fortitude, the steadfast hate, and the implacable resolution which are founded on despair;[46] qualities that cannot be imitated or admired; qualities that can be noticed in the characters of Merridew and Mugo.

Alienated from what he deems as his rightful place, the Satan figure transforms into a representation of the force that opposes the good doer, the hero and the achievement of his task or of his libido as antagonist to the superego. It is symbolic of evil and darkness, often including destruction, descent, and death. This antagonism of the hero turns this proud character into the archetypal antihero. The satanic element within one will attempt to submerge the heroic unless it is recognized and controlled. The outcast has strong affinities with the satanic antihero such as Ishmael or Captain Ahab. However, the outcast often becomes the conscience of the community by becoming its destructive force. Characters such as Hawthorne's Ethan Brand, Ngugi's Mugo and even Claude McKay's Outcast in the eponymous poem fulfill this role.

Cain and the Wandering Jew can also be taken as a prototype of the antihero. As pariah, this social outcast was cursed to wander the ends of the world without finding solace for his anguish. This prototype of Cain corresponds, in the 20th century, to the victim of the exiles and diasporas who are left free to roam the world but cannot claim any piece of earth as home.

Confounding the hero and the outcast is the scapegoat, who takes upon himself the sins of the people and who thereby removes it from the people. He himself is sacrificed, most frequently through his death, but at least through his destruction, as a potential hero. In one way, both Samson and Hamlet were scapegoats but whose antitype is Jesus Christ himself, who is the archetype of the incongruously ironic, the perfectly innocent victim excluded from human society.[47]

Thus, according to both Frye and Hassan, the opposite of the incongruously ironic is the inevitable ironic. Hassan cites Adam as an example of the latter, of human nature under the shadow of death. Between Christ and Adam, between incongruous ironic and inevitable ironic, lies Job, "A would-be rebel whose failure, unlike that of Prometheus, is more absurd than tragic." It is him, in his self-taught irony, who represents the latter than Christ and Adam the archetype of the existential man,[48] the antihero.

Georg Buchner's *Woyzek* (1837)[49] illustrates the picture of the man as unheroic, as pawn, and as a born loser, just as the same picture Bellow depicted of a man in *Herzog* (1964). Eliot's *Prufrock* (1918) shows us ordinary men beaten and bogged down by the sheer weight of life—its repetitions and darkness, and its meaninglessness.

Singer's *Gimpel* (1957)[50] personifies the Wise Fool, who perhaps with Lear's Fool, maintains innocence and does good through a lack of knowledge of evil, which nonetheless is not fully the case with the latter. Generally, the Wise Fool has no knowledge of the negative aspects of life and from his own innate goodness tries to discover the essence of the soul image.

The Great War, 'the war to end all wars', 'the war to make the world safe for democracy' shattered many of the assumptions of the Christian nation, and the phrase 'special providence' all but dropped out of the devotional literature of the mainline Protestant dominations. In *Archetypes of the Collective Unconscious*,[51] Jung demonstrates that our spiritual poverty and our symbollessness have brought us to the verge of the silent void. During and after the war psychologically battered soldiers mingled with the disillusioned, expatriated American intellectuals in the European coffee houses of Paris, London and even Madrid, re-examining with cynicism the old verities and truths of the heart that were worth writing about, worth all the agony and the sweat. World War I had the hero adrift across the sea of ambiguities and irreconcilable ironies. Often this is the content of the antihero. The ironic antihero usually acts without cause or value, staring at nothing, and trying to find meaning in the dark corners of Eliot's Wasteland.

It was perhaps natural that the war should have provided writers who had just climbed out of their uniforms with an experience large and trembling enough to compel the fictional imagination. Novelists of the generation of Hemingway and Dos Passos found in the war a symbol of general collapse as well as personal disillusionment. But the next generation entered World War II with few illusions, what they saw before them was not only the collapse of the old order but also a frightening prophecy of the future. The legacy of war, senseless violence, alienation from self, society and nature threatened to define the condition of man in the contemporary world.

Dostoevsky's hero from the underground reveals that it is perhaps upon itself that the modern self likes to gnaw. He knows that "there is no one even for you to feel vindictive against, that you will have not...an object for your spite...".[52] The hero understands a revolt against "the whole legal system of Nature, but then there is no one to blame".[53] This is what Camus describes as "metaphysical rebellion",

> ...rebellion though apparently negative, since it creates nothing, is profoundly positive in that it reveals the part of man, which must always be defended. Rebellion therefore is an aspiration to order, a means of lifting pain and evil from personal to collective experience. For the rebel-victim, the Cartesian argument is 'I rebel, therefore I exist'.[54]

When the forces of moral energy move so far from the centre of human effort in the world, losing itself in the domain of holy silence or demonic violence, it is then that anxiety takes over. The disassociation of action is nowhere more evident than in Dostoevsky's *Notes* and in *Molloy* where the protagonists condemn active life. The consequences also involve the alienation of the moral and aesthetic imagination from things in this world, often leading to a criminal state of autonomy. For Golding's Merridew, action does not necessarily mean welfare. He is one who reaches the domain of demonic violence, and tries to exculpate himself of his crimes by hiding behind the painted mask externalizing the non-existent Beast.

In Joyce's *Ulysses* (1922), the propositions of the hero are further shrunken; his self pushed further underground into the world of memory and fantasy. The element, to which Bloom submits himself, in humour and humanity, is the ignominious element. Insult and pathos, loneliness and failure are his familiars. Leopold Bloom, wandering Jew, mock Odysseus, and lonely Christ, finally appears as "Everyman or No man".[55] It is perhaps on *Ulysses'* odyssey that Beckett models his *Molloy*. A lonely and forlorn man is the antihero as described as the modern self under recoil. He not only abandons the idea of living a normal life but also goes to the extent of negating everything around him. In a way, he is a metaphysical clown. The heroes of Dostoevsky, Joyce and Beckett show that humanity lies on the other side of spite.

The idea of man as a transient compromise in the universe entails the acceptance of permanent outrage. However, writers like Mauriac, Bernanos and Graham Greene sought for their characters a solution more commensurate with their religious faith: for as Colin Wilson has noted the "problem of the modern man, rebel within and outside, lends itself to an intense religious apprehension...".[56]

Another important aspect of the antihero is role-playing. Ihab Hassan, who described the antihero as a rebel-victim, also regards him as an actor and a sufferer. An outsider, a demonic and sacrificial figure, anarchic, grotesque, innocent and clowning, the antihero wavers between martyrdom and frenzied self-affirmation.

> Thus the rebel-victim incarnates the eternal dialectic of the Primary Yes and the Primary No, and his function is to create those values whose absence in culture is the cause of his predicament and ours.[57]

His morality is essential, full of ironies and contradictions. According to Hassan,[58] like the ancient hero with a thousand faces, the rebel-victim too has many guises, among which are cited the relevant ones:

I. The young lover/dreamer, caught in the opposition of instinct and society, in those of his own dreams;
II. The comic rogue, traveling through a crowded life with nerve, but finding for himself neither home nor mate;
III. The grotesque, insisting on his particular vision of things, thrusting reality to confirm to the distortions of his own spirit;
IV. The stubborn underdog, the poor and the under-privileged, defying the oppression of some systems;
V. The disinherited man, finding no end to alienation;
VI. The Black, outsider within his own country, trying to create for himself, beyond hatred and guilt, an identity;
VII. The nihilist, cosmic and futile jester, vaudevillian of the dark calling all life into question.

To this exhaustive list we can also add the following:[59]

- The hero in the guise of the self-deprecating eiron, enjoying a limited degree of freedom, he makes an uneasy truce with necessity. However, the ironic mode hovers between comedy and tragedy.
- The hero in the guise of the rebel, rouge, picaro or the self-inflating alazon. Enjoying a considerable amount of freedom, he gives the illusion of escaping from reality.

The antiheroes here, especially Seaton, Mugo and Biswas, are a curious combination, having the qualities of both an eiron and an alazon.

At a simultaneous level as the development of the antihero, there is also the rise of the antiroman; while the former defies the novelistic content, the latter may be regarded as a protest against the pattern of novelistic forms. It was in postwar literature that the antihero became a predominant character in fiction and stage plays, especially in the ones by Amis, Wain, Sillitoe, Osborne, Pinter, Beckett and Braine among others. Antiheroes generally reject the codes and standards of conduct or social behavior formerly held to be essential in civilized society. Some deliberately revolt against the standards and regard the modern world as a jungle in which the law of tooth and nail prevail (Arthur Seaton, Jack Merridew); others are unaware of even the presence of standards (the Beckettian tramps); others having been taken away early from proper environment, become stranded intellectually and emotionally, turn bitter and despise what they cannot grasp (Mugo). Antiheroes of another sort appear in the novels of Graham Greene (Henry Scobie) where addiction to sin, mortal or merely shabby, but always unheroic, is the doorway to redemption.

The fictional antihero is an outsider because of the very condition of life of his consciousness requires estrangement. The forms of estrangement, however, evolved curiously in the postwar years. This period was a spent universe, ruled by entropy, and seemingly moving towards apocalypse. Caught in the web of metaphysical absurdity, as the ironic hero attempts to mediate between the contradictions of culture and to create a new consciousness, so does the form of the novel attempt the same task on a deeper level. Hassan describes the condition by which the alienated man dictates the form of the novel:

> The dialectal forces of history and society affect our idea of the self. A new type of hero emerges, and from the two critical moments in his encounter with experience, and the moments of initiation or defeat, the form of fiction takes shape.[60]

According to Walcutt,[61] this is clearly a condition in which the situation of the hero is a plight, a spiritual tension, rather than a place in an action. The disparity between the innocence of the hero and the destructive nature/character of his experience defines his concrete or existential position. Realism and surrealism, comedy and tragedy, expression and symbol tend to fuse in evasive forms equal to the complexities of the day. Between the irrational force of the human instincts and the insane powers of the world, the novel strikes its own incongruous bargains with terror and slapstick, poetry and fantasy. The language of the novel mimes its way to desperate truths, dangerously veering towards absolute silence.

Again, literature of the 1945's postwar era began to open itself to a jagged and grotesque sense of reality, and the novel leading the way, reinvents the gothic and the picaresque modes. The religious will of the 1950's, even where it was self-transcendent, implied sometimes a self-rejection of the western consciousness. The philosophical ideas of Sartre, Camus and Freud took hold strongly during this decade. Compared to this implosive decade, the 60's could be called explosive. The social, religious and the existential interest continued through into the 60's though, according to Malcolm Bradbury,[62] the temper of the times became more antinomian and more experimental. World War II was a shock to western cultural values, creating a new ideological and intellectual environment, leading to new forms of society, new balances of power and new difficulties. In fact, the immediate effects of war were succeeded and contained by the complex consequences of twenty years of uneasy peace that followed it. It was a period where one could see the rise of new forms of mass society, liberal, capitalist and communist; a new type of economic growth and expansion that insisted our world is one of constant materialistic modernization. More antinomianism and less morality led to a shift in their notions of ethical responsibility, social obligation and personal identity. The mood of the period was one of mental ferment and the generation seemed to have been caught in a kind of mid-century limbo.

The absence of marked cultural positivism and norms are perhaps reasons why contemporary arts have not created those epical images of modern man or the modern world that one associates with the highest powers of modernism. Modernism's tendency towards an epical conclusiveness is associated with its conviction that art was a priestly vocation. But postmodern contemporary literature, more exposed to time and history, has claimed a lesser separateness and independence; it has been art less as an eternal species or a timeless court of appeal, worried with the problem regarding loss of meaning and identity in a modernized society.

Moreover, of all the literary genres, the novel came to be regarded as the proper domain of both postcolonial and the postmodern period. It contains both the spirit of variety and multiplicity. However, the line that separates comedy from tragedy, pathos from irony, which distinguishes the rigid from the improvisational forms, tends to blur. In the 60s, literature showed increased tolerance for chance and incongruity and instances of eroticism, fantasy, black humour, comic surrealism and the absurdist manner prevailed. At ease in the void and with nothingness and erudite in its absurdity, this existential, postmodern vision finds its inspiration in something other than contemporary nihilism; it was to re-form human consciousness, even while it made its own art expendable.

The development of the novel seems to be a continuous movement from realism towards surrealism, silence, self-parody and the loosening of forms. According to Colin Flack,[63] the postmodern art form has an echo of the communicative despair. Modern violence and evil are generated, in part, by a repressive culture, which denies form to our instinct and therefore turns over unchanneled emotions. Literature has to try to make sense of the condition by revealing possibilities within us, which transcend the existing order. A heightened linguistic awareness has, thus, become a part of our modern sensibility. Our postwar world has a sense of *post historie* where representation fails before the rupture of the past and we are left with only elegiac memories of the past glories, nostalgia, and a sense of waiting for the apocalypse.

The form gradually moves towards silence, a silence which derealizes the world, which fulfills the extreme states of the mind-void, madness, outrage, ecstasy, and mystic trance—

when ordinary discourse ceases to carry the burden of meaning.[64] It is in these extreme states of mind mentioned above that we frequently find the antiheroes in. Though all the six antiheroes discussed here may not reflect these states of mind simultaneously yet they personify one or the other of these mental states, with some even personifying multiple states of mind. Almost all of them encounter the void at one time or the other. Biswas suffers from madness and nervous breakdown while at Green Vale. Mugo is obsessed with his future and is almost paranoid in protecting it. Molloy exists in a limbo, a void where nothing has meaning, Seaton feels outraged because he feels cheated of a better life. Scobie rebels metaphysically as he almost denies the divinity of God and treats Him as human. Merridew in his frenzied madness destroys all human values.

These antiheroes personify irony because irony isolates the element of unpredictability, the sense of isolation, the demonic vision from the tragic situation; from comedy, it takes the Quixote motive of the picaro, the savagery and the grotesque scapegoat ritual of comic expiation; and from romance it adopts the quest motif turning it into a study in self-deception and the dream of wish fulfillment transforming it into a nightmare.[65]

Most of the antiheroes here understand the great irony of life, but some understand it rather late. They can perhaps envision an ideal, but fail to achieve it. The contemporary novel concerned with pathos, thus, sums up the experience of the isolated hero. Recent fiction has correspondingly changed its form along with the changing features of the antihero. With absurdity of chance and the chaotic nature of reality becoming a part of life, a perpetual debate exists between intentions and fulfillment, dream and fact. As such, the fictional novel recognizes disorder, demonic intrusions and obsessive nature. It has become saturated with "Moha"—"the basic irremediable, irreplaceable characteristic and contemptuous stupidity of man confronted with choice or purpose".[66] The idea of causality is carried to the depth of casualness and the novel becomes an extended metaphor of duplicity and unreason.

Neither comic nor tragic, the fictional pattern shows the 'hero' to be a child of ironies, a mediator of polar claims, parodying man's quest for fulfillment. The form provides him with more freedom than tragedy allows, and less freedom than comedy persists. Form, then, as an ironic mask, leers in one concerted grimace at the proud fallibility of man. The postmodern world no longer lends itself to assured definition. The heroes of contemporary fiction not only struggle against the world but also they struggle for and against themselves. Their pressing concerns with love and interpersonal relations in an age of pure group dominance do not obviate their regard for the perennial interest of the self, something which the treachery of Mugo illustrates when he places his personal well-being above the life of his friend and even the freedom of his country.

This 'hero' is perhaps too much of a victim to be considered tragic; however, he is too much of a rebel to meet the requirements of comedy. Comedy is nowadays as ambiguous as tragedy. It is a sign both of anger and despair. It accepts the absurdities of our life even as it repudiates it at the same time. It leaves us face to face with the preposterous, the trivial, the monstrous and the inconceivable.[67] Laughter in our time is sickly, savage, self-ironic, feeding upon deformity, and thriving upon unreason.

The traditional way of seeing a character as a whole is no longer possible. These changes are backed by inchoate feelings about the changed nature of reality arising from the decline of religious and metaphysical certainties, and the growing influence of psychology, and the traumas of the 20th century:

> The crisis in character obviously corresponds to similar crisis in the concept of Man. Modern man can be seen as a mere numerical entity within the most terrifying collectives that the human race has ever known. He had been seen as existing not for himself alone, but as a part of something else, of a Collective feeling, idea and organism. It is very difficult to create a character, out of

> such a man, at least in the traditional sense of the word.[68]

Postmodernism's apostle Allan Robbe-Grillet had the notion that the creation of characters in the traditional, heroic sense is no more than presentation of puppets in whom the artists no longer themselves believe in.

> ...our world today is less sure of itself and more modest perhaps because it has abandoned the idea of omnipotence of the individual, but it is more ambitious too, as it looks beyond it. The exclusive cult of the 'human' has given place to a vaster, less anthromorphic perception. The novel seems unsure of its step because it has lost what used to be its great support—the hero. If it does not manage to get back on a proper footing it will mean that its life is intimately linked to a bygone society. If it does manage it, on the other hand, a new path will be open to it, with the promise of new discoveries.[69]

One of the essential functions of the artist is the assertion and creation of a personality in a profounder sense than any non-artist can attain. We, as readers, ask of the artist a definition of a man, at once profound and abstract, stated and acted out. It is often impossible to draw a line between the work an artist creates and the life he lives, between the life he lives and the life he writes about. One must thus be prepared to move constantly back and forth between life and art, not in a pointless circle, but in meaningful spiraling towards an absolute point. It is, but inevitable, that a writer's life should have a strong influence upon his life. Though a great writer, Naipaul needed to understand the intricacies of life in the unheroic Trinidad to create a Mr. Biswas. Golding's schoolteacher background provided the foundation upon which he built the dystopia of *The Lord of the Flies*. Moreover, one can also state that the moral and spiritual confusion of Henry Scobie is as much Green's as Scobie's. This is true of almost all writers. If they perchance happen to be too objective as Beckett, even then traces of influence of the life lived is evident.

Leslie Fiedler,[70] states the necessity of biographical information even in this age. One may often object as to why should there be any necessity of dealing with writers' biography if one is concerned with postmodern art. Any kind of art, postmodern or otherwise, is created by the artist when she/he has been deeply impressed or affected by some external stimuli or an internal thought. The artist's life is the focusing glass through which pass the determinants of the shape of his work: the tradition available to him, his understanding of the 'kinds', the childhood experiences and the impact of social, cultural and political experiences among others. Biographical information helps us to understand the underlying philosophies and the nature of art.

Fiedler asserts that the response of the artist to his archetypal materials gives it a unique stamp—the artist signature—to his work. Moreover, a study of any literary work provides useful insights into the individual psyche of the writer and vice-versa. According to Fiedler, a study of a writer's life is useful, for art combines the uniqueness of the writer (the signature) and the collective experiences of the race (the archetype). The three main aspects—experiences, communication, and initiation—all possibly imply a necessary interconnectedness between the art object and some other area of experience, which essentially intend pointing outward or inward toward some independently existing otherness.

Antiheroes abound in contemporary literature; however, this study attempts to delve into the character of six antiheroes. It also attempts to find out why the modern heroes are really antiheroes, and to understand as to why there is a proliferation of such characters in contemporary, postmodern literature, a question that the introductory chapter has tried to find an answer to. How do these characters—the moral and spiritual derelicts—that are focused upon, conform to the pattern of the archetypal antihero? What is it that categorizes the protagonist to the status of the antihero? Does this figure have a choice? What characteristics make us empathize with them? It also seeks to find answers as to how important are the outside influences—political, cultural, and literary, not to say the least, personal, to the author and how subjective or objective is he in the treatment of his characters.

Mention of the characters has been made earlier in the chapter. But taking into cognizance the assemblage of the creations of several writers it would be imperative to do that again. The first discussion focuses on Golding's Jack Merridew, the Satanic, frenzied Dionysus incarnate antihero, and Alan Sillitoe's Arthur Seaton, the defiant antihero opposing society's conventional definition of goodness and heroism and how he deals with the theme of regression and social and moral anarchy.

The second chapter deals with characters scarred by colonialism and oppression: V.S. Naipaul's Mr. Biswas, the boorish, rebellious, unaccommodated and unnecessary unheroic man; and Ngugi wa Thiong'o's Mugo, the imbalanced schizophrenic selfish antihero suffering from paranoia.

The penultimate chapter deals with two failures—Samuel Becket's Molloy, the denied antihero who tries to grapple with nothingness; Graham Greene's Henry Scobie, the scapegoat/ weak antihero who tries to take all sins upon himself and who in the process virtually damns himself.

All six antiheroes are angst ridden, suffering from a feeling of dread, anguish and anxiety. This anxiety brings them face to face with the void. As nihilists, they grapple incessantly with the meaninglessness of life, trying to find moral justification for the choices they have made.[71] The alienation deepens the experience of affinities between the characters as well as the fact that they belong to a paradoxical world which is "extensively homogenized yet intensely fragmented".[72]

NOTES

1. T.J. Shawcross, D.J. Burrows and F.R. Lapides (ed.) *Myths and Motifs in Literature*. New York: The Free Press, 1973, Preface.
2. Stated in Jung, *Contributions to Analytical Psychology*; trans. H.G. and C.F. Baynes, Kegan Paul, 1928, *ibid.*
3. Archetypes: "Archetypes of the Collective Unconscious", Jung, 1953, *20th Century Criticism: The Major Statements*. (ed.) William J. Handy. Max Westbrook, Life and Light Publication. N.D., 1974, p. 206.
4. Included in *Contributions to Analytical Psychology*, quoted by Maud Bodkin, "Archetypal Patterns in Tragic Poetry", Shawcross, *op. cit.*, p. 4.

5. Joseph Campbell, *The Hero with a Thousand Faces*, 1949, World Publishing Company, Meridian Books, pp. 3-4.
6. R.P. Blackmur, *The Lion and the Honeycomb*, Harcourt, Brace and World, Inc., 1955, pp. 45-46.
7. Leslie Fiedler, "Archetype and Signature—The Relationship Between Poet and Poem", *The Sewanee Review,* L X 2, Spring 1952, Anthologized in Shawcross, pp. 22-36.
8. *Chambers Concise 20th Century Dictionary,* ed. G.W. Davidson, M.A. Seaton and J. Simpson, Allied Publishers, New Delhi, 1986, p. 39.
9. *The Dictionary of Literary Terms and Literary Theory*, ed. J.A. Cuddon, 4th edition, 1976, 1998, Maya Blackwell, G.B., pp. 42-43.
10. *The Concise Oxford Dictionary of Literary Terms*, Chris Baldick, 1990, Oxford University Press, p. 11.
11. M.H. Abrams, *The Glossary of Literary Terms*, 6th ed. Prism India Ltd. Holt, Rinehart and Winston, Inc., 1993, p. 214.
12. Erich Fromm, *The Anatomy of Human Destructiveness* (New York, 1973), p. 225.
13. Ihab Hassan, *Radical Innocence*, Princeton University Press, 1961.
14. *Ibid.*, p. 21, Lionel Trilling, *Freud and the Crisis of Our Culture*, (Boston, 1955), p. x.
15. Campbell, *op. cit.*
16. *Ibid.,* p. 316.
17. Shawcross (ed.), *op. cit.*, p. 225.
18. Northrop Frye, *Anatomy of Criticism*, Princeton University Press, Princeton, 1957, pp. 33-35.
19. Shawcross, *op. cit.*, p. 225.
20. Yiddish—A clumsy person, Shawcross *et al.*, *op. cit.*, p. 225.
21. Campbell, *op. cit.*, p. 316.
22. David Wagoner, "The Hero with One Face", *A Place to Stand*, Indiana University Press, 1958. Anthologized in Shawcross, p. 133.
23. Shawcross, *op. cit.*, p. 130.
24. Raymond Giraud, *The Unheroic Hero*, New Brunswick, 1957, Referred to in Hassan, *op. cit.*, p. 21.
25. Mario Praz, *The Hero in Eclipse in Victorian Fiction* (New York, 1956), p. 383.
26. *Dictionary of World Literary Terms: Criticism, Forms, Techniques*, 1972, Joseph Twadell Sinpley, Little Field, Adams, p. 15.
27. Aldoux Huxley (ed). *The Letters of D.H. Lawrence*, London, 1956, p. 198. Hassan, *op. cit.*, p. 22.
28. Shawcross, *op. cit.*, p. 450.
29. Hassan, *op. cit.*, p. 6.

30. *Ibid.*, p. 21.
31. Shawcross, *op. cit.*, p. 450.
32. William Golding, *Pincher Martin*, 1956, Faber and Faber, London.
33. Hassan, *op. cit.*, p. 121.
34. Nietzsche, "The Death of God", *The Madman From Modernism to Postmodernism: An Anthology*, (ed) Lawrence Cahoone, 1996, Blackwell Publishers, p. 102.
35. Hassan, *op. cit.*, p. 18. Nathan A. Scott, Jr., "The Broken Centre: A Definition of the Crisis of Values in Modern Literature," *Chicago Review* 13, Summer 1954, p. 196.
36. Freud, *Civilization and Its Discontents*, 1930, Cahoone, *op. cit.*, p. 213.
37. *Ibid.*, p. 214.
38. Hassan, *op. cit.*, p. 18. Theodore Reik, *Of Love and Lust* (New York, 1957), p. 366.
39. V.V. Subbarao, *William Golding: A Study*, Delhi, 1987, quoting Gabriel Josiporici, p. 31.
40. Hassan, *Radical Innocence*, pp. 31-32.
41. C.C. Walcutt, *The Diminished Self: Man's Changing Mask—Modes and Methods of Characterization,* University of Minnesota Press, (Minneapolis, 1966), p. 334.
42. Hassan, *op. cit.*, pp. 19-20.
43. Joseph Conrad, *Lord Jim*, Harmondsworth, Penguin, 1949, p. 214.
44. Hassan, *op. cit.*, p. 112.
45. *Ibid.*, p. 114.
46. B. Rajan, "The Problem of Satan" (1947). A.E. Dyson and Julian Lovelock (ed.) 1973: *Milton's Paradise Lost,* (Casebook Series), London: The Macmilian Press, Ltd.
47. Northrop Frye, *op. cit.*, p. 42.
48. *Ibid.*, p. 121.
49. Georg Buckner, *Woyzek* (1837). Anthologized in Shawcross *et al.* (ed.) *Myths and Motifs in Literature*, pp. 280-303.
50. Isaac Bashvis Singer, "Gimpel The Fool" (1957, trans. Saul Bellow), *Ibid.*, pp. 322-33.
51. Jung, "Archetypes and the Collective Unconscious", William J. Handy, Max Westbrook (ed.) *20th Century Criticism: The Major Statement*, Life and Light Publication (New Delhi, 1974).
52. *The Short Novels of Dostoevsky*, Introduction by Thomas Mann (New York, 1945), p. 137.
53. Dostoevsky, *Notes From Underground*, p. 140.
54. Albert Camus, *The Rebel: An Essay on Man in Revolt* (trans. Anthony Bower), N.Y. Vintage, 1956, p. 19.

55. James Joyce, *Ulysses*. Quoted in Hassan, *op. cit.*, p. 24.
56. Hassan, p. 28. Colin Wilson, *The Outsider*, p. 261.
57. Hassan, *Contemporary American Literature, 1945-72* (New York, 1973), Fredrick Unger Publication, pp. 25-26.
58. *Ibid.*
59. Northrop Frye, *Anatomy of Criticism*, 1957.
60. Hassan, *Radical Innocence*, *op. cit.*, p. 87.
61. Walcutt, *op. cit.*, pp. 333-34.
62. Malcolm Bradbury, "The Novel", C.B. Cox and A.E. Dyson (ed.) *The 20th Century Mind, History, Ideas and Literature in Britain III*: 1945-1965, London: Oxford University Press, pp. 319-47.
63. Colin Flack, *Myth, Truth and Literature: Towards a New Post-Modernism*, Cambridge, Cambridge University Press, 1989, p. 164.
64. Ihab Hassan, *Dismemberment of the Orpheus*, Oxford University Press, 1971, p. 13.
65. Hassan, *Radical Innocence*, *op. cit.*, p. 121.
66. R.P. Blackmur, *The Lion and the Honeycomb* (New York, 1955), p. 294.
67. Wylie Sypher, *Comedy* (New York, 1956), p. 196. Quoted in Hassan, *Radical Innocence*, p. 119.
68. Alberto Moravia, *Man As An End,* Seeker and Warburg, 1965, quoted by Bernard Berzongi, 1970: *The Situation of the Novel*, London, Macmillan, p. 70.
69. *Ibid.*, Robbe Grillet, *Snapshots and Towards a New Novel*, 1965, p. 37.
70. Leslie Fiedler, *op. cit.*
71. Hassan, *Contemporary American Literature: An Introduction*, *op. cit.*, p. 3.
72. Hassan, *Radical Innocence*, *op. cit.*, p. 328.

2

The Radical Rebel: Jack Merridew and Arthur Seaton

Gilbert Phelps in "The Post War English Novel" asserts that the trend of the English novel since the war has, as a whole, been "...a turning aside from the mainstream of European literature and a tendency to retreat into parochialism and defeatism."[1] However, this tendency apart, how can one relate the postwar novel with postmodernism? Edward Smyth[2] argues that though there are several characteristics of post-modernism, i.e. fragmentation, pastiche, plurality, decentering, and parody, yet by common usage "postmodernism" has been adopted by several commentators to describe the contemporary novel in general, whether individual texts may exhibit these traits or not. He writes "It has thus come to be regarded as synonymous with the contemporary literary period, as a whole, in addition to being used as a synonym for *avant garde* experimental writing." Thus, one may question as to whether the authors being discussed in this study are really postmodernists if one uses only the stylistic technique, i.e. formlessness or grammatical deviation, etc. as a standard. Critics like Jeremy Hawthorn[3] categorize postmodernism into three groups. He uses the term not only to include the extreme extension of certain modernists characteristics, but also uses it to refer to aspects of a more general human condition in the late capitalist world of the post-1950s which had an all embracing effect on life, culture, ideology and art. Postmodernism therefore has not been exactly defined though it is largely accepted as a term to designate the cultural epoch in which we are living and largely viewed in apocalyptic terms.[4]

In the mid-50s, two new writers came into prominence with their realistic novels. Golding's *The Lord of the Flies* (1954) was an adventure story reversed to reveal the dark underside of human nature, whereas Sillitoe's *Saturday Night and Sunday Morning* (1958) was a working class Booze and Bash novel with stark realism. The latter was described as "the raw, robust novel of a working class heel on the hell of a spree".[5] A dominant metaphor in the works of these novelists is that of a jungle where the rule of might prevails.

The new society, which everyone was looking forward to in 1945, seemed, in the 1950s to be picking up the threads from the 1930s. As a result genuine feelings of anger and resentment were generated, reinforced by critics like Kenneth Tynan, who were themselves challenging an old style mandarin journalistic establishment. *Lord of the Flies* (1954) reflects the mood of the postwar and post-Hitler years; and also epitomizes mid-20th century disillusionment with the 19th century optimism.

There are differences between the writers before the war/ modernists and the postwar/postmodernists, the major being the latter's tendency to describe their perspectives more truthfully. This is not to say that the earlier writers were less truthful but there was a tendency among them towards nostalgia, either to complicate their expressions with their stream of consciousness technique, or to view things from a tinted glass. Comparatively, one can see that the postwar writers have been objective in their depiction of their views and their expressions, be it social realism in Sillitoe; or metaphysical probing and its resultant horror in Golding. In literary terms, the majority of accounts of the development of postmodernism is couched in historical language; postmodernism is seen both as a continuation of modernism and by some, as a rejection of it.[6] If Forster can be a modernist without the *avant-garde*, experimental style of Woolf and Joyce, then Sillitoe and Golding similarly can be classified in the postmodern period. There are, moreover, incipient traces of postmodernist elements in these writers, and they are able to accommodate within their writings these strains, especially fragmentation, multiplicity of consciousness and absurdity *et al.* They also inquire into ontological and epistemological uncertainty as both Golding and Sillitoe constantly question accepted social and metaphysical beliefs and values. As such these writers reveal themselves to be more aware of the rift between the self and the world. However, present in Sillitoe especially, but absent in Golding is the pull between artistic vocation and political commitment.

If postmodernism is rejection of modernism, then the depiction of social reality becomes a postmodern feature because in modernism the stream of consciousness was used to transcribe an inner mental world at the expense of external social reality. But this can also be true if postmodernism is taken as an extension of modernism wherein one often finds that depiction of reality is taken to its extreme point. In modernism, one frequently finds that there is the abandonment of chronological sequencing of events. Both the novels under discussion present the events in chronological sequence.

The novels reveal powerful anxieties at work. Authors show at various points of their career an attraction towards experiment as well as tradition and realism. Golding creates comparable combination between these experimental anxieties and the narrative style. Phelps' statement that the English novel tends towards defeatism and parochialism, nevertheless, fits both Sillitoe and Golding. Sillitoe situates his story in mining Nottingham in capitalist England; *Lord of the Flies* (1954) is localized in a desert Pacific island which in certain instances looks dangerously like the world in microcosm, or Eden just before and after the Fall.

Novelists are themselves products of their times and societies. They perhaps are the best spokesmen of their period, giving voice to the events and beliefs and often creating characters to represent what they see around them. Golding emerged as a powerful writer in the 1950s, almost simultaneously as the Angry Young Man movement but he is more in the line of Conrad and Melville, probing hidden terror, betrayal, sin and damnation. On the other hand, although unacknowledged, Sillitoe is strongly associated with the above-mentioned movement. Nonetheless both Sillitoe's and Golding's stories tread the fatal thin line between potential heroism and actual anti-heroism.

Who is a rebel? What is rebellion? A rebel is a man who says 'no',[7] one who resists or resents authority, one who refuses to conform to the accepted modes of behaviour, and rejection of accepted conventions. Rebellion can broadly be categorized into two parts—negative and positive. Positive rebellion arises from the spectacle of the irrational coupled with an unjust condition.[8] In its negative aspect, rebellion thrives on chaos, negating all that is good around it. Unlike positive rebellion, this is bereft of meaning, as it does not herald new and positive changes. Rebellion cannot exist without the feeling that one is, in some sense, justified. But this justification is a paradox in itself as it may be right, as with Prometheus, or it may be wrong, as with Lucifer. Rebellion for Satan started when he felt that God denied him a position, which he proudly thought, was his. But the involvement of pride and envy deviates it from a heroic assertion to antiheroic Satanism. On the other hand, Prometheus's rebellion results as a desire to help mankind. In a way he is considered as a Christ figure through his compassion for mankind and his gift for man.

The characters under discussion here, Golding's Jack Merridew and Sillitoe's Arthur Seaton are rebels, but whereas Jack's rebellion, like Satan's, results from pride and anger, Seaton rebels out of frustration with his prevalent condition of life. In this context, David Elloway's[9] comment fits Seaton's rebellion to a T. He says that rebellion in the case of the working-class protagonist emerges from a sense of isolation and insecurity and that the adoption of a cynical pose is a defence against this insecurity—a pose that increases the isolation of the antihero.

The first part of this chapter focuses upon Jack Merridew, the other central character in *Lord of the Flies*, the antithesis of

Ralph. Both Ralph and Jack seem to be an extension of an incomplete self; they are potentially alike but diametrically opposite of each other, in that Ralph represents heroic qualities, rationality, and order, whereas Jack, the antiheroic nature, irrationality, chaos, anarchy and evil in its purest form.

Jack is Golding's representation of evil in human nature, specifically showing that it exists even in innocent bodies often unaware of it. Golding asks several, often ignored, questions which are relevant to the portrayal of Jack as an antihero. What would man be like if there were no rules and values to govern and regulate his life? Would man still remain human if he were to be stripped clean of his humanness? The question-answer works out as a sort of parallel between the existential conditions of Ralph and Jack. Both of them have recognized darkness within themselves, but for Jack, it has opened the doomed doors to a void where the presence of values and restrictions are taboos. Ralph has been discussed to a large extent because it is mostly in comparison to him that one perceives Jack. Identical yet opposite, mirror images of each other, the two parallel characters of Jack and Ralph converge up to a certain point and then suddenly move in opposite directions with near fatal consequences. They are the two parts of the splintered ego—the divided self-competing with and yet incomplete without each other.

Jack grows as an antihero as he steadily degenerates in the social scale. From the beginning, he is different from other boys, differentiated both by his anger and by his idealism. Jack identifies himself as Merridew, not as Jack, which he believes to be a childish identification. As Jack, he reverses the folk tale myth of Jack, the Giant Killer, for he himself regresses into the proverbial, symbolic giant creating havoc in the idyllic island. Early in the story, Jack and Ralph recognize leadership qualities in each other. It stands in a sharp contrast to the later experience when the polarities surface and they stand divided. If there is anyone who can either complement or challenge Jack, it is Ralph. In their hostilities later, they were like "two continents of feeling and experience, unable to communicate" (p. 60).

Jack's transformation from a prefect and chorister to a demoniac antiheroic warlord is startling. He is the one who in his English idealism cries for rules and the need for them to be obeyed. Even as a child he carries a dual burden—first the White man's burden of the British as belonging to a superior race, and secondly, the awareness of the evil in him and the ensuing consciousness of being aware. Jack, a boy of twelve, a fact which one is led almost to forget, is a literary descendent of the satanic antihero. In his role of a satanic antihero he fulfills Shawcross's[10] definition of an antihero, as he tries to subvert and thwart the goals of the hero and destroy him in order to assert his own self.

Howard S. Babb[11] brings out the comparison between the inherent evil in Shakespeare's *King Lear* and the characters in Golding whose innate evil often seems to scare themselves too. Gloucester states that our world is cruel, governed by malevolent gods whose delight is to torture humans; if one wishes to see an image of the dark gods one needs only to examine "the ghastly and ferocious play of children",[12] "We are to Gods / As flies are to wanton boys / They kill us for their sport" (*King Lear*, IV, i) where they mercilessly torture flies for fun. From both within and without man is beset with evil. From this point of view it is evident that Golding holds that in human nature there is a terrible propensity towards cruelty and evil. He presents a savage close up of human nature, a stripping down of man to what he essentially is. The result is both appalling and humiliating: man is not close to the heroic idealized self; rather man is antiheroic by nature.

Jack's evil is comparable to the burgeoning evil of the pelican daughters of Lear. Evil and its justifications are often inexplicable but Golding is determined to show that Jack exist within every man's heart, "the reason why it is no go" (p. 158). Golding has spoken about the characteristic determination to anatomize "the darkness of man's heart" (p. 223). In the *Moving Target* (1981), Golding[13] writes:

> What man is, whatever man is under the eye of heaven, that I burn to know and that—I do not say this lightly—I would endure knowing. The themes closest to my

> purpose, to my imagination have stemmed from that preoccupation have been of such a sort that they might move me a little nearer that knowledge. There have been themes of man at an extremity, man tested like a building material, taken into the laboratory and used to destruction, man isolated, man obsessed, man drowning in the literal sea or in the sea of his own ignorance.

It is a sad irony that Jack's natural, potential leadership qualities are wiped clean when he is seduced by power and irrational savagery. "What intelligence had been shown was traceable to Piggy while the most obvious leader was Jack" (p. 19). Jack's intelligence is revealed when he finds a way to light the fire using Piggy's specs, when Ralph makes the last confession of incompetence. But his pride and aggression overshadows his intelligence and heroism turning him into an antihero. As his lust for power grows he is unable to accept opposition from any position. His antiheroism is further ascertained by his pride, subconscious guilt and hatred. Jack's hatred for Ralph arises from the fact that the latter possess some innately good qualities, which Jack wants, but cannot possess.

Polarities between Jack and Ralph are stressed from the very beginning. Whereas Ralph is "the fair boy" whose eyes and mouth "proclaimed no devil", Jack's introduction heralds sinister connotations. The choir group dressed strangely in black cloaks looked like a creature "something dark" (p. 20). When he comes forward unto the platform with his cloak flying, his movement is almost bat-like.

Golding views man as a being tortured by pride and guilt, one who has faith in his power but continually runs into conflict with other men and with his own human limitations. Awareness of this limitation, of evil, is in Golding's view intrinsically related to the primal human sin. The concept of *Corrupto Optimi Pessima*, that "the corruption of the best is usually the worst" holds especially true of the satanic antiheroes from Faust to Kurtz down to Jack Merridew. Circumstances are greatly responsible for bringing out the latent instincts in man. Situating the story in a desert island allows the sudden freedom from civilized restrictions, which in turn allows full play to suppressed desires. However, Jack simply cannot be labeled as an antihero because of his regression to primitivism, which resulted because he is stranded in an adult-less island without anyone to reinforce rules and regulations. The situation is much more dangerous and complex because Ralph, Simon, Piggy and Samneric are able to hold on to rational beliefs until they are subjugated, killed or hounded off by Jack and his savage brood. Jack fails as an actual hero and becomes the antihero because of the choices he makes and because of a failure in moral vision. One cannot deny the fact that he has the true potential of a hero that has unfortunately been diverted to the wrong path.

According to Gindin,[14] Golding raises the question: Is the Faust legend an adequate expression of the problems of the contemporary, guilt-ridden man? It is Conrad's Kurtz that Jack resembles most. Though Golding claimed that he had never read Conrad's *Heart of Darkness*,[15] there are resemblances between the two novels. Both symbolically explore the darkness within man, the atrocities within history, the powerful forces of the unconscious and the mystery of evil. Golding saw man as a morally degenerate creature and Jack represents his picture of the morally degenerate man with Kurtz as his precursor. There is an underplayed similarity in Jack's placating the pig's head and Kurtz's impaling of the skulls. As a potential adult with more propensities towards evil, Jack has in him the seeds of evil, which if unchecked would turn him into another Kurtz, corrupted by absolute power. His disdainful disregard for authority, flirtation with and lust for power and his transformation from a chorister to a warlord points him out to be the symbolic descendent of the archetype Satan. Utterly depraved, Jack echoes the spiritual void within. The emptiness he faces within himself drives him to gain ascendancy over others. Like Kurtz, in the beginning, he is remarkable in his intelligence and finally, in the unspeakable, unimaginable depth to which he sinks. As C.C. Walcutt[16] asks—Is Satan himself redeemed by the intelligence that accompanies his pride?

Evil is one of the aspects of the satanic antihero and Jack's image gives a terrifying insight into the human capacity for evil. Interestingly Golding follows Conrad in deliberately situating the novel where people are free from the confines of routines, manners and social security. How do people act when they are on their own? *Lord of the Flies*, like *Heart of Darkness*, probes the uncertain area between the myth of society's values and the actuality of their meaning. Without restraint, morals and values burst into flowers of evil, industry turns to greed, idealism and progress become an insane lust for power, courage and bravery is reduced into anarchy and cruelty, and adventure becomes irresponsibility. Idealism is worst affected as it turns to lust for power; especially so because the gulf between myth and reality becomes so wide that it leaves one to wonder about the connection between such extremes.[17]

Jack is brilliant yet depraved, without restraint; corrupt yet fascinating. Jack's anarchic rebellion against the order established by Ralph and Piggy aligns him to the rebellious Satan. Jack like Kurtz, is a modern Faust "who has sold his soul for power and gratification".[18] What does an antihero do when equipped with absolute power? Once power becomes real to Jack, the rules become meaningless, and he embodies the urge to appropriate power and to orgy. Of the antiheroes here, Jack, like Ngugi's Mugo comes close enough to be identified with the villain. Though he is not tactless or incompetent, he lacks the magnanimity of the truly heroic and his inadequacy is exposed when he succumbs to the pull of power.

An antiheroic escape to primitivism such as one attempted by Kurtz and by Jack unleashes brutality, greed for power, and sadism in the barest form, it leads to the horror of murderous, ritualistic midnight dances and skulls stuck on poles. Jack's degeneration offers a grim and dark view of the human condition. One way to deal with the darkness within man is to weep over it like Ralph does; another is to accept the darkness, hide away from it and unleash the horror as Jack does. Jack symbolizes, like the New Men and Pincher Martin, the descent of man, the loss of innocence, the burden of self-knowledge, consciousness and guilt, and the assertion of his will at all costs.

Golding focuses on the aspect of man questing for order on various levels and encountering chaos within and without. On the social level, it is seen in the violence resulting from the clash between different types of order. It is also experienced as a moral evil resulting from the over assertion of the ego, as in the case of Jack Merridew.

Though Jack seems to be equally capable, his thinking is crooked and it is the possession of the conch rather than his capabilities as a leader that crowns Ralph to be the chief. The seeds of dissent by what he sees as unjust deprivation are already sown by this incident and he is jealous of Ralph without knowing the reason why. Jack also symbolizes the various pulls and pressures that man experiences on the existential level because of his fragmented consciousness. As one progresses in the novel, one can see that in Jack, the heroic and the idealistic yields to the perverted. In *The Inheritors*,[19] Golding demonstrated that it is the fragmentation of man's consciousness into ego and superego, which constitutes the Fall of man, unchaining dark and irrational forces and resulting in anarchism, which seeks to destroy the remaining harmony.

The conflict between heroism and antiheroism, if taken to the societal and personal level, becomes a conflict between the rational and the irrational will, one aiming at a decent, democratic leadership based on reason and the latter seeking to establish an authoritarian regime based on power and brutality. Subbarao[20] quoting Erich Fromm gives a description of the former as an energetic effort to reach a rationally desirable aim that requires discipline and the overcoming of self-indulgence, whereas the irrational will is powerful but not subject to man's control. Apparently, Ralph symbolizes the former and the antiheroic Jack, the latter. In fact, even when being hunted and smoked out of the jungle, Ralph is concerned about the welfare of the boys. Contrastingly, Jack is so obsessed with the pig hunt that it almost consumes his spirit and energies. His sadistic and destructive nature overwhelms his personality and he confesses to a feeling of "being hunted" as if "something is behind you all the time in the jungle" (p. 57). The beast, which Jack tries to propitiate, is non-existent, and is a projection of "the age old tremors" (p. 139), which Jack is subject to as he hunts in the forest.

The four assemblies simultaneously chart the steady decline and degeneration of the Jack from anger to aggressive regression and chaotic anarchy. Later, as Ralph is hunted down, he glimpses with horror the darkest aspect of man, and is faced with the "wide grin of the skull" (p. 217). Jack's destructive anarchism makes him, metaphorically, a human counterpart of the Lord of the flies (Beelzebub). In his frenzy, Jack becomes the "dark culture hero"[21] symbolizing the darkest side of human nature which had been suppressed by centuries of restrictions, civilization and social nurturing.

The presence or absence of evil is also a factor in deciding the heroism or antiheroism of a character. As such, it is Jack who registers the dark and haunting creepiness of the forest. For him evil and destruction are live forces, powers stronger than man and they can be appeased and propitiated by ritual, ceremony and sacrifice. Jack has been open to some kind of human experience that Ralph and Piggy have not and thus his reaction to the same stimuli is extremely different to theirs. Jack's rebel-victim image is different from the other antiheroes. His rebellion, one can see, is not metaphysical, but personal, and he is victimized not by external forces as by his own fears and delusions. But still he negates all social values like friendship, sharing and humanity. Furthermore, his acting, role-playing as proper chief gets so internalized that he is unable to separate himself from his chieftainship.

Though he suffers considerably from guilt, he refuses to acknowledge it. It arises from the shame of self-consciousness and the presence of dark impulses. Freud traces the evolution of guilt back to the primitive period,[22] when people lived in communes. The beginning of guilt in man seems to be of a complex nature. Freud states that when an individual's desire for aggression is rendered harmless by civilization, his aggressiveness becomes internalized, and is directed towards his own ego. A part of the ego sets itself over the rest as the superego in the form of a conscience. The tension between the ego and the superego is the sense of guilt. Thus, it is the remnants of civilization in Jack that forces guilt in him and in order to hide that guilt, he paints himself in savage colours. Freud describes the two origins of the sense of guilt: one arising from the sense of authority, and the other from the fear of the superego, each stressing on the renunciation of instinctual satisfactions and the need for punishment. In the case of the superego, even with the renunciation, the wish persists, unconcealed from the superego. Thus, a sense of guilt emerges. A threatened external happiness—punishment and loss of love—is exchanged for a permanent internal unhappiness, for the tension of the sense of guilt. Freud traces this evolution to the primitive period, the traces of which is often seen when a modern child reacts to his first instinctual frustrations with excessive aggressiveness and with a corresponding severe guilt. His stand cannot be easily justified for he is going by what Freud terms as the "phylogenetic model".[23] The prehistoric times father has been attributed with a terrible aggressive personality. Man's sense of guilt springs at the killing of the father by brothers banded together. On that occasion the act of aggression was carried out; but ironically it was the same act of aggression whose suppression is supposed to be the source of the sense of guilt. If the killing of the father is a plausible piece of history then the case of a person feeling guilty because he has really done something which cannot be justified occurs.

Later the superego, vested with the father's power created restrictions, intending to prevent a repetition. Since the hatred against the father persisted, so did the sense of guilt. Thus, according to Freud, whether one has killed the father or abstained from it is not really the decisive factor, one is bound to feel guilty in either case, for the sense of guilt is an expression for the conflict due to ambivalence, of the eternal struggle between Eros and Thanatos. When an attempt is made to widen the community, the same conflict is continued in forms, resulting in the further intensification of guilt. Fear for Jack arises from the fear of the hero/superego/father/Ralph figure. Thus, he tries to hide from his guilt behind the mask of savagery and daubs paint all over his face masking his social personality and revealing the savage within. Fear and guilt can result in unimaginable consequences. Jack's regression to an utter savage is one of them.

Golding convincingly delineates Jack's regression from idealism to antiheroism as he charts the graph of Jack's behaviour as it goes from bad to worse to insufferable. Jack uses his predatory instincts, aggression and intelligence not only to alienate Ralph from the group but also to prey on him; gripped by paranoia he sees anything external to himself as a threat. Freud's belief that there is an inborn human inclination to badness, to aggressiveness, destructiveness and cruelty is proved to be true here.[24]

Jack's courage and heroism is overshadowed by his sadism, anarchic tendencies and antiheroism. Like Satan who in his pride rebelled against the authority of God, he rebels against the rational set-up of Ralph and Piggy. Aggressive, ruthless and an ambitious self-seeker he is the opposite of the "meek inheritors of the earth". Ralph and Jack are vitally different in their attitudes and perceptions, their worlds are essentially incompatible: "the two boys faced each other. There was the brilliant world of hunting, tactics, fierce exhilaration, skill, and there was the world of longing and baffled commonsense" (p. 76). At cross-purposes, the first note of antagonism is struck on the question of priorities. While signal fire, shelter, and rescue figures first for Ralph, Jack is obsessed with hunting. But meat is only an excuse, Jack hunts for the pure thrill that it offers him. Even before he paints his face, Golding identifies him completely with evil; there is the "hiss of indrawn breath", the serpent-like connotation prefigures danger in the Edenic garden. Again he is "a furtive thing, ape-like among the tangle of the trees", with "bright blue eyes that in frustration seemed bolting and nearly mad" (p. 50).

Ironically, in the beginning, there is innocence even in Jack. He is unable to kill the pig because of "the enormity of the knife descending and cutting into living flesh, because of the unbearable blood" (p. 30). A streak of mercy in him exists in him, a taint that he is ashamed of. But Ralph and Simon know and Jack unconsciously hides his face from them so that they should not see the shame. Later, it is the same Jack who hunts the sow with sadomachoistic gusto, disembowels, decapitates and impales the head of the sow to placate the beast as a gift. In his killing of the matriarch sow, he destroys the familial system, thus freeing himself from responsibilities and obligations which would tie him with rules. The idealistic chorister paradoxically does not behave like a God-fearing English gentleman, but manifests a moral corruption, out of tune with the natural environment.

If one takes Nietzsche into consideration, a different perspective of Jack begins to emerge. Nietzsche's[25] insight into the self-destructiveness of guilt shows the need to replace one's guilt with self-responsibility, for without it, the unleashed energies of man would become bestial. This is the fallacy that Jack is guilty of. His irresponsibility makes him unable to replace his guilt with self-responsibility and thus there is bestiality in his behaviour.

Irresponsibility and ignorance liberate a power that is more savage in the boys themselves. Whereas Ralph's instincts are to domesticate and civilize, to ward off evil by forming social relationships, Jack rediscovers in himself the instincts and compulsions of the hunter that lies buried in every man. The rediscovery is another dimension of awareness, deeper than "the compulsion to track down and kill" that was swallowing him up. For Jack, the forest becomes not only a place to hunt but also a place where one sometimes feels hunted, a place where the human being momentarily locates his intuitions of evil. In a way, the jungle reflects his inner changes; for along with his personal degradation, the jungle acquires an equivalent sinister quality. His reversion to primitivism and atavistic tendencies are aggravated by the fact that rescue does not mean anything real to him anymore. By page 55 of the novel, "Jack had to think for a moment before he could remember what rescue was". Ironically, Ralph undergoes a similar experience when he forgets the urgency of lighting the fire. Time and again he is left wondering why, what and who?

He too, perhaps, would have regressed back but for Piggy and Simon's ominous portends, and his personal hell of responsibilities. But all the while Jack is acquiring a kind of experience that Ralph singularly lacks. Jack not only understands the fear of the littluns but also learns to exploit them to his advantage. The fear, he says, exists "because you are like that".

It is man's nature to be frightened when it is dark and man is by himself. In the dark, man is faced with his own internal darkness. The children's fear is vague, coming with the darkness, from the depth of their unconscious, and assuming the shape of a mysterious beast. Whether the universe is malign or benign depends on the perceiver's psyche. Man projects his psyche into the environment and feels certain hostility towards it, putting an end to all meaningful relationship with the universe. Being an existential antiheroic character, Jack feels the hostility and alienation more sharply, leading him to assert his will over others.

Revealing his insatiable thirst for evil, Jack becomes guardian of a regime where the only existing rule is one of sadism. Evil has its attractions and Jack's absolutist tyranny has greater attraction for the boys who desert Ralph's tribe in hordes. Even though he satisfies what is only a short-term basic and base human craving, but ironically, his government is much more effective than Ralph's. He gives the boys meat; he is able to keep them in order, to put a stop to quarreling and sheer laziness in a way in which Ralph is not, whom he has reduced to a one-man tribe. This leads him to proudly declare, "See they do what I want?" (p. 198).

Jack exemplifies Thomas Hobbes's[26] pessimistic observation that human fractiousness requires to be governed by an absolute monarch, a power wielder. Jack's monarchy panders to and is an expression of the worst aspects of human nature, greed, cruelty and lust. Babb compares Jack to the vicious Roman emperor who provides food and entertainment for his mob. Here entertainment takes the form of beating littluns and murderous ritualistic dances. But when Jack gains power, he does not use it to lead the boys out of the wilderness as Ralph had attempted. Rather, he consciously exploits the vilest elements in human nature, and he delights in his obscenity, which is a symptom of man's essential illness.

For Golding, morality is a matter of conditioning and memory but savagery is innate in human nature. The frail conditioning of civilization that suppresses this element breaks in down Jack's case. As long as the remnants of civilization persisted, Jack's degeneration was incomplete, causing him shame and self-consciousness from which he wanted to hide. Once painted, he finds that an awesome stranger reflects back from him. Twice Golding stresses, "he looked in astonishment, no longer at himself, but at an awesome stranger behind which Jack hid, liberated from shame and self-consciousness" (p. 67). Jack discovers that it is not difficult to invent the devices whereby man can be released from shame. With the killing of the piglet, he gains new experience that "they had outwitted a living thing, imposed its will on it, and taken its life like a long satisfying drink" (p. 75). His anger erupts as he attacks Piggy and smashes his lens, as fresh from the total imposition of his will, he cannot brook moral condemnation and humiliation at the hands of Ralph and Piggy.

Present in the novel are multiple points of view. Ralph is perplexed, as things look different in different lights and from different points of view. "If faces were different when lit from above or from below, what was a face? What was anything?" (p. 84). He questions the nature of essential reality. Despite his age and immaturity, Ralph ask ontological questions about problems conveniently neglected by grown ups, or shut up in the back of their minds. Moreover, if there are various points of view, how can one verify that one opinion or belief is more correct than the other? In fact, who decides what or who is right?, what right does an individual have to judge another with his personal set of assumptions and standards? In "Archetypes and the Collective Unconscious",[27] Jung questions what men call the reason. Man's ability to think is "in point of fact nothing more than the sum total of his prejudices and myopic views". So can Ralph, or for that matter, we, judge Jack to be essentially bad? Is Jack's compulsion to hunt more defective than Ralph's rescue ideas to a world where anarchism, murder and mayhem will be played out on a macrocosmic level? This questioning of the multi-faceted reality and the corresponding uncertainty becomes in a way, the novel's postmodern feature.

In the midst of his anger, Ralph too betrays the beginning of a diminished sense of civilization. His experience at the hunt is also a revelation of his own darker side: he discovers in himself the fright, the apprehensions, and the pride that the others have known. It is this dark underside of Ralph that Jack personifies. The difference is that heroic Ralph maintains restraint on but the antiheroic Jack lets go of restraint, plunging into the dark world of his sadistic indulgences.

Jack's use of a prohibited word reveals that once he is free of restrictions he breaks all rules. He is antinomian, acting as if the rules are not for him and that he is beyond punishment. Hunting now becomes a form of power assertion, of exercising control. In a strongly visualized scene, the "once angelic" hunters chase the sow in oppressive heat, and the violence with which they hurl themselves at her, has unmistakable sexual undertones; finally the sow "collapsed under them, and they were heavy and fulfilled upon her". Without Ralph's and Piggy's moral condemnation, Jack and his followers revel in the dark and dangerous world of hunting and orgy. There is an impulse both in lust and in killing that seeks to obliterate the other as the most complete expression of the self. The first killing of the piglet satisfied Jack's bloodthirstiness "like a long drink" and now his bloodlust is fulfilled in a wedding-killing.

Jack feels justified for his violent outbursts. The outside world had recognized his qualities, thus he feels unjustified when Ralph and not he, is elected the leader. In his overconfidence he had arrogantly taken the leadership for granted to be his. He is, no doubt, endowed with an angelic voice but he has more of the darker shades of the other angel, Lucifer as pride, anger, and violence, coupled with the sense of not being granted what he thinks is rightfully his position. His offhand authority that disturbs Piggy recalls a military world of authority, arrogance and callousness rather than singing hymns which his ecclesiastical uniform suggests. His angry blue eyes, and his habit of driving the sheath knife into tree trunks hints at his capacity for rapacious violence, ungovernable energy, and perpetual restlessness. Though he has a strong determination to survive, his nature is fierce, snarling and predatory, making him a very frightening protagonist. Ironically, Jack compels a very strange attraction from the boys, his dogmatic authority and sadistic cruelty has a deeper hold on the man's nature than Ralph's sensible regulations.

Jack never accepts democracy as real, or the leadership of anyone else; he does not even feel the need for a responsible thought. All that makes sense to him is his own need to control others and impose himself. Symbolically, he stands for totalitarianism but the sudden humiliating tears, when his leadership claim is rejected, tell a different story—it, for the first time, brings the realization that this bogey-figure is only a child.[28] Establishing his antiheroism further is the fact that though in his frenzy Jack nearly represents "Power Urge" yet critics such as Kincaid and Gregor find him too diminutive to represent such spirit fully.[29] Thus, one sees that Jack who could have personified a great passion is denied even the position.

Jack's education has instilled in him the belief that it is his right to give commands, to rule. His arrogant "I ought to be chief," (p. 19) is strikingly similar to Pincher Martin's "I am Prometheus." Jack himself is a Prometheus-like character, a rebel who brings fire to the group of boys, by using Piggy's glasses. But unlike Prometheus, his rebellion is bereft of heroism and the desire to serve. Howard Babb quotes John S. Whiteley's comment "this assumption of leadership, bred in part of being civilized elite, is maintained when he becomes a member of the primitive elite. The perfect prefect becomes the perfect savage".[30]

Jack is "brilliantly happy" once his leadership is assured. Having renounced communal decision, and having no interest in rescue, the idea of the tribe becomes a satisfying way of life. His malevolence shows itself most fearsomely through mob atrocity and in the misuse of power. Whenever his power is challenged he uses fear and frenzy as his weapon. His antiheroism becomes an established fact as several times he sabotages any possibility of responsible decision insisting on turning it to a personal challenge.

Jack signifies the beast within, the innate susceptibility towards cruelty and self-destructive wickedness that makes any optimistic scheme incapable of realization. The boys, intrinsic products of the current society, convert an Edenic island to an abattoir. What they fail to see that the beast which is so hysterically externalize, can, and does have a human face.

The identification with Lucifer is furthered when Jack tempts the boys to join him. He stages a feast with meat and the incantation against the beast and gives a concrete shape to the vague evil by placating it as the other. The infernal incantation, "kill the pig, bash her in", is but a disguise, like the paint, for his emotional indulgence. His desire for malignant power sets no store for the conch. With the final break-up with Ralph, he shows himself to be susceptible to the totalitarian temptation for he empowers himself with titanic evil. "Power lay in the brown swell of his forearms; authority sat on his shoulders and chattered in his ear like an ape" (p. 168). Jack as an antihero is situated in the postmodern space as he reveals the catastrophic tendencies of man in his destruction of the island, which sustains him and the other boys.

The transformation of Jack is complete. Anthropologically, he is the victim of Durkheimian anomie, the boundless desire unchecked by moral restraint coupled with total breakdown of rules. Jack's uncontrolled pursuit of his desires makes him morally deficient and underplays his heroic potentialities. Marlow's comment, in *Heart of Darkness*, on Kurtz fits Jack only too well.

> They only showed that Mr. Kurtz lacked restraint in the gratification of his various lusts, that there was something wanting in him, some small matter when the pressing need arose, could not be found under his magnificent eloquence.[31]

The same is true with Jack. Even though he is very capable, he lacks essential goodness. Halfway through the novel the boy who had cried for rules screams, "What rules, who cares? Bollocks to the rules" (p. 100). With power, he has ceased to be Jack; power does not transform him into a leading hero but into an antiheroic warlord. Personality is overcome by power, and like Kurtz, he begins to adopt ritual and oracular speech. He sits throned "like an idol" waited on by acolytes. In his use of power over the boys, Jack's antiheroism is further stressed as he abuses power to indulge himself.

Simon, the wise fool locates evil in the constitutions of man's psyche, in "mankind's essential illness" (p. 97). When he comes to share the truth with others during the storm, staggering out of the forest, it proves fatal for him. In a frantic savagery born out of fear, and the agitation of the ritualistic dance reminiscent of the bacchic frenzy of the Dionysian followers, Jack forces him to enact the role of the beast and kills him. Later, he attempts to prove that it was the beast disguised as Simon. In fact, it is an attempt to exonerate himself. In doing so, Jack rejects the message that Simon brings "that we must acknowledge the thing of darkness as our own"; symbolically it is also a rejection of the means of salvation. For Jack and his tribe, Simon's death acts as a catalyst, releasing their inner darkness, and they proceed to build a tribal strategy for coping with the horrors of the island. However, if the world is one of power, Jack finds there is no power to be accountable to. He has to answer no one for beating Wilfred, thus revealing to Roger "the possibilities of irresponsible authority". Jack's awareness of darkness within himself disturbs him and in fact he realizes the truth of the tenet but refuses to acknowledge it.

Not content with isolating Ralph and Piggy from the group, Jack steals Piggy's glasses with utter callousness. It is in this context that Ralph calls him a "bloody, bloody thief". It is true that in bringing fire to his group, he is Prometheus-like, but his act diminishes in stature if we remember the fact that he steals from one who is incapable of defending himself. Jack's selfish behaviour, which is never a heroic feature, seems to preclude redemption. Sinister in his power, the symbol of his regime is the totem pole—the stick sharpened at both ends, the support of the Lord of the flies.

Scientifically, there have been hypotheses that relate the mental state of a child with that of savages and criminals. This point is significant because Jack is a child with strong criminal tendencies, which make him antiheroic. In the Victorian period, comparative studies were made between criminals and savages. J.W. Griffith[32] uses Lombroso's explanation that the criminal was only a reversion to the primitive type of his species. The relation between Jack's criminality and his regression to the primitive can be explained to a large extent by these findings. The Lombroson theory points out the mental anomalies visible among the primitive and the criminal; these are, an absence of moral sensibility, instability of character, vanity, irritability, love of revenge. As such, the anomalies pointed out by Lombroso, and those present in Jack are strong characteristics of the satanic antihero. Moreover, Jack's regression includes love of orgies and the irresponsible carving of evil for its own sake, he desires not only to kill the victim, but also to mutilate the corpse, tear its flesh and drink its blood (pp. 14-15). He also gives in to temptations and ill-balanced impulsiveness.

> These facts clearly prove that their most horrible crimes have their origin in the animal instincts of which childhood gives us a pale reflection. Repressed in civilized man by education, environment and the fear of punishment, they suddenly break out in the born criminal without apparent cause, or under the influence of certain circumstances.[33]

The child is thus proved to have a sinister capacity for evil. This perhaps explains why Golding uses children as representatives to symbolize inherent, yet hidden truths about human nature. Always a little nearer to raw humanity then adults, they slip easily into a condition of animality depraved by mind, into the cruelty of the hunters with their devil liturgies and tortures.

Golding uses the Nietzschian dichotomy of Apollo and Dionysus to explore the tension between the Apollonian Ralph and the Dionysian Jack. Jack the modern militant incarnation of Dionysus thrives on chaos and on freedom from institution. Ralph stands for the enlightened self-interest of Hobbes, Bentham and Miller, and by going against this enlightenment, Jack becomes an antihumanist. Between them, it is the conflict between lawmakers and lawbreakers, between the champions of order and of anarchy. Jack proves himself to be a product of the post-Nietzschian and post-Hiroshima age whose symbol is the sow's head on a stick. Through his actions and belligerence, Jack reveals aggression, sadism and irrationality, which pulls him strongly towards antiheroism. As a Dionysian he symbolizes Nietzsche's will to power. Nietzsche possibly would not have found any fault, moral or otherwise, in Jack, for he endorses an antinomian morality. Adults are seen by children as sensible creatures—by extension, almost God, so without God in the island, everything becomes permissible. He insists on a multiplicity of morality expressing the various energies of human life.

Often feeling desperately alone, Jack wants a connection with others, so in words and action he tries to find his way back to a common ground with others—the ground of old values. For this reason, the translation of values is always contaminated, impure. Goodheart[34] feels that in order to retain the connection with the outside world, one may be perverse and diabolical; an antihero implicitly recognizes the existence, despite his nihilism, by behaving rebelliously and contrary to law.

If Jack is the antihero, Ralph, the hero, is his conscience. In fact, both Ralph and Jack, as leaders are under twin compulsions, both have to succeed in what they undertake and at the same time contend with the alternative game the other offers. Jack will not be free completely until he kills Ralph, that way he can obliterate his conscience. Ralph's morality brings Jack face to face with shame; the ensuing tension between the harsh superego (Ralph) and the erring ego (Jack) that Jack's conscience is subjected to, increases his guilt. However, instead of accepting guilt, Jack turns the harsh aggressiveness upon another, extraneous individual. There is moreover, that "undefinable connection between Ralph, the good side of Jack and Jack himself, who therefore will never let him alone, never!" (p. 209). Kincaid and Gregor[35] support this idea "Jack can never be free from the Ralph in him till Ralph is dead." To be completely free from his guilt, Ralph needs to be silenced. Ralph, aware of the antagonism that Jack holds against him asks, "Why do you hate me?" (p. 132). Hostility between them brings the problems but the answers lie deep within man's primitive psyche, in the ancient tug-of-war between reason and passion. Thus, as a satanic antihero Jack tries to supplant Ralph and assert himself.

Martin Quinn's[36] essay "The Unheroic Hero" points out that in each of his first three novels, Golding situates his stories in such a way that allows him to strip man down to his barest essentials, revealing the central characters to be antiheroic. In each the characters wear a minimum of clothing so that one can observe clearly "bare, fork'd" animal that is "unaccommodated man".[37] Freed from the complications of social life, the boys gradually reveal deeper barbaric instincts Golding sees his characters somehow free, somehow guilty, intelligent and yet so capable of evil.

Like Conrad, there is a preoccupation with guilt and desperate technical resources like the sudden changing of view and paradigmatic time shifts. Frederick Karl[38] writes that Golding strives to pull the veneer behind the conventional matter of the conventional novel to view what man is like when the façade of civilized behaviour pulls away. The myth of progress has failed, but the rival myth of necessary evil has come back without bringing God back with it.

If Jack is taken as a representative of the degenerate man, with the seeds of Satanic antiheroism in him, how does Golding reach such a conclusion? The moral crisis brought about by the war, illustrated how man with his intelligence and material progress became more corrupt, violent and destructive. Civilization has not been able to restrain man's depravity and destructiveness; rather it arms him with a greater power of destruction. In Golding, guilt, the taste of isolation, good and bad, are made actual, like vomit in the mouth. In the novel, the increasingly tribal seeming activities of schoolboys on the desert island serve to trace the harsh diagrams of human history, charting man's evolution as a grisly decline from fruit eating commune to totalitarian butchery. The tale of a corrupt and decadent genius repeatedly seems to have heralded 20th century cultural preoccupations. Freud's emphasis on the divided self, of the striving, lustful, anarchic id, seeking gratification despite the countervailing pressure of the superego had been anticipated in the depiction of Kurtz's ferocious fulfillment in the Congo and later dramatized in the chorister-war lord Merridew.

Is the writer free to pursue his beliefs and visions, and more often than not, can he cross his limitations? At a certain level, there is a similarity between Conrad's Kurtz's plight and that of dedicated artist. In *A Personal Record,* Conrad offers reflections on his own aim as author:

> In that interior world where his thoughts and emotions go seeking for the experience of imagined adventures, there are no policemen, no law, no pressure of circumstances or dread of opinion to keep him within bounds, who then is going to say Nay to his temptations if not his conscience?[39]

But as a serious artist of contemporary anxieties and malaise, Golding feels moral accountability towards his work. He explores the moral conflicts with the full and tragic awareness.

Lord of the Flies combines present day confusion with the Faust myth. Characteristics of both Postmodernism and Modernism strain the tale with its sense of absurdity and meaninglessness, of human isolation and the problematic nature of communication and also the sense of defilement of the natural environment by man. From the very outset the narrative probes, questions and subverts familiar contrasts between the savage and the civilized.

It is by his use of language that Golding enters the perceptions of the children. His achievement in the novel is the creation of a complex character, Jack who, though a child, reflects the reason why Golding essentially sees "man" as an antihero figure, a morally diseased creature. The final jolt comes for the reader when he/she is suddenly distanced from the happenings on the island. The reader is pulled, as it were, outside the novel, and suddenly seen from the outside, the predatory hunters are seen as a semi-circle of dirty little boys in need of a wash. On the narrative level, there is a structural repetition, with the second half repeating the structure of the first, not revealing new things, but showing us the real depth of what the reader already knows. The novel fits the bill of being an anti-allegory, which according to Frye, is another way of saying serious parody. Parody is a postmodern feature because it totally denies the possibility of a pure autonomy, as it is already parasitic upon an earlier text. Again, anti-allegory is a peculiarly modern form that connects the imagery of traditional allegory so that instead of becoming exemplary and doctrinal, the imagery becomes ironic and paradoxical. It is, thus, the reversal of traditional, classical allegory based on the enlightenment, which teaches us that human nature is perfectible. It rather teaches the opposite, that "it is no good".[40]

In "Pain and William Golding", V.S. Pritchett writes that the modern realist faces problems when he fails to describe the features of a changing, violent or collapsing society. Concerned with the anarchy of a poisoned future, Golding is starkly bare, scarcely using any lecture or argument; he simply shakes us until we feel in our bones the persistent agony of our species. He is a pragmatic story-teller intensely concerned with the fundamental problems of human existence "of man's first disobedience" and the resultant tension of knowledge and guilt, conscience and in short, Golding's constant and penetrating focus on the antiheroic Jack shows that he has understood and laid bare the moral pulse of the fragmented, postmodern age. In the end, Golding must be placed in the context of his own generation, disoriented by war, and by philosophic beliefs that discouraged faith in God and man. His diagnosis of the divided, distorted and dehumanized self personified by Jack is informed by nostalgia, a recollection of the fundamental decencies, forgotten and neglected by now, the ceremonies of innocence which "support and sustain this frail but human frame".[41]

Be drunk and be happy.

Saturday Night and Sunday Morning,

In Alan Sillitoe, art is realistic and intrinsically related to the social atmosphere surrounding it. In an interview with John Halperin[42] he professes that his novels came from experience, though not exactly biographical yet they were sort of against the backdrop of what was "my reality in life". The introduction of the protagonist in *Saturday Night and Sunday Morning* (1958) is particularly interesting. Sillitoe does not idealize Arthur Seaton or even remotely try to project him as an epical character. Rather, the opening paragraph introduces Seaton as a drunkard, unable to hold himself up after eleven pints of beer and seven small gins.

> The rowdy gang of singers who sat at the scattered tables saw Arthur walk unsteadily to the head of the stairs, and though they must all have known that he was dead drunk, and seen the danger he would be in, no one attempted to talk to him and lead him back to his seat. With eleven pints of beer and seven small gins playing hide-and-seek inside his stomach, he fell from the top-most stair to the bottom. (p. 7)

Arthur Seaton belongs to the race of jaunty antiheroes, who people most of the literature of the Angry Young Man period. He is perhaps the most fully realized of the antiheroes of this movement. He is one of the first Teddy boys—the first real postwar workingclass youths in Britain, a type figure of the post-1945 industrial welfare state working man, born into an economic fabric against which his impulses strongly rebel.

Protesting against the genteel Bloomsbury, the postwar workingclass writers like Amis, Wain, Wilson and Sillitoe demanded that art deal with concrete, real life, the tangible, that art shape, and direct the multiplicity of contemporary experience instead of chasing phantoms of trite visions of the past. The postwar period was one of cultural and spiritual disillusionment. Contemporary society forced the intelligent person to limit his scope to more specific social problems because of its intelligibility rather than metaphysical discussions. One should not forget the fact that Seaton belongs to a milieu and society that is intricately related to an industrial mechanical life where the main concern of the individual is the question about the next meal or the next drink.

Arthur Seaton is representative of the workingclass man content to spend his 14 pounds a week on clothes, women and Saturday night binges at the local pub. However, this limited liberty is highly valued for this would have been impossible almost two decades ago and Seaton sympathizes with his father who had been on the dole during the war years. For a man so deeply rooted in the practical realities of life as Arthur, war is nothing associated with heroism and bravery. War is bad because it forced mobilization on people and meant less money and a hard life. He says: "Churchill spoke after the 9 o'clock news and told you what you were fighting for, as if it mattered" (p. 114). During his two years stint as a soldier, Arthur used all his cunning on the army people. He would be "so neat and tidy" that the sergeant even stated that Arthur would make a good soldier. However, inwardly Arthur responds, "You bastards won't get me down."

> But let them start a war, he thought, and see what a bad soldier I can be. "Them at the top" must know that nobody would fight, and he supposed that because of this they weren't so anxious to rely on them in another war. In the army it was: "F—you, Jack. I am all right". Out of the army it was: "Every man for himself." It amounted to the same thing. (p. 114)

Arthur Seaton represents nihilistic hedonism, which is an aspect of the ironic antihero as he not only revolts against the established authority but also celebrates his rebellion. His drinking, spending on clothes and women so recklessly are proofs enough. Seaton does not respect authority for they only serve to rob the happiness of the workingclass. Like Smith in *The Loneliness of the Long Distance Runner* (1959) Seaton has a strong sense of his personal worth. In the novella, Smith's deliberate loss at the race involves no histrionics, and though he suffers, he does so undramatically; the world can do very little for him. Similarly, Seaton feels that he is as good as any other man. His workingclass environment and painful memories may have bred defiance but they have not bred humility. The practicalities of a hard life have taught these defiant men that heroism is a hollow concept and does not pay for the basic amenities of life.

Seaton can understand others, sympathize, can react honestly and directly, yet he is incapable of heroic action. Born into a hard and difficult world, given little, pursued by the forces of an oppressive society, he grabs what he can and rarely reveals his emotions. Heroism is either a folly or a game calculated to delude the authorities and government officials who believe in such nonsense. Heroism and idealism can be practiced only in a world where there is, at least, a replication of order. But cultures of survival through struggle has made man realize the futility of heroism where man stands to gain nothing and lose everything.

As an antihero and an existentialist, Seaton exemplifies pure anarchism. He frequently experiences the desire to blow up the Parliament and the war ministry. Once walking along the street, Arthur hears the sound of breaking glass "it synthesized all the anarchism within him, was the most perfect noise to accompany the end of the world and himself" (p. 94). Sillitoe presents the destructive energy of Arthur in various ways. Even when he dislikes the army, the firing range holds his interest and provides an outlet for his pent up anarchism,

> He liked firing he had to admit. It gave him satisfaction to destroy, if only the board perched above the butts. He would rather destroy something more tangible, houses or human beings, but that was impossible, yet. When it was not his turn at the sandbags he loved to stand and listen to the total bursting of bullets from the dozen guns firing. Hearing the lifting and falling of sound, the absolutely untamable rhythms that ripped the air open with untrammeled joy. (pp. 120-21)

The people of the postwar period were deeply disillusioned by the improper functioning of the welfare state. Developments since the war were felt not to have contributed to a social revolution as promised by the Labour Government of 1945, but to a modified stasis, in which even the two leading political parties seems to have grown indistinguishable. The society was divided between the powerful rich "them" upper class and the workingclass poor "us" proles. Arthur believed that the two parties, the big fat Tory bastards and the Labour bleeders would bleed the people dry with their policies all the while telling them that it was for their own good. Like his creator, Sillitoe, Seaton indulges in protest politics.

Though it was Kingsley Amis's Jim Dixon who inaugurated the trend of the bumbling antiheroes of the workingclass, it was Seaton who is a truer picture of the angry young man. Though Sillitoe maintained that at that time he was in Majorica away from the movement, yet his and Seaton's sullen indifference to the establishment reveals that they were not very far away from the socio-literary happenings in England. Seaton is in fact one of the fifties' more genuinely stone-throwing-angry man, a self-conscious rebel infuriated by the raw edge of fang and claw on which all laws were based, law and order against which he had been fighting all his life. He is a rebellious antihero rebelling against the hypocritical institutions of English society. He fits Ihab Hassan's description of the antihero as a rebel-victim. But though a victim in the upper class dominated world, he refuses to cling on to this label. He is one in line with the brooding, volatile antihero Jimmy Porter, who along with Jim Dixon best depicted the rebellious, the angry and the hilarious moods of the period respectively. Like Porter, he complains about being a rebel in a bland atmosphere, in which there seemed to be an older instinctive workingclass anarchism and a gut resentment of all authority "don't let the bastards grind you down". He means to have his fun and cheat the world before it cheats him. Sillitoe's antiheroes are given to tough talking, drinking, screwing, stealing and insubordination. For such rebellious, anarchic men who refuse, both literally and metaphorically to play the games of the establishment, there is only one rule. "If it moves, screw it, if you can't screw it, steal it, if you can't steal it, set fire to it."[43]

Seaton wants to cheat the world because it is cheating him. Even Sillitoe does not debunk the idea that the world is the kind of place, a world of enmity, a world you have to keep looking over your shoulder.[44] Throughout the novel the feeling is "you are ok if you don't weaken". His feeling of frustration, disappointment and anger fits the picture of the angry young man. Kenneth Allsop's *The Angry Decade,*[45] describes the Angry Young Man:

> The phase the Angry Young Man carries multiple overtones, which might be listed as irreverence, stridency, impatience with tradition, vigour, vitality, vulgarity, sulky resentment against the cultivated.

However, a major difference separates Sillitoe's characters from that of other workingclass writers. Sillitoe solidly situates his protagonists in the workingclass environment strongly identifying them with the class structure. What makes Seaton likeable in spite of his anti-heroism is his defiant honesty. Unlike the resentful, malicious John Braine's Joe Lampton of *Room at the Top* (1957), who yearns to belong to the affluent middle class that he hates, Seaton has no such hidden motives. Most of the protagonists of this period were social climbers unconsciously aiming to identify with the ruling class. Though there was a consistent tension between rebellion and conformity, it seems that most of these men were rather disgruntled with their present position in the society. Compared to their dissentience, Seaton, Porter and Smith are really angry and helpless to bring about the change they want so badly, but they also have the realization that there is not going to be much of a good change even if there is a revolution. Sooner or later, things would be back on the same beaten track, same old policies and frustration with the hypocritical religion and same dissatisfaction with the meaninglessness of life. Not having much choice, the unconforming rebel settles for compromise, and in some cases, social acceptance.

Often with the exception of Sillitoe's and Barstow's characters, the angry young men were seldom genuinely critical of the forces shaping contemporary life, and personal success largely terminated dissentience. Whereas protagonists of Amis and his type largely choose the easy way of social conformity ready to pay the price to scale the social ladder, Sillitoe and his brood chose to rebel. Choices remain open but are not entertained: it is a hard way of life, it is their anti-heroism they thrive upon, but it is the only way of creating and holding on to their hard found identities.

Among the antiheroes, Seaton became the most fully realized antihero of the period, the representative of the angry decade. The lathe worker who perceives that the benefits of full employment are both partial and precarious, senses an unspoken comradeship between himself and his fellow workers directed against a vague 'they' of employer and the state and is dimly aware that all is not well either with the society in which he lives or with his personal values.[46]

Bred by long years of want, poverty and misery, Sillitoe's antiheroes seek self-realization not so much in a philosophical search for a meaning for life like the bourgeois heroes, but in the concrete experience of physical delights and private happiness. Happiness here is largely dependent on money that provides for the food, drink, sex and television. Sillitoe is not guilty of romanticizing the life of the workers even when they are relatively well off then their predecessors. For Seaton, happiness does not come by adhering to the traditional heroic conduct or following established conventions. With Seaton's realistic view of life, happiness in fact means a large pay packet which would provide tangible and concrete comforts like a holiday or a packet of cigarettes. As one who can be described as an eiron,[47] Seaton is not one of the idealistic heroes to show the ill effects of smoking or drinking, rather he would provide it to others as it affords an outlet for their pent up frustrations and energy. However, to their painful astonishment, happiness does not always follow automatically. According to Richard Hoggart, Sillitoe's antiheroes reveled in what he termed as "workingclass hedonism"[48] fostered by the new prosperity of the class. Hoggart regretted this new attitude, fearing that the workingclass would lose its solidarity. But the heroes who stay in their class, like Seaton, aren't much happy as well. Spending their fairly good wages on clothes, girls, and pubs, are means of escape not only from the drab eight hour job on the lathe, but from the narrowness of home as well. In some ways, in the novel, Sillitoe offers a terrifying glimpse into an age where booze, work and sex were all that Britain's young men had to look forward to.

David Holbroke[49] in his essay "Prostitution, Politics, and Egotistical Nihilism" states how Nietzsche's "God is Dead" implied that the church and all its moral injunctions and theology had gone dead. Conscience became outdated in the mechanical amoral society, except for the existentialists who insisted that a man can only find himself through hearing the call of conscience. He also suggests that Seaton in his hedonism follows the egotistical nihilism of Max Stirner, a German philosopher. The Stirnerean nihilistic egoist is the centre of his world which perpetually re-creates from the nothingness to which it is perpetually consigned.

Holbroke[50] also uses Anthony Wilden's argument from *Systems and Structure* that the fundamental ethic of our civilization is exploitation, that we everywhere internalize its 'ethic of disposability': the concrete jungle, popular hedonism, sexual opportunism—these are manifestations of the ruthless egoism of such a nihilistic philosophy. 'God is dead' and everything is permissible. This is also the initial point of existentialism. Indeed everything is permissible if God did not exist, but consequently man becomes forlorn and hopeless, because neither within him not without does he find anything to cling to. Thus, the only convincing philosophy for a man to follow remains the amoral nihilism on Stirnerean lines.

If one views Seaton through Stirnerean philosophy, it would not be a disservice. As an egoist, Seaton is immersed in his own world. For him, as for Stirner, the individual self is its own justification. That way he is much closer to Nietzsche's Dionysian immoralist. According to Stirner,[51] the idea of man under the modern dispensation has replaced the idea of God and the uniqueness of the individual is now denied in favour of the essence which each person must realize. It is hedonistic nihilism. In his view, I, the ego is a consumer, an appropriator of people and things for the satisfaction of its desires. Stirner's doctrine, with its faith in extreme economic individualism is the consumers' counterpart of the doctrine of productive economic individualism. So in the bourgeois world, the individual becomes gaudy, bragging and impertinent. His materialistic solipsism and practical egoism strives to negate authority and so creating a radical individualism. However, Camus[52] is critical of Stirner's ideas on nihilistic egoism. In *The Rebel*,[53] Camus consigns Stirner to dwelling in a desert of isolation and negation drunk with destruction branding him to be the direct ancestor of terrorist anarchy; he proclaims that Stirner is intoxicated with the perspective of justifying crime without mentioning that the latter distinguishes between the ordinary criminal and the criminal as violator of the sacred. On the contrary, when Stirner talks of egoism as the ultimate definition of the human essence it is not a question of moral category but of a simple existential fact. Stirner's idea fits the world of Seaton because the latter's reality too is the world of his immediate experience. On the reverse side, Seaton's hedonism illustrates Stirner's view that the individual must find his entire satisfaction in his own life.[54] Stirner's philosophy makes the fulfillment of one's will and interests the centre of the world.

Most social deviancy and perversion results from the unnatural circumstances modern humans are forced to live in. The urban jungle, the rootless cosmopolitanism, overcrowding and the stresses of a money culture create a bewildering array of unhealthy stimuli. Perversion and deviancy are just human responses to these uncontrollable forces. Ronald De Vareka's[55] study of Sillitoe's political fiction illustrates that a Marxist approach is valid for his fiction. His sympathy for a Marxist perspective is evidently clear. His realism also fits the definition provided by Georg Lukaćs that the Marxist conception of realism is realism in which the essences of reality are exposed perpetually and artistically. Seaton like Smith in

The Loneliness of the Long Distance Runner is a poverty grown and factory-formed rebel. Seaton and Smith, "the Borstal Boy" fight with the only tool available to them "their cunning" against the oppressive society that would, if it could, assimilate them, turning them into collaborators in the charade of benevolently despotic capitalism.

In his interview with Halperin, Sillitoe makes his stand clear that he is "anti-establishment, anti-privilege, anti anyone who achieves a certain position which is due mainly to their having been born in a particular way. I am against inherited wealth which gives power over other people."[56] In creating the anti-everything character of Seaton, Sillitoe personifies this stand. One fact clearly establishes the connection between two fundamental issues—the first is Seaton's anti-heroism and secondly, Sillitoe's Marxist leanings. For Seaton, all poll systems are fraudulent rhetoric to cheat the workingman; nonetheless, he has some sympathy for the communists, because in the 1950s, they were so universally despised or ignored. Justifying his voting for the communists, even as he was under twenty-one, and casting his Dad's vote, he says: "I did it because I thought the poor bloke wouldn't get any votes. I allus like to 'elp the losin' side" (p. 31). Apart from this, Seaton has no idealistic objective of voting for the Reds.

Sillitoe was deeply influenced by the two phenomena that probably made the greatest impact on the people's lives of the period, which at first sight bore rather conflicting implications; first, the fear of the atomic bomb and second, the new affluence of the upper classes. In the novel, the fear of the atomic bomb forms a gloomy shadow in the background. Still neither Sillitoe nor Seaton appears to revel in bleak despair, but react like the majority of men have reacted to the present day, "by psychological repression and escape, turning their attention to the more immediate problems of everyday life".[57] Arthur finds it useless to save money. "You never know when the Yanks were going to do something daft like dropping the Hydrogen bomb on Moscow" (pp. 27-28). Instead of looking forward to the future he believes in living in the present and enjoying it, and this attitude highlights his existentialism which can be seen from his behaviour as a careless spender, a rootless hedonist, engrossed in booze, fights and dangerous sex. Seaton's antiheroism is further established when he shoots Mrs. Bull, the street gossip for spreading nasty news about him. Ironically, these stories are rather true. When her husband comes to enquire, Seaton first mimes his action from the kitchen window and later even physically threatens him. Even his brother, Fred, at times, is forced to admit that Arthur was not a very nice bloke. In fact, at times he could be "a real bastard" (p. 102).

In the novel, Sillitoe had put his own personal experience of working in the Raleigh factory. Even though he did not loathe it, but in his words "work is work". The nauseous oil fumes and the vigilance from the management were major problems faced by the workers. The latter led a perpetual struggle between the workers and the management. Seaton is aware of the conflict between the two, the cold struggle that keeps class antagonism active and allegiance firm. The worker's newly found paradise of liberty and large pay packet is relative. Seaton sums up the anti-heroic life of the factory worker at the end of the novel:

> Born drunk and married blind, misbegotten into a strange and crazy world, dragged up through the dole and into the war with a gas-mask on your clock, and the sirens rattling into you every night while you rot with scabies in an air-raid shelter. Slung into khaki at eighteen, and when they let you out, you sweat again in a factory, grabbing for an extra pint, doing women at the weekend and getting to know whose husbands are on the night-shift, working with rotten guts and an aching spine, and nothing for it but money to drag you back every Monday morning. (p. 239)

Working in the factory since he was fifteen has made Arthur tough and realistic. He is aware of both the advantages and the disadvantages of being a factory worker, "Hard work and good wages, and smell all day that turns your guts" (p. 25). The standards set were entirely material, the only end was self-gain. For Seaton and others like him, coming from the underprivileged end of town, memories of empty bellies and inability to pay the rent were still sharp.[58] Nothing matters except money.

For the protagonists of the workingclass novels, paradoxically, work is not worship. The antiheroes did not adhere to a particular trade, in which they could take pride like the traditional heroes, but in accordance with the conditions of full employment, would wander from job to job, none of which is described as holding any interest in itself. The only aim was to earn money for "money is considered as the key to the gratification of the deeper longings stirrings obscurely in the hearts of the 'juvenile heroes'".[59]

The new prosperity had produced not only positive results, but had in an unforeseen way created a set of new difficulties for the workingclass, more or less psychological in nature. For the elderly, after the war, the predominant feeling was one of relief, like Harold Seaton, grateful for the greater sense of security and small luxuries. But for those growing up, like Seaton, it was an altogether different world. The unprecedented flow of money provided the means for unwonted pleasures but it also became a source of confusion. The mindlessness of their routine work, their frustrated aspirations for self-fulfilment along with their rebellious attitudes and their pursuit of small activities took up their already depleted energies. Their protest was partly social and partly cultural. Nearly all of them were too young to have seen war services and were impatient of the war mystique cherished by their elders. The main force of their anger was directed against those who still constituted a powerful, though outdated establishment, the largely upper class Bloomsbury intelligentsia. Moreover, the behavioral pattern, created by the earlier generation for the sake of necessity, had lost its inevitability for them and they began experimenting with new forms. Once the basic need for food, clothes and shelter were gratified, more complicated and subtler needs made themselves felt. Like many of the bourgeois individuals before them, in literature as well as in real life, these men now launched on a search for self-realization. But while the traditional set of behaviour had offered a certain psychological stability, the new prospects brought feelings of disorientation, insecurity and loneliness along with the promise of new pleasures. This slight shade of ambiguity of feeling and perception is present in the characterization of Arthur Seaton.

Unlike Smith, Seaton is not a "Borstal boy", though several of his cousins are. He is a prototype of the workingclass angry young man, rebellious and contemptuous towards authority in the form of the management and the army; the only way to vent his energy and frustration is to unleash it on women and drinks. His existence in a mindless state is consequent of the mechanical work that he does, and it is also a necessary state to tide from one weekend to the next, which helps him to retain his sanity. Ill-equipped for anything except drinking, noise and sex, his very recklessness, at once aggressive and evasive is summed up in his reaction to the sergeant major. "I am me and nobody else; and whatever people think I am or say I am, that's what I am not, because they don't know a bloody thing about me" (p. 120). This is his way of holding on to his identity. Though there is a lot of vitality, yet he has, like some antiheroes of the period, a distinctive blend of gaiety and suppressed menace around him, which is apparent in his shooting of Mrs. Bull, and the toppling of the car, which had hit him while walking back home one night.

But even complete and heroic rebellion is denied Seaton. His rebelliousness is diminished by several incidents. The first is Brenda's pregnancy and the resultant back-alley abortion. The near fatal beating that he receives from the two swaddies after his complicated relationships with both Brenda and Winnie shocks him into the realization that the world is a jungle where only the strong survive, culminating finally in his marriage with Doreen and his acceptance of the prescribed social roles. The last incident comes when Arthur slowly realizes that he is fighting a losing battle and that his aggressive attitude and stone throwing anger serves only to alienate him further from others. In the end, like a true existentialist and Sisyphus-like figure he accepts that he is the fish in the fang and claw jungle, bound to be caught in the bait, one day or the other.

The main problem Seaton faces is one of identity. How can he assert and hold on to his identity in a world opposed to his values? As a human he is often involved in a search for identity, and affiliations which help to define him. He longs for the security a specific relationship can give him while he finds that the complexity both within himself and the world cannot be easily expressed through any specific translations. Man has always felt the need for tangible identity, for reassurances of meaningful human existence. To this problem, several postwar British writers adopted the existential attitude. Sartre points out that often man accepts definitions of himself within a vacuum, and sometimes can define himself only in a vacuum. Often the breakdown of personality may leave the individual in uncertainty and confusion.

Gindin[60] asserts that collapse in beliefs and in public relations may often lead a man to rely only on himself. Existentialists hold on to the doctrine that man must see things himself. However, the clash in points of view, and the impact of contradictory definitions underline the complexity and confusion that the individual faces. He can only subjectively try to work his way through it. The existentialists insist on dealing with the concrete facts of experience though they may be multiple and chaotic. However, they tend to regard facts as less certain, less amenable to arranging of the perplexing and easily distorted images. In Sillitoe, the sensible man deals concretely with experience whereas the man who fits experience into an abstract essence is made ludicrous or vicious. But though Seaton in *Saturday Night and Sunday Morning* may be sensible in this regard, yet he has none of the heroic features. So in spite of this fact he remains an antihero. Sillitoe's antihero does not find the virtue of simple perception so rewarding. His world is more difficult, the facts are hard to understand and arrange. Man is caught up between the vast possibilities and his economic limitations. As a nihilist, Seaton, like Nietzsche, insists on what things ought to be rather than what they are, and the world as it ought to be does not exist.[61]

Seaton is the kind of antihero who has a quirky and individual code of his own, deriving a strong class identity from the workingclass solidarity. Of course he steers away from being sentimentally attached to anything, but he is a strong believer in community ties and its rules. It is evident in his relations to his deserter cousins, to Ambergate and even to Doreen, and in his silent respect to Robboe.

However, Sillitoe's antiheroes not only bring out several questions regarding identity but have disturbed many critics as well. The main source of controversy is the protagonist's unrepentant attitude towards his chosen life of aggression and often of crime; the critical question remains whether or not Sillitoe sanctions the values of his protagonists or somehow exposes the limitations of those blatantly anarchistic values. In *The Loneliness of the Long Distance Runner*, Smith declares:

> And if I had a whip hand, I wouldn't even bother to build a place like this to put all the cops, governors, posh whores, pen pushers, army officers, Members of Parliament in, no, I'd stick them up against the wall and let them have it. (p. 164)

Smith's expression of what he would do with power has an uncanny resemblance to Seaton's declaration that he'd never let anyone grind him down. If somebody offered him dynamite to blow up the factory, which provides him with his earnings, he will not back off:

> I'd do it because that's something worth doin'. Action. I'd bale out for Russia or the North Pole where I'd sit and laugh like a horse over what I've done, at the wonderful sight of gaffers and machines and shining bikes going sky high one wonderful moonlit night. Not that I have got out against them but that's just how I feel now and then. (p. 34)

Sillitoe's fiction has disturbed critics because he makes Seaton, once described by his brother as a "real bastard" at times, sympathetic and even seems to offer his anarchistic views and shrewd cunningness without ironic qualifications and with much sympathy. No external philosophizing comes over Seaton. He follows the rule of the jungle, getting what he wants either by deceiving weaker men like Jack, or by force and destruction. Though there is an air of cheerfulness around him, he also has a deep sense of nihilism. Seaton contends that the one way to assert his identity is to hold on his honesty and to his class.

In the novel, Sillitoe directly uses the imagery of a fang and claw jungle. Seaton gives voice to this belief when, late in the novel, he is bashed up by two swaddies for his complicated affairs with two married women. Both affairs on the whole failed to provide him with permanent bliss, though it provided him with temporary pleasures. For almost three days, he lay in half sleep overcome by inexpressible melancholy. Everything seems alienated, distant to him and he is unable to pin-point his malady exactly. The realization hits him:

> He knew it was no use fighting against the cold weight of his nameless malady, or asking how it came about. He did not ask, believing it to be related to his defeat by the swaddies, a fact that did not call for much speculation. He did nor ask whether he was in such a knocked out state because he had lost the rights of love over two women, or because the two swaddies represented the raw edge of fang-and-claw on which all laws were based, law and order against which he had been fighting all his life in such a thoughtless and unorganized way that he could not but lose. Such questions came later. The plain fact was that the two swaddies had got him at last—as he had known they would—and had bested him on the common battleground of the jungle. (p. 155)

Seaton attempts to fight his way out of the jungle and, he has no weapon except cunning. He uses his cunning in his dealings with the management and the army. In his defiance he asserts the only means of transcending the jungle. Sillitoe, like Osborne found the factory working man relegated to a reasonably clean ash can, sitting on a pile of rotten culture and debased values that should have been destroyed long ago. But Sillitoe's protagonists chose to remain where they are, however, uncomfortable it might be, and refuse to play by the societal norms.

The idea of class and the divisions of society by means of background, occupation or geography has been a strong influence on English literature. Man's social environment largely conditions his attitudes and responses to the world. Time, place, family, occupation, both mould and explain the individual. A comparison of the general conditions the protagonists of the 19th and the 20th century novels might shed some light on the pathetic condition of the present-day antihero.

Frequently, in 19th century bourgeois fiction, the unique hero was set against an impotent society and rigid class forms. The hero symbolized virtue, the others represented vice or benevolent mindlessness. Class, by then, had become a convenient way of explaining the frequency with which the social environment defined the individual, for the antiheroic heroes of contemporary literature bring into focus the problems cast by the fluidity of class structure. Why are the contemporary characters antiheroic as compared to the traditional heroes? One of the parameters of measuring the quality and greatness of a person, according to Gindin, is in the depth of his struggle. The Dickensian heroes struggled to fit in on to a higher society. The contemporary antihero in Osborne or Sillitoe struggles less and is considerably the lesser hero. Unlike the heroes of Dickens or Fielding, the ironic antihero is not the rare spirit who is inexplicable in terms that account for the mundane majority, linked to the rest of us only as an image of what we would like to represent. He is rather the illustration of one of the central issues of the volatile, changing society. When social values were more fixed, writers dwelt on the energy and exceptional quality of the hero characterizing the society. Now these are dealt with in a peripheral manner; the fixed alternatives seem far less fixed and the hero, neither exceptional nor exceptionally virtuous, is himself both a product and the problem of the society.[62]

Reading the literature of the period one comes to the conclusion that by the end of World War II, the antiheroic figure had become the standard fictional representation of the age in Britain. Without a rigid class structure enabling him to display his virtue by romantic opposition, without even a fixed definition of virtue at all, the exceptional and heroic figure has become the fool, the man living in terms of an outmoded ideal or a hollow pretense. Furthermore, socially British postwar era was dominated by a mood of defiance and bitterness on the part of the lower workingclass. Military conscription was compulsory, diverting the young men away from the money they could have earned during this two-year period. The army was regarded as a part of the Kingdom-cum-Establishment. But life within and outside the army was the same: Might, Savagery and jungle law prevailed. In the army it was "F—you Jack, I am all right". Out of the army it was "every man for himself". Both of it amounted to the same thing. Seaton feels that "every man for himself" is the best and the sanest way of survival. The Establishment invariably stifled and restricted the workingman by binding him in cruel and irrelevant laws. Seaton prefers the military world to his own because there the hostilities were open and one could be always on guard. But the welfare state was unable to assure the safety and security of the workingman. The antiheroic stance of hit-and-run of Seaton and other Sillitoe characters becomes sort of a defense mechanism against external danger.

> No place existed that could be called safe, and he knew for the first time in his life that there never had been such a thing as safety, and never would be, the difference being that now he knew it as a fact, whereas before it was a natural unconscious state. (p. 157)

Seaton sympathizes and identifies strongly with Ada's sons, most of whom belonged to the Royal Corps of Deserters, one serving three years in Borstal for stealing to provide some proper food for his family. The sympathy between them exists on the similarity in background and attitude. Workingclass families subscribed to the hostile attitude, for them, heroism, bravery and ideology are useless because they do not provide for the basic amenities of life. During the war, men were required to defend their country. Idealistic exhortations obviously did not matter to the workingman because once the war would be over, class discriminations, slightly forgotten during the war, would raise its ugly head again. Thus, the defiance of authority and the attitudes of resentment persisted even in the postwar years. An unspoken bond exists between the workingclass people. Seaton appreciates the plight of the waiter sent to throw him out; he recognizes the grim job that the waiter has to do while the latter recognizes and sympathizes with Seaton's gestures of defiance in getting drunk. A similar drunken scene ensues when he goes for his two weeks military training and has to be tied down to his bed.

He holds integrity and honesty in high respect but rarely follows it himself. While he can also sympathize with Brenda, Jack's wife whom he has impregnated, there is certain lack of sentimentality. For a moment, during her abortion he understands the agony he has caused another person. Yet Seaton does not dwell on the sentimental side of the revelation. After a sudden glimpse of understanding he goes to the pub and ends up with her sister. There is nothing as heroic loyalty. Brenda's cheating on her husband prompts Seaton to cheat on her. Strangely only some of Sillitoe's characters entice this occasional burst of sympathy for others. On the whole Sillitoe's stories are full of antiheroic, brutal and malicious men. Maliciousness, cruelty and brutality are part of the *Saturday Night and Sunday Morning* world.

While Seaton is presented as a boor and an oaf, a vainglorious individual, testing his endurance with gin and beer, yet there is in him a form of mental unpreparedness. Anxiety propels him to grab whatever he can. In order to be honest with himself as a representative of the workingclass factory man, and to his class, he must deceive, lie, steal and even throw himself against the very structures that will eventually crush him.

Energetic, yet irrational, Sillitoe's characters pit their skill, power and cunning against each other. Seaton uses his charm, without conscience to win over other men's wives and Smith challenges the Borstal governor with his cunning. Seaton shares an ambiguous relationship with Brenda. Although he feels guilty for cheating on Jack but he justifies it stating that it is men's bad luck who were unlucky enough not to be able to keep their wives. Nonetheless though he wishes to marry Brenda, he hates her for deceiving her husband so cruelly. On the other hand, he also feels fear when he has to keep a look out for strong and angry husbands. And if Jack was ever to ask about their affair, Seaton, though he loves Brenda would prefer to give her back rather than fight over her. It is one of his rules. Idealistic love does not hold any meaning for him.

The pressure of circumstances and a struggle in a hostile world binds the Sillitoe characters into a kind of unity and secondly directs this unity against the powerful establishment. However, this unity does not arise from any idealism or love, rather it springs from necessity. There is no hypocritical talk of charity or brotherhood; the acceptance comes because they recognize that everyone of them is caught in the same way. Each man for himself, and if "you don't look after yourself, nobody will". If he won a football pool, he has one goal:

> Do you think if I won the football pools I'd give yo' a penny on it? Or gi' anybody else owt? Not likely? I did keep it all mysen, except for seeing my family right. I'd buy 'em a house and set 'em up for lif, but anybody else could whistle or it. I've 'eard that blokes as win football poolsget thousands o' beggin' letters, but yer know what I'd do if I got 'em? I'll tell yer what I'd do: I'd mek a bonfire on 'em. Because I don't believe in share and share alike, Jack. Tek them blokes out as spout on boxes outside the factory sometimes. I like to hear 'em talk about Russia, about farms and power stations they 've got, because it's interestin', but when they say that when thy get in government everybody's got to share and share alike, then that's another thing. I ain't a Communist, I tell you, I like 'em though, because they 're different from these big fat Tory bastards in parliament. And them Labour bleeders too. They rob our wage packets every week with insurance and income tax and try to tell us it's all for our own good. I'd like ter go round every factory in England with books and

> books of little numbers and raffle off the 'Ouses o' Parliament. 'Sixpence a time, lads', I'd say. 'A nice big 'ouse for the winter'—an then when I'd made a big packet I'd settle down somewhere with fifteen women and fifteen cars, that I would. (p. 30)

This passage exposes not only the unidealistic nature of Seaton, unwilling to charity and generosity; it also reveals his political views and his form of protest politics. The statement "I'm all right, Jack" is in Sillitoe's world partly comparative. Partly it is his pose, partly his acquired defiance thrown up as a wall against a class with values and interests opposed to his own. The fact that he is unable to change the society around him leaves the workingman less of a patriot and an idealist. Skepticism about the possibility of positive change makes Seaton see that he must get the best for himself while prosperity lasts. The feeling of uncertainty that so little comes under their control makes the workingclass eager to do what they can while they have the power and the energy.

It is a fact that the workingman guards his attitude and position jealously. Generations of economic inequality followed by a decade on the dole before the war gave the workingclass a constant antipathy towards the established in the society. Opposed to a society that he cannot conquer or defeat, the factory man must often settle for preserving himself, keeping himself from knuckling under the power of government officials. The workingclass man views the world as a chaotic jungle, which works for the benefits of the moneyed, and feels that the best he can do is to preserve himself in the midst of the jungle. Sillitoe aptly feels that the workingman must keep himself alive in the jungle without any hope of transformation or reform.

Historically, most of the urbanized British workingclasses did not aspire towards the vague ideal of education or of gentility. It was sufficiently difficult to maintain themselves without the additional burden of aspiring towards some unreachable ideal. The workingclass ethos, as it were, dwelt mainly on the preservation of a rearguard action stolid, refusing to yield an inch of identity opposition. Hoggart maintains that they have always been like this.

> There are many thrifty workingclass people today as they always have been. But in general the immediate and the present nature of workingclass life puts a premium on the taking of pleasures now, discourages planning for some future goal, or in the light of some ideal. "Life is no bed of roses" they assume; but "tomorrow will take care of itself," on this side the workingclass have been cheerful existentialist for ages.[63]

As a factory man, Seaton's lack of faith in the future, his insistence on preserving his identity are all essentially defensive measures in the midst of a society in which he does not have the upper hand. Because no system or allegiance can assure the future, the working classes are apt to attribute a good deal to luck. Seaton believes that pure chance has the largest share in determining what happens to a man. The one who feels that he has little control is not likely to ascribe good fortune to his virtue or be responsible for his bad fortune. Existentialists do not believe in the presence of a supreme being. For them the individual must work his way through concrete experience because there are no specific standards for the human being. This is so because there is no God, no realizable essence to suggest values and standards. Allan Sillitoe explicitly develops the theory that the idea of God, the human persistence in adhering to an abstraction has done enormous harm to society. In *The Writer's Dilemma,* Sillitoe puts forward the idea:

> The idea of God is man's fatal neurosis, and war, as one sort of psychoanalysis, has certainly failed to cure him of it—though the next one might not. As soon as God is disregarded, and human contest becomes one of man against nature, then the battles between men will cease, and be replaced by the simple problem of getting enough food and shelter for everybody.[64]

A non-believer in religion and dogmatic church Christianity, he has gone on record stating that he is not a Christian, but that he believes in the biblical precepts and social organizations as outlined in the Holy Scriptures.[65]

Life, he believes, is still a long distance run, especially from emptiness.

With the passage of time man has gained flexibility but there is no assurance, that in the 20th century man can survive at all without compromises. With the social designations becoming less meaningful definitions for him, he has less faith in himself, less sure of progress, of virtue, of God and the uniqueness of his own soul. Maybe people in Sillitoe's throbbing world are unaware of philosophical developments, about Nietzsche, Camus, Sartre and existentialism, but the atmosphere of nihilism is all-pervasive in them too. Unknown to the call of the death of God, these people have stopped believing in God and the Church. In the novel, Seaton declares his disbelief in God

> ...you could say 'ta ta' to everybody, burn your football coupons and betting slips and ring up Billy Graham. If you believe in God which I don't, he said to himself. (p. 21)

Sillitoe, like Seaton, is a very strong believer in chance and ascribes his never been taken to prison to inordinate good luck. As ill-luck would have it, his father and his cousins had been to prison, the former for being unable to repay his debt. Chance thus governs Seaton's life to a great extent. Luck could crush or elevate man, raising him to pleasures of good wages and women and also lower him to the miseries of war, bad health and angry husbands. Seaton is aware of his considerably good position as compared to that of his predecessors. So there is a lot to do while the going is good. He thinks:

> No more short time like before the war or getting the sack if you stood ten minutes reading your "Football Post"—if the gaffers get on to you now you could always tell him where to put the job and go somewhere else. (p. 23)

The bomb presents a less horrible danger then further evidence of life's essential uncertainty, another unpredictable possibility that must be lived with. Still for the antiheroic hedonist, Seaton, no bomb has fallen yet and the wages are still good.

According to Sartre, man is free to create his own values. Camus also talks of a free man committing himself despite the fact that the things that he commits himself to never achieve the status of absolute authority. Sillitoe finds the use of "freedom" ironical:

> Freedom! Why do you keep on using such a false and stupid word? Freedom, freedom, freedom! Listen to it. Doesn't it have a meaningless sound? It's been twisted, hammered, burned and dragged into out. It's caused so much suffering in the world in these many disguises for tyranny that the soon people forget that it ever existed the better.[66]

Seaton may be free but there are not many choices that he can opt for. As an existentialist he believes a person must assume his existence and the existence of other things rather than posit abstract natures of things and people. This is so because existentialism insists on dealing with concrete facts of experience, multiple and unsystematic though they may be rather than theorizing about the general nature of essences.

The common man refuses to follow the patterns of the society, reacting negatively to the easy abstractions around him. The antiheroes of this period can define their antipathies more clearly than their affirmations and sympathies. For them, freedom is a sort of burden, dreadful and absurd. Seaton has the freedom to act but no certainty exists regarding its consequences. That he must act when he knows so little is dreadful: that he must act when the effects of his actions are so trivial, yet the action so meaningful, is absurd. The heroism of a freely acting individual is severely limited once the dread and the absurdity of the situation are clear. Though he sympathizes with them, Sillitoe gradually diminishes the heroism of his characters. They are not heroic in the sense of being admirable and effective leaders of society or champions of a new cause. Man's situation and his problems in addition to his own fallible humanity, make heroic action unlikely. Moreover, when heroic action is barely possible, no one else is able to acknowledge or realize it. The problematic contemporary world not only makes heroism dubious and unlikely, but also completely fails to notice even its rare emergence.

The diminished hero, the complex world, and the presence of numerous variations of abstracted folly all provide material for unexpected and incongruous clashes. Man's position is itself comic, vulnerable, incongruous. The existentialists have always viewed man in a similar way. Sartre's dread in the midst of significant action and Camus' absurdity also acknowledge the comic ambivalence of man's position. The comic and the unheroic hero can make choices, qualified, but he has no stirring message with which to lead his people out of the wilderness, literal or otherwise. He has only a limited, comically qualified control in the midst of twentieth century chaos.

According to Sillitoe, a writer writes for himself. In his interview with Halperin, he explains that the novels came from experience. "As far as the background was concerned they weren't autobiographical, but they were the sort of backdrop of what was my reality in life." "I put all my experience into the novel, which really doesn't span decades at all, you see. I never look at things in this way" (p. 176). A writer, he affirms, is idealistic in a sense, which, he says is true of all writers. He is not only one thing, but hundreds of things, not a single entity, or even a schizophrenic, one is a trizoprernic, or a dedacaphernic, or "you have so many selves in yourself that you are not one person ever".[67] In his *Modern Essays*, Frank Kermode talks about a linguistic phenomenon, present in Sillitoe, called "Rammel".[68] It is what Kenneth Burke calls 'Joycing'—strength and sweetness: violence with a sexual note and certain sweetness, and the whole thing against a background of urban and industrial waste.

Conflict is an essential part in this malicious world. But whenever there are conflicts, the results are always tragic, because in any conflict there are no winners, only losers. Forster's dictum "only connect"[69] does not hold much ground here, as connection seems to be difficult when one is in any kind of conflict. It becomes a condition of existence. "A sense of conflict is with you from birth—even as we are born we struggle for air" and as a writer "when you write a novel you sweat blood for a year or two". In his writing, Sillitoe developed a combatative, irreverent, defiant, edgy and ironic mood. The postwar English novel was heavily concerned with the social alterations and social viewpoints, often from the workingclass perspective. And in their concern not to be associated with the genteel Bloomsbury tradition of fine writing, Sillitoe, along with some Angry Young Man writers, developed a deliberately slapdash, honest-Jack style of writing with a loose picaresque structure.

The novel with its realism, along with its subject, is opposed to the traditionally heroic and legendary subject and treatment. Asked if he projected a pessimistic view of the world, Sillitoe maintained that he was interested in realism, but "realism was probably pessimism" (Halperin, 184). The realist is far willing to recognize his limitations, and to recognize how little of him is not dependent on his family, his social environment and his class. Again there is a huge difference regarding heroism in the 19th and 20th centuries. These differences are brought to focus time and again because all of these ideas contribute to the development of the present-day protagonist as an antihero. In the 19th century, the intellectual frequently asserted heroic quality that was innate as a primary virtue. The 20th century man looks at the heroic and the unique as myths, while regarding the class as shaping forces, making man what he has become today. For the contemporary writer too, class has become an element to be analyzed and worked with rather than as a barrier that an individual faces. Arthur Seaton is, thus, Joseph Campbell's ordinary man with whom legends "open in the recorded histories of time".[70]

As a novel *Saturday Night and Sunday Morning* was a piece of writing about a certain section of people, "which didn't write them down". It was a sort of thing that even Arthur Seaton himself would prefer. It wasn't the sort of thing they distrusted automatically, simply because someone who wrote it lived among them for the first twenty years of his life. Sillitoe's interest in provincial life shows his deep respect for D.H. Lawrence—but whereas Lawrence saw it romantically,

Sillitoe viewed it as drab and mechanical. Stylistically, Sillitoe uses the simple mode of narration—that of the first and third person alternately. The personal point of view is chosen as a logical consequence of the interest focusing upon a single individual. But unlike in the bourgeois novel, this perspective is not used for the illustration of subtle mental processes: the 'hero's' thoughts are for the most part determined by his experiences in the outside world, thus, providing an insider's view of a slice of social reality. Sillitoe transcribes the thoughts of his characters and he relies heavily on the colloquial inner voice. The reader might ask 'what is the relation of Alan Sillitoe with Postmodernism? Is this realistic mid-20th century novel a postmodern one?' Being a novel of the postwar period, it comes, according to Jeremy Hawthorn,[71] under the time frame which is accepted by critics as postmodern, as it is the periodising concept of postmodernism that has gained wide acceptance. Edward Smyth[72] also agrees that by common usage "postmodernism" has been adopted by several commentators as a means of describing the contemporary novel in general, whether individual texts may exhibit certain specific traits or not. Moreover, continuing with Hawthorn's definition of the term, one sees that the novel not only includes the extreme extension of certain modernists characteristics, like alienation and the questioning of the relation between man and his society, but also uses it to refer to aspects of a more general human condition in the late capitalist world of the post-1950s. Again, in the novel, modernist institutions and establishments are mocked as elitist. Sillitoe constantly question accepted social beliefs and values. However, one also finds the presence of postmodern irony in the character of Seaton. This irony, as opposed to modernist irony, is suspensive, dealing with an indecision about the relations or meanings of things which is matched by a willingness to live with uncertainty.[73] This apart, Seaton is seen to tolerate and even welcome a world seen as random and even absurd. This is made evident through his compromise with life and his final identification with the fish ready to be caught.

Many readers have seen Seaton as an alter ego of Sillitoe himself. He is deeply sympathetic to Seaton's temperamental nihilism and anarchism. He talks about the relation he shares with his characters:

> Every character you write about, no matter what they are, you are sort of half in love with, to the extent that you will have to respect their views in order to get the most out of them, and to drive them to their limits, their fullest extent. You can't look down on somebody and distance yourself. If you are writing about a person they are a part of you. You have to look upon them in this benign spirit to a certain extent. You have to accept their foibles, and even what other people might consider their criminal propensities. You can't really divorce me from the people I write about. There is always an inherent feeling in my fictional people that protection and caution are called for.[74]

Sillitoe is often criticized for being too emotionally committed to the negative values he sought to illustrate. There is no doubting of the talent of the writer but there are times when one feels that the vitality of the talent has been sapped by a profound distrust issuing from a wilful creative self-destructiveness. After the novella, Sillitoe tended to turn to a vaguely defined anarchism of the "rebel without a cause" type as in *The Death of William Posters* (1965).

Seaton remains a rebel throughout though the degree of his rebellion varies. His pay packet, his sexual adventures, his taste for expensive clothes and his workingclass codes place limitations on him. The hungry desire for freedom is stifled in the end, as he becomes a caught fish, readjusted to society through marriage. Though fishing provides a means of escape for him, he recognizes, ironically, his own identity in the fish. In the world,

> ...mostly you were like the fish, you swam about the freedom, thinking how good it was to be left alone, doing anything you wanted to do and caring about no one, when suddenly: SPLUTCH!—the big hook clapped itself into your mouth and you were caught. Without

> knowing what you were doing you had chewed off more than you could bite and had to stick with the same piece of bait for the rest of your life. (p. 236)

All jungles are not simple statements of man's nature-some, codified and institutionalized—become the framework where man's predatory instincts operate and man struggles with others are regularized. These institutions constantly block off man's abundant energy. Seaton understands the antagonism of the factory life but he also understands that he cannot exist outside this world. Deep within him, he suffers from alienation and longs for peace, which cannot be obtained either through complicated affairs or through mindless revelry. Seaton is as alienated as the other antiheroes. He finds himself lonely and empty in a crowded pub. Again, after being beaten up by the swaddies he exists in a "soulless vacuum". Pointing out the relation between the mechanical life and the position of the antihero, Sillitoe depicts the jungle not only as a permanent part of man's life but also as an outgrowth of the Industrial Revolution. Yet if the concrete jungle is specifically a 20th century phenomenon, Arthur is a 20th century man, part of the jungle and fully aware of the issues it forces on man to take sides of.

Though the novels of this period were similar in their theme, they did not deal with the same story. Some were more pessimistic than others. Some like *The Loneliness of the Long Distance Runner* and *Saturday Night and Sunday Morning* leave the antiheroes after a series of upsetting adventures, all turning out to be frustrating in the end, leaving them high and dry in a state of either bewilderment or utter cynicism. Seaton realizes that his hopes and his despairs are not at all related to what happens to him. He goes with the tide, having learnt the lesson too well, compromising a bit, showing his defiance but attempting little to change the situation.

The racy story of the new affluent worker whose life is divided between slavery at work and weekend pleasures is a negative picture of drab squalor in a grimly hostile society. The resolution of the novel is the way in which its odious antihero, Seaton begins to move from a jungle like milieu through marriage and becoming a charge hand. What is activated here is a kind of half thought anarchism, an ideal of personal freedom, seemingly but ambiguously sacrificed at the end as marriage makes its claim. It is as if modern society, with its pleasures stifles humanity and vitality and violates some half glimpsed freedom.

Many workingclass members try to escape from the negative aspect of their class—poverty, narrowness, and try to achieve associations of the upper middle class—wealth, education and status. But the price they have to pay is considerable—it is usually attained at the expense of the workingclass community. Aware of this incomprehensible predicament, the worker feels uneasiness and strangely isolated from the rest of the familiar world. Sillitoe makes anger a matter of individual consciousness, indeed a point of definition and identity, an existential coordinate.

Though the end of *Saturday Night and Sunday Morning* may show the hero conforming to the social role of a husband, but in the words of Seaton, they are content with "the conventional end".[75] The voluntary reintegration into the traditional code of social behavior of the class on the private level appears as the only guarantee left to protect the young people from the loneliness and confusion created by the postmodern world. It would be wrong, though, to have the impression that the novel is basically acquiescent. The very resignation is voiced with such bitterness and fury that the criticism is obvious. It is a story of individual rebellion and told in a very impressive way even if the outcome is one of defeat. Finally, after his compromise, with his position of a caught fish, Seaton turns happily to catch the fish foolish enough to be baited and caught.

In the end, one might ask if the systematic acceptance of defeat, uncertainty and the acceptance of the position of a baited fish by Seaton make him antiheroic. To a great extent, yes, for to a life of radical rebellion, one at least expects a bang, if not a blast; but both the novel and Seaton's rebellion actually end in a whimper. One might also feel disappointed by his final compromise with the chaos around him. He is not the ideal rebel-hero, denied, as he is, the heroic proportions of his rebellion. This is a very antiheroic conclusion to a life that has been so full of rebellion and assertiveness. True, the fact should be conceded that throughout his actions and attitudes are antiheroic, and which eventually does not end in complete defiance like that of Prometheus, but at least he has chosen an optimal way out. He might no longer be rebelling radically but life still remains divided between aggressor and victim. As a Sillitoe man, Seaton's behaviour is in complete conformity with the unpredictable world around him—sometimes a predator, sometimes a victim, all depending on chance. Yet, his antiheroic stance throughout his life comes as a reaction to what he experiences around him. His way of life is that of a happy-go-lucky existentialist, eager enough to cash on life as it comes, and as long as possible. His antiheroism helps him to accept, and adapt, without illusions, to the fragmented, chaotic and uncertain place that is our postmodern world. But, in all he does, he tries to remain, and succeeds in remaining in a position where he can say, "I'm all right, Jack".

In the end, both Merridew and Seaton can be defined as radical rebels; for them, rebellion has become a way of life, the only way that they can assert their identities. For Merridew, rebellion means the removal of every obstruction that lies in his path; for Seaton, it is the assertion of his self and it comes through drinking, puking, fornicating, and fighting. Both are antinomian, anarchists to the very core, nihilists, rejecting every form of authority and order, but it also needs to be pointed out that Merridew is of a more satanic character than Seaton. Both of them are passionate, but their method of rebellion does not, at times, exactly seem correct. However, one can also say that they don't have many options available to them. They may differ in their modes of rebellion, but their actions and attitudes reveal them very much to be antiheroes.

NOTES

1. Gilbert Phelps, "The Post War English Novel", *The New Pelican Guide to English Literature*, ed. Boris Ford, 1983, Penguin Books, p. 413.
2. Edward Smyth, "Introduction", *Postmodernism and Contemporary Fiction*, ed. Edward Smyth, London, Batsford, 1990, p. 9.

3. Jeremy Hawthorn, *A Glossary of Contemporary Literary Theory*, 4th edition, N.Y. Arnold, London, p. 216.
4. Patricia Waugh, "Introduction", *Postmodernism, A Reader*, ed. Edward Arnold, G.B., 1992, p. 3.
5. Alan Sillitoe, *Saturday Night and Sunday Morning*, Signet Books, 1958.
6. Edward Smyth, *op. cit.*, p. 10.
7. Albert Camus, *The Rebel*, trans. Anthony Bower, Penguin Books, 1973, p. 19.
8. *Ibid.*, p. 16.
9. David Elloway, "Introduction", *Billy Liar and the Loneliness of the Long Distance Runner*, Keith Waterhouse and Alan Sillitoe, Heritage of Literature, Longman, p. 202.
10. *Myths and Motifs in Literature*, ed., J.T. Shawcross, et al., The Free Press, N.Y., 1973, p. 450.
11. Howard S. Babb, *The Novels of William Golding*, Columbus, Faber Publication, Ohio University Press, 1970.
12. Golding, *Free Fall*, Faber, 1961, p. 130.
13. Golding, *The Moving Target*, p. 199.
14. James Gindin, "Gimmick and Metaphor in the Novels of William Golding", *Post War British Fiction: New Accents and Attitudes*, London, Cambridge Univ. Press, 1963, p. 204.
15. Fredrick R. Karl, "The Metaphysical Novels of William Golding", *A Reader's Guide to Contemporary English Novel*, Rev. Ed., Octagon Books, 1975, p. 334.
16. C.C. Walcutt, *The Diminished Self: Man's Changing Mask—Modes and Methods of Characterization*, Univ. of Minnesota Press, Minneapolis, 1966, p. 99.
17. *Ibid.*, p. 101.
18. Cedric Watts, "Heart of Darkness", *The Cambridge Companion to Conrad*, ed. J.H. Stape, G.B., 1996, p. 47.
19. William Golding, *The Inheritors*, Faber, London, 1955.
20. Erich Fromm, "The Anatomy of Human Destructiveness," quoted in Subbarao, *William Golding—A Study*, 1987.
21. Bernard F. Dick, *Twayne English Authors Series* (William Golding), Revised, Twayne Pub. 1997, p. 14.
22. "Civilization and Its Discontents", Chap. VI and VII, (pp. 64-80), trans. James Starchey, N.Y., *From Modernism to Postmodernism: An Anthology*, ed. Lawrence Cahoone, Blackwell Press, Massachusetts, 1996, p. 213.
23. Freud, *ibid.*, p. 215.
24. Freud, *ibid.*, p. 213.

25. "Nietzsche and the Aristocracy of Passion", *The Cult of the Ego: The Self in Modern Literature*, Eugene Goodheart, University of Chicago Press, 1968, p. 127.
26. Howard S. Babb, *op. cit.*
27. Carl Jung, "Archetypes of the Collective Unconscious", *20th Century Criticism: The Major Statements*, ed. William J. Handy, Max Westbrook, Life and Light Publication, N.D., 1974, p. 212.
28. Kincaid and Gregor, *op. cit.*, p. 41.
29. *Ibid.*, p. 20.
30. Howard Babb, *op. cit.*, p. 12.
31. Conrad, *Heart of Darkness*, p. 57.
32. Cesare Lombroso and William Ferrero, *The Female Offender*, London, 1895, pp. 112-13. Quoted in J.W. Griffith, *Joseph Conrad and the Anthropological Dilemma,* p. 161.
33. Lombroso, *Crime*, p. 336. Quoted by Griffith, *op. cit.*, p. 173.
34. *The Cult of the Ego: The Self in Modern Literature*, Eugene Goodheart, University of Chicago Press, 1968, p. 130.
35. Kincaid and Gregor, *op. cit.*, p. 60.
36. Martin Quinn, "The Unheroic Hero—William Golding's Pincher Martin", *The Critical Quarterly*, 4, 3, Autumn, 1962, pp. 247-56.
37. William Shakespeare, *King Lear.*
38. Fredrick R. Karl, "The Metaphysical Novels of William Golding", *A Readers Guide to Contemporary English Novel*, Rev ed., Octagon Books, 1975, p. 258.
39. Conrad, "A Personal Record", p. 18, quoted by Cedric Watts, "Heart of Darkness," *The Cambridge Guide to Joseph Conrad*, ed., J.H. Stape, Cambridge University Press, 1996, p. 49.
40. Bernard F. Dick, *op. cit.*, p. 29.
41. V.S. Pritchett "Pain and William Golding", *William Golding: Novels 1954-67*, ed. Norman Page, Casebook Series, Macmillan Press Ltd., Hampshire and London, G.B., p. 140.
42. John Halperin, "Interview with Alan Sillitoe", *M.F.S.*, Vol. 25, No. 2, Summer 1979, pp. 175-76.
43. Frank Kermode, "Briefly Noticed—Alan Sillitoe", *Modern Essays*, 1071, Fontana, Collins, G.B., p. 284.
44. Halperin, *op. cit.*, p. 182.
45. Kenneth Allsop, *The Angry Decade*, Peter Owen, London, 1958.
46. Gilbert Phelps, "The Post War English Novel" in Boris Ford ed., *The New Pelican Guide to English Literature: From Orwell to Naipaul*, Penguin, 1983, p. 425.

47. Northrop Frye, *Anatomy of Criticism*, Princeton University Press 1957, p. 40.
48. Richard Hoggart, "The Uses of Literacy", quoted by Ingrid von Rosenberg, "Militancy, Anger and Resignation: Alternative Moods of the Working Class Novel of the 1950s and early 1960s" in Gustav Klaus, ed., *The Socialist Novel in Britain*, Harvester Press, 1982, p. 176.
49. David Holbroke, "Prostitution, Politics and Egotistical Nihilism", *Critical Quarterly*, Vol. 16, No. 3, Autumn 1974, pp. 227-29.
50. Anthony Wilden, *System and Structure*, quoted by Holbroke, *ibid.*
51. Eugene Goodheart, *The Cult of the Ego, The Self in Modern Literature*, University of Chicago Press, 1968, pp. 117-18.
52. Sidney Parker, "The Egoism of Max Stirner: Some Critical Bibliographical Notes", Mackay Society of New York; Source: The Internet.
53. Albert Camus, *The Rebel: An Essay on Man in Revolt*, trans. Anthony Bower, N.Y. Vintage, 1956, pp. 105, 213.
54. Eugene Fleischmann, "Stirner, Marx, and Hegel, Hegel's Political Philosophy, The Role of the Individual in Pre-Revolutionary Society", Cambridge University Press, London, Quoted by Sidney Parker, *op. cit.*
55. Book Review: William J. Palmer, *M.F.S.*, Vol. 25, No. 4, Winter 1979, p. 681; Review of Ronald De Vareka, "Commitment as Art, A Marxist Critique of a Selection of Alan Sillitoe's Political Fiction", University of Uppasala, Stockholm.
56. Halperin, *op. cit.*, p. 184.
57. Rosenberg, *op. cit.*, p. 159.
58. James Gindin, *Post War British Fiction: New Accents and Attitudes*, London, Cambridge University Press, 1963, p. 15.
59. Rosenberg, *op. cit.*, p. 159.
60. James Gindin, *op. cit.*, p. 230.
61. Sishir Kr. Ghosh, *The Malady of the Modern: Modern and Otherwise*, 1974, p. 17.
62. Gindin, *op. cit.*, p. 91.
63. Richard Hoggart, Quoted by Gindin, p. 97.
64. Alan Sillitoe, "The Writer's Dilemma", first printed in *T.L.S.* as "Limits of Control", pp. 68-69, quoted by Gindin, p. 232.
65. Halperin, *op. cit.*, p. 188.
66. Sillitoe, *The General*, p. 68, Gindin, p. 20.
67. Halperin, *op. cit.*, p. 184.
68. Frank Kermode, *op. cit.*, p. 284.
69. E.M. Forster, *Howards End*, Epigraph, Penguin Books, 1941, Edward Arnold, 1910.

70. Joseph Campbell, *The Hero with a Thousand Faces*, Meridan Books, 1949, p. 316.
71. Jeremy Hawthorn, *A Glossary of Contemporary Literary Theory*, 4th edition, N.Y., Arnold, London, 2000, p. 216.
72. Edward Smyth, *Postmodernism and Contemporary Fiction*, 1990, ed. by Edward Smyth, London, Batsford, p. 9.
73. Alan Wilde, "From Modernism and the Aesthetics of Crisis" in Patricia Waugh ed., *Postmodernism: A Reader*, Edward Arnold, London, 1992, p. 14.
74. Halperin, *op. cit.*, p. 188.
75. Rosenberg, *op. cit.*, p. 163.

3

The Search for Identity: Mohun Biswas and Mugo

> I knew Trinidad to be unimportant, uncreative, cynical. We lived in a society that denied itself heroes...our known past was buried and no one cared to dig it up.
>
> V.S. Naipaul, *The Middle Passage*, 1962.

Helen Tiffin[1] writes that the label "postmodernism" is increasingly being applied hegemonically to cultures and texts outside Europe, assimilating postcolonial works whose political orientation and experimental formation have been designed to counter European appropriation. However, they have themselves provided the cultural base and formative colonial experience on which European philosophers have drawn apparent radicalization of linguistic philosophy. She distinguishes two different kinds of postcolonial circumstances. These distinctions are based on the examination of the ways in which postcolonial writers have challenged the western master narratives of history, while continuing to fracture it.

The first includes the postcolonial areas of Indian subcontinent, Africa and Australia. Here writers were and are able to challenge European 'westernized' viewpoints with their own metaphysical systems. The second includes areas like the Caribbean and the non-indigenous populated parts of Canada, Australia and New Zealand. In the Caribbean, strategies are made to promote polyphony, eschew fixity and monocentricism. Here writers have had to act subversively through what Michael Dash has termed "the counter culture of the imagination".[2]

Colonizers not only colonize the history of the colonized but also subjugate their imagination as well. Writers in the commonwealth have dealt with the lives of people whose selves have been altered by colonialism and the subsequent multinational capitalism. Some of these novels merge the fictional with the factual and dramatize the tensions that result from the effect of socio-political change on the individual and collective sensibilities. Literary creative interrogation in the form of a quest for both self and collective identity may be defined as the consciousness of a writer taking form. African novels especially may be considered as postcolonial writing because they attempt to dismantle and decentre European hegemonic authority.[3]

For Freud, the exploration of one's personal history is vital for self-actualization and is ultimately of commensurate importance to the health of nations, families and that of the individual. The history of the west and of the non-west is irrevocably different and irrevocably shared. Both have shaped and been shaped by each other in various ways. Postcolonialism is most frequently used and mis-understood as a temporal concept associated with the time colonialism in a country has ceased to exist. It is rather an engagement with and contestation of colonialism's discourses, power structures and social hierarchies. Languages, education, religion, artistic sensibilities, psychology of the colonized and popular culture are affected by colonialization. The agenda in postcolonialism is to dismantle hegemonic boundaries and the determinants that create unequal relations of power based on binary opposition such as 'them' and 'us', and 'first world' and 'third world'.[4]

Simon During[5] writes that the postcolonial desire is the desire of decolonized communities for an identity. During also states "in both literature and politics the postcolonial drive towards identity centres around language, partly because in postmodernity identity is barely available elsewhere". For the postcolonial "to speak or write in the imperial tongue is to call forth a problem of identity, to be thrown into mimicry and ambivalence."[6]

The characters discussed in this chapter, Mr. Biswas (Naipaul, *A House for Mr. Biswas*, 1961), and Mugo (Ngugi, *A Grain of Wheat*, 1968) are scarred, directly or indirectly, by colonialism. They share similarities in their aspirations for success and attempts to achieve concrete identities; but fate, chance and personality combine, not only to shatter their dreams but also to reveal them as essentially antiheroic. They are marginalized characters resulting from colonialization and social, cultural and personal deprivation. Trouble erupts for both of them when they try to fashion their futures individually in traditionally communal societies. As marginal men they are products of two social worlds and they are placed in the psychological uncertainties of both these worlds. They are also schizoid characters and in this regard they remind the readers of Prufrockian man. Biswas remains an outsider to both the cultures being neither assimilated by the idealized Western society, nor being able to accept the rigidity and hypocrisy of his own society.

A House for Mr. Biswas is mediated through the sensibility of the antiheroic Mr. Biswas. Born with an extra finger, indicating endemic bad luck and malnutrition, he reacts to his adversities with a defensive and self-destructive clowning. Throughout the novel, his search for a house of his own is an attempt to find both independence and meaning for his life. He is always associated with failure, futility and ordinariness. As a small boy, he is regarded as ill-fated, a harbinger of tragedy. Whatever he touches has unfortunate consequences, and he is, indirectly, the cause of his father's death. Though he is for the most part passive, he is not able to escape the assigned role as the generator of tragedy. John Thieme regards it as a fitting beginning to a life history of dependence, antiheroic ordinariness and a dignity denied.[7]

Critics agree on the point that Biswas is an ironic antihero. He is physically runtish, emotionally beset with doubt, fears, hysteria, and an overpowering sense of futility and failure. As if to underscore his rootlessness, Naipaul discloses the fact that he was not born in his father's house. For thirty-five years he lives the life of a wanderer, shuttling from one house to another, none of which belongs to him. Empty of religion, which he frequently derides, and also of original creativity, he is a victim and a prisoner of his own passage on earth. His story is largely an odyssey of restless questing. He is Naipaul's "compassionate version of a being condemned to wander the world on the *Narrenschiff* of his own psyche".[8] Life is actually not the problem for him; the problem is making a world to live in.[9]

According to Robert Frazen, often when we observe the protagonist of one book we repeatedly notice the outlines of the antihero of another, incongruously standing behind him.[10] Critics have noted affinities between *A House for Mr. Biswas* and H.G. Wells' *The History of Mr. Polly* (1910) Biswas is similar in many ways to Mr. Polly. They are marginal figures enduring social and cultural obscurity. The argument can be taken further by stressing a similarity in situations stemming from alienation and comic degradation produced by the industrial and colonial systems. Anthony Boxhill[11] refers to the similarities between Biswas and Mr. Polly. By giving the title 'Mister' Naipaul emphasizes Biswas's lack of real childhood. Naipaul gives a very frustrating education to his hero, paralleling the pain in his hero's mind with acute stomach pains, using the common but excruciating pain to reveal the pain of mental indigestion and frustration. Boxhill further writes that unlike Wells, Naipaul does not allow him to achieve contentment in the end. He lets Biswas glimpse romance, disillusions him into marriage and finally half permits him to escape.

No doubt, Mr. Polly has had a frustrating life but his life is lived against the background of established society. Biswas, as a Hindu in Trinidad, has to forge for himself the standards by which he is going to live. What he is struggling against is a profoundly unstable world. John Thieme[12] states that Naipaul offers none of the solace of the happy ending that Wells affords his hero. The novel represents a fragmented colonial world and employs a fictional form that is its co-relative, as it suitably undermines the sense of comic prudence that underlines its European equivalent.

Biswas's description as a boy is certainly no description of a hero. He is dusty, unwashed, with eczema and sores that swells and bursts repeatedly. His poor physique with a shallow chest, thin limbs and stunted growth makes him a picture of absurdity. Every time one imagines Biswas as an antihero, we see an image of Biswas lying down on the floor and playing with what his wife, Shama calls "hammock calves". His entire growth is marked by grotesque comedy and frustration. At Pt. Jairam's, he quickly falls into superficial routines, but transgresses in a humiliating way, is disgraced and thrown out. From the very beginning his antiheroic status is confirmed. His ignoble return home to Bipti is an inversion of the Biblical Prodigal Son parable for he is attacked by Bipti's hostile questions rather than be rewarded for his contrition.[13]

At Ajodha's rum shop, Biswas is subject to ridicule and humiliation for he smiles as if he were a spy. He avenges himself by spitting in the rum he bottles every morning. This foolish and unknown revenge gives him pleasure, as there is little that he can do. This incident further strengthens the impression of his antiheroic buffoonery. This is an everlasting process because after his marriage his status is further diminished by his ridiculous fashions and by Seth's intimidating presence; he uses this ridicule as his own defence in situations he cannot otherwise dominate.

Biswas's antiheroism stems as a reaction to non-belonging, and his being a victim of determinism. His life is a deterministic tragicomedy, where he is forced to choose an identity for himself, but invariably denied the opportunity. This inevitably brings us to another antiheroic feature in Biswas's character, as all his 'heroic' efforts to assert himself and find his identity are ludicrously clownish. Consequently, he exists as a picaro drifting from one experience to another. The events in the Biswas's life are picaresque and episodic. Biswas is thus a drifter, a picaro, trying to find footholds in society. As an exile in a "picaroon society",[14] Biswas is a stranger to himself. Sandwiched between an old identity in a

Trinidad community and a new identity in a post-industrial society, Biswas becomes an exile trapped in the cultural collusions of his epoch. Without a stable identity, empty and fragmented, he simply drifts in the cross-cultural current of a transitional society.

Socially, in colonial Trinidad, the Tulsis are a mushroom growth, without any real autonomous cultural life, and 'Hanuman House' is a monument that is inwardly hollow. For Frazen, Biswas is its stooge, an unwilling partner, a jester in its court of mimicry. In his life, there are existential situations with comic overtones. The 'insuranburn' business only shows how redundant Biswas is to the people around him. He is only curiously consulted and treated as non-existent and it is far from obvious that Biswas grasps the full import of Seth's suggestion. The harsh laughter that seizes the family group during this discussion is provoked not by their planning but by the absurd notion that Biswas, the focus of the operation, should take any active part in it at all. The epitome of all this facility is the 'insuranburn' trick that totally leaves him aside. Frazen writes, "Mohun Biswas, the ultimate cipher of colonialism, is denied even the ownership of his own failure, the elementary dignity of true and conscious anguish."[15]

The world of Biswas has no magic and human relationships are never a source of sustenance here. He belongs to a multiracial and stunted society without any core in it, a society of failures without heroes. A major problem faced by the inhabitants in such a society is the lack of central tradition. Writing in such a tradition, Naipaul's work treats peripheral, amorphous social groups without a discernable core, who are seemingly anarchic and chaotic. His work therefore deals with men whose ordinariness never fails to astound us. With Biswas, he portrays the anonymous man and his desire for security and fulfillment. As a Hindu in Trinidad, Biswas is the rootless derelict man in search of an identity, inheriting the sense of insecurity of the exiled/transplanted Indian with an ambiguous identity. Consequently, Biswas lacks the true place of belonging unsure of himself and his fate. It is no coincidence that Mr. Biswas is in search of a home, which he can call his own. In archetypal terms, it is his journey and his quest for fulfillment. Home is not only a place where one lives. It is an extension of one's identity—personal, cultural and national. Exile, the loss of home, reveals the meaning of what is lost. It entails both physical and emotional alienation:

> A derelict man in the derelict land: a man discovering himself with surprise and resignation, lost in a landscape which never ceased to be unreal because it is the scene of an enforced and always temporary residence....[16]

Naipaul speaks of Trinidad's anarchic character, the cult of eccentricity and the admiration for the sharp character. Biswas cultivates his eccentricity as a means of ascertaining his self in a world that refuses recognition. Reading *The Middle Passage* gives an insight into the psychological and sociological compulsion behind such eccentric behaviour:

> In the colonial society every man had to be for himself ...corruption, not unexpected, aroused only amusement and even mild approval. Trinidad has always admired the sharp character who like the 16th century picaroon of Spanish literature, survives and triumphs by his wits in a place where it is felt that all eminence is arrived at by crookedness.[17]

Biswas is faced with a mental breakdown under cultural and material dereliction. His life is a continuous story of failure and loneliness, from one end to the other. Anand realises the loneliness of his father very early. When Shama leaves Biswas behind in the Chase, Anand refuses to do so, not out of affection, but because "they were going to leave you alone". Rather than manifest dignity or heroism, Biswas presents a weak and unreliable picture in need of his son's protection:

> Father and son, each saw the other as weak and vulnerable, and each felt a responsibility for the other, a responsibility which in times of particular pain, was disguised by exaggerated authority on the one side, exaggerated respect on the other. (p. 374)

Certainly, had Biswas been an ideal heroic figure, Anand would not have felt the need. As a father, he is seen as defenceless by his son, unable to defend his family or himself. He fits the description that Chris Baldick gives of an antihero, one who "is an example of antiheroic ordinariness and inadequacy".[18] Instead of manifesting dignity, and valour in the face of fate, Biswas is petty, reprehensible, ineffectual, and passive. Bullied as he is by the women during his stay in Hanuman House and even beyond it, and dominated for the most part of his life by Aunt Tara and Mrs. Tulsi, Biswas belongs to what Northrop Frye[19] calls the "Omphale" archetype.

When the novel first appeared, an early reviewer remarked "Mr. Biswas is simply not worth all the detail that Mr. Naipaul spins so laboriously around him...he is a rather stupid man...also cowardly and ugly, definitely not the kind of stuff heroes are made of."[20] Joshi quotes Gordon Rohlehr[21] who points out the archetypal roles filled by Biswas—"he represents man at the most vulnerable—physically weak and ugly, socially powerless because he has neither money nor status nor family support". He often takes up the buffoon's role as a cover for his helplessness, making laughter a means of defence, an escape from intolerable reality. Interestingly, Seepersad Naipaul, upon whom Biswas is modeled, responded in a similar way to personal failure. Naipaul says: "my father had a prodigious sense of irony, a way of turning all disasters into comedy which he transmitted to his children".[22]

For Thieme,[23] colonialism and determinism go together in Naipaul; the essence of the colonial mentality is the renunciation of the freedom of choice—Biswas not only suffers from the colonial mentality but is also emotionally colonised by the Tulsis: "...to be colonial, is, in a way, to know a total kind of security. It is to have all decisions about major issues taken out of one's hand".[24] The novel sees the treatment of the determinist man at its best. His antiheroic tragic-comic struggle to attain dignity becomes a parody of the attempt to emancipate oneself from colonial/determinist dependence. Although Biswas has resistance in him, it does not negate his essential passivity in most instances, especially when he is confronted by the existential void. He tries to live his unfulfilled life through his son Anand, but it is Anand, who, in the end, by rejecting him, relegates him to the position of a failure, an antihero. He never fails to remind Biswas of the failures he has suffered and equates Biswas with weakness. By leaving Trinidad for London, he makes true his declaration: "I don't want to be like you when I grow up" (p. 465). During the depression after his Exhibition exam when Biswas attempts to cheer him up by saying that true efforts is never wasted, Anand retorts back "what about you?" (p. 477).

Biswas's life is the book's most grotesque irony; he is central to the action and yet dissolved by it. Futility governs the results of an odyssey within a small yet disjointed society. Biswas remains a deterministic prisoner of this society, as symbolized by the houses in which he lives. In this context, Thieme quotes Gordon Rohlehr's comment:

> The description of the Hindu family in Trinidad exactly parallels all the descriptions of the Hanuman House, the Chase, the Barracks, Green Vale, and finally the house in Port of Spain around which the Tulsis built a wall. The whole story has shown the difficulty of escape and the uselessness of rebellion.[25]

The marked signature of failure that accompanies Biswas's effort throughout the novel strongly reiterates the suggestion that familial and colonial dependency breeds circumstances in which it is far more difficult to sever the relation between the old and the new, or the past or the present, than a simple desire to do so may imply. Furthermore, one finds that whenever Biswas attempts "to paddle his own canoe", he faces harsh derision from the Tulsis, and he is contemptuously referred to as "Biswas the paddler". The more he tries to tackle the problems of life, the more exacting it becomes, demanding more than the amount of energy that he has in him. Biswas fits several of Ihab Hassan's description of the rebel-victim—the fool, the clown, the poor and the outsider.[26] It becomes easier for the reader to identify with Biswas for his experiences are a mirror to our fragmented, real world. His attempts at fulfillment and self-definition always end in drastic failure. His world and the conditions surrounding him challenge him everyday and he is never able to match up to these challenges. Biswas's initiation into rebellious adulthood is visualized in terms of a house: "I am going to get a job on my own. And I am going to get my own house too" (p. 66).

Alienated by his sensitivity and his diverse readings, he is stalked by the fear of poverty, starvation and unemployment. However, he leads a precarious life, living from one venture to another, hoping for elusive success. He realizes that he has been a weak man throughout his life. Bullied into marrying Shama, "how often did he regret his weakness, his inarticulateness that evening. How often did he try to make events appear grander, more planned and less absurd than they were" (p. 91). Through this reflection of weakness, Naipaul exposes that even Biswas himself realizes that he has been a less than ordinary individual.

According to O.P. Juneja, the outsider figure in West Indian fiction tends to be existential in nature. Being preoccupied with his helplessness, he tries to define the 'absurdity' of his condition through the existential paradigm of the human condition. Often, the colonized begins to see himself through the eyes of the ruler; the more he tries to emulate and assimilate the Western fashion, the more he rejects himself, leading to the development of existential tendencies. Juneja shows Biswas's identity as an outsider as he quotes A. Sivananda's statement in *Alien Gods* (1974).

> On the margin of European culture, and alienated from his own, the coloured intellectual is an artefact of colonial history, marginal man par excellence. He is a creature of two worlds, and of none. Thrown up by a specific history, he remains stranded on its shores even as a world of false shadows and false lights.[27]

The urgency of Mr. Biswas's action surfaces from his desperate efforts for acknowledgement, so as to have validated his human necessity for himself. His acting as the licensed buffoon and absurd behaviour are attention-grabbing techniques, used consciously or unconsciously, without it, he has the persistent feeling of disintegration. Biswas, unlike a traditional hero, has his restlessness and dissatisfaction, and an urgent longing to make a dent, an impression in the world, to be acknowledged, appreciated and overcome the limitations imposed on him by the circumstances.[28]

Though he has escaped realities of slavery, Biswas carries the schizoid personality within him. He feels a need to be appreciated. M.I. Singh[29] quotes Naipaul attesting the fact "The world is what it is. Men who are nothing, who allow themselves to become nothing, have no place in it." Unfortunately, Biswas is nobody and all his attempts to become somebody come to naught. His flashes of clownish wit, his buffoonery, his exhibitionism are at bottom attempts to relieve his own anxiety. Aware of his own absurdity, he increases his clowning and also tries to extend it to Anand. When a teacher at the school humiliates Anand, Biswas becomes the licensed buffoon, revealing his own misadventures at Jairam's "caricaturing and ridiculing Anand's shame". But his clowning is no ordinary clowning. Garebian points out that Biswas is not the ordinary classic fool, the one who destroys and subverts conventional reality and turns the world upside down in order to assert the basic properties of the universe. Using Richard Pearce's[30] *Stages of the Clown: Perspectives on Modern Fiction from Dostoevsky to Beckett* (1971), Garebian argues that rather Biswas is the type of clown whose result is chaos. He makes everyday life comic by his mimicry and by his farcical misadventures. Throughout, he carries on the role of a victim and a clown. He does not choose the role of the clown deliberately, but a variety of absurd experiences thrusts this role upon him. At times he appears to live before a mirror, inventing an identity that lacks conviction because it is mechanically assumed. By his need to be seen and appreciated by others, one can well discern that he is what Albert Camus[31] describes as "a dandy". In *The Rebel* (1956), Camus writes "the dandy creates his own unity by aesthetic means", He not only musters his forces but also tries to create a unity for himself by the very violence of his refusal. Further, Camus writes, "Disoriented like all people without a rule of life, he is coherent as a character. He can only play a part by setting himself up in opposition." Biswas exactly conforms to the role of a dandy. When he dresses up in a new suit to go to a cricket match, "he is the clown as the dandy, the rebel as a mimic exhibitionist",[32] looking at himself in the mirror, he finds the "cascade of brown" grotesque. But as a dandy he is compelled to show off and he attempts to find himself in the reactions of the crowd to his exhibitionism, but this mirror refuses to give him back his self-image. Camus' statement on the dandy as the hero in his own romance is pertinent to Biswas. "He plays at life because he is unable to live it" (p. 52), this dandyism is rebellion of sorts because it creates an aesthetic to define an attitude against the public norm. In Biswas's case, however, dandyism is foolish because the display isolates Biswas as a self-caricature. He tries fashionable outfits, but ends feeling foolish without gaining appreciation or even acknowledgement from the ones for whom he made such a show of himself. A dandy Biswas can only be sure of his own existence by finding it in the expression of other's faces:

> It must be carelessly stimulated, spurred in by provocation. The dandy is, therefore, always compelled to astonish. Perpetually incomplete, always on the margins of things, he compels others to create him, while denying their values. He plays at life because he is unable to live it. He plays at it until he dies, except for the moments when he is alone and without a mirror. For the dandy, to be alone, to be alone is not to exist.[33]

Perhaps this is why insecurity turns to hysterical paranoia when he is alone. Ultimately, the form Biswas's action can take is tragic farce. He grows increasingly grotesque because his alternatives are both absurd and irrelevant. Yet it is necessary for him to go through this, even when it is not reasonable at all. Unaccommodated and alienated, Biswas is compelled to be a tragic clown. At Sikkim Street, he discovers that the romance of the house is destroyed by the disappointing reality of disrepair. The catalogue of disasters is emphatic to a purpose. The house is an emblem of the loss of the El Dorado "the golden dream of his life".[34]

For a third world character, the need of "sense of place" is the sharpest experiences of inferiority in all forms, social, racial and intellectual. It is the equivalent of being a metaphorical slave, and life becomes filled with role-playing. It leads to the desire to be a sophisticated man in the modern world. Ironically becoming modern also means being aware of time as concrete reality and this denotes ageing, wasting and absurdity. Naipaul's characters are solitary creatures conscious of their alienation from their surroundings. L.R. Anderson[35] states that far from being able to accommodate themselves socially, they experience these societies as the hostile environments in which their identities are perpetually opposed. The discovery of a social role, therefore, does not coincide with the discovery of a self; rather it inspires the maintenance of a mask. Anderson[36] quotes Erving Goffman's distinctions between the performed self and the real identity. His statement is very germane to Biswas's role-playing. A person who is conscious that he is appearing before others will intentionally project a definition of the situation, in which a conception of himself is an important part. He will act out the part assigned by his situation rather than express his true identity. This "dramaturgical principle"[37] which informs the way a person acts before others reflects the alienation of subject from the object. Naipaul expresses this duality by creating the sense that his creators are also actors coinciding with Hassan's similar statement about the rebel-victim. Anderson illustrates the example of what Marlow says in Conrad's *Heart of Darkness*, "people do not express their true identities but rather the roles assigned to them by their cultures". So, in a culture bereft of heroes and full of failures, the only role that Biswas can assume is that of the clownish antihero. Robbed of identity, the hollow space is often filled with role-playing.

Biswas's antiheroic position is further established with his resemblance to the Sisyphus-victim figure. He is the absurd, ironic antihero that Camus talks of in his *Myth of Sisyphus*. Camus writes, "his passion for life won him that unspeakable penalty in which the whole being is exerted towards accomplishing nothing". Similarly every new attempt by Biswas to start afresh is like the figure of Sisyphus, straining to push the huge boulder up a hill, only to see the whole effort collapse into nothing. Biswas "powerless and rebellious" knows the whole extent of the wretched condition. Absurdity in Biswas's life is strongly akin to the one experienced by Camus about man's experience of absurdity.

> ...in a universe suddenly divested of illusions and lights, man feels an alien, a stranger. His exile is without remedy since he is deprived of the memory of a lost home or the hope of a promised land. This divorce between man and his life, the actor and his setting, is properly the feeling of absurdity.[38]

A rootless man commits a fallacy by supposing that the search for an authentic life will be easier in the contemporary world provided he has the sensibility. For Naipaul, sensibility is not hereditary. Rather one acquires sensibility when one lives within a viable and cultured tradition. Paradoxically, tradition and freedom must co-exist within the same person if he is to live a full life. In his confrontation with the vicissitudes of life Biswas expresses a keen awareness of the absurd. The absurd man feels within him a longing for happiness. The absurd is born of the confrontation between the human need for happiness and the unreasonable silence of the world. Absurdity arises for Mr. Biswas because he knows that all his acts and its consequences are meaningless, but he is also under the compulsion to act, even though these acts do not have any meaning in itself. In a meaningless world, Biswas is left to invent his own personal meaning for his existence. He tries to understand the absurd world through journalism, painting, and writing short-stories which are always aborted.

Biswas deliberately cultivates eccentricity. In the Chase, he devotes himself to absurdities, growing his nails to extreme length, holding them up to—startled customers. He picks and squeezes at his face until his cheeks are inflamed and the rims of his lips are like welts. Garebian situates Biswas as a colonial grappling with his identity and traces the grotesque nature of his character, projecting him as a victim of absurdities. Evidently, he is on his way to a state of madness; his bizarre behaviour is a futile version of metaphysical rebellion against the compulsion to become a Tulsi.

In a way, Biswas is a postmodern protagonist as his very indecision about meanings of things is matched by a willingness to tolerate the uncertainties of life and welcoming a world seen as random and multiple and even at times absurd. The grotesque in his character and his life is the result of collusion, multiple intrusions and shocks, which are psychologically threatening to Biswas. These devices serve to show him as irrelevant to the natural order of things.[39]

Garebian refers to Biswas's behaviour as a manifestation of the symptoms of the mad, the neurotic or the temporary irrational. The savagery and violence of some of his acts are consequences of his intemperate passions. At the Chase, when profits plummet he blames his failure on Hari's blessings. "Hari blessed it", the words standing in his disordered mind for the curse of orthodoxy on his efforts to establish himself in the new world. His fear causes severe stomach problems and he develops fear of dirt growing unnecessarily hysterical. His self-imposed seclusion is surrender to paranoid irrationality. Biswas sees the future as "a void like those in dreams into which past tomorrow and next week and next year he is constantly falling" (p. 190). He sees all his actions as futile and he is constantly tired, restless, and indecisive. Garebian also brings forth the point that Biswas's encounter with madness is one of the basic experiences of the grotesque, an attribute which definitely points towards antiheroism. Biswas oscillates between two extremes of intermittent gay vitality, which often veers towards the borders of terror. His mimicry and buffoonery are playfully funny whereas his paranoid seclusions and violent outbursts are fantastically sinister. Playfulness and sinisterness, resulting in the grotesque, are aspects of the same absurd experiences from which he cannot escape. Naipaul thus reveals different facets of Biswas's nature which range from comic and eccentric to the neurotic and disconcerting.

It is perhaps significant that the crisis in breakdown in Biswas is prompted by an unusual moment of insight on his part, that he is a nomad, a wanderer who can find no rest. It is also the predicament of the frustrated West Indian artist whether he is B. Wordsworth producing one passionate line a month or Mr. Biswas who worked "more and more elaborate messages of comfort for his walls with a steady unthinking hand, and a mind in turmoil" (p. 259). The mental image that he has of himself as a civilized man in the centre of a jungle changes to an image of a man surrounded by a huge black billowing cloud, the void into which he finally tumbles. The breakdown comes during a storm in the Green Vale. Behind Mr. Biswas's terror are traumatic personal memories haunting him—the voices outside his house after his father's death, Bhandat's violent treatment, the menace of Mungroo and Govind—come back to attack his gesture of individuality. Naipaul ably conveys the oppressive weight of Biswas's unraveling. The devolution of his fears is precise involving fear of being alone, threatening labourers, of bodily harm, of people; his obsessions with the newspapers on the wall, the house, the asphalt snakes, his dreams, his wife and his children.[40] Completely insecure, he loses the power of evaluation and rationality. During his nervous breakdown ants and dribbling tar assumes threatening surrealistic shapes creating visual and auditory hallucination. Anand's unceasing chant of "Rama, Rama, Sita, Sita" remains his last contact with reality.

The storm plunges Biswas into the most serious existential crisis of his life. Though at first, the decision to free himself from the limitations of the past gives him a new found awareness of life's possibilities, a series of setbacks soon tempers the exhilaration and leads to bouts of psychosomatic malaria. With the storm, he breaks down completely. His first attempt at liberating himself ends in total failure and he is forced to regress into a total kind of security "of the colonial mentality".

In Shakespeare's *King Lear*, one sees the furious protest of a mad man raging against nature's cosmic violence. A similar situation takes place in the novel but with diametrically opposite reaction. The relationship between Lear's mad scene at the height of the storm and Biswas's mental breakdown under similar conditions has been variously noticed. Anthony Boxhill[41] compares Lear with Biswas revealing the latter as a considerably weak man. But the point of emphasis is that while Lear competes with the storm in power, Biswas only mutters and cringes. Even while Naipaul is drawing attention to the similarities and to the predicaments of Lear and Biswas, he is emphasizing that Biswas is no Lear. The fact remains that while by his assertion, Lear is a hero, Biswas is not; he is an antihero whose assertion, rebellion and aspirations, all remain half established.

His crisis in identity comes from his critical experience of being an indentured slave's descendent. Quoting Walsh, S.P. Swain[42] states that the faith of Biswas is the faith of the despairing and the excruciating lot who "carry about them the mark in their attitudes, sensibilities and conviction of the slave, the unnecessary man". The reference to Lear's "unnecessary and unaccommodated" is correct because like Lear, Biswas too is a derelict, living for thirty-five years of his life in the houses of others as a temporary resident. In none of these places his presence is appreciated and he realizes that his absence would not make a difference for "in none of these places had he been more than a visitor, an upsetter of routines" (p. 132). In isolation he suffers from bouts of panic and anxiety. He rebels against being reduced to a Tulsi without any individuality, against the disorder and lack of privacy in communal existence at Hanuman House but frequently his gesture of defiance ends in humiliation, and in defence and in aggression, he begins to clown. But given the chance to "paddle his own canoe" he discovers the horrors of loneliness, the abyss that opens under the rootless man when exposed alone. Unfound, between several worlds, he is "a sardonic contrast with Prospero or Crusoe."[43]

L.R. Anderson finds the idea of freedom paradoxical. One can project oneself beyond the restraints of ordinary life and free himself from every social relation. But the catch is that it brings a terrifying sense of isolation and emptiness. In his desire for freedom Biswas attempts to break every social tie, but the feeling of terror and loneliness intensifies to such an extent that he becomes morbid and he devices macabre designs to free himself from his family by killing them.

Biswas's nervous breakdown is brought about by alienation; disgruntled, he finds that there is no one to kill. The rage turns inwards, becoming self-destructive. Alternating between self-disgust and anger; he gives in to humiliation and feels aggression towards those who humiliate him. It is an aimless cycle in which the individual is both victim and aggressor. Anderson's essay also brings to light the relation that exists between inner degradation and outward violence. A victim is at once potentially capable of violence and his self-abnegation may also inspire violence and contempt in others. Contextualizing this in the novel is the incident where Biswas is badly beaten up by Govind.

Biswas's varied readings of Hall Caine, Marie Corelli, and Samuel Smiles nourish his fantasy and make him "despair of finding romance in his own dull green land" (p. 78). "Real life was always to begin for then, soon and elsewhere" (p. 147). His remoteness from the events in his life is aggravated through his fantasies and his readings. The literary heroes he admires in Samuel Smiles live in countries where ambitions have meaning and can be pursued, but Biswas is trapped in an absurd place without any romance. It is from an early phase in his life that he begins to wait out of anguish, "not only for love, but for the world to yield its sweetness and romance" (p. 80). For support he turns to the stoic Marcus Aurelius, in ironic counterpoint to his own neurotic fear of life. His smattering of Western education propels him to think of himself as an individual, giving him ideas of self-development, ambition and romance, for which his actual situation provides no such outlet. Again reality and the myths fed by these books are in conflict. He imagines himself to be the Samuel Smiles hero—young, poor and struggling, but here the comparison ceased. Trinidad was no magic land offering opportunities to men like Mr. Biswas, ready to take off into the skies but lacking the foundation of the runway. Biswas's world as opposed to the world of Samuel Smiles is characterized by dependency, poverty and ceaseless worry. His collection of books reflects his tumultuous inner life. One may laugh at the alternating comic and pathetic collusions between his sense of himself and the actualities of his environment.

Books have a strong but negative effect on Biswas, as Peter Hughes[44] points out, Biswas reads books about politics, but their presentation of misery and injustice leaves him feeling more desolate than ever. He is neither a thinker, nor a planner who can exercise conscious direction over the direction of his life. He indulges in fantasies to relieve depression and boredom. His sensitivity to his environment and his imaginative capacity to identify with heroic character in books are major causes of his problems. Biswas realizes that the romantic sagas of self help make sense only in countries where ambitions are credible, where heroes can propel themselves up ladders already in existence. For Biswas, reality lies somewhere beyond Trinidad. Swain writes "his dark humour and brooding unhappiness lends him to the distanced 'exotopic' perspective of an exile".[45] His dreams to be somebody beguile him and isolate him from others. His inner and outer worlds have a separateness, which does not co-exist.

Biswas's changing perceptions of the Tulsis result in existential suffocation and this ambivalence is insufficient to end the existential fear of extinction. His alienation is the consequence of his vivid imagination and fantasy sustained by the alien influences of his readings that channelise his ambitions unrealistically. Ironically, Biswas develops an idealized image of himself, which is in fact, a sharp contrast to his real self. His real self, the image that the Tulsis have of him is in conflict with his self-image as a person with a high and sub-lime ideal, a dignified individual whose real life of accomplishments and enterprises is yet to begin.

It is an irony that Biswas, who always strives for an identity, does not have any proof of his birth and childhood. Industrialization has removed all traces of it. The world carried no witness to his birth and childhood. It is as if his very past is erased. In doing so, the world denies all the individual's attempts to assert his dignity. Biswas personifies an individual's attempts to fight against the cosmic denials of his very existence. The consequence of the parodic discovery of

El Dorado is that, Mr. Biswas loses all contact with the past. Eraser of the past is a typical postmodern feature. With the creation of his false "buth certificate", his entire past is falsified.

> Throughout his life Mr. Biswas is filled with a despairing sensed of his own insignificance. Suppose, "Mr. Biswas thought in the long room, suppose that at one world I could just disappear from this room, what would remain to speak of me? A few clothes, a few books...he had lived in many houses. And how easy it was to think of those houses without him. (p. 131)

So overwrought is he by this feeling of insignificance that he tells Anand: "I am nobody, I am just a man, you know." Seth's remark, in sharp contrast to his idealized heroic self, becomes a bitter reminder of his insignificance "Your father is a damn funny sort of man. Behaving as though he owns the place. Let me tell you that when you children were born your father couldn't feed you." (p. 387)

Biswas's awareness of the irony of his situation comes to the highest point when he becomes the investigator of the Deserving Fund. Insecure in his work and racked by the shame of poverty, surviving on Tulsi charity he mocks at his own condition. He calls himself "Deserving Destitute Number One, Mr. Biswas, Occupation: Investigator of Deserving Destitutes!" (p. 441). He sees his ownership of the house and the winning of Shama's loyalty as triumphs. However, comparative to the exulting antiheroic Biswas and his achievement, the house is revealed to be a squat sentry box like structure, with a staircase seemingly attached as an afterthought, and a door that wouldn't open. An ironic intention of the use of epic conventions in the novel becomes apparent when the epic hero is revealed to be the runtish, antiheroic Mr. Biswas. The double edged device of an epic prologue made it possible for Naipaul to write about Biswas in the epic mode and simultaneously undercut his achievement by implicitly acknowledging the absurdity of the comparison.

Through Biswas, Naipaul confronts us with the truth of an individual agitated by a culture he is born into, but cannot respect. Biswas is maddened by the circumstances but is totally helpless to change or counter it. There exists a huge gap between the protagonist's desire and his life of responsibilities and limitations. Naipaul does not allow him to attain great heights, financially or socially, in his exhaustive fight with the Tulsis. He is denied the satisfaction of being absorbed into the Hindu world or to represent it in the outside world.

Biswas is a boorish man, an oaf without etiquette, but such behavior steems mostly in reactions to situations where he is powerless to do anything. However, this boorishness in his character aligns him with the antihero. He mocks the Tulsis by renaming them in animal terminology. Powerless, he throws food on others' heads deliberately, even washing his hands and gurgling from the upper storey window with the full awareness of people passing beneath the window. He tries to attract attention through his deviant and aggressive behaviour but after his rebellion he slips into his role of a licensed buffoon. As the protagonist of the novel, he has none of the characteristics associated with a hero. Even his son views him as a whiner and tormentor of Shama. He accosts Biswas with the astonishing judgment summing up Biswas's life as a fastidious never-getter. "Once upon a time there was a man who...whatever you did for him was never satisfied" (pp. 378-79). To a certain extent, Biswas is self-centred, often resisting reciprocity and inclining towards suspicion and paranoia. Moreover, in spite of his professed concern for his family's welfare, he remains solitary with a subjective view of others.

Biswas's comic defiance always springs from the feeling that he belongs nowhere. Moreover, his rebellion too does not bring him complete selfhood. It only gives him a sense of having made his point several times only to himself. Meenaksi Bharat[46] points out that in the long run it is quite ineffectual. His rebellion, which consists of secret revenges of spitting into drinks, rejecting Tulsi food and eating inordinate quantities of salmon, confirms his comic meanness from which he gains so little, "Secret eating had never done him any good" and by doing this he is only doing a great disservice to himself. In Hanuman House his antiheroism and lack of sympathy is clearly exposed. When Mrs. Tulsi falls ill, Shama urges Biswas to see her; he rebels by playing with the sag of his hammock like calf muscles. He fails to show concern and worst of all displays no contrition at all.

Politically and sociologically, Biswas is a victim of cultural racism.[47] A refined form of primitive racism carried to its logical end, it makes the individual hate his dress, value system, social institutions, historical past, religion and practically everything not connected with the colonizer. Biswas's colonial embarrassments are exposed in his encounter with Ms Logie, the Welfare Development Officer and he is absolutely servile in her presence. Biswas's nervous condition and sickness is borne out of a psychological yearning for an independent identity. Alienated from the self he fights against an irrational fear wherein he feels mentally and physically threatened. Covering his vulnerable parts, he screams, "I am not whole." As if in chain reaction, one thing invariably leads to another. Menace, panic and continuing sense of futility bring about a sense of uselessness in him. Hysterical, he sinks further into disorientation "a condition typical of the colonial subjects, wherein he displays contradictory urges".[48] Lacking the conviction to commit even the most ordinary action, he is confronted with a complex and obsessive decision involving his broken tooth. Deciding firmly that he would throw it, he keeps it with him.

His life is a series of disasters, each of which can be taken as his angry rebuttal of an uncongenial society which exhausts him by the time he is middle-aged. His final peace is a consequence of a limited personal triumph but it is also one of exhaustion, sickness, and failure rationalized and accepted. He is quick to acquire what Naipaul has described as "the exile's compensating sense of temporariness".[49]

Landeg White[50] writes that by 1964, Naipaul saw himself as a person utterly displaced, connected by birth and education to three different societies but unable to establish living contact with anyone. A displaced man himself, Naipaul has a deep understanding of the effects of displacement and subjugation. That Biswas seeks to transcend the impermanence of his life is also characteristic of Trinidad. "So Trinidad was and remains a materialistic immigrant society, continually growing and changing, never setting into any pattern, always retaining the atmosphere of a camp...."[51] Biswas's attitude throughout life was that "it was temporary and not quite real and it didn't matter how it was arranged" (p. 147). In such a society, Singh finds Naipaul's Biswas "wasted, decentred, unwanted".[52] This attitude of impermanence and instability is so ingrained and internalized that when in the end he finds himself in his own house, "He grew dull and querulous and ugly, living had always been a preparation, a waiting. And so the years had passed; and now there was nothing to wait for" (p. 586).

He is a rebel but since his rebellion comes in strange and grotesque forms, his assertions constantly fail. His life is a reversal of his dreams. Instead of taking Shama to his house, he becomes the Dolahin, the bride, occupying the subservient position of the Hindu daughter-in-law.[53] Though his life is governed by "amazing scenes were witnessed" statement there is nothing amazing about Biswas; his life is unremarkable, as his curt obituary shows. The last phase of his mediocre life is marked by waiting and postponement, two of the most insidious elements of his life. He waits and worries for his debt, for his job and his son, Anand. When he falls into the void of his own being and dies suddenly, there is little or no impact.

From the beginning, friction prevails between Biswas's desire and the lacerating milieu around him. Naipaul presents a very bleak unromantic portrait of the colonial split self and its quest for wholeness. Unlike a hero, Biswas finds that it is the fragmented events of his life that shape and mould his mind and thought. His attempts to break free to an independent imaginative life through writing are through sterile imitation of western literature with which he cannot identify in his unromantic surrounding. A journalist of mediocre talents, his articles mirror his longing for wholeness and also reveals his attraction towards the grotesque and the absurd. His newspaper essays depict the lives of "Trinidad's richest, poorest, tallest, fastest, strongest men". It is then followed by another series on men with unusual calling: "thief, beggar, night soil remover, mosquito killer, undertaker, lunatic asylum warden" (p. 352). As a journalist he writes facetious stories through which he obliquely expresses his anxiety. In his attempt to be a writer, his earliest stories feature reports of "a wife and four kids" later replaced by stories of barren heroines.

His need for identity and dignity and the constant pressures on him reverse his intentions and undermine his vision of an El Dorado. From a disappointed bus conductor to an overseer in the Tulsi estate, Biswas does not belong anywhere. Biswas is an orphan, a stranger unrelated in a world of relationships. Insecure societies can only hope to imitate and remain second or third rate societies lacking all role models.

Journey is one of the literary motifs which reveal character. Biswas's momentous journey begins and ends with darkness. If Biswas has triumphed we are left in no doubt how little has been won, how, as Alan Wilde[54] has stated, uncertainty is preferable to what has been lost. By the time he acquires the house, Biswas is beaten down, exhausted and handicapped by his paranoia, and he becomes a passive voyeur faced with the spectacle of his own empty achievement. For his achievement Biswas pays with his life dying a premature death, sick, exhausted, receiving only humiliation from society. Left with no cause to fight, and without any income, he is once more, as he began, alone and unimportant. All that is meaningful, the presence of Anand and Savi is once more out of reach. "Anand's letters grew rare again. There was nothing Mr. Biswas could do but wait. Wait for Anand. Wait for Savi. Wait for five years to come to an end. Wait, wait" (586-87).

He is a victim of manipulation of those seeking to keep his rebellion at bay, but his sensitivity to his existential and human desires, separates him from others who have accepted their marginalized state. His emotional urge for freedom, his sensitivity to humiliation and slavery are signs of a rebellious and subversive temperament. The 'little man's' quest for independence is characterized by disgruntlement and menacing inner violence.[55]

Gradually, Biswas is transformed from a buffoon to a sub-human victim. Forcing him into the security of the colonized he finds that even in choosing names for his children, decisions have already been made for him. Biswas tries to choose for himself but his choices are rather a negation than an affirmation. His rebellion assumes the form of ridiculous acts, such as his spitting into drinks at Ajodha's rum shop and swinging his hammock calves. His clowning fury reduces him to the level of a vindictive vulgarian. Quoting from Harvey Cox's *The Feast of the Fools* (1969), Garebian[56] shows how Biswas steadily degenerates under mental pressure. His buffoonery is what Cocteau says of a man who is really incapable of originality; it is the painted smile on the terminally sick.[57]

His fluctuating states are consequences of a lifetime of struggle and unrelieved tension. In his own home, he is trapped by his material inadequacies and his emotional dependence on his children. The ultimate trap is the vast gap between struggle, ambition and the actual achievement. The energy spent in the struggle to survive, to avoid failure is completely out of proportion with his actual achievement. Biswas has no doubt achieved his own half plot of land, but can this success be qualified as success in its complete meaning? Can it be described as a heroic achievement? Even as we appreciate his achievement, doubts are raised about it. Readers are made aware of the fact that Biswas has just lost his job and he cannot pay for the mortgaged house, and that the house itself is uncomfortable and jerry built. It is also revealed that he got the house not because of his wisdom but because the solicitor's clerk was looking for someone to swindle. Moreover, as Fawzia Mustafa[58] points out, the third person narrative also contextualizes Biswas's success by portraying the paucity that underlies Biswas's claims. The mortgage on the house, the solicitor's clerk's scam, the neglect of Bipti, Biswas's mother, and his own illness all announce the limitations to Biswas's sense of achievement.

There is no "lived happily ever after" end to the story. Biswas enters the house under the shadow of death, irritable and dissatisfied. Illness, disappointment in Anand and anxiety dim much glory from his achievement. Even the final triumph seems short-lived because Biswas dies estranged from his son Anand whose comprehension and love is the thing he needs most. When Savi returns, "Mr. Biswas welcomed her as though she were Anand and herself combined...."

Through Anand, Biswas tries to achieve a sense of wholeness but with his departure even this attempt at wholeness ends in failure. In the end true freedom remains elusive as ever. The ending is ambiguous because it does not depict Biswas as being exceptionally happy and proud of his marginal achievement. Like his life, his achievement too is ordinary, passable for others, a laudable achievement only for himself.

Despite his weaknesses, Biswas remains radical, he is also an artist who insists on "paddling his own canoe", however, disastrously. He is, in fact, a representative figure of everyman. In fact, Biswas combines in him, "a tragic and a doomed man unable to find a portion of the earth". His vision is absurdly out of sorts with the reality around his landscape. Biswas's world is a fragmented and disturbed. He is a misfit in his society because he leans towards a rebellion directed towards forming a separate individuality based on western models. He is rejected by his family, but even with his job as a Reporter, which gives him some solace, he finds that this inferiority complex cannot be ignored.

> And so he rode on to his Reporter's job and its curious status: welcomed even fawned upon, by the greatest in the land, fed as well as anybody and sometimes even better, but always finally, rejected. (p. 347)

Biswas's neurotic personality results from psychological factors. He lacks motherly love and security. He ambivalently hovers between the poles of idealization of the mother's image in his fantasy and rejection of her in reality. In this context, Sudha Rai[59] quotes Gordon Rohlehr's observation that "Biswas needs to be mothered...he needs a mother as well as a wife. He is in a state where he can neither give nor receive the love he needs."

Biswas attempts to construct his identity as a writer but fails, succeeding only as a sensational news writer, reporting what often came close to the incongruous, absurd, and sordid. Through writing, he takes hold of his world, seeing and defining it in his own eccentric way; as a feature storyteller, he imaginatively plays out the dark possibilities of his own life. In Biswas, Naipaul brings out the shame, the contempt and anguish that he resolved in himself through the grotesque and patois of his early Trinidad fiction. He struggles to acquire a professional identity in a colonial society but his career is fraught with insecurity and fear. Again the role-playing aspect comes to the forefront. In this context, it is his fear of being sacked from his job because he has the feeling that he is masquerading as a journalist.

The novel's multivalent vision focuses on the protagonist as a man grappling with defeating circumstances, yet refusing to yield to them. Biswas is a man who, in the contemporary cosmopolitan context, is hardly worth noticing about. His achievement and fame are thin and as brittle as his personal identity. From his birth to adulthood and later death, one can see the emerging pattern of his personality in conflict with his society. Determined to be himself, he is shamed yet does not submit to the ridicule and humiliations thrust on him by his family as they perceive him with Tulsi eyes.

The prologue and the epilogue serve a limiting, deflating purpose—in keeping with the relentless unsentimental view of things preserved throughout the novel. It is also an irony that Biswas's roots as a writer are in imitation. A journalist with mediocre talents, he copies the styles of London papers before turning them into presentable imitation. But with the change in editorship, even self-expression is denied Mr. Biswas, and his writing becomes laboured, dead. The policy of *The Sentinel* "news not views" (p. 369) muffles his personality and "he had not so much to distort as to ignore, to forget the bare toughened feet of children in an orphanage: its sullen looks of dread, the shameful uniforms" (p. 375). The cause of failure here is also replicated in Biswas's abortive attempt to write for British and American magazines through a course from the ideal school of journalism. Garebian quotes Naipaul regarding the relation between a writer and the society in which he lives, how society is responsible for moulding a character into a hero or an antihero. "No writer, however, individual his vision could be separated from his society."[60]

In deliberate contrast to Seepersad Naipaul, Mr. Biswas's fiction never goes beyond the first line of the story called "Escape". To Biswas, Naipaul allows only limited achievement. Here facts mock fiction because unlike Seepersad Naipaul, Biswas's stories do not move beyond the first few lines of the abortive escape stories.

Partly responsible for Biswas's character is immigrant ancestry and partly it is his personality; born in extreme poverty in a family of sugarcane workers, Biswas's life is exposed to the worst economic stresses of an immigrant's life. Throughout his life he is mocked at for being a have-not in a materialistic society. Several times he is derided for having possessions, which could be hung from a one-inch nail. Most of his antiheroic stances are reactions to this constant derision. Biswas is denied the possibility of revolutionary or epical transformation. A runaway husband and father, Biswas seeks new life in the city. He becomes a roving reporter for a yellow newspaper making a living out of a rootless man's facetiousness and fantasy, but his own life is precariously balanced over an ever widening void. By the time Biswas becomes the community relations officer all real sense of community is gone.

Mental and physical chaos dogs Biswas. The play of chance, chaos, anarchy, and fragmentation, which according to Hassan,[61] play important roles in post-modern writing, creates havoc in Biswas's life. In the novel, the fluctuations in his state, the noise and the sight of children shouting and elders quarrelling, unhealthy competition, the noisy chattering, all combine to create chaos around him.

In his essay, Garebian[62] traces David Ormerod's observation on the question of identity in the novel in terms of vegetative imagery, connecting it to the theme of social frustration and personal failure. Though Biswas attempts to create order in the surrounding chaos, it comes as a dismal failure. The changes in Biswas's fortunes are marked by the state of vegetation which surrounds him. As such, the locales in the novel have their own symbolic connections with Biswas's psychopathology and descent into the void. The epical stature of the novel is supported by the conflict ridden trajectory of Biswas's wanderings from place to place without finding a resolution to his problem of identity. By the time he gets to Sikkim Street, fear has taken root rendering him powerless to fight it. The house has a real significance with regard to the existential phase of the detachment. It is a place "as wild and out of way as he wished, unpainted the house starts to decay even before it is completed" signifying the futility of his greatest act.

Father and son share a very problematic relationship. That Biswas is a dismal failure is reflected in Anand's remark "when I get to your age I don't want to be like you" (p. 46). It is an irony as Biswas himself is the living embodiment of his disappointment of efforts. Anand rejects the coarseness of Biswas's domestic life, and is angry when Biswas takes his frustration out on Shama. Biswas's behaviour continues to perplex Anand. In the foreground, there is the perpetual chaos of Biswas's house building, and beyond that, his domestic and professional frustration. "Self-disgust led to anger, shouts, tears, something to add to the concentrated hubbub of the evening, the nerve torn helplessness" (p. 438). Mr. Biswas dies after writing hysterical, complaining and despairing letters to his son, perhaps in the same frame of mind in which he had looked at his mother's corpse "oppressed by a sense of loss, not of present loss, but of something lost in the past". With his death, he does not even achieve the individual obituary he had fashioned for himself "Roving reporter passes on". Rather it is the only brief "Journalist dies suddenly" mentioned and forgotten.

Biswas's fight for identity and roots become ridiculously futile. Every burst of his rebellion against his humiliations is derided upon. His atheism is partly a pose and partly his rebellion. When he realizes that he has been trapped into marrying a Tulsi only because of his caste, his rebellion against Hanuman House grows into a rebellion against all things traditional. Though he is expelled from his birthplace, he does not leave its darkness behind, rather it surrounds him everywhere. Lack of a solid foundation, thus, may make a person react antiheroically, for to a man dispossessed there is nothing which creates meaning for his existence.

In the novel, Naipaul uses dramatization, reflection, the centre of consciousness and the third person omniscient narration to create an overwhelming mood of minor irritation turned major crisis. The third person omniscient narrator focuses on the manner in which the protagonist handles the society, and directs his irony at the man and the society. The narrator shows him as essentially incapable of meeting the demands of his times and so partially responsible for his alienation in his self-centred universe.

Memory, imagination, history, and tradition are examined as organizers of a personal vision. The novel becomes a vehicle for man's ontological need for a personal order. Naipaul, Biswas and the narrator share a common existential and physical heritage in varying degrees. All three are rootless men whose feelings of unimportance express itself as a desire to leave a mark. The mood of the novel is that of absurdity and existential despair. Biswas's moods of dissatisfaction and his compulsion to escape are expressed through a subtle underplay of moods. In Biswas he creates an awareness of terror which underlies the third world situations and which erupts unexpectedly into uncontrollable and unexplained violence.

Biswas carries the mark of a slave. Walsh's observation may be relevant here.

> ...the palpable absence of external institutions does not mean that slavery had not afflicted an incurable wound on the national consciousness...even those like the Indians who were exempt from formal, historical slavery, carry about with them in their attitude and posture, in their management of life and feeling the indelible mark of the slave.[63]

Purabi Panwar[64] mentions that the novel narrates the tribulations of a weak and vulnerable man in search of freedom. There is a sense of half wasted life and half thwarted aspiration. Joshi concludes that Biswas's attempts to take lessons from a London school of journalism make a point about the absurdity of trying to live by alien/western standards. This episode also illustrates the "predicament of the artist in the colonial society".[65]

The novel is completely epical in form, framed by an epilogue and a prologue which in the prescribed epic manner gives a summary of the entire action of the novel, except the ordinary, antiheroic character who is the focus of this mock epic. Andrew Gurr[66] notes that fearing emptiness Biswas spends his entire lifetime as a fantasy man, an escapist. Both the prologue and the narrative are equally dispassionate, the former is an impartial assessment of Biswas achievement at his death, in the latter we find the irony "gentle and the effect comic".[67]

With the passage of time, disaster looms close, quickly devouring Biswas's ordinary life. Biswas is compared to an old tired machine, his heart failing him at last, like one overusing one's limited resources, and destroyed by the accumulation of forces against him.

> His complexion grew dark; not the darkness of a naturally dark skin, not the darkness of sunburn: this was a darkness that seemed to come from within, as though the skin was a murky but transparent film and the flesh below it had been bruised and become diseased and its corruption was rising. (pp. 587-88)

Reaffirming Biswas's antiheroic position Naipaul measures his achievements in such petty acquisitions as second-hand Slumberking bed, an old hat rack and a jerry built house. The search for self-identity seems endless; the basic compulsion towards finding a sense of identity brings other compulsions in its wake. The search is conscious of his lack of affinity with his time, his place and history. During his visit to India, Naipaul came in contact with people who were diminished and deformed, men who begged and whined. It can be mentioned again that Anand too sees his father, the antiheroic Mr. Biswas, as frequent whiner.

Finally, Biswas reaches the point of detachment of non-doing, non-interference, and social indifference. It is one position that Alan Wilde speaks of as a postmodern acceptance of the quotidian, yet chaotic, nature of the world. He reaches Hindu state of understanding, "...the knowledge of the abyss, the acceptance of distance as the condition of man."[68]

Referring to an interview that Naipaul gave in 1968, Gurr makes a point, which is exactly applicable to this process of composition. To a question, he replied "there is something absurd about the fictional form". In fact:

> It's an artificial activity, made up people taking part in invented actions. The first thing for the writer is to understand why he is setting all these people in motion. Which leads to the second problem: I didn't know who I was.[69]

To quote Garebian again,[70] Biswas's claim to a portion of the earth "shrinks to a succession of frustrated gesture and compromises". Biswas is a combination of the factual and the fictional. Naipaul, of course, makes no attempt to present Biswas as a traditional heroic figure. Biswas attracts both our attention and sympathy because Naipaul creates in him an enduring pattern of our common humanity. He is not an ideal hero but in his final acceptance of the chaotic nature of life he emerges as the perfect Sisyphus figure, victim and rebel in equal proportion, engaged in futility, losing much more than what he finally acquires, enduring but paradoxically antiheroic.

In ancient shadows and twilights
Where childhood had strayed
The world's great sorrows were born
And its heroes were made
In the lost boyhood of Judas
Christ was betrayed.

A.E. Germinal, 1947

In the novel *A Grain of Wheat*, the theme of betrayal is intrinsically related to the characters, especially to the antiheroic Mugo. The poem at the beginning of the chapter refers to the betrayal of Christ by Judas which had been influenced in a way by the latter's childhood. This is mentioned because it is in similar lines that one can trace the cause and effect of Mugo's betrayal.

Arthur Ravenscroft writes in his "Novels of Disillusionment"[71] that the African novels present a serious questioning of the idealistic euphoria that accompanied independence. In the marginalized third world countries, especially, it is not an attack upon the necessity of independence, but a refusal by conscious artists to be diverted from examining those realities and dilemmas that are the most inescapable and cruel inheritances left by former colonies of any imperial power. The postmodern world no longer lends itself to assured definition. The heroes of contemporary fiction do not only struggle against the world, they struggle for and against themselves. Their pressing concerns with love and interpersonal relations in an age of pure group dominance do not obviate their regard for the perennial interest of the self, something which the treachery of Mugo illustrates when he places his personal well-being above the life of his friend and even the freedom of his country.

Only a little more than a decade after a vicious colonial war, Ngugi wa Thiong'o, a Kenyan colonized subject wrote a novel that did not romanticize the struggle for independence. In fact, Ngugi starkly concentrates on the characters' human feelings and weakness to demonstrate the need for individuals to come to terms with the truth about themselves. He emphasizes the urgent need to confront the unhappy truths about themselves that crisis and action inevitably bring. *A Grain of Wheat* (1967) is a great advance in Ngugi's development as a novelist and this appears in the complex orchestration of the four different common but interrelated betrayals and the subsequent corrosion of selfhood. Even as the country gains its freedom there are already hints of incipient betrayals. The four characters who have each been involved in the events that led to Uhuru are now slaves to the memories of their own personal inadequacies.

One of the rebel-victims as cited by Ihab Hassan,[72] is the black, often seen as an outsider in his own country. The prototype here is the native African who after acquiring western education rejects his native culture and tradition. As a result he becomes a misfit in the society, as the very basis of African society is the community. Consequently, anyone who rejects the society, with or without the influence of western education, rejects his selfhood as the self is strongly identified with the community. Mugo, in Ngugi's *A Grain of Wheat*, represents the black as the native, thus becoming an outsider in his own community. He is not the former type of outsider but it is his ambitions and dreams as an individual, which makes him so. As an antihero, Mugo is one of the types who having been transplanted away from the early environment becomes stranded both emotionally and intellectually, embittered and despising what he cannot grasp.

The novel, laden with Biblical symbolism, alludes to Moses with reference to two characters, Mugo and Kihika, the nationalist, and Mugo's antithesis, who helps to define Mugo's character. Standing pre eminent among the villagers, seeing the vision of an independent Kenya and hoping as Moses did, to lead the people to freedom and in dying a heroic death, Kihika with his glorious actions becomes the hero of the novel. Panduranga Rao[73] points out that the sense of commitment that radiates from the spirit of Kihika proves that he is the representative consciousness of the Ngugi strongman, "the beacon hero". By contrast, Mugo who has messianic ambitions of leading the people to the Promised Land turns out to be a false prophet, a delusive daydreamer whose dreams and reality lie between two irreconcilable parts of a deep chasm. He is also a victim of absurdity, as Camus puts in the "Myth of Sisyphus". Absurdity arises in a situation where man's idealized projection of himself is opposed to his basic actuality of life. Put very simply, by going against Ngugi's 'beacon hero' Mugo in a way becomes the novel's antihero. When the novel opens, the reader comes face to face with Mugo, a very reserved young man who wakes up every morning, as we soon find out, in despair. Even in the dream he has just before he wakes up he is threatened by drops of water, which look as if it will stab him.

Critics have debated on the question as to whether Mugo is an antihero. His position, indeed, seems very ambivalent. Of course, he is the hero of the novel but not in the sense of being traditionally heroic, rather he is the opposite. He is the central consciousness and he owes his designation as a hero solely to the fact that he is the book's central character.[74] It is through him, as the central consciousness that the story unfolds. He is also the repository as both Mumbi and Gikonyo confess their guilt to him. This confession comes forth as the people see Mugo as emotionally and mentally strong, as the man who will not betray the faith reposed in him. All the while Mugo is trying to contain his inner turmoil as a result of betrayal. It is an ironical fact that Kihika too had reposed immense faith in him. Mumbi makes this apparent. Kihika was very wrong in his judgment. "Do you know, no, he said it often when...he would confide in someone like you" (157).

By his betrayal of Kihika, Mugo comes to be labeled as a villain, comparable to Judas. But another perspective points out that by his final, public confession, he purges his guilt and also serves to bring a community closer. If Mugo were any ordinary villain, he would have swallowed his guilt and enjoyed the enviable position offered him which he had always yearned for. Contrarily, Mugo cannot do even this. Quoting Francis Ki Lubuka, Panduranga Rao cites that Mugo is both guilty and self-aware.[75] Having never anticipated such a turn of events, the sudden proposal from the party to lead the Uhuru celebrations throws him off balance creating further panic and turmoil. Since he betrayed the people's hero Kihika, the veneration showed by the people who now choose him as their leader plays such havoc with his mental makeup that he suffers from false pressure on his bladder. Fear and suspicion splits him into a "bundle of raw nerves" and makes him shirk with lame excuses.

Ngugi brings to light the mental and psychological divisions created by social pressures between the members of the colonized society. The psychological effect of colonialism and its associated traumas is dramatized through the central protagonists in the trilogy and it is also no coincidence that these characters are often antiheroic. Loneliness, which is a neurosis in *The River Between*, becomes a condition of life by *A Grain of Wheat*, where Mugo betrays Kihika because the latter threatens the loneliness, which is Mugo's sole refuge. And with this loneliness comes guilt, the consciousness of failure, and the neurosis, which grows in the cracks of society, once cohesion is gone. The movement of the three novels traces the descent from little defined heroism to total antiheroism. Even the setting of the novel at a point of maximum social disintegration and the shifting methods of narration reflects the isolation of the characters. As the focal consciousness in the novel, Mugo is found wanting, disintegrating, unheroic and vanishing. Perhaps as Edith Kern,[76] has maintained, the position of the hero changes according to the changing reality.

It is Mugo's fear and single act of cowardice that thrusts him deep down the abyss of guilt and makes him an antihero. A rethinking of Kihika's proposal would have certainly fulfilled his messianic ambitions. However, there are various causes leading to Mugo's act of collaboration with the oppressive colonizers. Both Mugo and Kihika have similar dreams. But Kihika braves to change them into action while Mugo watches with jealousy as Kihika's fame spreads far and wide. The readers are given one insightful glance into this self-destructive emotion of jealousy. A meeting that Kihika is addressing draws huge crowds. Mugo, as one of the listeners is absolutely overcome with jealousy. Even here he tries to justify to himself that Kihika could reach this position because he had everything whereas Mugo had nothing. His reaction to Kihika's proposal to lead the underground group of forest fighters reveals that he suffers from an obsessive unwillingness to participate in community affairs, to be involved and committed to his social environment, its past and present history. This proposal is like a two-edged sword, fraught with dangers and opportunities at either ends.

The voices Mugo hears, psychologically may characterize him as a victim of auditory hallucination, which is also correlated with his schizophrenic character. But the voices he hears and the visions and dreams he has before and after Kihika's intervention in his life urge and diverts him towards a different part. The voices often fade and merge into the voice of God "calling out Moses, Moses!" (p. 214). And Mugo is ready with the answer "Here I am Lord" (p. 214). The proposal offers Mugo the one chance to answer this call but he blunders out of fear and a subconscious hatred for Kihika. Often the visions would make him walk the edge of revelations in which he remembers the words marking him out as the chosen one; he shall save the children of the needy. It must be him; it was he, Mugo, spared to save people like Githua, the old woman and anyone who had suffered. In dreams he sees himself as a man sought to save; one shouts, "Mugo, save us, the cry was taken up by others Mugo, save us. The suppliant voices rose to a chanting thunder; Mugo, save us" (p. 146). Ironically as it turns out Mugo is not the saviour he sees himself as, but a coward who is under the delusion of his own self-importance. From his dreams and visions, it may be ascertained that he entertains personal ambitions of probably becoming a political patriarch to his people in some distant future. This commitment to a course of action that may possibly be taken in the future rather than in the immediate present is the key to his failure he shares with the other antiheroes of the previous two novels. In his betrayal of Kihika, he betrays and endangers the lives of the people he actually dreams of leading.

Ngugi's Mugo is an alazon,[77] self-deceiving young man. A lonely, reserved and withdrawn member of the village, he is honoured as a former detainee. A deputation from the Party's village branch invites Mugo to lead the Uhuru Celebrations. But his reputation is a lie, the details of which are revealed very gradually as Ngugi relates the full story of Mugo's loneliness, jealousy and the heavy burden of unshared guilt.

Mugo's antiheroic irresponsibility is also highlighted when jealousy and fear prompts him to settle his jealousy at the expense of the national cause. His childhood experience, the sufferings and humiliations he suffered at the hands of his distant aunt has alienated him from his surroundings. He is a troubled man who is afraid of losing the little that he has got—the little strip of shamba and his crops. He is restless, gnawed by jealousy and humiliation, and later by guilt, undermined by the feeling that he can do nothing both against the British colonizers and Kihika's Forest Fighters. The former will detain him if he associates himself with the latter, and the latter will drag him to the confusing and dangerous vortex of politics from which he can never escape.

The reasons of Mugo's touch-me-not attitude are not far to seek. By nature he is very shy and avoids getting into any kind of conflict. Moreover, his treatment by his aunt is abysmal. His parents had died leaving him, an orphan, penniless, with an aunt, who when drunk, reminded him of this fact. At times, he slept among the goats. Once she puked after heavy drinking and in the morning, forced Mugo to pour soil on the filth. "Disgust chocked him so that he could not speak or cry. The world had conspired against him, first to deprive him of his father and mother, and then to make him dependent on an aging harridan" (p. 7).

Her derision at his every attempt began to haunt Mugo with the images of his own inadequacy. Her questions and statements about his clothes or even his face made all his pride tumble down. "His one desire was to kill his aunt" (p. 7), and her seeing into his desire was a painful and humiliating experience. In a way when he betrays Kihika to the authorities, the anger towards his aunt and the desire to kill her is directed as anger towards Kihika. But when Waitherero died, there was no one to claim him, leaving him alone, an outsider to his community. It is this lost innocence and lost childhood that holds the germ that led to the betrayal, turning Mugo to Judas, not to Moses.

His only dream is to be someone, a recognized individual. He would force people, through labour, sweat, success and wealth to recognize him. So obsessed is he with his ambitious dream that he rarely mixed with other boys for fear of being involved in brawls, and ruining his chances of a better future. He only carved a better future for himself but with Kihika's entry, he feels the dream that he valued most in his life is in danger of being destroyed.

It was two years that Kenya had been in a state of emergency. Mugo, untouched by this, continues to work on his strip of shamba, forgetting that the individual does not and cannot exist alone, except corporately, in the African society. Faint-hearted that he is, Mugo shirks further and further to fortify his future by not taking part in the national freedom struggle. For all practical purposes, he turns a blind eye to the events and turns to the soil, to bury the seeds, to tend the plants to ripeness; they were part of a world he had created for himself and which formed the background against which his dreams soared to the sky. Mugo, reveling in his dreams is often transported from the present to the future. Thus, when Kihika suggests that Mugo lead an underground movement, it frightens him. He sounds mad to Mugo,

> ...why should Kihika drag me into a struggle and problems I have not created? Why? He is not satisfied with butchering men and women and children. He must call on me to bathe in blood. I am not his brother. I am not his sister. I have not done harm to anybody. I only looked after my shamba and crops. (p. 194)

Fear surrounds him from all sides. "If I don't serve Kihika, he will kill me. They killed Rev. Jackson and Teacher Miniu. If I work for him, the government will catch me. The white man has long arms. And they will hang me. My God, I don't want to die" (p. 194). Mugo cannot afford to lose his future. Kihika could play with his death because "he had a family, people who would mourn his end, who would name their children after him, so that Kihika's name would never die from men's lips. Kihika had everything. Mugo had nothing (p. 145).

Essentially, Mugo is the uninvolved Gikuyu who has a glimmer of hope for a better future. When he searches his soul for sympathy for Kihika he finds only disgust. He believed "if you don't traffic with evil, then evil ought not to touch you; if you leave people alone, then they ought to leave you alone" (194). But Kihika's proposal filled him with fear and paranoia. In the first place, he had never wanted to be dragged into the evil vortex of politics. Now hatred for Kihika filled his heart. On his way to the D.O's office to reveal Kihika's whereabouts, Mugo is filled with the delusions of his own self-importance.

> I am important. I must not die. To keep myself alive, healthy, strong—to wait for my mission in life—is a duty to myself, to men and women of tomorrow. If Moses had died in the reeds, who would have ever known that he was destined to be a great man. (p. 197)

Mugo, the antihero, both hates and is jealous of Kihika as he lives by the words of sacrifice and love for the country's freedom. Mugo's betrayal is thus a betrayal of friendship, of family and communal values and of the nation itself. By handing Kihika over to the authorities, Mugo believes that he will achieve unquestioned authority and power. "To be great you must stand in such a place that you can dispense pain and death to others without anyone asking questions. Like a headmaster, a judge, a Governor" (p. 197).

In the African communal life, Mugo is an anomaly, deviating towards a selfish, lonely life which will only afflict him with further loneliness. As an antihero, he represents the betrayal of the implicit faith of the people.[78] He is a problematic outsider who strongly resists ideological and political manipulation, but in doing so marginalizes himself from the immediate society. A fundamental loneliness is a basic trait of such a problematic outsider, aggravated by social pressures, which have affected the relationship between the individual and the society. He marginalizes himself from society. Like Naipaul's Mr. Biswas, Mugo is a marginal man, a product of two social worlds, poised between the psychological uncertainties of these two worlds. Mugo's failure to communicate in a society where human communication plays an integral part also makes him an outsider. The communal life at Thabai is a kind of extended family where the feeling of we-ness is so strong that no one can remain isolated even if he wants to. This goes on to heighten Mugo's sense and problem of isolation. He succeeds in gaining a freedom that can only be termed as negative. Even in the beginning of the novel, Ngugi brings out Mugo's neurosis and guilt with clarity and it has reached such an extent that every day begins in despair pushing him to the edge of a breakdown.

He is obsessively attached to his shamba; it is through it that he wants to realize his dreams. Why is land so important to Mugo? A major problem faced by the peasants was that of land alienation, which would not have happened if they had had education. Mugo's attachment to the shamba and the security that he derives from it obfuscates even the nation's need of freedom for him. Mugo's action is not a direct, but an indirect effect of colonialism. Land is, after all, the key to people's life, providing them with a peaceful tillage and their material needs, in undisturbed serenity. His collaboration with the colonizers is not only a result of his insecurity, as Ngugi also shows that one purpose of Mugo is to achieve recognition and power. On his way, he already starts thinking of using the monetary reward for improving his future.

Traumatized as he is by his childhood experience, he suffers extensively from angst and alienation. This sense of alienation in man, from all that surrounds him is exacerbated by an awareness of one's precariousness in a changing world. One is assaulted by a general apprehension of threat that prompts angst as understood by existentialists, not as something that derives from any particular quotidian care but as a pervasive uneasiness or malaise of indeterminate origin. The source of anxiety is often indefinite; it is usually an intrinsic part of the basic condition one finds oneself in.

Existentialists view anxiety as a valuable indicator of an individual's need to modify the circumstances he finds himself in. It also reveals a manifestation of man's sense of radical insecurity and his precarious and contingent condition. Anxiety offers one of the most far-reaching and primordial possibilities of disclosure about man and his position in the world. Mugo seeks detachment from the world, but in the African society, and as any existentialist would point out, man is inextricably a being in the world existing in unavoidable contingency with all that surrounds him.

Mugo can be defined as a homo-duplex, divided between romantic heroism, ambition and practical sense. His is a wilful self-destructive individualism, existing in a literally empty world, bereft of meaning or any social relations. On the one hand, he romantically imagines himself as Moses leading the people out of servitude to freedom. On the other hand, practical sense and dreams of material success leads him to a solitary life dedicated to labour and success, cut off from all kinds of social relations. So isolated is he that he avoids all contact with the Emergency, avoiding the difficulties of the anti-colonial struggle, nurturing his dreams of a distant future. At most, he represents the trauma, and complexities of the non-combatant.

Like the antiheroic Munira[79], his fictional descendent in *Petals of Blood*, Mugo is afraid of being drawn into others' lives and struggle. Without a sense of coherence and integration with the community, Mugo suffers from self-alienation. He is ambivalent in his character as he longs for passivity rather than dynamic action. His inability to act or to participate fully in life or in the community affairs signals a profoundly disempowered state, a figure whose lack of fixed identities and allegiances leads to a sense of continual self-inflictive stasis.

What makes Mugo an antihero springs not only from his own character but also from his reaction to the encounter with crisis. It should be mentioned that both Kihika and Mugo entertain dreams of leadership. The former turns it into a reality, overcoming the obstacles, whereas the latter defers it to a distant future. How Mugo reacts to this proposal is totally unexpected of him, especially by Kihika who has always admired him as a self-made man. Mugo betrays him; his fear, his hatred of Kihika, his neurosis, and his selfish nature, all go on to show that Mugo who is seen by others as a stoic hero is in reality a weak man, an antihero.

Several times, Mugo refuses to take responsibilities for his actions. The philosopher, Nietzsche believed that irresponsibility of any kind should be replaced with self-responsibility. Though it is the community, which gave a sense of meaning to the people, Mugo refuses to accept his responsibility towards the community. Later when he realizes what he has done by betraying Kihika, he becomes conscious of the full extent of his horror, and does not want to face the truth. "He did not want to know what he had done" (p. 200). Later on, in order to exculpate himself from the crime, he reasons that Christ would have died on the cross anyway; Judas should not be blamed for it. By comparing his act of betrayal to that of Judas, Mugo indirectly compares Kihika to Christ, the true leader ready to sacrifice his life for the sake of the people. The recognition of Kihika as the true Christ is made apparent in Mugo's painful questioning as to why Judas, "a stone from the hands of a power more than a man" should be blamed for Kihika's crucifixion as Christ would have died on the cross anyway (p. 199).

Though he considers himself as an instrument of the Lord "to save the children of the needy...break in pieces the oppressors" (p. 142), "the Chief who would lead his people across the desert to the new Jerusalem" (p. 153), yet the appearance of Kihika brings to light Mugo's self-deception, weakness and the inconsistency of his position. When the opportunity offers itself, he takes the road of retreat and betrayal. Henceforth he is a tortured soul, in the anomalous position of being a hero in the eyes of the people but a traitor in his own. Thereon, he is pursued by an oppressive sense of alienation until the last day when he makes his public confession.

For Ngugi, individual betrayals are representative of the whole society by the powerful. He effectively portrays the influence of the Emergency on the individual psyche. Eustace Palmer[80] states that Ngugi presents "indecisive young men who called upon to play a major role in the society are unable to do so successfully because they are plagued by a sense of insecurity and guilt". Mugo turns a blind eye to the Kenyan War of independence in preference to the bogey of status. And in comparison to the protagonists of the novels, before and after independence, one finds that while the pre-independence ignorant Ngugi hero is struck by colonialism and made to feel degraded, the post-independence informed Ngugi hero is shaken by neo-colonialism and rendered far more degraded. In other words, the pattern of Ngugi intimates that the psychologically damaged hero of colonial Gikuyuland reaches the modern free Kenya not as a positive hero but as an ungainly non-assertive antihero.[81] In himself, Mugo exemplifies the atypical problematic hero who experiences a radical rupture between his ethical vision and the real/fictional world. Mugo with his torn and clouded conscience, embodies in him the major conflicts that has been troubling African young men. A hero of a cowardly nature, showing how weak he is, how perplexing his contradictions are, is a warning that Kenyans should abhor miniature heroes. In a way, Mugo's personal history is related to the history of Kenya as a nation. Ngugi's trilogy (*The River Between, Weep Not, Child*, and *A Grain of Wheat*) delineates a movement from relative stability in a rural culture to a state of alienation, strife and uncertainty.

Preoccupied with the means of improving his status, Mugo creates a gap between himself and his community. His position is similar to Goethe's Werther, who in his inordinate concept of himself severs the traditional bond between himself and the society and which points out the way to instances of complete alienation as such found in Byronic heroes. Indeed, in his brooding, reserved attitude, Mugo does really come close to the Byronic heroes. He is of the people but he has no relation with them. Separated from a meaningful relationship with the society, loneliness has become a burden for Mugo. "How time drags, everything repeats itself; the day ahead would be just like yesterday and the day before" (p. 3). Everyday he wakes up when dawn diffuses through cracks in the walls, but each day begins with pain and despair. Mugo can be compared to Munira. As David Cook and Michael Okenimphe[82] point out, Mugo shares a multiple sense of guilt. "Life...has always been a strain."

A point made by Kathy Kessler[83] can strengthen the fact that Mugo is not a psychologically whole self, a major precondition of the hero, and that he is unable to mediate between the contradictions of his own self with that of the world. His withdrawal from a positive assimilation with society not only shows alienation and misanthropic nature, but it also points towards an ill balance in his mental psyche. Kessler draws attention to Fredrick Jameson's idea of the co-relation between psychology and semiology which is pertinent to Ngugi's portrayal of Mugo. Is Mugo schizophrenic? Schizophrenia is classified as a mental disorder involving deterioration of/or confusion about one's personality. It also involves contradictory behaviour and attitudes, often veering towards obsession. Kessler refers to Jameson's thoughts on schizophrenia as a symptom of the postmodern experience. He argues that the schizophrenic experiences a breakdown of the relationship between signifiers and "that the experience of temporality, human time, past, present, memory…is also an affect of language".[84] Further, in Jameson's theory:

> The schizophrenic…is condemned to live a perpetual present with which the various moments of most of his/her life have little or no connections. In other words, schizophrenic existence is an experience of isolated, disconnected, discontinuous material signifiers which fail to link up into a coherent sequence. The schizophrenic does not know personal identity in our sense, since our feeling of identity depends on our sense of the persistence of the 'I' and the 'me' over time.

These symptoms relate to a dual situation, one, to Mugo's personal situation and two, to the Kenyan national situation. When Mugo speaks publicly of his experience in detention and the longing for home and family, the linguistic gap becomes apparent, as he reveals that his speech is virtually empty of any personal referent. There is no home for Mugo to go back to, no family to reclaim him. His is a terrifying loneliness, and he is a victim of both circumstances and of his own delusions. After he describes the detention experience in short, passionless, declarative sentences, such as "we only thought of home", and abruptly breaks off, the linguistic problem becomes evident:

> At first Mugo enjoyed the distance he had established between himself and the voice. But soon the voice disgusted him. He stopped in the middle of a sentence and walked down the platform towards his hut. (p. 58)

His inability to speak further and later his refusal to lead the people during the Uhuru celebrations lead the people to view him as a legendary figure who has suffered greatly. This, ironically, is far from truth. He is reluctant to accept the position given him. Despite the perception of the people around him, he does not suffer for the community. In this respect, he is diabolically selfish. In constructing a hero out of Mugo, one sees that it is the need of the community to construct the legend of a hero it so desperately needs. At the linguistic level, we see Ngugi demonstrating how language functions as a vehicle for both constructing and disrupting meaning.

The community, however, seeing him as a stoic survivor, transforms him into a hero. Having been present at the famous Rira uprising which resulted in eleven prisoners being brutally beaten to death, and having somewhat mechanically intervened when a home guard was whipping a pregnant woman in an enforced labour camp, and again having spoken, rather mechanically again, at the party meeting, unintentionally arousing the resistance spirit, Mugo comes to represent precisely what he is not. It is also an irony that the woman whom Mugo attempts to save is Kihika's girlfriend, Wambuku. Perhaps it might be deduced that Mugo is responsible for her condition. Mugo becomes, in effect, a material signifier for the needs of the people. The large gap between the signifier, Mugo and the signified, the need for heroism, is apparent to the reader and it becomes a cause for guilt in Mugo. The villages misinterpret virtually all his actions as they construe a hero out of a man who had actually betrayed them by giving Kihika, their heroic Mau Mau leader to the authorities.

What Mugo wants to avoid is making decisions, taking responsibilities for any choice or action. Like Munira in *Petals of Blood*, he dwells on the "twilight of doing or non-doing" fated to watch adrift, but never to make things happen. To choose between anything involved effort, decision, preference to one possibility over another and this could be painful, so he chooses not to choose. Both Mugo and Munira are casualties of colonial history and lack the capacity to engage in a world of adult endeavour and thus drift from one failure to another.

His obsessive insecurity afflicts him with paranoia. This along with the personal sufferings that he underwent are factors that lead him to believe that Kihika's intrusion was a threat to the little glimmer of hope he had for a better, secure future. Having lived a dependent life on indifferent relatives, Mugo's attachment to his shamba symbolizes for him, filial bond, love, security, and his own identity. He hates Kihika and despises politics and the freedom struggle because he cannot grasp the concept of patriotism and love for the nation. Kihika's intrusion into his life, he feels, threatens the very essence of his life, and his loneliness which is his sole refuge. He suffers from "moral imbecility"[85] the selfish condition of a man who refuses to accept his own complicity in his condition of life. His betrayals are consequences of unique, personal reasons, unlike Gikonyo and Karanja. His sense of personal guilt results in his experience of oppression as an indication of the worthlessness and self-contempt.

In his desire for power and recognition, Mugo attempts to identify himself with the white colonizers. Mentally, he strives to reach the position of unquestioned authority where he can choose life and death for others. The most potent weapon in the hands of the oppressor, significantly, is the mind of the oppressed. Colonialism has impressed a very different mental psyche on the colonized people. Their freedom is just an illusion, a burden which they can neither carry nor give up. The change, which affects the individual, occurs at multiple levels: at the personal level, disturbing social forces shape the individual psyche. Secondly, it also brings a change in the individual's relationship to the community. This often creates conflicts in the individual who is often compelled to make a choice. At the social level, tension between the two cultures often leads to conflict. These levels of conflict in varying degrees, affect the individual's choice of action either positively or negatively. However, in Mugo's case, this choice of action brings only fatal and disastrous consequences.

To achieve success, Mugo avoids complications that might involve him with the political complexities, and resents Kihika's demand that he make his choice of sides immediately. He realizes, too late, the meaning of General R's ideological conviction that an individual cannot escape from social responsibility without paying a terrible price. Gikonyo had once told Mugo "you want to be left alone, remember this, however, it is not easy for any man to be left alone, especially a man in your position" (p. 24).

As we have seen by now, Mugo is necessitated to error by the fear of seeing his dreams shattering. In Kenyan society, the very nature of the years of struggle, with its conflicts of values and its betrayals, has precluded the birth of heroic figures. Eustace Palmer states "Ngugi is concerned not merely with the wickedness of the oppressors but also with the weakness of the indigenous people themslves."[86] Panduranga Rao further goes on to quote from Leslie Monkman[87] the statement that Ngugi in *A Grain of Wheat* demonstrates the need for a complete re-examination of the traditional concepts of heroism, martyrdom and villainy.

Ngugi depicts Mugo's trauma and paranoia with intensity. Mugo feels haunted, watched. For Kessler,[88] a relationship exists between postmodernism and paranoia. She refers to Jerry Fleiger's paper where she says that the postmodern texts characteristically contain projected modes of behaviour involving grandiose and uncontrollable projection outward. The experience of paranoia, like Mugo's, in which "the protagonist feels watched, haunted...menaced from without by what he can't figure out" becomes for Fleiger, an important element of/in postmodern texts.

When Mugo goes to meet the DO, he is in a paranoiac state, choosing "an unusual path across the field", to avoid meeting people (p. 221), and arrives at the office only too soon. The proposal had filled him with "a foamless fury, a tearless anger that obliterated other things and made him unable to sleep" (p. 195). As is his habit in such an uncontrollable condition, as if by instinct from setting in motion a course of action whose consequences he could not determine from the start, he allows himself to be driven off to the DO's office almost by impulse.

> Mugo's heavy eyes discerned nothing. And his mind was a white blank dazzling the eye like the sun at midday. He was in that stage of exhaustion that comes from the accumulation of sleepless nights, heated, ceaseless and directionless thoughts—that stage in which man is irritable, ready to break at the slightest provocation without he himself realizing the danger. (p. 195)

Mugo's inability to associate himself with the position of others, Gikonyo's outburst against Karanja's betrayal and his unforgiving nature towards Mumbi filled Mugo with horror and recoil. In a way, Mugo's position is similar to that of Sisyphus—during and after his detention he has the realization that all struggle is in vain and that whatever he does, nothing is ever going to change. Life has become absurd and he has to continue living but his guilt mocks his every effort at living it. He is tormented by a sense of inadequacy, humiliation, fear, suspicion, and isolation. Guilt and the pressure of outside events impinge on him, and his reminiscences reveal his torn and clouded conscience. Psychologically, he exists in a state of limbo, as Panduranga Rao,[89] quoting Robson puts it, "being poised between the stances of a betrayer, a sufferer, a hermit, and a hero".

On Mugo, the effect of Mumbi's account of the villager's suffering is profound. He is finally able to connect his act of betrayal with the ruin in Wambuku's life and the lives of others in the village. "Mumbi's voice was a knife which had butchered and laid naked his heart to himself" (p. 199) revealing the brutal selfishness of his act.

The African novel has a very distinctive flavour setting it apart from its European counterparts. In the event of a clash between an individual and the society, in the latter tradition, the scores would be settled on behalf of the individual whereas the reverse would be true in the case of the African novel. Here, society, which is the larger entity, emerges triumphant against the individual who disassociates himself from the society to assert his individuality. The individual has practically no stake against the society. It is the unifying center, and the individual derives its strength from it during the hardest times. Mugo attempts to break away from this crucial centre.

Mugo is one of the millions of men who have been disillusioned, their psyches damaged by inferiority complex and despair. It is evident, by now, that during the betrayal, Mugo is in a state of catatonic fear. In his novels, Ngugi exposes the colonial subjugation of the Kenyans by presenting before every Kenyan what he was, what he is and what he is being led into. The Ngugi hero thus is at the most confused in *The River Between*, utterly passive in *Weep Not, Child*, paranoid in *A Grain of Wheat*, and degenerating in *Petals of Blood*. In the novel, Ngugi effectively portrays a major reason for the weakness of the character, showing him to be antiheroic rather than heroic—the influence of the emergency on the individual psyche.

Gurr[90] states that African literature suggests that the modern African individual is almost by definition a schizoid person. It arises from the fact that whenever the individual has apparently shaken off the operational aspect of the communal ethic, it returns to haunt his memory. The individual in African fiction is an exception and atypical. He is often regarded as an outsider, striving to assert his point of view in a society which is compact, integrated, but under stress due to colonial intrusion. Coupled with this, if the character fails to communicate, the problem worsens. Similar is the problem with Mugo. As the problematic, ironic antihero, he embodies the rupture between the self and the world. An instance of this is present in the beginning of the novel. When Warui, the village elder, greets and talks to Mugo when we first see him, his reaction is almost as if he is afraid, and forced to share the life of the community. Family and religion are often the only source of refuge for the oppressed. But even this refuge is denied Mugo, as he has no family to fall back upon. Religion, instead of supporting him becomes the very foundation of his fantasizing and his delusions.

Tim S. Woods,[91] in the *Encyclopedia of the Novel*, writes that the novel's planned and constructed narrative represents a departure from the disjointed scenic structure of Ngugi's previous fiction. He acknowledges that the novel departs from the linear and biographical unfolding of a story in favour of "telling stories within stories in a series of flashbacks". Ngugi develops a complex narrative structure that moves backwards and forwards oscillating between the various time periods. In *Decolonizing the Mind* (1986), Ngugi writes "the multiple narrative voices, apart from helping me in coping with flexible time and space, also has helped me in moving away from the simple character novel. In the novel all characters are of equal importance and the village people, in their motion in history are the real hero of the novel".[92] By this statement, in going against the community, Mugo becomes the antithesis of the hero. Mugo's troubled and neglected childhood should definitely be taken into cognizance. In a way, he is the troubled "Blakean divided man". His sin is what Blake called 'selfhood'—a fall into division—the proud attempt of the part of the whole to be self-sufficient and to subordinate other parts to its own desires and purposes.[93] So alienated is he that he has lost the sense of identity which comes from the feeling of belonging to a family and thus by extension to the community.

David Cook[94] regards this interlocking of different phases of time, as essential to Ngugi's juxtaposition of the various aspects of the characters' lives, since he is concerned to "move out of a period of simple heroics into much more baffling and complex realities of our independence". The novel also indicates Ngugi's growing interest in the psychological profiles of his characters as he traces their moral and emotional responses through a variety of personal struggles deriving from the Mau Mau emergency. Construed as a montage of narrative passages, interior monologues, dialogue, recollection and anecdotes, the novel attempts to demonstrate how each character's present state of mind is the result of numerous past events and circumstances.

Unlike Ngugi's previous fiction which sought messianic heroes, *A Grain of Wheat*, consciously reveals the weakness and limitations of its characters to be the result of material and social conflict. Simon Girandi[95] writes that the novel is the story of a man's mistaken heroism, and the capacity for betrayal came to be read as an allegory for the culture of post-colonialism.

Mugo's personal suffering and outward behaviour are essentially different in character and cause from what is perceived from those around him. Despite their perception, he does not suffer for the community; he has not lived through social oppression, as others have, with hopes of receiving "leaves of victory", for enduring "the ills of the white man...in their cause for African freedom" (p. 91). He is contrasted to Kihika who truly "lived the words of sacrifice he had spoken to the multitudes" (p. 15). After Kihika's visit to his hut, Mugo reflects,

> A few minutes ago, lying on the bed, in this room, the future held promise. Everything in the hut was in the same place as before, but the future was blank. Kihika was a man desperately wanted by the government especially after the destruction of Mahee. To be caught harbouring a terrorist meant death. Why should Kihika drag me into a struggle and problems I have not created? Why? He is not satisfied with butchering men and women and children. He must call on me to bathe in the blood. I am not his brother. I am not his sister. I have not done harm to anybody. I only looked after my little shamba and crops. And now I must spend my life in prison because of the folly of one man. (pp. 168-69)

These are ruminations of a man who far from being his brother's keeper is also contrary to his own vision of himself as another Moses. In fact, he is unable to differentiate between his personal experience and the immediate political situation governing his life. He is an ultra sensitive young man whose life is a failure; he wishes to be left alone as a deliberate policy in order to guarantee success. He despairs in daylight because it brings the realization of the betrayal and guilt. He literally bolts himself inside his hut in order to secure himself against the encroachment of the outside world. His position is contradictory and ambiguous. It is as if he relishes darkness because "it provides the darkness in which he can lose himself", merge with it and thus attain anonymity.

Ngugi demonstrates sure psychological insight into the presentation of his protagonists. The reader gets access not only to the thoughts of the protagonists but also to the forces which condition him. Ironically, Mugo possesses a certain degree of idealism, but it would be a mistake to suppose that his withdrawal from involvement is due to an idealistic revulsion against a corrupt society. It is rather more due to cowardice than such delusive idealism. The removal of bravery and idealism from Mugo's character and steeping him in cowardice and indecisiveness points to the fact that Ngugi portrays the central protagonist in the novel as an antihero.

Govind Narian Sharma points out to Ngugi's use of the biblical text and symbols to a large extent but it exposes a curious and baffling ambivalence in his attitude towards Christianity and religion. In *Homecoming*, Ngugi categorically declares, "I am not a man of the Church. I am not even a Christian.[96] The message in the novel is profoundly Christian—the duty of each man and each society is to work out its own salvation. In African society, it can be attained through the service of the community. One of the elements of the antihero is the rejection of the ways of personal salvation. The Christian way of the attainment of salvation is through suffering, especially for others and also through sacrifice. Mugo conforms to the role of an antihero as he rejects his duty to society and in his betrayal of Kihika, rejects his personal salvation. He is alone, alienated from society bereft of all meaning, he dreams of leading his people into freedom and salvation. It is an irony, a paradoxical situation which is starkly opposed to the above-mentioned fact. But he tries to confer meaning on his loneliness, as he rationalizes that, Moses too was alone keeping the flock of Jethro, his father-in-law (p. 143). Mugo has a compelling sense of his own election:

> In the miraculous escape from death, he now saw the guiding hands of fate. Surely he must have been spared in order that he might save people like Githua from

poverty and misery. He, an only son was born to save. (p. 153)

But, as the story moves back and forth, Mugo is revealed to be a self-centred youth with messianic dreams like Waikayi in *The River Between*. Mugo has a peculiar similarity with the antiheroic Mr. Biswas, in Naipaul's *A House for Mr. Biswas*. Stomach pains upset both of them when they are faced with dilemma or by incomprehensible circumstances. When the Party members come to visit Mugo, he suddenly develops an upset stomach. Excusing himself he goes to the toilet to relieve himself but realizes that it is only a false call. He feels alienated from the people around him and is obsessively concerned with his personal objective.

His problem of a schizophrenic, split personality has remarkable affinities with the absurd position as described by Camus in the *Myth of Sisyphus*. As we have seen, Mugo's personal suffering and outward behaviour are essentially different from what is perceived by those around him. Absurdity arises for Mugo because there is a gap between man and his world, an actor and his setting. Absurdity is born because of the confrontation of the two diverse elements—Mugo's obsessive dreams and his subsequent act of betrayal. Camus also declares "man is only what he has become by his actions".[97] As one can see, there exists a major discrepancy between Mugo's reality and the projected, idealized image of himself. Going by this declaration, Mugo, a man who could have been a hero if he could be his idealized self, becomes an antihero because of his spineless and vicious action. Several times, he sees himself as deserving punishment. The drama of mental and spiritual struggle is enacted in its most graphic form in the development of Mugo, a highly complex character, sensitive, thoughtful, and imaginative, but also a nervous and a restless soul. It is this radical freedom that makes Mugo terrifyingly responsible for his actions.

Reason in any sense can be understood as part of a broader historical, political and social struggle over the relationship between language and power. In the novel, the struggle is illustrated primarily through Mugo's insinuating presence which informs the novel with the author's sense of resistance to inscribing any single articulating principle. The primary characteristics of Mugo's psychosis and its effect upon others correspond to a retheorising, which is a postmodernist concept of mythology (Mugo/Moses as Saviour) and language (misconstruction of behaviour and words).

The institutionalized concept of heroism and bravery is questioned and mocked. Ngugi questions the concept of heroism as an invention so that one does not see the horror and chaos of life, but it is also a way of creating meaning in an otherwise incomprehensible, chaotic world. The truth about Githua exposed by General R disappoints Mugo as he too had seen an idealized figure in him.

> It makes his life more interesting to himself. He invents a meaning for his life, you see. Don't we all do that? And to die fighting for freedom sounds more heroic than to die by accident. (p. 152)

This statement is almost a mirror reflecting Mugo's thoughts as he still remains in the belief that he is the elected one to lead the people to freedom and salvation.

In her essay Kessler[98] also refers to the fact that in the context of shifting social, political and linguistic relations, Ngugi problematizes concepts of authority and submission, individual and community, dependence and freedom, fidelity and betrayal. He consistently disrupts the binary opposition in the narrative, allowing the readers to see relations that are unstable and not firmly attached to an ideology of the whole self and a unified self.

Simon Girandi[99] also writes that the novel marks Ngugi's break with cultural nationalism and his acceptance of Fannonist Marxism, and describes how he attempts to come to grips with the difficulties and possibilities of modernist ideologies. The characters in the novel, and the text itself, vividly dramatize the rupture and transition from colonialism to post-colonialism. Containing multiple points of view, the narrative moves forward and backwards in time, disrupting the linearity in movement, yet becoming complex and involved. The complexity occurs due to its interweaving narratives. In the text, as Pandurang[100] points out, characters and the situations are examined in the light of the neo-colonialism experience of socio-political-personal betrayal and cultural hybridization.

It is agreed that postmodernism is much concerned with fragmentation. Either it sets the world fragmenting or it sets out to discover modes which will break and dissolve old and supposedly exhausted unities. Mugo's urge to power and to destroy Kihika can be explained in postmodern terms. Patricia Waugh[101] feels that this urge to break and fragment/fracture can be viewed in psycho-analytic terms. The desire to destroy that which we cannot possess has been long recognized as a child's strategy persisting into adult behaviour. As a marginalized, dispossessed person, Mugo's betrayal and obsessive, neurotic and often destructive behaviour has its seeds in his deprived and neglected childhood. Comparing himself to Kihika, Mugo always finds that he is lacking in all levels, "Kihika had everything, Mugo had nothing." However, Waugh also mentions that the destruction of the other cannot be accomplished without an accompanying effect of the fragmentation of the self. Mugo's fragmented personality and schizophrenia is thus a direct result of his betrayal. Waugh[102] also points out to Melanie Klein's idea about the fragmentation of subjectivity as a final defense against the fear of annihilation/total destruction. It is often preceded by a desire to destroy that which threatens to annihilate oneself.

Ngugi has brought a new dimension to African literature with his introspective protagonists, giving much importance to dreams, inner uncertainty, and moral questioning. He is describing a society in transition, sharing a strong emotional commitment to his people, an embedded source of his identity. He is a novelist of the 'we', creating for the readers, from the inside, a communal vision of the village and the world.

Ngugi's protagonists have a restless consciousness, meditating in silence, alone, which is unusual in a traditional community. Moreover, as individuals, they are driven by blind desires, aspiring towards personal success, and obsessed with introspection and self-searching. The consequences of these searches are often horribly unbearable for the 'heroes' themselves, the reality of the motives and their selves too frightening to bear. By looking too deeply into his own motives, Mugo sees only meaninglessness, his own valuations having totally disappeared. Their thinking can be paralyzing, their assessment of others and of their own intentions can defeat their purpose. Ngugi unremittingly shows the abysmal gap between self-heroisation and effective deeds and reality, even between clear analysis and the difficulty of final commitment. This perhaps makes Mugo's mind a battlefield, containing dialectic between two contradictions never coming to a fruitful resolution. The ordinary people in Ngugi's novels find themselves trapped in their own complex motives and values. The heroic simplifications become inadequate to account for what the Kikuyu people went through.

Ngugi's pessimistic view and his opinion of unheroic people are born out of his assessment of the present social imbalance and of the personal weakness of individuals. Each character in the novel is free at some point to make a fundamentally moral choice. Ngugi has a sense of urgency of 'here and now', of a society threatened with fragmentation. He traces the path of individuals of a world which has grown formless and chaotic.

Mugo suffers from anguish and the inability to make a choice. Sartre locates the origin of anguish in this feeling of a being which, because of its frightening freedom to choose one form of action over another, is responsible for what it makes of its existence. However, the moral freedom, existentially, makes each individual a responsible agent in his life, with a potential for good and harmony on the one hand, and evil and fragmentation on the other. This responsibility forces Mugo to face his condition—that it is his own choice that has brought him to his fate, that of a betrayer, a Judas. Gareth Griffith suggests that the novel is "haunted with a feeling of discrepancy between false rhetoric and what actually happened".[103] The novel ends with two images suggesting continuity, one of the rains, and two, of Gikonyo's thought of creating the figure of a woman heavy with child,—but both images arise as a response to a series of troubled experiences. Ngugi writes: "what I remember was the energy and the hope and the dreams and the confidence after all, we were a part of a continent emerging from a colonial era...into...what? We never answered the question."[104]

The essential thematic force of the post-independence novels dwells on the psychology of neo-colonialism, the "sickness of subservience" that arises from neo-colonial psychological and ideological dependence on the west,[105] and its adverse effect on identity. *A Grain of Wheat* follows the central protagonist's dilemma of guilt, betrayal, indecisiveness and cowardice, Ngugi not only questions the Uhuru but also the consequences of Kenya's independence. Independence gained, but at what cost? The dilemma exists because the ordinary peasants have to make a choice between passivity, active fighting and loyalty to the existing order. And they also realize that neither of these options would ever lead to happiness in life. Ngugi does not simplify the issues; neither does he use the retrospective vision of a happily decolonized country, nor he does create the confused tangles of personal and emotional motives among which human beings have to take a stand. David Cook[106] comments that in the novel Ngugi is chiefly "concerned with discerning connections and patterns amidst the apparently mass of day-to-day quotidian experiences and examining the relationships between one event and another".

In novels such as *A Grain of Wheat*, Ngugi presents a world which calls for historical and cultural repositioning, denying what Henry Giroux[107] calls a "comfortable sense of time and place", encouraging us to ask questions which are essential in postmodernism's "redrawing and rewriting how individual and collective experiences might be struggled over, felt and shaped".

Injury and illness, mental or otherwise are consequences of the traumas undergone by the colonized. Mugo, with others like him, is caught between the two opposing forces of war. His deeply problematic character acts as a mythologizing feature which is central to Ngugi's dialectic of language, history, and power. Through him the narrative enlarges the experience of the alienation of the marginalized people by interweaving the acute agonies of a tormented individual psyche and a ravaged national psyche.[108] The novel examines the meaning of individual and collective commitment to cultural and political revolution. Nonetheless, it simultaneously explores the psychology of the defranchised, whose personal struggles to serve, like Mugo's, can become destructive forces which undermine the endeavours of the freedom movement.

Values and ideologies and their importance in one's life are also questioned. These inquire into meanings which are often necessarily attached to the problems of relationships. In the novel, as Kessler[109] highlights, several such questions are asked. Just before the betrayal, Kihika asks, "but what is an oath? For some people you need the oath to bind them to the movement" (p. 167). Later on, Karanja asks, "What is freedom?" as he recalls his first job as a home guard. Dressed in a white sack, with only eyes cut out, he denounced those guilty of being involved in the struggle. Again, in contemplating the senselessness and cruelty surrounding Kihika's death, General R asks, "What is a prayer...it did not help Kihika. Kihika believed in prayer" (p. 21) and on his way to the DO's office, with a dual vision of himself as Abraham and Moses, Mugo asks, "what is greatness but power? What is power? To be great you must stand in such a place that you can dispense pain and death to others without anyone asking questions (p. 171). What happens subsequently afterwards is absurd, incongruous, because Mugo attains neither greatness, nor power. What he receives instead is a slap, and a spit in the face. Nevertheless, one begins to feel that he deserves it, and he loses the respect and the position that he longed for as well as any tragic sense of dignity. Nevertheless the questions are not answered definitely because there can be no absolute answers to these questions and each man has his own interpretation which, of course, would change according to their change in situation.

The world seems logical because we make it seem logical. The real world is characterized by change, multiplicity, contradiction, horror and absurdity. In such a situation, no man feels easy. One is attacked and overcome by a presiding sense of alienation in knowing that he is a separate entity, separate from all that surrounds him, left alone to create his meanings and values. Ngugi's ideal, Conrad regarded the individual as a solitary being hurled by chance into an irrational world, fighting against the irrational obstacles that follow his pursuit for/of a fuller life and inducing in him an alienating state of anxiety and the tragic awareness of his own fixitude and limitations. In *Heart of Darkness*, he says "we live as we dream, alone".[110]

Ngugi also uses the strategy of double coding, contrasting fidelity against betrayal, individuality against the community, and the traditional against the modern. The novel shows the effect of colonialism of the traumatized people. Colonialism degrades not only the society but also the colonizers and the colonized. Using Freud's concept of the alienated psyche and Marx's concept of alienation of labour, Ngugi describes colonialism as a wholly alienating form, infecting the economic, psychological and cultural aspects of the society. Freud evinces the idea that the sense of guilt is an expression of the conflict due to ambivalence, the eternal struggle between Eros and Thanatos, the life and the death instinct. The accumulated guilt of the colonized is a social reality, which manifests the influence, again, of Conrad. Ngugi went to Leeds presumably to write a thesis on Conrad, but by 1964, he describes that his interest had narrowed down to Conrad's concern with the morality of action. He writes:

> Reading Conrad one feels struck by the man's capacity for bearing suffering, but more than this, he questions what appears on the surface. He questions what I would call "the morality of action". What is success...is failure to make a decision a moral failure or not?[111]

In the delusive, antiheroic character of Mugo, Ngugi was addressing this very question. The novel, as such, is concerned with his outlook of the dilemma of guilt, betrayal, cowardice and moral action. Mugo's self-delusive nature remains with him up to the very end. When he first thinks of making a public confession at the Uhuru celebration, he sees himself in the role of a saviour, the cleanser of the people's guilt. But when he realizes that it is Karanja who stands accused, his vision alters. Finally, as he eventually makes his confession, it is simply an acceptance of personal responsibility. It is his own soul that he cleanses of the guilt, which has isolated him for so long, and not anybody else's.

Mugo is strained between two opposite pulls, and between these two, he has nowhere to go. The insecurity of homelessness is a powerful influence on exiled writers and this is often reflected in their characters. On the one hand, there is the need for individuality, on the other hand, the counter pull of communal identity, which has shaped his identity, drags him in the opposite direction and it grants him a communal identity. In the end, it is an irony that the individuality and his future, which he so wishes to preserve, are totally erased. After his confession, and later, his trial, he is killed but without anyone knowing about it. Mumbi looks everywhere for him, but all traces of Mugo, the person, are, as if, gone, non-existent, something, which has been erased off the face of the world.

The extreme stances of Ngugi's characters are shocking. Earlier in the story, when Mugo is unable to speak at the meeting, people declared that these were the words from no ordinary heart, misinterpreting his shame as an expression of unspeakable pain. Later, when he walks alone in the market during a very heavy rain, he is watched by all and wondered upon. Finally, during the meeting, when General R asks the betrayer to come forward as a sign of repentance, instead of Karanja, Mugo takes the microphone and suddenly the image of Moses changes to that of Judas: "You asked for Judas, you asked for the man who led Kihika to this tree here into all these years" (p. 252).

The man who was seen as a hero by the community had turned out to be an antihero. In a Black Books Bulletin interview, while talking about the direction the Black aesthetics were taking on the African continent, Ngugi says, "while we still sing about our oppression, we must sing beautifully. A death dance must be danced beautifully".[112] And about Mugo, the antihero, he gives a critical comment, "If *A Grain of Wheat* is a song sung as an accompaniment to one such dances, Mugo, the hero, is its burden."[113]

To conclude, one can say that Mugo fails to attain the stature of a heroic leader because of his moral failings, selfishness, indecision and cowardice. The potentiality of leadership, the energy and devotion for success which could have propelled him to be a hero, is selfishly misdirected. There is a sense of waste and by the time, he realizes his moral weakness, it is already too late. One can contend that the desire to lead a singularly successful life, to carve for a better future is no crime. Nevertheless, it is also true that the life of a friend and the freedom of the nation is too valuable and cannot be so easily bartered for a selfish interest. However, in doing so, he becomes the opposite of "Mugo—a medicine man, a healer", and transforms himself from a hero, a latent Moses to a Judas.

NOTES

1. Helen Tiffin, "Post Colonialism, Postmodernism and the Rehabilitation of Post Colonial History", *Journal of Commonwealth Literature*, 23/2, 1988, pp. 169-81.
2. J. Michael Dash, "Marvellous Realism: The way out of Negritude", *Caribbean Study*, 13/4, 1973, p. 66; Quoted by Tiffin, *Ibid.*
3. Mala Pandurang, *Post Colonial African Fiction: The Crisis of Consciousness*, 1997, p. 5.
4. Gilbert and Tompkins, *Post Colonial Drama: Theory, Practice, Politics*, 1996.
5. Simon During, "Postmodernism on Post Colonialism Today", *The Post Colonial Studies Reader*, ed., Bill Ashcroft, Gareth Griffith, Routledge, 1995, p. 125.
6. *Ibid.*
7. John Thieme, "V.S. Naipaul's Third World: A Not So Free State", *Journal of Commonwealth Literature*, 10, 1 Aug. 1975, p. 14.
8. Keith Garebian, "The Grotesque Satire of a House for Mr. Biswas", *Modern Fiction Studies*, 30, 3 Aug, 1984, V.S. Naipaul Special Number, p. 492.

9. C.B. Joshi, *The Voice of Exile*, 1994, Sterling, Delhi, p. 127, Bernard Krikler, citing Dan Jacobson, "V.S. Naipaul's *A House for Mr. Biswas*", *The Listener*, 1964, p. 270.
10. Robert Frazen, *Lifting the Sentence: A Poetics of Post Colonial Fiction*, 2000, Manchester University Press, p. 196.
11. Anthony Boxhill, "Mr. Biswas, Mr. Polly and the Problem of V.S. Naipaul's Sources", *Ariel*, 8, July 1977.
12. John Thieme, "V.S. Naipaul", *Encyclopedia of the Novel*, II, Ed. Paul Schillinger, p. 891.
13. Keith Garebian, "The Grotesque Satire of *A House for Mr. Biswas*", *Modern Fiction Studies*, 30, August, 1984, p. 491, V.S. Naipaul Special.
14. Naipaul, *The Middle Passage: Impressions of Five Societies, British, French, Dutch in the West Indies and South America*, Andre Deutsch Ltd., 1962, p. 78.
15. Frazen, *op. cit.*, p. 200.
16. Naipaul, *The Middle Passage*, p. 200.
17. *Ibid.*, p. 72.
18. Chris Baldick, *The Concise Oxford Dictionary of Literary Terms*, 1990, OUP, p. 11.
19. Northrop Frye, *Anatomy of Criticism*, 1957, p. 228.
20. "High Jinks in Trinidad", *TLS*, 29th September 1961, p. 641, Joshi, 136.
21. Gordon Rohlehr, "Ironic Mode", *Critical Perspectives*, ed. R.D. Hammer, p. 19, Joshi, p. 142.
22. Charles Michener, "The Dark Vision of V.S. Naipaul", *Newsweek*, Nov, 1981, p. 108, Joshi, p. 143.
23. Thieme, "V.S. Naipaul's Third World: A Not So Free State", *Journal of Commonwealth Literature*, XI, Aug 1975, p. 13.
24. Naipaul, in conversation with John Hamilton: Without A Place: *TLS*, 30 July, 1971, p. 897, *ibid.*
25. Gordon Rohlehr, "Predestination, Frustration, and Symbolic Darkness in Naipaul's *A House for Mr. Biswas*", *Caribbean Quarterly*, 10, March 1964, Thieme, p. 11, *ibid.*
26. *Radical Innocence*, 1961, p. 21.
27. O.P. Juneja, *Post Colonial Novel, Narratives of a Colonial Consciousness*, 1995, p. 28.
28. Joshi, *op. cit.*, p. 123.
29. M.I. Singh, V.S. Naipaul, *Writers of the Indian Diaspora*, ed. Jasbir Jain, 2nd edition, 2001, Rawat Pub., p. 159; Naipaul, *A Bend in the River*, p. 9.
30. Richard Pearce's *Stages of the Clown: Perspectives on Modern Fiction from Dostoevsky to Beckett*. 1971, Keith Garebian, "The Grotesque

Satire of *A House for Mr. Biswas*", *Modern Fiction Studies*, 30, August 1984, p. 57, V.S. Naipaul Special.

31. Albert Camus, *The Rebel: An Essay on Man in Revolt*, trans. Anthony Bower, N.Y. Vintage, 1956, p. 47.
32. Garebian, *Op. cit.*, pp. 494-95.
33. Albert Camus, *Op. cit.*, p. 52.
34. Garebian, *Op. cit.*, p. 494.
35. L.R. Anderson, "Ideas of Identity and Freedom in V.S. Naipaul and Joseph Conrad", English Studies, *A Journal of England Language and Literature*, Vol. 59, No. 6, 1978, p. 510.
36. Erving Goffman, *The Presentation of the Self in Everyday Life*, London, 1969. *Ibid.*
37. Anderson *Ibid.*, p. 510.
38. Albert Camus, "The Myth of Sisyphus", *Images of Man: Selected Readings in Art and Ideas in Western Civilization*, Sidney Thomas, Syracuse University, Holt, Rinehart and Winston Inc., 1972, p. 418.
39. Garebian, "The Grotesque Satire," p. 488.
40. Fawzia Mustafa, "V.S. Naipaul", *Cambridge Studies of African and Caribbean Literature*, 1995, Cambridge University Press, p. 72.
41. Anthony Boxhill, "Mr. Biswas, Mr. Polly and the Problem of V.S. Naipaul's Sources", *Ariel*, 8, 3, July 1977, p. 134.
42. S.P. Swain, "The Crisis of Identity: V.S. Naipaul—*A House for Mr. Biswas*", *Commonwealth English Literature*, ed. M.K. Bhatnagar, Atlantic Publishers, Delhi: 1999, p. 183.
43. Kincaid Weeks, "Bone Flute or the House of Fiction, the Contrary Imagination of Wilson Harris and V.S. Naipaul", *The Uses of Fiction*, ed. Douglas Jefferson and Graham Martin, Open University Press, 1982, p. 146.
44. Peter Hughes, *Contemporary Writers: V.S. Naipaul*, Gen. ed. Malcolm Bradbury, Christopher Bigsby, Routledge, London, 1988, p. 38.
45. S.P. Swain, *Op. cit.*, p. 190.
46. Meenaksi Bharat, "Colonial Maladies, Post Colonial Cures? Sick Politics in *A House for Mr. Biswas*", from *V.S. Naipaul—An Anthology of Recent Criticism*, ed. Purabi Panwar, 2003, p. 69.
47. O.P. Juneja, *Post Colonial Novel; Narratives Colonial Consciousness*, 1995, New Delhi, p. 5. Fanon's speech which he delivered before the First Congress of Negro Writers and Artists in Paris, 1956. Here he analyses the relationship between culture and racism and divided it into two categories—primitive and culture racism. The latter is a more refined form of the former.
48. Bharat, *op. cit.*, p. 70.
49. Naipaul, *The Loss of El Dorado*, p. 276, Joshi, *op. cit.*, p. 129.

50. Landeg White, *V.S. Naipaul: A Critical Introduction*, Macmillan, London, 1975, p. 3.
51. Naipaul, *The Middle Passage*, pp. 57-58.
52. M.I. Singh, *op. cit.*, p. 115.
53. White, *op. cit.*, p. 110.
54. Alan Wilde, "Modernism and the Aesthetics of Crisis", *Horizons of Assent*, 1987, pp. 41-49; from *Postmodernism: A Reader*, ed. Patricia Waugh, 1992, Routledge, Chapman Hall Inc., pp. 14-21.
55. M.I. Singh, *op. cit.*, p. 115.
56. Harvey Cox, *The Feast of the Fools: A Theological Essay on Festivity and Fantasy*, 1969; Keith Garebian, "The Grotesque Satire of *A House for Mr. Biswas*", p. 492, *MFS*, 30/3, 1984.
57. Garebian, *Op. cit.*, p. 498.
58. Fawzia Mustafa, "V.S. Naipaul", *Cambridge Studies of African and Caribbean Literature*, 1995, Cambridge University Press, p. 59.
59. Sudha Rai, *Homeless By Choice—Naipaul, Jhabvala, Rushdie and India,* Jaipur, 1992, p. 125; Gordon Rohlehr, "Character and Rebellion in *A House for Mr. Biswas*", *Naipaul*, p. 85, ed. Hammer.
60. "Words on Their Own", *TLS,* 4th June, 1964, p. 472, Garebian, "V.S. Naipaul's *Negative Sense of Place*", *JCL*, 10/1, Aug. 1975, p. 25.
61. Ihab Hassan, "Paracriticism": "The Seven Speculation", From Patricia Waugh (ed), *Postmodernism: A Reader*.
62. David Ormerod, "Theme and Image in V.S. Naipaul's *A House for Mr. Biswas", Texas Studies in Literature and Language*, 8, 4, 1967 (p. 601) in Keith Garebian, "V.S. Naipaul's, *Negative Sense of Place*", *ibid.,* p. 30.
63. William Walsh, *Novelists*, ed. James Vinson, p. 893, Joshi, *Op. cit.*, p. 21.
64. Purabi Panwar, *V.S. Naipaul: An Anthology of Recent Criticism*, 2003, p. 18.
65. Chandra B. Joshi, "Autobiographical Elements in *A House for Mr. Biswas*", *ibid*, ed. Purabi Panwar, p. 80.
66. Andrew Gurr, *Writers in Exile, The Creative Use of Home in Modern Literature*, 1991, Harvester Press, Sussex, G.B., p. 71.
67. *Ibid.*, p. 79.
68. Naipaul, *A Wounded Civilization*, p. 27, Sudha Rai, p. 29.
69. *The Sunday Times*, 10.9.1968, Gurr, *Op cit.*, p. 82.
70. Garebian, "V.S. Naipaul's *Negative Sense of Place*", *Journal of Commonwealth Literature*, 10/1, Aug., 1975, p. 32.
71. Arthur Ravenscroft, "Novels of Disillusionment", *Readings in Commonwealth Literature*, ed. William Walsh, Clarendon Press, Oxford, 1973.

72. Ihab Hassan, *Contemporary American Literature, 1945-72*, 1973, pp. 25-26.
73. Panduranga Rao, "The Resolution of the Hero Identification in Ngugi's *A Grain of Wheat*", *Recent Commonwealth Literature*, Vol. II, ed. Dhawan, R.K., Dhamya, P.U., Shrivasta, A.K., Prestige Books, N.D., 1987, p. 141. See "The Hero 'Beacon Hero' Complex in Ngugi's Major Fictional Writing", *Commonwealth Essays and Studies*, 8, 2, Spring, 1986, pp. 113-17. He further writes that in Ngugi, the beacon hero can be a trouble-shooter, a pathfinder, and a guide. On the other hand, the hero, here the central protagonist, stumbles on his way with a torch in his hand.
74. Quoted by Panduranga Rao, "The Resolution of the Hero Identification in Ngugi's *A Grain of Wheat*", *Recent Commonwealth Literature*, Vol. II, ed. Dhawan, R.K., Dhamya, P.U., Shrivasta, A.K., Prestige Books, N.D., 1987. See Edith Kern, "The Modern Hero-Phoenix or Ashes", *Comparative Literature*, 10, 4, Fall 1958, p. 326.
75. Panduranga Rao, *ibid.*, p. 147. Francis Ki Lubuka, "Ngugi wa Thoing'o: The Novel as an Instrument of Social Criticism", Paper read at The Third World Ibadan Annual African Literature Conference, 10-14 July, 1978, p. 11.
76. Panduranga Rao, *ibid.*, p. 134, Edith Kern, *op. cit.*, p. 326.
77. Northrop Frye, *Op cit.*, p. 39.
78. Mala Pandurang, *Post Colonial African Fiction*, 1997, p. 32.
79. References made from Mala Pandurang's *Post Colonial African Fiction*, 1997, and David Cook and Michael Okenimphe, "Post Colonial Literature", Casebook Series, Eustace Palmer, "Ngugi's Petals of Blood", *African Literature Today*, 10, 1979.
80. Eustace Palmer, "Ngugi's Petals of Blood", *African Literature Today*, 10, 1979, p. 153.
81. *Ibid.*
82. Ngugi, *Petals of Blood*, London, 1977, p. 91, quoted in David Cook and Michael Okenimphe ed., "*Post Colonial Literature*", Casebook Series, p. 103.
83. Kathy Kessler, "Elements of Postmodernism in Ngugi wa Thiong'o's Later Novels", *Ariel*, 25, 2, April 1994, pp. 75-90.
84. Fredrick Jameson, *Postmodernism and Consumer Society*, Forster, pp. 111-25. Kathy Kessler, *ibid.*, p. 86.
85. Thomas A. Harris, *I'm Ok, You are Ok*. Avon Books, N.Y., 1967, p. 73.
86. Eustace Palmer, *An Introduction to the African Novel*, London, 1972, Quoted by Panduranga Rao, *op. cit.*, p. 130.
87. Leslie Monkmann, "Kenya and the New Jerusalem in *A Grain of Wheat*", *African Literature Today*, 7. p. 112, Panduranga Rao, *ibid.*, p. 134.

88. Jerry Alise Fleiger, "The Postmodern as Paranoid: Vian. Aueneau. Perec", Dec. 1992, MLA Conf. N.Y.: Kessler, *op. cit.*, p. 89.
89. C.B. Robson, *Ngugi wa Thiong'o*, Macmillan Commonwealth Series, 1979, p. 58. Quoted by Panduranga Rao, *op. cit.,* p. 156.
90. Andrew Gurr, *Writers in Exile, The Creative Use of Home in Modern Literature*, Harvester Press Ltd., 1981, G.B.
91. Tim S. Woods, "*A Grain of Wheat* by Ngugi Wa Thoing'o", *Encyclopedia of the Novel*, I, Paul Schillinger, p. 503.
92. *Ibid.*
93. M.H. Abrams, *Natural Super Naturalism—Tradition and Revolution in Romantic Literature*, W.W. Norton and Company, New York, 1971, pp. 256-64.
94. David Cook, 1977, "A New Earth, A Study of Ngugi's *A Grain of Wheat*", *African Literature: A Critical View*, London: Longman. *Encyclopedia of the Novel, I.*
95. Simon Girandi, *Encyclopedia of the Novel*, II, pp. 934-35.
96. Ngugi, *Homecoming*, p. 31, Fifth General Assembly of the Presbyterian Church of East Africa at Nairobi, quoted by Govind Narain Sharma, *African Literature Today*, ed. Eldred Durosimi Jones, 10, 1979, p. 169.
97. Albert Camus, "The Myth of Sisyphus", *Images of Man: Selected Readings in Art and Ideas in Western Civilization*, Sidney Thomas, Syracuse University, Holt, Rinehart and Winston Inc., New York, 1972, p. 408.
98. Kathy Kessler, *op. cit.*
99. Simon Girandi, *op. cit.,* pp. 934-35.
100. Mala Pandurang, *op. cit*, p. 6.
101. Patricia Waugh, "From Modernism, Postmodernism and Feminism: Gender and Anatomy Theory," *Postmodernism: A Reader*: ed. Patricia Waugh, Edward Arnold, 1992, pp. 190-91.
102. *Ibid.*, p. 131.
103. Gareth Griffith, *A Double Exile*, p. 37, quoted by Mala Pandurang, p. 32.
104. Ngugi, *Detained*, 1981, pp. 63, 142, quoted by Mala Pandurang, *op. cit.*, p. 35.
105. Mala Pandurang, *op. cit.*, p. 55.
106. David Cook, *African Literature: A Critical View*, 1977, London. Quoted in O.P. Juneja, *Post Colonial Novel*, p. 35.
107. Henry. A Giroux, "Postmodernism as Border Pedagogy: Redefining the Boundaries of Race and Ethnicity", p. 230, Kathy Kessler, *op. cit.*
108. Kessler, *op. cit.,* p. 82.
109. Kessler, *op. cit.,* p. 87.

110. Joseph Conrad, *Heart of Darkness*, p. 172.

111. *African Writers Talking*, London, 1972, p. 124, Andrew Gurr, p. 103.

112. Panduranga Rao, *Op. cit.*, Interview with Dr. Betty J. Parker in 1975, B.B.B. Interview, Ngugi Wa Thoing'o. *Black Books Bulletin*, 6, 1, Spring, 1978, p. 49.

113. *Ibid.*

4

The Urge to Fail: Molloy and Henry Scobie

Suffering, metaphysical alienation, failure and the anguish of the divided self are the major themes in the *oeuvre* of both Samuel Beckett and Graham Greene. These are present in several aspects—metaphysical, social, mental and spiritual. However, an important similarity between these two writers is their obsession with the experience of failure. Starting to write before World War II, the unjustified suffering of the innocents cloud their vision and consequently their work appears bleak and hopeless. This chapter discusses two ageing, spiritually complex and problematic characters as antiheroes. One is Beckett's eponymous *Molloy* and the other is the reticent Scobie in Graham Greene's *The Heart of the Matter*.

Major contemporary novelists of the period sought realistic explanations of the social and political conflicts of the period, whereas some placed importance on characterization and situation, others stressed on the depiction of the socio-political situation. Some renounced the outer world in favour of the inner man, and vice versa. According to Fredrick Karl[1], Greene and Beckett attempted both. Karl also states that it was as if the tumultuous war years, despair, frustration, the postwar years with its increasing anxieties and the sense of possible world destruction left the novelists with no choice but to retreat to the individual.

Both Greene and Beckett are thematically similar, but if Beckett is reticent about his personal life, Greene gregariously speaks about his childhood and the influences he had been open to. Religion and spirituality play a very important role in the work of these writers. From their work one can construe the idea that Greene and Beckett have found it difficult to accommodate the fact of death and suffering with the traditional idea of a benevolent God. Beckett, more so than Greene, continued to be preoccupied by a fundamentally religious question concerning the existence of God, His justice, and mercy. In a sense, both Beckett and Greene are Augustinians. Beckett follows St. Augustine in his saying that man cannot be a light unto himself, and suggests that being is only possible because of God's intervention. But both Greene and Beckett, in their respective novels, allude to the fact that a cruel God has failed in their case to intervene. Rejecting the philosophy of meliorism, Beckett is preoccupied with the passivity and potential non-existence of human existence. St. Augustine remains a strong influence because Augustinian theology talks about "the contradiction between the goodness of God and the misery of the world. If God exists, He must be omnipotent and omniscient. For Beckett,[2] only one half of the divine contract was fulfilled. He is just but not merciful.

Scobie and Molloy, are middle-aged and in the process of disintegration, Molloy, physically and mentally, and Scobie, spiritually. In rendering the descriptions of their protagonists, the writers have brought out the consciousness of their age. They are to a great extent influenced by existential philosophy. Though existentialism is one of the main reasons of antiheroism in almost all the protagonists under study here, it is more so in these two characters their immersion in existential philosophy contributes to their antiheroic nature; it emerges in their relation to God and His inexplicable method of running the world.

The works of Samuel Beckett are relevant to our twentieth century situation. His tramps and outcasts, in their fantastic settings are concerned with the problems of time and eternity and of human suffering, of the purpose and the nature of the real self. Beckett is disillusioned with the hopes the previous generations have had for ameliorating their lives by making changes in the world around them and with the religious systems or metaphysical theories that previous generations used to have to enable themselves to feel more or less at home in the universe.

The antiheroes in Beckett (they can be taken as a specie because Beckettian characters are interchangeable) are very different from the other protagonists under study here as antiheroes, first, because they have a very weak identity in the spatio-temporal frame, and secondly, because there is a total rejection of the condition one finds oneself in, along with a paradoxical acceptance of the abject condition of one's existence.

Beckett is influenced by Geulinecx's rejection of the Pythagorean claim that man is the measure of all things.[3] However, he differs in certain ways from Greene, whereas Scobie seeks escape and solace in suicide, Beckett's Molloy does not regard this as a happy issue out of all afflictions. Suicide provides no way out because it involves a making a God of oneself in a situation in which God has already been seen to be useless. All one can do is search for the self. Molloy's condition, like that of other Beckettian characters, is like Sisyphus, damned to an eternal but futile existence.

If the idea of God did not exist, none would feel the pain of its absurdity; if the idea that life has meaning did not exist, the meaninglessness of life would not be painful. However, these ideas hurt Greene and Beckett and, they express through their fictions this meaninglessness and godlessness. These are made absurdly painful by perpetual reminders of conceivable but non-existent alternatives. Thus, painfulness comes from what things could be, but are not.

A God who could create a world of suffering, absurdity and death, and yet still give man an inherent notion of beauty, happiness and significance can only be a cruel being and utterly cynical as to pass all human understanding. Again and again, Beckett's characters reveal the "divine spark" in them by their causeless and wanton sadism. If such is the nature of God then most of the deliberate evil and stupidity in the world arises when men seek to imitate Him. If God's attributes are to be deduced from the *prima facie* evidence of his creatures and their suffering, He seems a being so monstrous that even man might come to pity him.

Through the experiences of their confused protagonists, both Greene and Beckett are trying to find answers to age long questions, Does God exist? and if He does, why does He not intervene and provide solace to those who seek peace in Him? Without any answers, the world is a silent and absurd place. This absurdity is impervious to human speech and reason. Beckett's Molloy disintegrates as he tries to confront this absurdity, whereas Greene's Scobie takes recourse to suicide. According to David. H. Helsa,[4] absurdity results because 'being human' and 'existing' are mutually contradictory. One cannot be both simultaneously. Helsa gives reasons for this.

- to be human is to be body and mind, but what one needs and wants as body is what the mind neither needs nor wants and thus rejects it;
- to be human is to want to know and to love others, but the other is precisely that which one cannot become;
- to be human is to want to say who one is, but one cannot exactly express oneself.

Molloy can be taken as an everyman, in Beckett's view every man is unheroic by nature, because, man is incongruous with the conditions provided for his existence. He and his world do not fit each other and so absurdity ensues. In both the novels, one can see the conflict undergone by the characters because of these contradictions. However, it can also be mentioned that these two characters are portrayed as very mundane and ordinary men, who seem, in one way or the other, to be attracted to the vocation of failure.

As a writer, Beckett has a radical effect on the development of fiction in the second half of the twentieth century. Brian Finney[5] points out that Beckett along with Luis Borges laid the foundation of postmodern fiction. Where modernists had experimented with new forms which lent itself to what Eliot called "the immense panorama of futility and anarchy which is contemporary history", postmodernism attempted to subvert all varieties of artistic form in order to render the reality of the abyss, the nullity of post war life. If, as Beckett believed, life constitutes an "issueless predicament" that amounts to a "meaningless void" how then is the postmodern writer to respond to the meaninglessness with words, those signs that cannot help but proliferate meaning? Beckett wanted to create what he called "a literature of the unword".[6] He wages a "lifelong war on words which led him to startling innovations in form and language. His fictions offer a record of his struggle to force words to yield to the silence that underlies them and that, for him, represents the only reality. He is the picture of a solitary artist who refused to compromise. In his belief, words can do anything; by the same token they can do nothing.[7] Since fiction is helpless in the face of reality, heroism has nothing related with it. Only the fiction of helplessness is real, and art, a mute cry of despair.

It becomes pertinent to understand the nature of Beckett's art, especially when one tries to understand why his characters are antiheroic. Beckett's art is an art of failure. He once told his friend Thomas McGreevy that he was "not interested in heroism or success. I am only interested in failure".[8] He praises Van Velde for being "the first to admit that to be an artist is to fail as no other dare fail, that failure is his world".[9] Beckett's art is by definition trying to do something which it cannot conceivably do—to create and to define that which created and defined ceases to be what it must be if it is to reveal the truth of human situation. His characters echo this theme of failure.[10] Publishers had rejected *Watt* saying that they were looking for something more positive and heroic. This goes on to show that Molloy and other Beckettian characters as well as the thematic contents of Beckett's works are the opposite of heroic.

Beckett's Molloy is truly "the non-hero or the antithesis of the old fashioned kind who were capable of heroic deeds, dashing, strong, resourceful...he is the person who is given the vocation of failure a type who is incompetent, unlucky, tactless, clumsy, backhanded and buffoonish".[11] Recoil, according to Hassan,[12] is a chief feature of antiheroism.

From the very beginning, Molloy recoils from the external world. However, it would be suffice to say that as a decaying character, obsessed with his self and his crippling body, his schizophrenic division of the self, which does not allow any mediation between the fragmented self and the external world, Molloy does not fit into the idealistic role of a hero.

In his *The Dismemberment of Orpheus* (1971), Hassan[13] gives a description of the Beckettian character that would qualify him as an antihero. He is a "metaphysical clown, morbid quietist, cripple, impotent, suffering from radical acedia", a testimony to the vanity of human effort. Hassan further says that Belacqua, the ironic hero in *More Kicks than Pricks*, reclining in Purgatory, becomes the archetype of the Beckettian antiheroic protagonist who delays his salvation through spiritual indifference.

An important fact that needs to be mentioned is that the term 'Beckettian protagonist' is frequently used. Readers are fairly aware that almost all the protagonists in Beckett share a similarity of fate, suffering, and disintegration. Although the study here concerns only Molloy yet he shares similarity with other characters like Murphy, Watt, Malone, *et al.* They are all characters on quests which are foredoomed to failure. The term Beckettian 'antiheroes' can be used interchangeably—be it Moran, Molloy, Watt, the Unnamable, as all of them are similar, the only difference lies in the degrees of their disintegration. In story after story, the details change, but the tone of detached hopelessness remains, and readers encounter a continuous hero in a continuous plight. Beckett's bums, tramps, and outcasts are beyond all hope of redemption; they can survive only as they are. Germaine Bree[14] also points out to the similarity in the clown like uniform worn by the Beckettian antiheroes—hats, stiff coats, odd shoes, ill fitting, cast off garments, white hair, dirty and matted with the accumulated filth of the centuries.

It is on Ulysses' odyssey that Beckett models his *Molloy*. But unlike the heroic wanderer, Molloy is a mock Ulysses, a parody of the spirit of adventure and heroism. En route to see his mother, he passes through such womb-places as ditches, caves, alleys, to arrive in his mother's room, Molloy reminds us of the archetype of the fabulous voyager, and in Western culture this suggests Ulysses, Aeneas, Dante, Christian.[15] To his destination, he encounters several trials and obstacles. Ulysses seeks knowledge within the known world and beyond it; Molloy too like the great adventurer, journeys to unknown quarters in quest of his mother, whose identity he is not exactly sure about.

A lonely and forlorn man, he is the antihero who can be described as the modern self under recoil. He not only abandons the idea of living a normal life but also goes to the extent of negating everything around him. From the very beginning, Beckett makes it certain that Molloy is not at all associated with beauty, wholeness or heroism. And as such, he is created with a body that is already in the process of disintegration. The decay of his body is slow but gradual, starting with the stiffening of his legs. At first, when he begins his epic journey, he walks, then cycles using a crutch, and crawling finally falls into a ditch from where he is rescued by unknown forces.

Molloy is symbolic of man isolated from his own kind. He has no possible identification with nature as a substitute for his failings or a solace for self-doubt. As one of the Beckettian bums, Molloy shares the same antiheroic description: the homeless, aging, wandering male, with hats, boots, long coat, infected scalp, inability to communicate, sensory confusion, hatred of sexuality, of conception and birth. However, what separates a Beckettian antihero from other protagonists is a rarely failing sense of humour in the midst of deprivations.

It is his sense of humour that makes Molloy supportable. Physically, as he progresses on his journey, he grows more and more repulsive, however, his sense of humour utterly fails him when he contemplates the human being responsible for setting him forth on the *Via Dolorosa* which is his existence. A mother, in the heroic tradition is a source of comfort and peace for the hero, but with a lamentable lack of delicacy, Molloy refers to his mother as a "poor old uniparous whore" (p. 19), who brought him out into this world of pain and misery.

Indeed, here, he comes out as obscene, cruel, blasphemous, and arbitrary character who in no way can be identified with the heroic or positive qualities.

He is also a story teller but an absurd narrator, who wants to tell stories not to entertain or to instruct, but as to set up a persona through whom he can hint of his own lack of identity. Confused about his lack of personal identity, and belonging to, what can be termed as the species of the Beckettian antihero, Molloy has nothing but his own resemblance to his species.

> And then I saw a little globe swaying up slowly from the depths, through the quiet water, smooth at first, and scarcely paler than its escorting ripples, then little by little a face, with holes for the eyes and mouth and other wounds, and nothing to show if it was a man's face or a woman's face, a young face or an old face, or if its calm too was not an effect of the water trembling between it and the light. (pp. 148-49)

Molloy's aimless tales are meaningless and egoistic ventures to recall the past, as the present heralds no pleasure. However, the past is painful, full of contradictory impressions, of misadventures and lost opportunities, of unsought, forced relationships, of jobs, of strangers coming up with strange requests and tortures. And there forever remains an absurd difference between his small expectations and even smaller fulfillment. For Beckett the use of the existential absurd becomes a metaphysical device to explore existence. Molloy exists in an absurd world. Absurdity puts man in a meaningless universe; it arises not so much from man questioning himself as from his interrogating the universe and adapting to its refusal to answer. It arises where man's demand for rational explanations go unheard by a deaf and purposeless universe. But Molloy also accepts that human experience is an experience of Nothing, the only reality it knows is the inability to interpret its own structure.

Molloy's relation with the objects around is full of conflict, suffering as he is from the Cartesian separation of mind and body, a divorce between him and the objects surrounding him. As an antihero, he fails to mediate between the inner and the external world, thus leading to recoil. He refuses complicity with objects; in every instance he is divided from the world.

Thus, it can be inferred that a Beckettian character clearly lacks concrete identity or a positive wholeness. As he is himself divided, he cannot identify what he is, and as the world is divided, he cannot identify with anything outside himself. The quest for identity in Beckett is almost cosmic in scope[16] as the character leaves the everyday world far behind. Molloy's quest is comic because even he knows that what he seeks cannot be recovered. When he constantly keeps seeking regardless of the outcome, the result is often comic. Thus, he becomes a particular kind of fool, subject to practical jokes, cosmic ironies and paradoxical experiences. Molloy knows that what he is doing is a part of a game, becoming, in a way, a metaphysical clown. But the clown in man has many disguises; the self in recoil cannot afford to be choosey.

In *Beckett and the Voice of Species* (1980), Eric P. Levy[17] shows the Beckettian protagonist as belonging to a species. By denoting Molloy as a part of the increasingly reductive species, Levy also demonstrates how he is an antihero. Though he specifically does not mention Molloy as an antihero, he lists a group of characteristics which can be identified as ironic and antiheroic. To quote Levy, "to consider man from the standpoint of species rather from individuality is to overthrow every traditional source of his greatness". The result is not only his abjection or humiliation but his futility as well. The species is totally helpless; it can accomplish nothing, not even its own termination. By pointing this out Levy also demonstrates the similarity of the Beckettian characters. Merging man with his species imprisons him in a changeless universe of abstraction where his noble properties still work but with nothing to work on. Consequently, they fall back on themselves in blind obedience to their functions.

Molloy is a bicyclical tale of two quest 'heroes', active but failed seekers, after the nameless joys of salvation. Beckett makes use of two characters, both incomplete, fragmented selves, who can be complete only when the quest is completed. Moran is both the antithesis and complement and the divided other self of Molloy. Like the latter, he too has been sent out on an incomprehensible task: to find Molloy, but without any details about the subject or his whereabouts. In the beginning, he is a normal person, situated in concrete time and space. According to John Fletcher,[18] Moran is a kind of private detective who shadows Molloy, but loses his vocation, abandons his assignment, and resigns his office. He is the kind of spy who is an antihero, and is characterized by its deliberate refusal of the romantic, of the prestige traditionally attached to the classic detective.

Both Molloy and Moran, having nothing to do with success, are aware and, in some extent, obsessed with failure. Their soliloquies are written compulsively, outwardly in subservience to a thirsty messenger, actually in obedience to an inner voice. Both soliloquies report of a quest in search of a human prey, but each of them ends in failure, but also without acknowledgement of failure. The presence of the inner voice within each man hints at the schizophrenic, and split personality. Fredrick R. Karl[19] writes, "had Stephan Dedalus failed at everything he tried and become a tramp, a bum", he would have been a Beckettian protagonist nearly all of whom are writers chronicling their weary odyssey.

In a meaningless world without punishments or rewards, nothing is attained. Does Molloy's quest serve any purpose? Do they succeed in gaining what they seek, thus helping the reader to identify them with the heroic and adventurous spirit of the wanderers they seemingly represents? Unfortunately, the answer remains negative. Moran searches for Molloy and becomes increasingly crippled, his quest ending futile. Aspirations and goals mean nothing to people for whom there is no purpose or connection to anything outside themselves. They ask what happen when belief in God has disappeared and man lacks the energy to seek death?

None of Beckett's characters wait for answers, not even Molloy. Operating with a strange intensity, heroism for him and his sort consists of hooking a chamber pot with a stick and finding a stubby pencil, making a continually deferred inventory of one's possessions, trying to cycle with a stiff leg and a crutch, or finding the perfect solution to the problem of locomotion if one happens to have two stiff legs of unequal length, finding the best way to suck sixteen stones one after another in perfect order, all of which end in failure. Enduring in a miniature world, his endurance is without any heroic connotations. And because endurance is meaningless, it is comic.

Endeavour is the keynote of Molloy, the incompetent tramp, however, this endeavour is not an attainment to be proud of. His inspection of the self only leads to further contempt of the self. Beckett further gives his character a Geulinecxian trait—indifference. Though he must act, the only consolation that he can derive so is that he cannot do what he does not know how to do.[20]

Molloy is a comic character in a tragic world. Beckett's bum is the Elizabethan fool who has been reduced by disintegration to a shadow of his former self.[21] As an outsider he is the norm of a declining world, the universal fool. Without standards, he is ridiculous, pathetic, and close to non-existence, astounding us with his vitality and by his failure to crumble in self-destruction. He is unaware of any standard of life—social or otherwise. Engulfed by the infinite universe, worn beneath his endless misery, Molloy is deprived of every characteristic, which would make him seem master of the situation. He embodies Beckett's parodic impulse in a complete form that scoffs at all possibilities of the human order. No longer do we find a clean and dashing hero, here we have an ironic hero, with an infected scalp expressing the shame he feels in doffing his hat.

Beckett's *déclassé*[22] character is truly a representative of the anti-hero—blind, will-less, impotent, spiritually and mentally morbid, always in search of something which remains ever elusive. The possibility of motion for the protagonists of the novel is severely restricted. Sealed up in their mental space, they move about, fading changing voice in the dark, constrained, they lack the constraints of particular identity. The 'hero', if we call him one, is the hero of all closed systems—subject to imperceptible decay. An instance of the

Beckettian tramp, Molloy feels the need to analyze simplest movements and prove what he is doing; in other words, he is a metaphysical clown, a casualty of Cartesianism, torn between his mind and body.

David Hayman[23] finds Beckett's misfit heroes trapped in an existential web, counterparts of Kakfa's faceless heroes in search of grace in a godless world. But whereas other writers permit their characters to experience hope, Beckett depicts creatures for the most part as despairing, agonizing, and irreverent. Molloy, the tormented ironic hero exhibits disgust for life to be matched only by the tenacity with which he holds on to it. With utter comic patience, Molloy dwells on the miseries of his body and the malevolence of the world. Strangely, he discusses his deplorable and repugnant condition very calmly, finds it tolerable and primarily concerned with the possibility of eviction, accepts its inevitable deterioration in good spirit.

Molloy is almost a Beckettian parody of Western humanism, idealism and heroism. In the novel, he rages at charity, reasons over the distribution of the stones and he is resigned to the idea of love. In Molloy's resignation, Beckett parodies love. Levy[24] demonstrates how Beckett mocks the traditional concept of rationalism relentlessly. Reason, the most renowned of human qualities, the center of experience in the humanist tradition, makes man a rational animal. Reason in Molloy and Moran is reduced to a relentless inquiry into its own nature. It is deprived of guidance and does not offer any assistance, so that it becomes totally directionless. Molloy rages and is furious but this is merely frustrated will.

Man's will, along with rationality forms the basis of his moral nature. But as such, both Molloy and Moran are will-less. The combination of will and reason can be found in a crude form in the antiheroes, so instead of will and reason, they have fear and fury. Reason and will, absent in Molloy will not help him to gain the Humanist ideal of beatitude. Freedom does not have meaning in a universe without choices, where acts can only reiterate their own moral impotence, but this is exactly what all the narrator's little stories do. These self-reflexive stories unfolding according to a cyclical epic pattern contain features, enumerated by Joseph Campbell[25] in his celebrated *The Hero with a Thousand Faces* (1949) as undergone by the hero. These stories thus contain voyage, quest, encounter, combat, separation and return. Both Molloy and Moran experience these events though in an ironical manner and each event unfolds to reveal their antiheroism. Their voyages are full of trivial incidents, parodies of great adventures, their quests end as dismal failures with no achievement, they encounter strange people, from which Molloy and Moran each kill a person because they feel menaced. Molloy clubs the charcoal burner because of unwanted attention. Again in a strange manner, Molloy's victim looks like him and Moran's victim like Moran. They are able to return, Molloy to his mother's room but she is absent, and Moran returns, thoroughly dehumanized and disintegrated, to an empty and similarly disintegrating house.

An important feature of the Beckettian antihero is of habit. Molloy, with others like him are conditioned by habit. As such, it designates the capacity of will and reason to respond to exercise and develop stable disposition. Whereas in the humanist thought, habit is the result of conscious application, according to Levy,[26] Beckettian habit is a passive acceptance of any restriction. There is boredom, which cannot be absorbed by habit. Molloy has no notion of fulfillment, knowing only tedious repetition, and no chance of improvement.

Molloy is afraid of pain, he thinks of, but does not have the courage to resort to suicide to end his absurd existence. He is merely disappointed that he persistently fails to commit it. Death for him is irrelevant and life is a long exile to be endured. Suicide in Molloy's world poses paradoxical questions; on the one hand, it implies that life and therefore suffering are useless and meaningless. On the other hand, "it provides no way out because it involves making a God of oneself in a situation in which God has already been seen as useless".[27] For Molloy, the universe is a vast auto-erotic ring, a serpent with its tail in the mouth, and thus there is no real difference between life and death.[28] Beckett does not allow any of his characters an abrupt termination of their sufferings. Death merely consummates the body's life-long putrefaction which began in the womb, it does not and cannot destroy the mind. Disappearance and anonymity are quite beyond the attainment of characters that must fight blindly against life even without the chance of a hopeful death. The Beckettian antihero is a haunted man devoted to an impossible task. The dilemma is 'whether it is better to live, to continue to exist, or to give up and die?' Both Molloy and Moran opt for the former, even though it is more difficult.

Moran compares himself to Sisyphus forever going over the same route, bound to a task that has no conclusion. Even Molloy, as part of the Beckettian species, duped by isolation into confusing his singular species with individuality, thinks that 'each journey is his first', or at least that it will be his last, and occupies a worse position than Sisyphus who has no expectation.[29] He says "to see yourself doing the same thing over and over again fills you with satisfaction" (p. 133). The simple pleasure of gaining identification is denied Beckett's Molloy, and his vehemence can be turned only against himself, and his struggle to survive in the destructive element of non-life is the only means of identification, hopeless though it is and helpless though he is. For Karl, the illusory gleam of hope that Camus sees in Sisyphus's absurd labour, Beckett transforms into man's desperate quest for answers that will forever be denied him (p. 39).

Beckett's absurd and ironic hero is also an unreliable narrator. Raymond Federman[30] points out that Molloy is responsible for his own fictitious existence but often creates flagrant contradictions. By his own admission, as narrator, he is untrustworthy to the point of absurdity. He usually negates in the following sentence what he has just expressed in the preceding one, creating confusion not only for the readers but also for himself. He contradicts his own attitude because he assimilates himself into nature, and at the same time, also tries to differentiate himself from it, which is indicative of his contradictory and unreliable nature.

Beckett's Molloy introduces the antihero as an absurd narrator, a voice droning in the wilderness of its solipsism. Molloy is a crippled, amoral tramp whose fear-ridden existence has led him finally to shelter, to an ironic rebirth out of the chaos of existence. In the story's beginning, Molloy examines his present condition and position as a bed-ridden invalid in his mother's room and as a wage slave for an unknown boss for whom he writes this tale. Molloy further admits that he is unsure of the facts and that he is beginning at an arbitrarily set point in his tale. With the beginning of his soliloquy, Molloy graduates from difficulties in narrating, even in thinking, to the beginning of a story.

Paul Davis[31] writes that Beckett's narrators embody the spiritual emergency of the Cartesian consciousness, split not only from the environment but also from its own organism, all it is left with is 'thinking'. Under the "hypnosis of positivism", or the rule of mechanistic reason, they can find no answer to the question "What am I?" other than "I am a thinking machine whose disintegration is inevitable and utterly gratuitous".

Insulated from author and from intruding conventions, Molloy is the perfect mouthpiece for a species isolated in its own uniqueness. He remains a purely literary figure whose existence is qualified only by his relation to his own words and estranged from himself in uttering them, he is completely alone. As such his is an existence only by dint of his words. In creating the character of Molloy, who is himself aware that he is a fictional character, Beckett is saying that the very foundation of personal identity has been eaten away, and it is easy to see why. According to humanism, the most important question is "what is man?" Beckett tries to demonstrate this for to know oneself, one must know first what a man is. When men cut away all external trappings what remains is the bum, the tramp, the outcaste. In the cycle of human experience, man's goals lose meaning. What are personal attainments? Who or what is a hero? What is character and what is society, with its restrictions and admonitions?

Molloy and Moran's existence are fraught with uncertainty. They do not exist as concretely as an Austen or Dickens character does with a revealable past, an available present, located in time, in space, in society, in relation to others. Molloy and Moran exist more tenaciously in an unreal world, each after his own fashion. They have their space—Molloy, his mother's room; Moran, his house. They are situated in fairly modern time—the bicycle, the Venus pencil, the autocycle attests this fact. They have a past which they analyze at length, the present is fully preoccupied with writing, but they don't seem to have a future. It is with the help of these coordinates and with the words that they are able to construe and hold on to these characters.

Perhaps Molloy has fallen into a dream about his identity, a dream that always moves on so that, unless he keeps on asking questions, he will fall behind hopelessly confused. Molloy suggests:

> ...ask yourself questions, as for example whether you still are, and if no, when it stopped, and if yes, how long it will still go on, anything at all to keep you from losing the thread of the dreams. (p. 49)

Molloy's burden is always to question and never to reach an answer for he has no means to grasp his experience. Moreover, in Molloy as a narrator, Beckett has found the means to express the experience of nothing, a flux of empty experience with neither subject nor object.

Hannah C. Copeland[32] delineates the character of the Beckettian antihero as a suffering artist. The creative acts that the antiheroes undergo are characterized by extreme mental and physical distress. She quotes Ruby Cohn's statement that "Beckett's haunted 'I's are in constant anguish", they are the images of the "strife torn artist".[33] Even as artists Molloy and Moran are in the distress of one caught up in a terrible dilemma, of one torn between the obligation to create and the inability to do so, with unreliability in their narration. So confused and divided are they that in their enclosed world they create the solipsism in which they keep talking, and trying to convince themselves of their existence.

Ordered by the voice, both within and outside them, Molloy and Moran write of their experiences, but without any clear motive for their actions. In spite of hating and the inability to create, they continue to compose and there is no choice but to mirror their agonizing state in their creation. They are compelled to do so, and before its demands, they maintain "an awareness of his inadequacies and ignorance" (p. 131). Molloy and Moran are victimized by words and they must contend with the voice. As characters, they are "entrusted with missions", an imposition upon them that cannot be avoided. Molloy, a vaguely defined character, is ordered by the voice to go and look for his mother, whereas Moran is asked to look for Molloy.

Torn between the obligation to create and the need to seek truth and the impossibility of accomplishing the creative act, of being one with himself, the artist—antihero suffers deeply and endlessly. Compelled by self-perception and the need to know oneself, he is forever paralyzed by his inability to express his inner vision, by his failure to find the self in words. Molloy and Moran thus can neither achieve success nor expiate themselves to gain salvation. Levy regards their condition, their search for themselves as beguiling and uncertain. Failure does not make this search less engaging, and they continue to devise new strategies to reach the center which can grimly be visualized but cannot be reached.

Molloy repudiates the heroic quality of the acceptance of love. Love for him connotes the Calvinistic Original sin—the primeval curse of sex and suffering. He rejects maternal love and holds his mother responsible for the decay, the progressive disintegration that he undergoes—the whole sordid, malodorous, obscene Calvary procession from womb to refuse dump. Physical disgust in Molloy centers on his mother, veiled with hair, wrinkles, filth, slobber. Beckett absolutely rejects seeing the body in a beautiful, heroic aspect as it is the base of all suffering, and the useless body with its functions is exposed to severe ridicule.

Beckett's ironic "heroes" often speak as though birth is something that happens to them. Whoever has no been fully born, i.e. not fully forgotten where he came from, will feel revulsion. Their peculiar love for inanimate objects makes sense when we understand the fact that they are furthest from fertility. Molloy's antipathy towards conception and his equating new life and the existing world with excrement and rubbish, puts him in a hopeless distance. It confers upon him a distanced privilege, which seems to be a bane. The external world, all exclusions to the private consciousness are considered as 'shit'. All this can only fail him in the end, turning his antipathy to guilt and then to grief at the resulting isolation.[34] His alienation and isolation is double because he is doubtful even of the existence of God. His isolation speaks for itself, so does his interest for stories. It is a way of recreating and completing one's fragmented self.

Normally, a hero tries and succeeds in extending his lineage, producing other heroes who will carry on the tradition. Not so with our antihero. For Beckett's antiheroes, the harm is in the descendents. Birth, the revival of life, descent, is the hated tragedy, the descent into the flesh via the slime and mucus of generation. Molloy speaks of birth in contemptuous terms, a torture he was subjected to. Virility, long associated with manhood, bravery and heroism is a bane. Molloy longs to see his testicles "gone from the old stand where they bore false witness, for and against the life-long charge against me" (p. 34). He even feels "remorse for having begotten" (p. 96) his son. Molloy horrifies the readers with his gross indifference to major human procreations, such as the will to live and the impulse to procreate, both of which provoke his pithiest ironies.

Molloy is virtually impotent; he can do without love, which for him is only an absence although he searches for it. Molloy finds his senseless kind, while Moran has barely enough energy to abuse himself. Love, the source of strength and hope for the traditional heroes has no importance in Molloy's unheroic, abnormal world. However, he finds his own senseless kind of love with an old woman no better than a goat. He strongly hints that Lousse keeps him for sexual purposes. But thoughts of Lousse lead him to the memory of an old woman called Ruth. Significantly, there are clues of suppressed incest in Molloy's personality. Whenever he thinks of Ruth or Lousse, he cringes "God forgive me, to tell you the horrible truth, my mother's image sometimes mingles with theirs, which is literally unendurable, like being crucified" (p. 59).

Molloy's fragmented and incestuous tendency comes to the foreground in relation to his mother. His mother lives in his imagination as a very old woman who confused him for his father, "I took her for my mother, and she took me for my father" (p. 17). In a way, this feeling of incest prevailed both ways. This is perhaps what Molloy has to settle between him and his mother. If she is wrong, even he might be wrong about her. He seeks her because she is the only imaginable goal for him, because all other directions would be *cul de sac.* His mother is a distorted mask of his point of origin to which he wants to return.

The Cartesian, split self is evident in the character of Molloy—he is after all a solitary self speaking about itself. The cut-off-ness that he frequently experiences from the surroundings around him can be attributed, according to Jung, and R.D. Laine,[35] to the phenomenon of schizophrenia. Often Molloy speaks of himself not as a whole self but as two split beings. Thus, he says "I woke up in my bed, in my skin" (p. 36).

According to G.C. Barnard,[36] an important feature of the Beckettian antihero is schizophrenia. It entails withdrawal of interest from the outside world and concentration upon the inner world of fantasy. In its catatonic form, the person goes into extreme, inert stupor to taking up bizarre postures. Paranoiac people suffer from delusions of persecutions or grandeur, hear inner voices and sometimes have visual hallucinations. One can also suffer from emotional poverty. In Freudian terminology, the libido is withdrawn from people to concentrate narcissistically on one's own ego.

The prognosis of schizophrenia has been elaborated because of its intimate relation with our antihero. A schizoid condition, as such in Molloy, seems usually to arise because a child fails to achieve a sufficiently firm and definite sense of his own identity, often caused by an imbalanced, disharmonious relationship with a parent, especially the mother. Eventually, it may destroy one's confidence in human relationships, leading to withdrawal from social contacts and escape into narcissistic phantasy. To counter the threat of social pressures, the ego is divided into inner self, a world of fantasy; and the outer or the false self. The false self directs bodily functions and enables one to perform external demands and cope with daily life, whereas the inner self is considered as the real self. In Molloy's case, the outer self has ceased to function completely, so that he cannot really differentiate between the real and the unreal.

The severe conflict between the deeply repressed incest-wish and the barrier of hatred that the ego has built as a defense against it are evident here, and this conflict is at the root of his mental disintegration.[37] It is the cause of his utter disgust with life, of his withdrawal from reality, and also the cause of his need to return to his mother, which he rationalizes as a need "to settle the matter between us". "I had been bent on settling this matter between my mother and me, but had never succeeded", though what the matter is, he does not explain.

To the schizophrenic whose self is disrupted, the external world is unreal. The ego that relates to the external world vanishes, internal chaos ensues and to his vision clouded with darkness, the universe appears hostile, evil and confusing. Molloy and Moran are full of this confusion and are acutely aware of the hostility of the outer world from which they seek to protect themselves by bodily flight from people and by mental flight into fantasy. But they are also searching for that immanent central self which they posit as the basis of those "homeless mes and unwanted hims" that are the manifestations of their fragmented personalities.

Molloy take up the issue of dualism. The body and the mind are firmly separate. Hugh Kenner[38] suggests the cycle represents an ideal body that the Beckettian hero seeks in vain to annex to himself, since his own is in full-scale decay. The brain, it is stated is by far the most reliable part of the body.

"Therefore there were days when my legs were best part of me, with the exception of the brain capable of forming such a judgment." Such a mind, self-sufficient, is detached from its accompanying body. Molloy sees his hand on his knee as an indistinguishable part of the external physical world, a foreign object and like a truly Cartesian machine, the body only works when instructions are sent from the brain. Descartes' idea of dualism is thus reflected in the chasm in the personality of the Beckettian protagonist. There is an ever-widening gap between the mind and the organic identity of the man. Molloy, like others, embodies the spiritual emergencies of the Cartensian consciousness, split from the environment but also from its own consciousness, so that all it is left with is thinking.

Molloy exists in a Purgatory, a limbo, a middle ground between the tortures of hell and the delights of heaven. In the Purgatory,[39] one has to gain or regain one's identity. Molloy will regain it only when he confronts his mother whom he loves and hates. The two are joined together by the venereal disease they share, a common bond of illness and pain. By extension, limbo means the edge of nowhere or oblivion. When man seeks to define himself by rejecting his surroundings, his memories and even his habitual language, he is at the edge of nowhere. In Molloy's misadventures, apparent hell and apparent heaven give way to the only reality which man knows, the constant purgatory of existence.

Deep within involuntary memory Beckett has discovered a lost paradise with memory as the only way of uncovering it. But it cannot be regained even in memory because, paradoxically, the irretrievability of the lost is what makes it a paradise. For Molloy paradise entails mother's memory, which he seeks to regain by setting out on his impossible quest. Intensely alienated, he carves for the fellowship of his mother, with its memories of intense love-hate; it is a journey he takes towards communion. But were he to come upon her, the reality would deny the existence of paradise, and therefore the quest must be unsuccessful and self-defeating. All quests in Beckett's novels, including Molloy, are foredoomed to failure.

Molloy is culturally and physically homeless. But evidently he has had a home, culture, parentage, education, and even a spiritual home.[40] His isolation is the isolation of separation—the wandering of mind and the fading of destination. The emphasis of separation leading to isolation is crucial, and is discoursed upon constantly, by Beckett's character-narrator. The predicament of all Beckettian antihero-protagonists is epitomized in the person of Molloy, whose relations with other people are drained of sentiment, but who still is attached to material, inanimate objects.

Molloy is a victim of two kinds of failure: the failure to possess, which is tragic, and the failure to communicate, which is comic.[41] Like other antiheroes in this study, Molloy suffers from the failure and the inability to communicate; "when asked something, I take time to know what" (p. 27): "so far from words so long in his rare conversations with men"—Molloy has to avoid speaking as much as possible. He finds conversations incomprehensible. He can talk about complex subjects but interestingly cannot answer a simple question. Molloy confuses objects and persons, and has the prodigious talent for forgetting his own name. His lapses are frequent: Molloy can scarcely remember his name "I had forgotten who I was (excusably) and spoken of myself as I would have of another"; "I shall recall my present existence compared to which this is a nursery tale" (pp. 31-32). When Molloy cannot recall his name, it demonstrates that he cannot prove that he exists officially. Traveling on the road of ego attrition for so long, Molloy has rid himself of all the excrescences that is deemed necessary for life. Thus, Molloy's journey becomes a psychological undertaking, a quest in search of his own identity. And when one has a mother, one has proofs of one's identity.

The physically repulsive, one-eyed, toothless Molloy is a stranger to everyone, a stranger even to the hand of his own body. Molloy does not tell us much, he is more interested in finding his mother "who brought me into the world, through the hole in her arse if my memory is correct. First taste of shit" (p. 16). Both Molloy and his mother are ageless cronies, sexless, sharing the same faulty memories, communicating by knocking on each other's skull. Molloy has trouble making himself understood through words and he does not use them for his messenger or his mother. Moreover, the mode of communication shared by the mother and the son is very strange indeed. Molloy communicates with his mother by knocking on her head, but even then, he is unable to get the message across because of her miserable memory. When Molloy talks to his mother by knocking on the skull, the whole interview is hideous and painful, laced throughout with outrageous indifference, an indifference that is deliberate.

Memory is uncertain and unreliable for Molloy. Ensconced within the castle of his mind Molloy cannot remember his name or the name of his hometown, and he confuses "several different occasions". His hearing is generally good; he registers well, but conversation is unspeakably painful to him because understanding the meaning of the words takes place some time after the registering of the sounds of the words. Similarly, he finds it hard to name what is mirrored in his eyes and he usually smells and tastes things without knowing exactly what.

> And even my sense of identity was wrapped in a namelessness often hard to penetrate, as we have just seen I think. And so on for all other things which made merry with my senses. Yes, even then, when already all was fading, waves and particles, there could be no things, but nameless things, no names but thingless names. (p. 31)

Most of the times when there is a conversation, it is *non sequitur*. The inability to converse normally fails because both Molloy and Moran have a continuous but disordered and chaotic chain of thought, usually broken by a sudden interruption of irrelevant ideas. This naturally leads to the negation thereupon of any positive statement previously made. Gradually divested of all human capacities, his increasing physical destitution indicates his growing insignificance and produces a clear image of the inescapable misery of existence. As Ruby Cohn puts it, "Gradually stripped of possessions and clothes, they grow larger in meaning as their silhouettes shrink."[42]

With no interest or activity to devote himself to Molloy kills time and distracts himself with theological and mathematical speculations. His lifetime is an incomplete process, diversified by learning, travel, sex, a desire to love, but dwindling into a mere existence sick with thought and fastened to a dying animal. Unworldly, without any attachments to material objects, Molloy is a 'holy fool' (p. 84). Molloy is at once impoverished and liberated; only one town is in his horizon, all people are strangers and events, disjunctive. Cohn thus points out that Molloy chronicles his own suffering so that we see him, in his journey, as a Christ-like martyr and fool.

Molloy is associated with a Caliban like intelligence rooted in a disillusioned reality. Frye[43] points out that Molloy is so crippled that he resembles mutilated animals; a lump of flesh that tries to establish how much life is consistent with death. Molloy vegetates and formulates his thoughts and "without much will left" wants to finish dying. Ruby Cohn[44] further says that Molloy's hesitations and self-contradictions are a concentration of Western intellectual anguish: What am I? Where does myself begin and end? Where does my freedom begin?

Molloy and Moran make a valiant but vain search for being, a search distinguished by fragmentation and chaos rather than freedom. They are paralytics living in a world where dreams, imagination, and reality mingle. They do not need to make decisions because they are puppets to the "voice"; they are no more than shadows drifting across the mind which creates them. Early in the story, Molloy declares:

> Free, yes, I don't know what that means but it's the word I mean to use, free to do what, to do nothing, to know, but what, the laws of the mind perhaps, of my mind, that for example water rises in proportion as it drowns you and that you would do better, at least no worse, to obliterate texts than to blacken margins, to fill the holes of words till all is black and flat and the whole

> ghastly business looks like what it is, senseless, speechless, issueless misery. (p. 13)

What freedom is it, when there is no choice at all to be made? In spite of Molloy's qualified declaration of freedom, he rarely knows crucial moments of decision. For Cohn,[45] he is neither mind nor matter, chattering in ambiguous monologues of startling existential immediacy, while being constantly haunted by being. Despite his ignorance and impotence, he is unable to relinquish the hopeless quest for the metaphysical meanings of the self, the world and God.

Beckett as well as his Molloy and Moran are non-believers in God. Beckett's attitude is Gnostic or Manichean. The God who created the world was Satan.[46] For Beckett, God is just, but cruel. Moran reveals that his beliefs in God are forced ones, "whom I had been taught to ascribe my anger, feelings, desires, fears, and even my body" (p. 156).

Beckettian antiheroes share a very complex relationship with God. Their lives are painful pilgrimages and progress is slowed by lameness and general debility. A cruel God rules over Molloy's universe, a God who does nothing to end the suffering of his creatures. It is a universe precariously balanced between the opposing forces of positive and negative, where both cancel each other leaving a void. Molloy's and Moran's attempts to escape from the arbitrary absolutes are futile; they become mutilated, losing arms, legs, becoming featureless, they stagger to a standstill, now bedridden, now propped up against a wall. This, in Beckett's universe, is the condition of man. Yet, they seem to have almost inhuman patience and endurance. Like other Beckettian antiheroes before and after him, Molloy waits incessantly and miserably for an end that does not come. Molloy and Moran cry out against God, yet they refuse to accept the evidence that they themselves have provided, and their indictment turns into an appeal for a different kind of God altogether, with a different kind of reality and a different kind of death. Molloy and the others, reach the ultimate realization "that they can never hope to understand God, His purpose, still less, His lack of purpose."[47] Unlike heroes,

Beckett's Molloy and Moran refuse to believe in a God they do not understand.

Molloy questions, but Moran, frustrated by the lack of meaning of it all, sinks from scepticism and despair to theological pruriency. Helsa[48] draws attention to Moran's question. He asks "did Mary conceive through the ear, as Augustine and Adobard assert? (p. 227) as he writes about his experiences he expresses his disenchantment with the Divine in stronger language, moving to revulsion. He screams, "I don't like men and I don't like animals. As for God, he is beginning to disgust me" (p. 141) he finally collapses to sullen blasphemy "there are men and there are things, to hell with animals and with God" (p. 225).

For Beckett, as for his characters, the problem is whether God exists. They have serious doubts about the vaunted rationality of human beings. Restlessness expresses itself in a search which is not outwardly directed but inwards. An inward search is generally the mark of one who is dissatisfied with the fruits of outward seeking. This dissatisfaction is reflected in Molloy.

The art that caricatures the current reality dignifies the comic as a gesture of despair.[49] One might call Beckett's art as an exercise in futility. Far from depicting them as heroes or even ordinary normal characters, Beckett is cruel with them, afflicting them with paralysis, blinding and muting them, sinking them into the earth and in the end, virtually eliminating them. It is as if he is playing the part of a malevolent God whose compassion matches his cruelty. Molloy and Moran, like other Beckettian characters, are invariably aged, or rapidly ageing, contemplating their lives from the edge of the abyss. What Beckett expresses is the ambiguous mood and the anguish of those who deprived of God, continue to seek Him even in the void.

Molloy's alter ego, Moran is a precise and punitive man who abuses himself and bullies his 13-year old son. As he progresses in his futile exercise, slowly changing to a Molloy-figure, he is beset with violence and fear. Till then, he has tried to exclude from his life all that is mysterious, incomprehensible, and irrational. He, at first, shows no such amoral indifference to the things that are supposed to matter. Entirely different from Molloy, he is fussy and self-important insisting on punctuality, disliking interruption and is immensely conceited; he prides himself on being a sensible man. He is, of course, very scrupulous in religion, assiduous in his attendance at mass and troubled if he misses his weekly communion. But, as a father, Moran is a complete failure, unable to evoke any kind of respect and love from his son. He has him brought in his faith, raising him with great firmness and little love, insisting on respect but doing less to earn it. To this calm and meticulous Moran, in all his shapelessness and restlessness, Molloy is a frightening creature, lacking all discipline, will-power and purposelessness.

Moran's relationship to his son is a mixture of mawkish sentiment, with a strong sadistic pleasure of domineering over him. He disciplines him mercilessly, actually because he delights in maintaining his authority as a father. He is a mean and restricted personality, solitary by choice; he is timid amongst other men, punctual, parsimonious and obstinate. Moran's exile is more a self-imposed alienation: his love is entirely devoted to his piece of land "my trees, my bushes, my flower beds, my tiny lawns". But once he has returned from his unsuccessful search for Molloy, he rejects his lost links with humanity. "I have been a man long enough…I shall not try anymore" and takes to living in his garden with his fowls.

Moran is aware that his real quest is to find the Molloy inside him, as a kind of Hyde to his Jekyll.[50] The quest is a dismal failure as far as both of them are concerned. Moran makes a mental picture wherein Molloy can be vaguely recognized. He pants and his walk falters, he is always on the road. He throws himself against enclosing walls, moves like a bear, utter incomprehensible words, fat and shapeless. By this abominable creature, Moran sometimes feels haunted, and he feels "uproar, bulk, rage, suffocation, effort unceasing, frenzied and vain. Just the opposite of me, in fact". This opposition does not last much longer. Moran's report is about the fruitless search for Molloy whose existence he does not understand.

There is no achievement and he returns home in a state of physical and moral reduction. The man of morals and means becomes Molloy-like, a crippled, asocial, impecunious vagabond.

In the end, both Molloy and Moran, in despair of their destination, assume the position of inhumanity. While Moran comes back home on the orders of Youdi, on crutches and losing almost all of his possessions, Molloy is brought almost to the verge of extinction. Being unable to progress upright, he begins to crawl on his belly and is reduced to a virtual reptile.

In a review of J. D.O'Hara's *20th Century Interpretations*, Maratha O'Nan[51] writes that Beckett's characters like Harlequins, contradictory and uncertain in an absurd world. They reveal themselves in their agony, suffering the inevitable, accepting the ignominious situation, the insult, turning more and more inward to find solace. They are uncared for, bullied, rejected and isolated. They respond with ironic speculation and with feelings of rage, contempt, and curiosity, undergoing manifold varieties of a few basic adventures. The two tramps are skeptics, and like the Greek cynics described by Lionel Casson, they "dress in rags, living off scraps, and limiting their possession to the old coat, sack, and staff, which were their standard accouterments". With total disregard to personal appearance, they are dirty and unappetizing to look at.[52]

After shedding most of his education as useless, Molloy approaches people and things without learned attitudes. Like all Beckettian ironic heroes he is an intellectual, or once was so; he speaks ironically of TLS, and he can quote scraps of Italian and Latin, and he is evidently familiar with Leibeiz and Gexlincx. He is in fact, a self-confessed former student of many varied disciples; "my head was a store house of useful knowledge". His dismissal of knowledge is Faustian—he has studied and rejected several fields of knowledge. Copeland compares Molloy to Faust as he too descends into "the mother of being, to the innermost heart of things".[53] Consequently, his language becomes the Dionysian's inarticulate cry of pain and passion. He can only muster contempt for the Apollonian language of reason, whose purpose is to arrange and create order.[54]

Beckett has created unforgettable details about Molloy's appearances; from his appearance itself, readers will not take him to be a normal heroic character. He is toothless, has a scant beard and wears trousers, hat, greatcoat and long boots. He sleeps very little and that little by day and he is a light eater, albeit a voracious and uncouth one. He combines nobility with sadistic violence. Having no moral standards, he steals without qualms and has no misgivings or shame in recounting to the readers how he had stolen silverware from Lousse. Towards the end, he meets a charcoal burner who offers him undesired attention; Molloy kicks and clobbers him almost to death, and then crawls back, via a ditch from where he is rescued, to his mother's room. Molloy comes across as a cruel man; cruelty which in word and deed is a Beckettian correlative of impotence.

Beckett's characters are racked with pain and anguish, they grovel in the mud, wander about aimlessly and miserably, torturing one another in the best infernal manner, but while in Dante's hell the damned are at least relieved of hope, in Beckett's hell it is hope that chains his creatures to their pain. This gallery of graveyard figures reflects the mood of a dying world. The protagonists are both submerged in and alienated from the world of objects representative of the urban environment. Molloy obviously is a misfit in the society of Bally. In the face of the increasing irrationality of the hero, the bicycle can come to represent that excess of form which is the other side of the coin of madness. Beckett's protagonists though form-ridden, demonstrate their incapacity or unwillingness to incorporate themselves into the societal machine.[55]

John Fletcher[56] compares the events in Molloy's life to a clown's act. The events form as integral a part of the Beckettian antihero's life as gags do in a clown's act. The comparison is not in fact far-fetched; the various episodes occurring in Molloy's history constitute the Beckettian clown's performance, each incident having become an unchanging item in his repertoire. One therefore almost expects the Beckettian antihero to execute certain ritual gestures to submit to certain regular happenings. Molloy is seen as in a circus act, riding a bicycle with crutches. He, like other Beckettian protagonists play, physically and intellectually, in such a way as to show that ordinary respected people, committed to life, are doing exactly the same thing. The most trivial actions are catalogued exhaustively in an elaborate pretence of obsessive realism. This realism pushed to such a logical conclusion, soon gives the effect of living in a kind of casual, surrealistic hell. Beckett's antiheroes share a long-standing relation with the clown. O'Hara states that in "Yellow" in *More Pricks than Kicks*, Beckett lists, "Bim and Bom, Grock and Democritus' Philosopher and clown together" (p. 10).

It is not only the character who is ironic, the world he lives in, is itself an unheroic world, devoid of humanity, much less of heroism. Comedy here is cruel, absurd. Vaudevillian and grotesque, Beckett's humour is essentially metaphysical; it assumes the absurdity of the universe and eludes conventional tragedy or comedy by confronting the automatism of number with the cruelty of nightmare. His is the satire of a man who tries to bear his own company. Because the humour is sadistic and reductive, it tends to focus on scatological functions. Copulation thrives but feebly, usually among cripples or octogenarians, as further proof of the mind's disgust with life. Beckett's three "modes of ululation", described in Watt,[57] are the bitter laugh in the face of evil, the hollow laugh in the face of falsehood, and the mirthless laugh in the face of human wretchedness. All three laughs howl at his alienation.

Molloy is the cursed Wandering Jew, destined to be isolated and lonely. However, he is not only alienated; he is also just as completely indifferent to his situation. He realizes the reaction he is liable to provoke in a stranger: "what is it I want? Ah that tone I know compounded of pity, of fear, of disgust." Being an outcast, he can freely indulge in irony at the expense of his persecutors: "he began to interrogate me in a tone which, from the point of view of civility, left increasingly to be desired, in my opinion".

The disintegrating hero, Molloy finds a refuge in old age, a retreat from the external world with its distractions. Age strips man of his vanity as it gnaws at his capacities. With a diminished body, one has fewer outward concerns. In the aged ironic hero, one begins to approach the fundamental element of being, hidden beneath superficial characteristics in younger men. The twin characters of Molloy and Moran are puppets of physical laws outside their control. They talk even when there is nothing to say; mostly about what could have been their alternate lives. Had they possessed teeth, they would have chewed, had they not been crippled, they would have walked, had they not seen love as a dirty act, they would have loved others normally.

The Beckettian antihero is caught between the friendly voice and the hostile spirits of darkness, yielding now to one, now to the other. He is therefore a flimsy creature crushed by powerful forces and crippled in his body by disease, in his mind by uncertainty. Even then he has not the courage or ability to seek death itself, perhaps because death is no solution to the really desperate. The speaker-antiheroes are all exiled beings, shadows representing the universal drama of the Self,[58] enacting, in the spirit of consummate parody, the ancient struggles between mind and matter, fiction and fact, others and self, word and silence. Like Cartesian clowns, they play out the farce of human identity in a cosmos turned inside out. They are total satirists of our condition, leaving nothing holy or intact.

The antihero in Beckett is left with the minimal state of being and with the mirror of self-consciousness to constantly remind him of his stark situation. Copeland,[59] quotes Willie Sypher's statement that in Beckett's theme, the consciousness of the central figure is vestigial, a vague residue of man's anxieties. Like Mugo in Ngugi's *A Grain of Wheat*, Sypher finds that Beckett "man is no longer the sole hero, but only the centre for what he sees"[60] Beckett's metaphoric hero reaches a state of absolute poverty and utter self-consciousness. Thus, it is significant that Beckett should devote so much space to descriptions of his characters' physical bearing—their gaits and means of locomotion. Natural to them, strange to us, they are both comic and puzzling. Molloy perched on his bicycle with his crutches and lame leg, the absurd Ubuesque structure formed by the Morans, father and son, cycling, along the roads that will not lead them to Molloy, are factual evidence of the absurdity of the characters who in no way can be equated with the hero.

Journey figures recurrently in Beckett's fiction, these journeys usually lead the hero nowhere. Molloy's and Moran's journeys are protracted and painful, leading nowhere except to the breakdown of each hero's body and the isolation of his mind. Such a journey, perhaps, is symbols of fruitless questing of the turning into derision of "seek and ye shall find". Jean Jacques Mayous[61] states that Beckett treats his characters cruelly, strongly refusing to grant solace to his protagonists. He is not content with portraying them as antiheroic, but also resorts to "mutilating, martyrizing, killing, and sometimes even eating them".

Beckett's use of the form confuses past, present and the future, and the logical relationships between them are negated. By doing so, he reasserts the disorderly nature of the universe. He posits chaos which man must subjectively order assuming that all ordering processes are self-deceptive. This is in essence the nightmare of the contemporary man. Man can only survive if he is able to accept the incongruous nature of the universe.

Writing for Molloy is the reason for his existence.[62] For that purpose, Molloy is rescued from the ditch into which he had fallen half dead, by those mysterious forces that, in times of need come to the aid of Beckett's antiheroes. But as a writer, he is not blessed with imagination or talent, or even with the certainty of what he is writing about. There is a variation of helplessness in Molloy's autobiography, for like his creator, he suffers under a condemnation to failure because there is nothing to say.

Molloy is compelled to write his experiences and he determines to carry it through "even through the whole world should enjoin upon me this or that, under pain of unspeakable punishments". Molloy has furthermore to keep reminding himself that he is only telling a tale, and has to be careful to remember what he represents in the story, so much so that he asks the reader to correct any lapses he may make.

> I cannot stoop, neither can I kneel, because of my infirmity, and if I ever stoop, forgetting who I am, make no mistake, it will not be me, but another.

Molloy is the ignorant narrator. Beckett has removed the omniscient narrator and replaced him with an ignorant, and uncorrectable narrating hero. This is a strange literary creature, a narrator who tells stories about his desire to narrate no more. Molloy is the ignorant but uncorrectable narrator, and both he and Moran are completely unreliable.

Dieter Wellershoff[63] sees in all the strivings of Molloy the triple ridiculousness of a fool who is looking, with inadequate strength, on the wrong road, for a goal that perhaps does not exist at all. But the intensity of his effort stops all laughter because this is serious monomania from which no laughter can liberate us. Seeking peace in entropy and silence, Beckett's anonymous antiheroes perform combinations and permutations, repeating words and varying their gestures *ad nausuem*, adding and tabulating all the trivia of existence. Molloy's and Moran's condition are what happen to the mind when it has nothing to contemplate but its own symmetry.

Not only are the characters ironic and antiheroic, the novel itself is an anti-novel. It is what Northrop Frye[64] calls a Menippean satire. Readers are struck by the fact that nothing happens. Two insignificant quest heroes, two suffering clowns are decomposing, one a noman, and the other, an everyman. However, there is a reversal. The quest hero is generally conceived of as going into darkness to retrieve light and achieve a meaningful existence. But the antihero Molloy is a shabby version of the shining knight-errant, achieving deeper darkness and meaninglessness.

The dislocation and alienation that characterizes Beckett's work goes well with the disintegrating nature of his solipsistic antiheroes. Apart from himself, nothing makes sense to him. Jongleurs of solipsism, even as fictional creatures, they see themselves as defective creatures and are suspicious of their creator, as they themselves are contemptuous of whatever they can create.[65] His narrator characters seem to create themselves and their own fictional environments, with a total disregard for their creator's responsibility towards the narrative. Beckett is subtly hidden in the voice of his protagonists to the extent that they are capable of speaking against their "irresponsible" creator, accusing him of trying to impose upon them a story when there is no story to tell, but also words when words are meaningless.

Existential reality is incommunicable, and Beckett insists that modern or postmodern man has no place in the scheme of things as envisaged by Shakespeare or Milton. Beckett's visualization of the predicament of man is as an unaccommodated, lonely man, waiting and yearning for a salvation that never comes. The world of the antiheroes, the postmodern world is inhabited by spiritual paupers, bankrupts in the inner man. It is a cheerless world, cold and grey, devoid of meaning, love and joy.

There are circumstantial evidences linking Molloy to Moran. Raymond Federman[66] explains that Moran becomes Molloy in the end. There is also a complete duplication of events in the two parts of the novel; yet, there is a perfect negation of one part by the other. Molloy's fiction negates Moran's report because it is unreliable, unconfirmed. Similarly, Moran's fiction negates Molloy's adventures because it is invented. Thus, when Moran reveals that at the end of his futile quest that he "had not been able to go to him, and grow to be a friend, and like a father to me" (p. 222), he is admitting, the failure of his quest, the negation of his fiction. Molloy and Moran try to break out of the solipsistic circle refusing to acknowledge that the language they use and intermittently understand is theirs. Wavering, staggering, they deny their words, and then themselves, as the circle of solipsism tightens like a noose around their neck.[67]

Beckett's vision of man, like that of Golding, is bleak and painful. His awareness of man is as an impossible anomaly in time and space. In the twentieth century, after the accumulation of too much history, man has lost the innocence to believe in any more explanations. In Beckett, the antihero often bravely raises the question of his own insanity only just as bravely to deny it. But he also abuses the people who cannot accept his vision.

> And in the evening I turned to the lights of Bally, I watched them shine brighter and brighter, and all go out together, or nearly all, foul little lights flickering lights of terrified men. (p. 162)

Levy[68] writes that Beckett's vision may be called post-metaphysical. It responds to the need for a universal ordering of being but knows that there is none. With Beckett, all the old assumptions of man and universe are vanquished so that human experience is left to formulate vainly its own resulting complexity. Beckett is a pessimist to believe in any new dawn: our only chance lies in a retreat, a retreat such as all his antiheroes seek and fail in different ways to do so.

About *Molloy* Germaine Bree[69] makes an important statement: these are undoubtedly procedures characteristics of the epic form—negative antiheroic, epics unfolding in an "immeasurable time", taken up over and over by a voice that animates these characters. They are vaguely aware that they are about to make the whole absurd repetition again. Descartes unintentionally prepared the way for Beckett's "great articulates"—creatures whose special articulation, in body, thought or defective speech, makes them forget that they are really "frightened vagabonds" regardless of dragging themselves aimlessly along, dying by degrees, while words and images spin round inside their skull.

In the novel, two of Beckett's obsessions are present: the ever present feeling of guilt, of life as a condition of guilt and the Protestant idea of predestination which joins with guilt, judgment and damnation itself to make it even more intolerable. Knowing neither pattern nor any purpose, Beckett's characters are subject to these continual changes for which the obvious metaphor is bodily decay, and they are repeatedly obliged to feel the pain of being. It tempts them into grandiloquent remarks like Molloy's descriptions of his life as "a veritable cavalry, with no limit to its stations and no hope of crucifixion".

Molloy is a novel, which thematically and technically can be called postmodern; as such there are several postmodern elements in it. Unreliability makes *Molloy* a postmodern novel and the characters, postmodern characters. Beckett attempts to counter the linearity of language by a circularity of structure and repetition of motifs. Beckett has the postmodernism penchant for self-referentiality, using language that mocks, outrages and exasperates, parody, slapstick, the delayed joke, the combinations of dissimilar—all aimed at creating a reality that is both fantastic and grotesquely true. Recurrence of names, words, situations, articles of clothing—recurrence in every possible way is common in Beckett and helps to sustain the novels without narrative force. Beckett warns, "Art has nothing to do with clarity."[70] Beckett's word on this issue would suggest that the Saussurean view of language disintegrates the psyche rather than answering its questions. The art of Beckett convinces us that parody is indeed the form our pain must now take.

An unreliable ironic relation remains between situation and characterization. It is difficult to believe that such well-spoken, well-educated men as Molloy and Moran, could come down from everything to nothing. For Beckett, literature does not contain the truth. Molloy's endless, futile speech, exemplifies the story of the human spirit all over again. It is now recognizable as the absurd efforts of a Sisyphus, who, thinking, wants to transcend thought and thus remains a prisoner of the fictions he produces. Thus, Wellershoff[71] compares Molloy both to Sisyphus and to Kasper Hauser, a human being who does not know himself and who cannot tell who he is, where he is and wherefore he is. Further, Molloy stands for something lost to which it wants to return. He wants to return from banishment, striving for a union that is always frustrated. With failing strength and inadequate means, he searches for something unknown in a sphere of permanent deception.

Unlike his literary Irish ancestor, Swift, Beckett's dark humour no longer implies a belief in man's ultimate salvation to be reached through the use of reason and ingenuity. Through his antiheroes, Beckett brings out both the pathos and the absurdity of our mental postures by grossly simplifying them and turning them into concrete situations which his characters act out physically. A sort of anguish hovers over this human comedy, creation continually menaced by abortion, failed enterprise, which must always be rebegun.

Graham Greene occupies a transitory position between modernism and postmodernism. His style is essentially conventional but his treatment of problematic subjects and enquiry into metaphysical uncertainties are postmodern inasmuch as it questions institutions accepted as established authorities. Greene's varied *oeuvre*[72] is informed by a unifying vision of a ravaged world through which God's love moves in terrifying ways. It was, Greene claimed, the sense of hell lying about him in his infancy that brought him to this bleak pessimism. His autobiography *A Sort of Life* (1971) delineates an appalling unhappy childhood, but these "facts" have recently been questioned. Nevertheless something happened within him to create the belief that his life did not matter and thus there was nothing to lose.

The relationship of Greene's Catholicism to his writing remains a central mystery, and the definition of his belief is also elusive. If marriage drew him to the church, Greene was not an easy convert. Paul O' Prey[73] refers to Greene's *Why do I Write?* (1948) in which Greene defended his right to be disloyal to the Church. As an artist, he wrote, he must be allowed to write "from the point of view of the black square as well as the white". This comes from his insistence on the individual's right to live according to the highest promptings of his conscience, whether those promptings be political, religious or social.[74] This attitude thus has a dual consequence: firstly, it often makes many of his most sympathetically drawn characters exist in a state of unbelief and secondly, it emphasizes his attraction to characters who inhabit a spiritual borderland embodying some form of paradox. His characters inhabit a shabby, seedy world without heroism. Few contemporary novelists have so faithfully depicted the outer squalor and slovenliness that accompanies inner degradation.

Religion plays an important role in Greene's life, conditioning his view of the world and the treatment of his characters. The experiences gained in childhood are scattered throughout his work. Boredom, the sense of injustice and unnecessary suffering form the base from which he views his characters and their situations. Like Beckett, Greene is concerned with the themes of failure and the divided consciousness, and like Golding, he is preoccupied with moral dilemma. J. Kurishmmootil[75] writes that the tensions burdened Greene during his adolescence leaving a permanent mark on his soul. Childhood, Greene states, is the first victim of a betrayal. Duplicity, treachery and betrayals definitely form a dominant motif in Greene. There are broken pledges and there are infidelities in love and marriages. In the novel, *The Heart of the Matter* (1948), there is a complex web of betrayals and the ironic hero Scobie is unable to work through the labyrinth woven around him.

Greene's preoccupation with his religion, sin and moral dilemma, with divided consciousness force his heroes reluctantly to be involved and take sides, not for ideological but for personal reasons. In Greene, the Christian hero is the embodiment of the scapegoat-antihero, with a soul to save or lose. He personifies what Kenneth Alcott and Miriam Farris[76] call the "divided mind", the inability to resolve the inherent contradiction in his character between the twin pulls of pity/love and duty.

Imitations of corrupt power and shabby glory shape the novel *The Heart of the Matter* set against the seedy fecundity of Sierra Leone and drawing upon Greene's association with the Secret Service, the novel follows Scobie, caught between his hollow marriage with the pious Louise and an adulterous love for the agnostic Helen through a crisis of faith that ends in suicide. The epigraph to the novel is a direct suggestion to the central character as a holy sinner. "The sinner is at the very heart of Christianity.... No one is so competent in matters of Christianity. None, if it is not the saint."[77]

Of Greene's characters, Henry Scobie is the most problematic and paradoxical, one about whom critics disagree most. Opinions about him range from sympathetic to downright harsh with Greene himself calling him "inordinately proud".[78] In himself, Scobie is such a curious amalgam of good and evil that it is difficult to label him as either hero or villain. Scobie is definitely a good, but weak man corrupted not by power or wealth but by pity, sentiment and a sense of responsibility for the happiness of others. He voluntarily damns himself so that others shall not suffer in this world. Unable to bear others' pain, he aggravates his problems, as he himself is the cause for the pain. He is trapped in an emotional dilemma that can only be solved by betraying and therefore hurting either Louise, his wife, or Helen, his new found love. Scobie is morally conscious of the fact that he is unable to reconcile his love and his duty—his infidelity to his conscience. This divided mind is an instance of indecisiveness and doubt, pointers to the antiheroic nature of Scobie.

John Spurling[79] writes that Scobie is a rare character in Greene's fiction, an ordinary man who is not obsessed with childhood or adolescence, who is not cynical, who does not flaunt grown-up vices as badges of maturity. Scobie is not only a good man, judged by Greene's scale of values; he is also an upright man. Although Greene sympathizes with Scobie, yet he disapproves of him; his character was intended, Greene says in *Ways of Escape* (1980) "to show that pity can be the expression of an almost monstrous pride".[80] Because of their amalgamation of good and evil such characters are known as "sinful saints" and "Holy atheists".[81] This makes Scobie one of Greene's most challenging characters. Graham Greene is a connoisseur not of good and evil, but of innocence and corruption. In his novels, Greene is obsessed with this moral paradox. Scobie, suffers "corruption by pity", and embodies the tension between dumb innocence and nihilism.

He is corrupted by sentiment and a sense of responsibility for others, and this leads to spiritual egotism, which is a form of pride. There are clues that Scobie is in two minds, as is Greene about whether God will damn him. Of all Green's characters, he is perhaps the most difficult for a non-Catholic to sympathize with.[82] Greene himself finds Scobie's religious scruples "too extreme". Greene's antihero is a hunted man, pursued by his deeds and conscience. Green himself wrote that Scobie's life illustrated the paradox that "the greatest saints have been men with more than a normal capacity for evil".[83] As an ironic hero, Scobie suffers from internal tension and lives in constant terror of infidelity as the temptation to which he inevitably submits. He belongs to a long line of seedy adventurers whose shabbiness is a kind of check against even failure swelling to heroic proportions. Greeneland is the world of the seedy, the tawdry, and a world of failures. Greene evokes the wasteland of modern society as his basic material with its atmosphere of seediness, degeneracy, disease and corruption. For Greene, the modern world has mechanized its creatures. He describes anxious, dissatisfied temperaments chronicling a period in time when the world is extraordinarily sad.

J.A. Cuddon[84] states that several of Greene's protagonists are basically antiheroes, surrounded as they are by the aura of failure as well as incompetence and in Scobie's case, by unconscious pride. Antiheroes in Greene's novels are addicted to sin. For Scobie, the sin lies in adultery, pride and despair. Greene is concerned with the fallen man and with the possibility of redemption. According to Philip Stratford,[85] Greene's hunted heroes are all sinners launched on a quest for salvation. A Christian hero is in Greene's sense, a man with divided consciousness and a sense of moral failure. Apart from being a social failure, he is a spiritual derelict, a victim of theology, spiritualism and the organized religion. For Anuradha Banerjee[86] in Greene's fiction, man is ill-placed and tries to go to the root of moral implication of his actions. Scobie lives a life of recoil because he has allowed his sense of pity to override his sense of duty. Morally and spiritually, he is a failure because there are inherent contradictions in his character; his duality makes him feel stoic about his own sacrifice but also lets him feel very strongly for others. Several external and internal factors—the mental and spiritual alienation, 'the ennui'—combine together to make him, a social outcast. In his marriage, he recoils internally, love having died;

he is forced down by pity and responsibility for his wife. Scobie's antiheroism emerges from his unassertiveness; he is one who has reduced himself to live with failure and insults. Louise's calling him "Ticki" recoils him internally but he never attempts to assert himself, knowing that it gives her some peace. He personifies Greene's sense of boredom, religious doubt, and the value of suffering, evil, and the divided self.

Though a good man, Scobie is confounded by confusion. Love is confused with pity in Scobie's heart and he becomes incapable of reconciling the emotional demands made on him by the women as well as of reconciling his infidelity with his conscience. He assumes responsibility for their happiness and his inability to hurt either of them involves him in lies and deception, which lead inexorably to his own death as he sees suicide as the only way out of a situation in which his very existence is a source of pain to those he care for. Killing oneself, in a sense amounts to confessing that life is too much and that it is beyond comprehension. In life, one continues making the gestures commanded by existence for many reasons, the first of which is habit. Dying voluntarily implies that one has recognized the ridiculous character of that daily agitation, and the uselessness of suffering.[87]

There is nothing extraordinary about Scobie. His personality is totally unheroic for a central protagonist; he is squat, grey haired and a middle-aged man. He sees himself as a dull failure, who has been passed over for promotion. His is the struggle between an insufficient man and an indifferent nature. His failure to be promoted leads to social and emotional frustration of his hysterical wife Louise, who appears on the verge of a nervous breakdown. She is a self righteous, pious woman whom Scobie does not love anymore but feels morally responsible for. To send her on a holiday, he borrows money from a corrupt Syrian, Yusef. Scobie assumes responsibility for order, for seeing that justice is done. His attempt to regulate justice backfires as he himself is the victim of that justice. His personal moral disorder, however, is great and too chaotic that he cannot perform his duties at the personal level.

Though Greene treats Scobie with sympathy, readers often tend to find Scobie's religious conscience over-scrupulous and his self-judgment pitiless, particularly one who is so concerned with pity for others, and one who believes in the mercy of God. His sense of pity leads him first to despair and then to blasphemy; first, in his note, telling Helen that he loves her more than he loves God, and in protecting Louise from the truth by going to communion with her even though he is in a state of mortal sin. The blasphemous note, the first sign of Scobie's spiritual corruption becomes the reason for his actual corruption when Yusef, who uses it to blackmail Scobie into breaking the law, intercepts it. The communion clearly exposes his weakness and we are given a glimpse of the limits to which his sense of pity will lead him.

Scobie makes even God a victim of his pity, for his decision to kill himself is due to a wish to spare God further suffering. He is undoubtedly not the normal sort of antihero, rebelling against everything authoritarian, nevertheless, his sense of pity and responsibility lead to an antiheroic feature of spiritual egotism. This pride also leads to despair, as he becomes not only his brother's keeper but pretends to be God's keeper as well. His relationship with God is paradoxical—if God created him then He must share the blame for the way Scobie is. "If you made me, you made this feeling of responsibility that I have always carried about like a sack of bricks" (p. 259). Secondly, his act of despair is also an act of atonement, an act born not out of a sense of evil or hatred of God, but out of a sense of goodness and love of God:

> Despair is the price one pays for setting an impossible aim. It is, one is told, the unforgivable sin, but it is a sin the corrupt or evil man never practices.... Only the man of goodwill carries in his heart this capacity for damnation. (p. 60)

Scobie cannot believe in a God "who was not human enough to love what he had created", and later he tells Helen "against all the teachings of the Church, one has the conviction that love does deserve a bit of mercy". Although "one pays terribly", he does not believe that "one will pay forever".

Among the ambitious Englishmen, Scobie is the wise fool, indifferent to material success and totally out of tune with the competitive life there. This perhaps accounts for his failure to acquire the coveted post as well as the house in which he is outmaneuvered by the sanitary inspector.

Suicide is an unforgiveable sin, but he justifies it by asking whether Christ had not killed himself? After Ali's death, Yusef is his sole companion. Yusef is a foil to Scobie; he is Mephistopheles to Scobie's Faust. He is in short the latter's evil aspect. Kurishmmootil writes that there are many facets of love. Scobie's love, corrupted to pity, has created a monster that would leave nothing and nobody unharmed in its trail.[88] He also draws attention to Greene's *Collected Works* (p. 15) where Greene states that suicide was Scobie's inevitable end; the particular motive of his suicide, to save even God from himself, was the final twist of the screw of his inordinate pride. So is Scobie an imperfect and a deluded hero?

Pride is a deliberate illusion. Scobie's moral dilemma is rooted in conflicts that he is unwilling to face. He lacks the courage to clear up the confusion of his motivations and beliefs. What he needs is an ordered moral conscience to untangle his confused and unbalanced sentiments. His decisions not guided by reason are themselves acts of despair. He is even doubtful of the sacrifices that he has made and whether it would have the desired effect. For him, the corruption of God in sacrilege is the most monstrous crime of all. Scobie is condemned eternally to an unrewarding task, similar to that of Sisyphus. Scobie thinks of God as enfeebled with an excess of compassion.

The world that Scobie lives in is significantly, morally and spiritually barren. There is extreme egotism, spite and malice, injustice, hatred and menacing violence. In a way both Greene and Scobie wonder how God could have conceived such a world, and left it so irremediably lost? But with God out of the scene and without responsibility, it is, he feels, Scobie alone who must bear the entire weight of the burden as best as he can.

Critics such as George Orwell and Judith Adamson have strongly criticized Scobie's character. One of the harshest critiques came from George Orwell, who thought the theological nature of Scobie's dilemma 'snobbish' and 'sinister'. He attacked Greene's concept of 'the sanctified sinner' as if there is something rather *distingué* in being damned. O' Prey[89] quotes from "The Sanctified Sinner", where Orwell ridicules Scobie:

> White all through, with a stiff upper lip, he had gone to what he believed to be certain damnation out of pure gentlemanliness.... If he were capable of getting into the kind of mess that is described, he would have got into it earlier. If he really felt that adultery is mortal sin, he would stop committing it: if he persisted in it, his sense of sin would weaken. If he believed in Hell, he would not risk going there merely to spare the feelings of a couple of neurotic women.

In spite of his best intentions, Scobie's actions always have negative reactions. His most vital act of pity is also his most disastrous: his prayer exchanging his peace so that the dying six-year old child may have peace. To lose one's peace forever is to be in hell and according to the Church's law, he has chosen hell when he takes communion in mortal sin and then again when he ends his own life. The problem lies in Scobie's ability to combine Christian charity with offences, his adultery and his bad communion. What Orwell says about him best illustrates the difficulty.

Scobie's love for the blacks separates him from the other expatriates; it is he who appreciates the beauty around him, even if it is the ephemeral, five-minute beauty of the sunset over the laterite roads, "so ugly and clay heavy by day". The same affection makes his betrayal of Ali the darkest moment of his despair, so that when he finds Ali's dead body, he thinks "Oh God.... I have killed you: you've served me all these years and I've killed you at the end of them" (p. 247).

For Scobie, God is a spent force, a failure. He reads failure as final meaning of Jesus's death. The Cross is the ultimate sign of despair and there is nothing further for him to invoke. His aspirations, his plans to help others thus depend upon his own resources. He imagines God to be in need of his protection and pity too. He alternately feels pity, shame and resentment. God is felt to be like a handcuff on his sense of pity. This peculiar notion of God is perhaps the projection of Scobie's own pathological image. Jung has described the working of this psychic process and he demonstrates how pervasive its incidence really is.[90] The effect on Scobie of his self-projection is to reproduce the pattern over and over again. The process entails the keen eye for the victim, the urge to help, the unreasonable demands made on self, the failure of the redemptive role, its recognition and, finally, resentment at what had first seemed an objective demand. The action is always triggered more often than not by a woman in distress, and ugliness is always a stimulant. This is Scobie's self, redeemer and victim; and his God, apparently, takes after him, as though He is none other than his own self projected outside and blown to cosmic dimension. Scobie evidently "knew" his God, for he does not "trust" Him for an instant. Evidently, he does not trust God, had his trust been complete, he would not have hesitated in transferring his burden of self-assumed responsibility to God. He cannot shrug off his part in Helen's happiness or Louise's unhappiness.

True, Scobie cannot bear to see others suffering. Judith Adamson[91] writes that Scobie's inability to refuse the pull of "the face for which nobody would go out of his way, the face that would soon be used to rebuffs and indifference" makes him appear to be a good man who is haunted to his doom by the harshness of his wife and the colonial experience. In fact his vulnerability to those who suffer innocently has more to do with his vanity than with his goodness. This is clear when the telegrams Louise sends about his daughter's death gets mixed up so that the first to arrive is the one saying that she died, and the second that there is still hope, Scobie feels disappointed. "That was the terrible thing. I thought 'now the anxiety begins, and the pain' but when I realized what had happened, then it was all right, she was dead, I could begin to forget her". This, Adamson points out, is certainly a monstrous pride.

Moreover, he exhibits a tortured individualism. His belief in the integrity of the individual is so radical that he is compelled to treat each person and experience in isolation and out of context. His is not the simple obsession with innocent suffering and the inability to watch it. It is coloured by his intense subjectivity and depends entirely on his individual consciousness. This leads him and others into moral complicacy and contradictions rendering him incapable of taking a decisive moral action. Pity for Louise and Helen binds him to Yusef, gets Ali killed, and complicates his own relation with his wife. It gets him nowhere, and he soon discovers that in helping, or loving, one he is often being destructive to the other.

Adamson's appraisal of Scobie dwells on his antiheroic characteristics. He is a good man whose concern for others is admirable but he is also shortsighted and selfish. Louise questions herself who is it that Scobie really loves, "Me, This Helen Rolt...? Or just himself" (p. 217). Scobie's myopia makes him incapable of disinterested action. He is so corrupted by sentiment that he manipulates reality—"The truth...has never been of any real value to any human being.... In human relations kindness and lies are worth a thousand truths"—and thus creating havoc in people's lives. Helen never asked for his pity but it is as if it were forced on her. "Pity smoldered like decay at his heart...the conditions of life nurtured it". He cannot leave her alone. His pride makes him believe that he is indispensable.[92]

Louise tells Wilson, "Love, love, love. It means self, self, self." "It was his favourite lie." She is right that Scobie's moral indecisiveness is self-protecting. Greene has all his sympathies with Scobie, but then again the novel does not end with some kind of approval. He ends *The Heart of the Matter* leaving us with a statement about man's inability to understand God's mercy. Greene definitely draws the readers' sympathy for Scobie but leaves his death unresolved.[93]

Chronically indecisive, he refuses to recognize cause and effect and commits extreme intellectual dishonesties. His confusion reaches the bottom when near the end of the novel he turns to the villain Yusef out of moral exhaustion. Returning from a brief, peaceful evening at Yusef's, he cannot face his own moral turpitude, a reality that includes suffering and Ali's death.

His corruption starts from a loss of innocence and a fall into experience. He finds peace in remembering his childhood and in memories of being alone with Ali on trek when things were simpler. After asking for directions from God several times, he kills himself, dying listening to his own voice to stop play-acting. In this respect he is very much like Somerset Maugham's Bob Forestier in "The Lion's Skin."[94] Forestier pretends to be a gentleman all his life and in the end is unable to discriminate between the real and play-acting. Maugham writes that he sacrificed his life to the ideal of spurious heroism.

Scobie falls back on a God he does not trust and feels that he has failed. "No, I don't trust you. I've never trusted" (p. 259). Scobie loves but does not trust Him. In the end he walks out of the Church because "I can't shift my responsibility to you...I'm responsible and I'll see it through the only way I can (p. 259). Paradox abounds in Scobie's nature. On the one hand, he believes in God but on the other, he is an existentialist, as shown by his above-mentioned statement. Father Rank's statement neither condemns Scobie nor resolves the tension in the novel between Greene's fascination with the dogmatic teachings of the Church and his insistence on the independence of the individual consciousness to interpret reality.

Scobie is faced with the trauma of having to make a choice where he can make none. He can live with Helen and leave Louise, or live with the latter and leave the former. Or he can leave them both, or he can wait for a miracle. The last not forthcoming, he kills himself. The choice to damn himself, for Scobie, is deliberate. There is only despair here at having to choose in a godless world. However, he has the existential freedom of individual choice and by killing himself, Scobie accepts it. He is also using his choice of freedom when he surrenders his peace to God in exchange for granting peace to the dying child. He has knowledge of the choices he makes and he is damned by his knowledge.

Freedom is a burden and has no meaning for Scobie as he is enslaved by a strong sense of responsibility for other's happiness. He suffers from guilt in his relationship with Louise because he believes that it was he who formed her face, as though he were responsible for something in the future he couldn't even foresee (p. 17). The realization of the futility of his attempts to bring happiness into other's life brings about a kind of weariness in him. "No human being can really understand another and no one can arrange another's happiness" (p. 81). This weariness in Scobie intensifies to such an extent that in place of human communication he longs for death and total effacement. This also reveals his existential attitude, as he is always aware of his own responsibility: that he had selected the experience. Failure to get the loan makes him doubt himself, "that he must have failed in some way in manhood" (p. 46). He knew that it was an absurd thing to expect happiness in a world full of misery (p. 123). Wilson too judges Scobie as insufferable, too honest, and too unbearable to live with.

Alienation occurs in a derelict world and Scobie's relationship with spirituality is full of complexity and doubts. Lamba[95] states that the sin of the fallen angels, i.e. pride and disobedience to the divine law—is the sin that besets Scobie. Out of hidden pride, he assumes the mantle of a father figure, but he lacks the sense to discriminate between right and wrong from good and evil. Fully aware of the consequences, he commits the sin, and he tries to replace God's mercy by inadequate human compassion. In his moral confusion and unconscious pride, he assumes the mantle of the dispenser of peace, occupying the space left empty by what he sees as God's absence or lack of intervention. He has the feeling of the loss of faith and trust. He feels that God has set standards that are totally beyond the bounds of an ordinary human. He is obsessed with the weight of his sin, the very nature of which implies an act of injury to God. The sin of deceit and adultery along with the tacit murder of Ali spurs him to despair and to suicide. He is a heretic even in his presumption of considering "God a failure" (p. 254). The fact that as a Catholic he sees God as a failure damns him. Though Greene sympathizes with the ironic antihero, he denies him the pleasure or tragic or heroic elevation or self-satisfying identification. Scobie inhabits a moral and physical no-man's land, carrying the border mentality, belonging nowhere.

Dicky Pemberton's suicide induces a sense of worthlessness in him, at this moment the very thought of the act of suicide frightens him, but his dream also gives a brief glimpse into his sub-conscious where suicide already figures as the solution out of his life. Greene offers no alternative for Scobie. For him, lack of liberty is an irreducible fact of life. All tensions impinge on him leading to his breakdown. Why is Scobie a failure? He acknowledges that he is a failure, appropriated by other men. Karl writes that Scobie is enduring a re-assessment of the self in which he is a focus of failure. Failure and the love of failure, becomes, for him, a way of life. Chance plays an important role in his life. He has elevated pity to the position of a passion. He is enfeebled by pity as it incapacitates both the giver and the subject. He is a weak man, with the burden of heaven and hell, a saint, but for the wrong reasons.

Given the premises of Scobie's character, personality and belief, there is undoubtedly an element of 'monstrous pride' in him, "God can wait, he thought: how can one love God at the expense of one of his creatures?" (p. 187). The possibilities here for self-deception and having it both ways are clear. Grahame Smith[96] writes that the artistic justification for such a problem is that one should be made to feel that it isn't an easy option for Scobie, that opting for it carried him to the outer limits of human suffering.

His questions about the innocent suffering continually nag the religious mind and like the neurotic who makes his own pain, Greene flogs Scobie to death with it.[97] God does not come forward to inspire trust, and Scobie cannot come to accept the world without Him so he lives and dies in a quagmire of skepticism. He does not learn to accept the anguish of modern life; moreover his suffering is introverted and suicidal. He is unable to accommodate himself to the collective moral complexity of the new world, which leaves him radically isolated and alone. A failure at every turn, Scobie is non-resilient, a post war character, challenging God to help him out of the terrible moral morass into which he has sunk. He is a man who cannot face the post war world where right and wrong are far from clear and for whom religion, which once was purposeful and gave a sense of communion, has failed to provide the comfort that had been expected of it.

As an antihero he is the opposite of the anarchic rebel, Arthur Seaton.[98] They are opposites because Seaton goes to extreme lengths to assert his identity whereas Scobie is absolutely unassertive and submissive, unwilling to defend himself against the attack of others. He has come to terms with defeat and lack of respect. Building "his home by a process of reduction" (p. 15) Scobie has cut down his personal needs to the minimum. He is totally disillusioned with life and prides himself on being a good loser. He is a man who cannot be bracketed as a radical rebel. He too is a metaphysical rebel seeking to find God in a Godless universe. In a way, he is similar to Beckett's Molloy[99] discussed earlier in this chapter. The ambivalence in his characterization along with his heretic like tendencies finds a parallel in what Hassan[100] says in his book, *Radical Innocence*:

> He is not exactly...the radical's idea of the rebel. A victim of angst and existentialism, perhaps he is all of these and none in particular. Suffering from dread and anxiety, he encounters the void and often fails to find justification for the choices he/she makes. His capacity for pain seems saintly and his passion or heresy almost criminal. But flawed in his sainthood and grotesque in his criminality, he appears as an expression of man's quenchless desire to affirm, despite the void and vicissitudes of our age, the human sense of life.

That Scobie is an antihero can be accepted if one takes into account the statement Greene makes about heroes. In *The Minister of Fear* (1943), Greene says "Our heroes are simple:

they are brave, they tell the truth, and they are never in the long run defeated" (p. 89). Contrarily in a society where man is measured in terms of social success, status and financial position, Scobie is a poor man, existing in a static state unwilling to move ahead. A postmodern antihero, he is a victim of alienation, cultural and spiritual sterility, seeking solace in social withdrawal and anonymity. He is an example of spiritual aridity, a mundane life, failure, and an unconscious attraction towards evil; he is the indecisive and ineffectual and clumsy protagonist. Life and the world for him are *de trop,* which exacts more energy than he has in his personality.

Afflicted with an uneasy sense of inconsequence, Scobie fascinates us with his pessimism and as an embodiment of an unqualified admission of defeat,[101] he has no belief in the future, very likely of an existentialist, and accepts the fact that there is no reason for celebration. Life is irremediably meaningless for him. Misery is accepted as a fact of experience. He finds no justification for the misery that he sees around him. "What an absurd thing to expect happiness in a world so full of misery" (p. 123). He resolves not to be taken by its experience. He is similar to Greene's other characters, especially Pinkie (*Brighton Rock*, 1938) and the Whiskey Priest (*The Power and The Glory*, 1940) in agreeing that the world is dying slowly. He knows that the hopes of a better world are futile. Fifty years of experience have led him to suspect ambition and hope.

Scobie's *hamartia*, his fatal weakness is that he cannot bear to hurt anyone. Pity drives him to borrow money from Yusef; he is the victim of his pity; pity for Helen from which his love springs, pity for the child hovering between life and death. The incorruptible man sees himself caught up in corruption. He cannot hurt Louise by refusing to go to Communion, he cannot hurt Helen by giving her up, and he is too honest to promise in confession to do something that he knows he cannot. And it is with the knowledge of damnation that he receives the Communion. Caught between pity and love, and knowing that he cannot continue to wound God—"striking God when he's down"—he plans his suicide in such a way that neither Louise nor Helen will know that he took his own life.

Probably the first stage in his disintegration is his failure to report the Portuguese sea captain's secret of a letter in a lavatory cistern, an offence which Scobie as a policeman should have transmitted instantly to the proper authority. The seeds of Scobie's downfall occur in a little exchange of dialogue: 'A man is ruined because he writes to his daughter.' 'Daughter?' (p. 50). This episode is important because although his departure from duty may seem a minor one, it is the beginning of a descent down a long slide and he sees it as:

> Frazer said cheerfully, 'Burning the evidence?' and looked down into the tin. The name had blackened: there was nothing there surely that Frazer could see—except a brown triangle of envelop that seemed to Scobie obviously foreign.... Only his own heart-beats told him he was guilty—that he had joined the ranks of the corrupt police-officers (p. 55).

Destroying the letter and borrowing money from Yusef is the point of his initiation into corruption from which he is unable to extricate himself. He has till now refused gifts from Yusef, but even with the perfectly proper arrangement on the surface, he feels that his moral status has altered and his descent continues. Superior to neither men nor to the environment, he is bound to frustration and absurdity of life. In fact, Scobie can be classified as a pharmakos.[102] According to Northrop Frye, the pharmakos is neither innocent neither guilty. He is innocent in the sense that what happens to him is far greater than what he has done provokes. He is guilty because he is a member of a guilty society, or living in a world where injustices are an inescapable part of existence. He inhabits an ambivalent space where one cannot exactly state whether he is dammed or saved. He is opposite of the God directed hero like Moses, rather, the more help he asks from God the more distant he finds himself from God. He is a *schlemiel*—an ironic antihero who is the apt representative of the society of failures. He is a scapegoat about whom it can be remarked that he is a "Christian martyr who can aspire to perdition."[103]

As Scobie plunges ever more deeply into his problems, he feels himself entering "the territory of lies without a passport to return" (199), which results in the sensation of his whole personality crumbling "with the slow disintegration of lies" (p. 209). Towards the end of his ordeal Scobie begins to sink into a quandary of moral and spiritual complexity. "There were so many lies nowadays he couldn't keep track of the small, the unimportant ones" (p. 231). He is a man who desperately desires to be good but who, through character and circumstances, finds himself enmeshed in evil. Smith points out that Scobie desires the eternal life of Catholic salvation, but cannot bear to inflict pain on others and his way of dealing with the second dilemma renders the first unachievable. There is clearly an element of absurdity and moral and spiritual confusion in these difficulties. A similarity with *Macbeth* comes to mind when on discovering Ali's corpse, Scobie wishes he could weep; it is similar to Macbeth's inability to say Amen at the sight of Duncan's body.

Scobie is living Greene's 'dangerous edge'.[104] Fixed within his character, Scobie is unable to change or resist what he is and what he is becoming. Only suffering, soul-searching tension and inner conflict can help a Greene character like Scobie by making him turn away from the devil. Contrary to Bunyan's *Pilgrim's Progress*, in Greene, it is the sinner who stumbles on his way to heaven "almost forsaking God and embracing the devil in his inability to fulfill what God requires".[105] In Scobie, Greene personifies the marginal, the weak in will, the poor in spirit, and the proud in the soul.

Greene quotes Charles Péguy in the epigraph to *The Heart of the Matter*: "The sinner is at the very heart of Christianity. No one is as competent as the sinner in Christian affairs. No one, except the saint." For many, the honorable police officer in the novel was a portrait of a saint. But Scobie's dilemma, torn as a Catholic between his duties to his wife and his promises to a desperate young woman with whom he is having an affair, may reflect ambivalence in Greene himself. Scobie's solution, suicide, recalls a constant temptation.

Scobie imagines his adulterous affair as an insult to God—like rubbing the face of the baby Jesus in the dirt of the Bethlehem stable. He believes himself damned but cannot cease loving God. Greene's hero is often the innocent, pursued by God, and characterized by a sexual traumatism of adolescence and a pessimistic view of the world. He is a Christian who believes more in the subterranean life of grace than in the facade of the visible Church.

Greene's frenzied characters possess a sense of inner fate, and are in conflict with God Himself. Scobie transgresses in forgetting that God has powers that go beyond his comprehension. Apart from taking communion in a state of mortal sin, Scobie commits suicide, the unredemptive act of despair. He undergoes a kind of re-evaluation of self in which he becomes the focus of a failure; and failure itself and love of failure becomes a way of life. He is a social and religious derelict; isolated and alone, Scobie is approaching a state of acedia[106] which places him outside the understanding of other men and which even denies the efficacy of God's grace. Unable to compromise his honesty and integrity, he gives up hope. He comes close to finding peace with Helen because she, like Scobie is another failure, a flotsam that floated in the open sea for forty days and right into his life.

Journey Without Maps (1936) brings up an important question:

> ...the boredom of childhood, that agonizing boredom of 'apartness' which came before one had learnt the trick of transferring emotion, of flashing back enchantingly all day long one's own image, a period when other people were as distinct form one self as this Liberian forest. I sometimes wonder whether, if one stayed longer, if one had not been driven out again by tiredness and fear, one might have relearned the way to live without transference, with a lost objectivity.[107]

John Spurling[108] asks whether by this 'apartness' Greene means that it is fatal to love other people or that it is fatal to think you love them when in reality you are using them only as a mirror for your self-love? This question is relevant to Scobie. His life, as the last sentence of the passage, suggests that it would be better if love didn't come into it at all, that one might learn to grow up away from love, even at the price of boredom.

After his first night with Helen, he thinks "Human beings were condemned to consequences. The responsibility as well as the guilt was his" (p. 154). Love is now recognized as pity—"the terrible promiscuous passion which so few experience"—and the dangerous qualities in the opposite sex are failure, ugliness and pathos, not beauty, grace or intelligence. Perhaps Greene really seems to have meant his readers to see Scobie's pity only as an emanation of pride and self-love and him as spiritually corrupt.

He is the embodiment of the scapegoat as the antihero. Scobie's character begins to reveal itself as it is constantly put in comparison with the environmental details. Environment and setting is taken as an extension of one's personality. In Scobie's case, his surrounding controls his behaviour to a great extent. Kurishmmootil[109] uses Austin Warren's defense of this mode of characterization. Setting describes one's personality and is an expression of the human will as much as it projects a man's inner states and emotions. Warren states:

> Environments, especially domestic interiors, may be viewed as metonymic, or metaphoric, expressions of character. A man's house is an extension of himself. Describe it and you have described him.... These houses express their owners: they affect as atmosphere, those others who must live in them.

Scobie's room defines its reclusive owner. Greene creates in Scobie, a man of scant ambitions, a very reclusive character. His withdrawal from life is not necessarily passive. He desires peace, but peace for him is not one of fulfillment or contentment but one of negation. In God-forsaken Sierra Leone, Scobie is a man divested of his faith, isolated both internally and externally. Like Greene's other ironic heroes, he is perturbed. His is a world where men are without hope, continually betrayed to self-destruction by whatever is best in them. Scobie's virtues are, paradoxically, his vices. What comes to mind here is Arthur Rowe's statement in *The Ministry of Fear*:[110] "It was not only the evil men who did these things. Courage smashes a cathedral, endurance lets a city starve, pity kills...we are trapped and betrayed by our virtues."

Incapable of heroic deeds, Scobie is the non-hero given to the vocation of failure. The colonial setting with its unbearable combination of heat, boredom, and isolation conjures up a condition which gives rise to despair. The vivid sense of wasteland, a place forgotten by humanity, the seediness and the sordidness combine to create a world abandoned by hope and God. Caught between different pains, tormented by pity, Scobie is a victim of his love of God. He continues his role-playing as husband and lover to serve the happiness of both women, and he goes to the altar with a clear expectancy of his own damnation. In *Saints, Sinners and Comedians* (1984), Roger Sharock[111] points out that Scobie's betrayal of God coincides with the final stage of his corruption as a policeman. Before delivering the diamonds he needlessly begins to doubt his loyal servant, Ali. Yusef ambiguously promises to take care of things, and has Ali murdered, but does Scobie understand the full implication of this reassurance? This remains a question. Probably he does, and what is sure is that he finds the body under the petrol drums and he holds himself responsible on account of his lack of trust, and this betrayal is intimately connected with his betrayal of God.

His suicidal urge towards self-destruction prompts Scobie to damn himself in preference to hurting either of the women. He transfers his own emotion of consuming pity to others he suffers in his person to their immense need as he imagines it, and in doing so-fails to grasp the facts of the case.

Unconsciously, Scobie is playing the role of a condemned Christ—atoning for the crimes of others. Damning oneself knowing its full implication is as daring an act of surrendering oneself to evil as it is to surrendering to total goodness. Scobie carries the opposing viewpoints of love and duty in him. He is intensely stoical for himself and intensely sympathetic to others. He follows the principles of disinterested duty, justice and responsibility and simultaneously has the urge to protect the ugly and the unhappy. His alienation arises out of the inherent paradox in his character—his limitless capacity to bear his own pain and loneliness on the one hand and on the other, his failure to bear other's pain and unhappiness.[112] He reaches an *impasse* because of his self-effacement and his inability to reconcile love and duty.

Pride is without doubt Scobie's great flaw but it commingles with a compassionate awareness of misery and unhappiness. His pride is suggested by a paradoxical readiness to accept the doctrines of the Catholic Church for himself but not for others. He does not so much fear hellfire as he does the permanent sense of loss that the church describes as one of the consequences of damnation. Scobie's sin is that he prefers to trust himself, in his limited knowledge of love, to God. He cannot put his faith in God, for his faith is love and pity its image. It is a paradox that Scobie flinches from the thought of a sacrilege, but not from the fear of retribution. Had he trusted God completely, he would not have hesitated in transferring his burden of self-assumed responsibility to God. He cannot shrug off his part in Helen's happiness or Louise's unhappiness. Without an ordered moral conscience to help and guide his confused sentiments, his responses to life are frightfully unbalanced and his decisions are often irrational.

For him, love and suffering are irreconcilable. He becomes at once a traitor and a scapegoat: his sense of pity, an image of his love for God, assumes the proportions of a tragic flaw. In the process of learning the wherewithal of his religion, he realizes the immensity of human commitment, but he fails to recognize the immensity of God's mercy. His pride and his humility conspire against him, and because he cannot trust the God he loves, he commits the sin of despair. With the smuggling of the diamonds he realizes that he is "one of those whom people pity" and he has the further awareness that his corruption corrupts others (p. 235). Now of the devil's party, Scobie knows that he will now go from "damned success to damned success" (p. 267). For him, love can only be aroused by pity. He is overcome by religious doubt, and boredom. In his case it is his combination of pride and his goodness that makes him an antihero. Greene offers no alternative for Scobie. For him, lack of liberty is an irreducible fact of life. All tensions impinge on him leading to his breakdown. He is an Everyman; his voice is a moral protest against the miserable condition of existence.

Scobie, like Ngugi's Mugo,[113] in *A Grain of Wheat* (1967), suffers from the inability to communicate; both domestically and socially, he is an absolute failure. Long out of love with his wife, he shares nothing in common with her. He recoils more in his shell as he encounters human snobbery, malice and hypocrisy. Disgust for "the grandiloquent boast of weak men" he is further alienated from the existing structure of society. He is a failure in that he is unable to discover any principle that would give meaning to his life.

Scobie wants to know who is responsible for innocent suffering. Greene has no answers to the question of responsibility that Scobie's ethical dilemma alludes to. Adamson[114] is critical of Greene and his religious beliefs. Catholicism may have carried him through the beginning of the war, but at its end it fails Scobie, and Greene is uncertain why. While insisting that man is defined by his choices, he insinuates that Scobie's actions are completely not his fault. Louise's conceited ambition causes his criminal negligence and spiritual self-destruction and Helen's childishness is responsible for his adultery. Scobie is responsible, but he is also a good man stretched to his limits, his goodness forms the base of his weakness in him. It is true that Scobie is an antihero but not a villain. According to Kurishmmootil, he is a sinner, and he is sinned against, but he is no worse than most of us; what evil he has caused is not self willed, though they might be self inflicted, it is the result of his confusion.

Scobie, whom circumstances and his own needs compel into sin has a question mark over his final end. What he desires and lacks most is peace. This he attains when, in his own mind, he thinks he has inexorably cut himself from God. The picture of a native porter bowing under his load enters into the imagery of the story. The image comes to be applied to Scobie himself who lives by shouldering other people's burden.

> He was surprised how quickly she went to sleep: she was like a tired carrier who had slipped his load. She was asleep before he had finished his sentence, clutching one of his fingers like a child, breathing as easily. The load lay beside him now, and he was prepared to lift it. (p. 44)

The metaphor implicitly hints at pain and burden of Scobie as increasing loads are thrust upon him until he can no longer bear them. Both Pemberton and the captain's daughter, indirect receivers of Scobie's pity, are shadows cast before the fatal catastrophe that culminates with the disastrous entry of the girl-woman, Helen Rolt.

Not only is scobie's spiritual destiny left ambivalent but questions are also cast over his character as a man. He has been judged as a moral failure, an inferior person, and even as a self-destructive neurotic.[115] As a twentieth century man he has a problematic relationship to his social and cultural environment, and moreover, the environment in the coast is a place that drives men to the breaking point.

Scobie the Just's (p. 18) fatal flaw of pity manoeuvres him to a position where he can be corrupted. This automatic terrible pity makes things difficult for him. Pity for the women is excited by ugliness and failure, never by attractiveness. "It isn't beauty that we love, he thought, it is failure—the failure to stay young for ever, the failure of nerves, the failure of the body. Beauty is like success: we can't love it for long". Scobie defines himself by pitying others. He has a painful sense of separation from other people which is masked by his steadily maintained life of pitying service.[116] This guilt of separation produced dual attitudes. Scobie treats the subjects of his love as inferior, and yet he feels, after all his day-to-day support for them, "the enormous breach of pity has blasted through his integrity" (p. 115). He exists as an isolated self but when he commits himself to other people it is destructive to the isolated self and its veracity. A paradox underlies his behaviour, a Christian morality involves sacrifice and this entails the abandonment of the implied compromises by which the lonely self tries to exist in society. His attitude towards the weak and the ugly can be seen a condescending and proud, ironical because he does not treat them with contempt. Rather he feels that without him, there would be no one to love them and feel responsible for them.

According to Francis Wyndham,[117] in Scobie's character Greene carries the character of Rowe in *The Ministry of Fear* to its terrifying conclusion. Greene creates a three-dimensional character in Scobie. A converted Catholic, he is an incorruptible man, but corruption does find a way in through pity and sentiment. He is also passed over for promotion and is expected to retire, but the burden of ennui makes retirement, for him, worse than death. "The thought of retirement set his nerves twitching and straining: he always prayed that death would come first".

Scobie, the errant soul, has often been seen as the tragic hero because of the tragedy that befalls him and also because his pity is akin to the Greek *Hubris*. Can Scobie be called a tragic hero? For an answer one can turn to DeVitis,[118] who quotes Martin C. D'arcy, who discusses the anatomy of the hero, albeit a little problematically:

> In the Christian scale of values the hero is not easily distinguishable from the saint; it is more a matter of emphasis than of division. The saint cannot be canonized unless he can be shown to have practiced heroic virtues, the man of heroic deeds cannot be called a hero unless there is evidence that his inner spirit corresponds with his deeds, and that his motives are pure. But whereas in using the word 'saint' the emphasis is on a man's relation to God and his spiritual work for his fellow man, it is prowess and self-sacrifice for others, for friends or for nation, which is uppermost in the thoughts of the hero.

The potentiality of tragic action in either the classical or in the Elizabethan sense is limited because the individual no longer finds means to battle such a complicated social organism. Lacking classical tragic proportions and often tending towards melodrama Scobie becomes the ironic hero. His motives are pure no doubt, but it presents a problem because he wants to remove himself, the source of pain to others. But his deeds do not correspond with his inner spirit of motive and thus are absurd.

Scobie is one whom Karl[119] calls Greene's "demonical heroes". It is a fact that the hero in major western fiction has more or less vanished, or become diminished in stature, somewhat unable to meets the demands of life. Often, he is now characterized as an antihero. He is no longer the romantic hero with simple purity, natural goodness of heart and action and Christian morality, a hero who was an aristocratic Christian knight. What does Greene do with such an ironic hero?

In Greene, it is the impotent, self-destructive, helpless character who has insight into the nature of spirituality or devilishness denied the man who is normal.[120] In an attempt to recover him, Greene has taken the fallen hero, peculiar to our modern times, and tried to raise him through suffering and pain to a heroic stature. Having understood that the romantic hero is surely dead, Greene still believes that man can be heroic, though in his terms heroism takes on a different shade from that of the previous times. In Greene, the hero usually has a demonical descent from the state of grace. By assuming different roles, the individual places himself beyond a force that may either lead to limited happiness or to severe unhappiness.

The idea that the failure is nearer to God, as Karl sees it, is close to the Greek idea of *Hubris*. Accordingly, the man of overweening pride challenges the order of the universe and when he comes to see himself greater than God, he is struck down. Within the Christian world too, God operates similarly, retaining pity and sympathy for the failure. It is an irony that God reveals Himself to the tortured deniers, to the ones who despair and are close to the devil. In every instance, Greene feels that God seeks out the ones who would deny Him, for they are probing the very roots of His existence.

Scobie is the virtuous sinner and an erring individual; what shocks the readers as well as Louise and Wilson in fact, is the extent of his goodness and of his sin. Indeed he can be described as a 'moral monster'.[121] In Greene's view of Christian morality, losing life to save it is a monstrous form of behaviour. At times, Scobie seems to be sharing the lot of the victim—at other times to be inflicting pain on Christ or joining in his betrayal. After his first night with Helen, he reflects on the impossibility of his dual responsibility and the lies that he will have to tell. He now interprets his action as treachery to God:

> He had sworn to preserve Louise's happiness and now he had accepted another and contradictory responsibility. He felt tired by all the lies that he would some time have to tell: he felt the wounds of those victims who had not yet bled. Lying on the pillow he stared sleeplessly out towards the grey early morning tide. Somewhere on the face of those obscure waters moved the sense of yet another wrong and another victim, not Louise, not Helen. (pp. 161-62)

Scobie's dilemma shows an irreconcilable problem for his creator. There is no answer to his broad philosophical problems about suffering. Scobie who tries to prevent it in an intellectual way by putting the welfare of others before his own is guilty of pride and of causing further suffering. As he says to God at the end of the novel: "you see it's an *impasse*, God, an *impasse*". He finds himself in a blind spiritual alley, and his suicide marks Greene's inability to get him out of it, either to take the leap of faith or to abandon Catholicism.[122]

Is it Scobie's arrogance that he tries to arrange other people's lives as if he were God? What propels the role of an antihero upon Scobie is the criticism that Greene has of the novel. Sharrock[123] states:

> Suicide was Scobie's inevitable end; the particular motive of his suicide, to save even God from himself, was the final turn of the screw of his inordinate pride. Perhaps Scobie should have been a subject for a cruel comedy rather than for tragedy....

For Greene, the essential human tragedy rises from the absurdity of the world, implicit in the gap between what man wants and what he is able to attain. Man's capacity and his limitation mock his desires. What Scobie longs for is peace, but it remains elusive as ever.

The Greene hero operates according to his religious beliefs. Moreover, the religious framework within which he exists is either non-existent or marginal. Karl points out that because Greene believes that from impurity comes purity, and saintliness from demonism, his 'heroes' often seem closer to demons than to saints. Scobie, like every other serious Greene protagonist, despite external experience and personal degradation, has a vision of saintliness. His inner conflicts results from his inability to live up to his ideal. Greene likens Scobie to Oedipus, whose pride has overwhelmed his sense of reasonableness. He recognizes how short he has fallen of the ideal, how mortal he really is. Karl[124] refers to Greene's retelling of the *Song of Roland* in *The Confidential Agent* (1939) to illustrate explicitly the theme of false heroism and pride which deceive men into thinking themselves to be God. By downgrading heroic roles in general, Greene leaves room for humility that is clearly part of a tragic vision. One can become truly heroic only by humbling oneself before God. The imperfect man, the one closest to the devil, is, for Greene, precisely the one who is in need of God. The devilish man, the failure, the seeming antihero is somehow unconsciously, approaching God; for in failure not success, we realize the depth of our sins and recognize our faults.

Greene has staked everything on his demonic heroes, who, by turning all accepted values upside down, come to understand God through the knowledge of the devil. They operate in a 'decay saturated' corrupt world and in their attempts to transcend themselves through knowledge of the God and the devil they try to regain a sense of betrayal in a corrupt universe. However, Greene's characters frequently cannot rise to the vision he has of their potential greatness. Greene's use of the 'demonical hero' raises several questions for the readers, because the characters attain salvation through

God's almost arbitrary use of grace. Karl points out a few questions: what is the use of legal boundaries placed upon man if they are merely temporary and finally meaningless, if God may choose to ignore them in his judgment? If forgiveness, as Greene indicates, is forthcoming according to God's wishes, which no one can understand, what is to prevent chaos of those who wait for God's judgment and flout Man's law? These and many similar questions are hinted at and curiously left unanswered. By indicating that God can save whereas man's devices fail, is Greene not claiming the inside knowledge of God that he states is impossible to understand? Is there not implicit an underlying arrogance in his message, a lack of humility in his claim that the Catholic is closer to the devil and so through him, to God?

In Scobie one sees the human capacity for love, pity and despair. He overreaches himself, but all in his attempts to arrange for other's happiness. He is conscious of the fact "that he had set himself an impossible task" (p. 211), a task in which he is destined to fail. He does not realize that his loyalties to Louise and to Helen are exacted by pity and has brought despair even before his suicide. Scobie's plans are doomed from the beginning since his pity is blind to consequences. It is a bitter joke that when he is at pains to keep his affair with Helen a secret, Louise should know about it, rejoin him from South Africa and hurry him off to Mass with her, thus starting his blasphemous communion and his suicide plans.

The partly natural and partly self-imposed isolation affects him negatively. He leads a mechanical life sustained by habits. But he does not see these flawless habits as virtue. "He didn't drink, he didn't fornicate, he didn't even lie, but he never regarded this absence of sin as a virtue" (p. 115). Sustained by a practice of habit, pity, and responsibility, his life seems to have been drifting purposelessly. In committing adultery, he has flouted the Church's law, he faces the unsolvable dilemma of being unable to choose over either the sacrilege of the church or the pain he will cause either Helen or Louise by desertion. When he prays to God for a miracle, it is an anguished cry of helplessness and loneliness trying to choose between human love and the faith that is the base of a codified religion. Alienated from religion, he cannot love a distant God at the expense of his creatures. He further develops a terrible guilt for desecrating God and takes God on human terms making God a partner in crime. Bogged down by doubt he takes a deterministic and pessimistic view of life further to the point of implicating Christ in His own betrayal and suggesting that He too committed suicide, for if God exists then he must be all-powerful, and man's sins must be an integral part of his plan. He puts a radically unorthodox implication of religion, implicating Christ in His own murder:

> God had sometimes broken His own laws and was it less possible for him to put a hand of forgiveness into the suicidal darkness than to have woken himself in the tomb, behind the stone? Christ had not been murdered: you couldn't murder God. Christ had killed himself and hung himself on the Cross as surely as Pemberton from the picture rail. (p. 182)

Scobie has been labeled a failure and an erring individual; his pity is questioned as destructive, as it causes more harm than good. Stratford[125] observes that the destructive power of pity is turned inward and the result is suicide. Had he been less good, a bit less pitiful, he would not have suffered. Indifferent to success, he might be even termed as ascetic, but his asceticism is corrupted by pity and by the inevitable interaction between man and woman. The dreary repetitions of his sins and those of others make him feel betrayed at all points and he sees death as the only release.

Greene's characters are insignificant people with little authority, forced to make a choice and to suffer the pangs of indecision and conscience. His Catholicism encourages him to see action as a series of moral dilemmas. Uncertainty seems to be the driving force for Greene providing him with a sense of real pleasure under which his characters are obliged to act. The narrow boundary between loyalty and betrayal is the paradox one carries within oneself. Scobie is broken by the impossibility of proving his love for God, because God's love has set standards out of his grasp as an ordinary man. Scobie is a neutral person; passionless, he has elevated pity to the position of a passion. Louise cannot accept the fact that he has failed to secure the coveted post, but Scobie loves failure and loves God because he rationalizes that He too is a failure. But this is a heretical presupposition that allows a man to think that God can ever be a failure. This conjecture is directly opposed to the view that a traditional hero might hold. For a traditional hero, however difficult the task, however complicated the moral dilemma, his belief in God and salvation always remains unyielding.

Peace is described in the novel in terms of "the great glowing shoulder of the moon heaving across his window like an ice berg. Arctic and destructive in the moment before the world was struck" (p. 61). Kurishmmootil[126] infers from this that it is an objective correlative to Scobie's compulsion to escape. Conventional society is too weird and complex for him. He is only at home in a world that has recognized its essential seediness and accepts it. Peace for him is a disavowal of certain of his association and his memories, entailing no emotion, and consequently he dreads occasions when other's expectations might make demands upon his compassion. But involvement is a part of his personality and he is unable to stand merely as an unlooker. "An obsessive pity and an urge to withdraw are complementary strains in his character."[127]

Scobie's disengagement from life is so nearly complete that he expects nothing from it. His wife, pathetic and ugly, is a responsibility to be born with patience. For his utter disregard for Louise, Scobie yet has an exaggerated sense of responsibility on her account. He blames himself for having failed her in her life. He is aware that no one can ever hope to understand another completely, and that no one can ever guarantee other's happiness yet her misery has a massive impact on him.

Kurishmmootil argues that if Scobie is viewed analytically, his confusion may be traced to a vaguely diagnosed nihilism. He persists in viewing life through the coloured filter of his fifty years of experience; at the root of his neurosis there is a deranged perspective. His life is blighted by the shadow of his own cynicism. The result is a misapprehension of realities and objective situations, and his response, in consequence, is miserably inadequate.

Pity "the terrible promiscuous passion" is an irresistible passion for Scobie. "It isn't beauty that we love", he says, "its failure, failure to stay young for ever, the failure of the nerves, the failure of the body".

> Pity smoldered like decay in his heart. He would never rid himself if it. He knows from experience how passion died away and how love went, but pity always stayed. The conditions of life nurtured it. (p. 205)

The degeneration of the hero is common to the whole of modern fiction. One can say about Scobie, as he says about Arthur Bishop, that he is a "soppy hero" (p. 129). Greene speaks of each new novel as "a different kind of failure"; to describe the modern man in all his misery as Greene does, is to reveal the chaos left in this world by the absence of God.

Greene holds the view that evil prevails in this world without God and hope. His view, Augustinian and similar to Beckett's, is unable to accommodate the idea of a benevolent God with the misery of the world. Going by Scobie's nature and his goodness, DeVitis finds, in his character, traces of Pelagianism. This approach insists that man is naturally good, "but is perverted by external forces, by society as such if he is an anarchist, by the capitalist system if he is a Marxist, or by the family".[128] This is acceptable because though Scobie is the farthest thing from an anarchist, one can easily see how he is perverted by the pity that he first feels for Louise and then for Helen Rolt.

Scobie is isolated from society and its values, from self and from God. His crisis in faith leads to the development of a sense of futility and purposelessness. An atmosphere of uncertainty and void in his life brings out the absurdity of existence. Greene brings out a world of destruction, decay, chaos and corruption, strongly characterized by an element of indifference. For Greene, isolation is a part of human nature that is aggravated by the vicious atmosphere and also by the destructive economic and political problems of the 20th century. Indifference and neutrality characterizes the system into which man is born. As a form of rebellion and also to relieve the sense of danger, man takes recourse to a life of violence and crime. Often trying to evade this indifference the character works out escape routes but eventually this evasion exposes them to the fact of isolation. The harder they try to work out the escape routes, the more their inner split widens frightening them. The escape routes involve the protagonists with dangerous acts and violence and generate, in turn, crime, violence, seediness, hatred and betrayal. The character in his behaviour reflects the inner boredom, frustration and anxiety of the disinherited self. In the face of acute dilemma, he has to make a crucial decision, and Greene does not allow his protagonists to escape happily.

Greene recurrently portrays the lonely man, crushed by various social, religious, and political institutions as his protagonists. In a violent and chaotic world, man feels relegated and this is experienced more strongly in the Third World countries, where Scobie is, with its wide range of exploitation. Scobie's heart is an arena of endless moral crisis giving rise to a strange dualism that grows out of a clash between the given violent surroundings and the desire for security. This crisis fundamentally consists of a split in human self caused by the opposition of moral failure and moral redemption, guilt and repression, isolation and a desire for involvement and companionship.

Scobie is confronted with the presence of two powerful forces. The first is the incomprehensible moral world; the other is the organized religion that proclaims itself to be the absolute judge of human actions and conduct. Scobie finds the orthodox religion too narrow in its view of life, and pledges his loyalty to moral truth. His commitment to the moral universe alienates him from the orthodox religion, bringing about a slow corrosion in his material condition. He challenges the standard of judgment of the organized religion but beneath this opposition, there is a complicated struggle between his traditional complacent self and the emerging awakened one. Scobie realizes that the real evil lies within him in the form of corrupting egoism and self-love, thus resulting in over whelming doubts, despair, and hopelessness.

The surprising element of pride in his pity makes him feel that it is up to him to relieve others' suffering. He keeps the pretence of love with Louise only because he presumes that kindness is worth a thousand truths. Furthermore, the open-endedness of the novel causes the uncertainty of his fate and the ensuing ambivalence. He constantly weakens himself by denuding his personality by love and pity. An imperfect character, he lacks determination and decisiveness so that his love is like a pendulum oscillating between pity and responsibility.

Among the religious, the saying goes that a Christian is a stranger in this world. Greene's antiheroes exist close enough to international trouble spots to see every horrific detail—as Greene, a sometime intelligence agent, did. But his characters are helpless to act on what they see. They are adulterers, caught by bonds of love. Addicted to sin, pity, or terror, they are impotent sinners, stuck in hellish situations as punishment. Greene brings characters into the world—complex, inscrutable and made unhappy by their lack of identity with the good and totally disenchanted with life thriving on and relishing his loneliness.

Scobie exhibits the savage incisiveness of a man who went to confession often, listing every sin. Scobie is not self-sufficient; he is plain ordinary, an exile from happiness, a failure and a tormented lonely figure. He has a sense of insufficiency, a terror of life, and a haunting preoccupation with death. The depth of his fall gives a measure of the vocation that has been betrayed. He is the fallen hero, and his misery results because he is unable, in this modern world, to cope with the chaos brought about by the absence of God. Scobie personifies the opposition between Greene's ironic antihero and the characters who aspire to certainty, justice, and social order. Scobie's lack of self-understanding and the brutal judgment that he passes on himself is meant to show the readers the distinction between pity and love and how pity spoils the capacity to love in Scobie. It shows how 'Scobie the

Just' yields to the temptation of melodrama, when, motivated by pity, not charity, he relies on his own justice and not on God's mercy.

To see the character in the correct perspective, one has to understand the exact nature of Scobie's religion. Let us consider his reaction when he is urged by his wife to go to Communion. Being in a "state of sin" he cannot go for Communion until he confesses and also undertakes to stop his illicit relationship with Helen. Scobie reacts to his wife's suggestion by driving frantically and unsteadily "down the road, his eyes blurred with nausea" praying "O God, the decisions you force on people, suddenly with no time to consider" (p. 256). Kurishmmootil contends that even if he is suffering from a real dilemma, his reaction is rather extreme. Helen's claims for him are more pressing than God's, but he cannot dismiss the thought that God may suffer even more because he is infinitely more vulnerable; it is impossible to protect all three at once. That to protect the women, he must desecrate God is the core of Scobie's tragic dilemma, and it is convincing if we accept his religious neurosis. The twin factors of his religious neurosis and the rigid attitude of religion impinge on him. This bargaining and haggling with God over 'other's happiness' is remarkable in one whose faith assures him that everything is in God's hands. He feels that he has been condemned to the role of an executioner. There is no end to this strange affliction until he is dead.

Although the novel's rhetoric supports Scobie's reading of his situation, nevertheless it does not excuse his indulgent pity. One could argue that if Scobie were right in that life is meaningless, then surely no one would be worth saving too. He would have known that his efforts would have been in vain.

It has been noticed, how "blind and prone to sentimentality" Scobie is. He is self-deceived in his very self-knowledge, and lacking in real moral courage. Kurishmmootil,[129] quotes F.N. Lees' remark that "curiously egoistic he takes no cognizance of fullness of other's existence". This probably is a correct estimation of Scobie's character. He also uses Auden's[130] description of pity as "a corrupt parody of love and compassion which is so insidious and deadly for sensitive creatures". He further explains it by stating "to feel compassion for someone is to make oneself their equal, to pity them is to regard oneself as their superior".

In fact, Greene offers Scobie's emotion as a corruption. The author claims that he meant it as a species of pride, since pity and pride are closely related. Scobie errs in not recognizing his limitations. Pity may be proper for the Gods but human beings do not have the means to satisfy it, and in pitying others, human beings tend to place themselves in the position of Gods. Compassion is a noble virtue, but to pity is never truly human.

His decision to send Louise on a holiday relieves him, cushioned on the knowledge of his awful sacrifice. Prone to disaster, Helen's affirmation of faith in him "I have a feeling that you'd never let me down", becomes a command "he would have to obey however difficult". With the beginning of the adultery, he is in the middle of a significant crisis, and his response to Helen's bitterness and frustration leads to heresy on his part, an act which even the secular church would condone.

It needs to be observed that Scobie's pity has implications of the most abject self-denial. Attempting to comfort his wife, he uses for himself a nickname that he detests but given Scobie's character, it is acceptable. It is the diverse expression of the same inner urge: compulsive, powerful and self-destructive.

The signing of the letter commits him inexorably to Helen as he is already to his wife by the bond of marriage. The letter to Helen also implies a conscious decision to sustain the complexity and the evasions to the very end. The implications of the responsibilities that he has accepted strike him with a startling finality. He resents all the exacting demands that are made on his compassion.

> Why me, he thought, why do they need me, a dull middle-aged police officer who has failed for promotion? I have nothing to give them that they can't get

> elsewhere.... It sometimes seemed to him that all he could share with them was his despair. (p. 219)

The character of Scobie is postmodernist as it poses several questions. Greene is questioning established institutions of religion and marriage and its validity and sanctity. In the novel, traits of modernism overlap with that of postmodernism. Toying with the idea of uncertainty and indeterminacy of meaning, Greene seems to ask the important question: does a person have an equal right to end his life, just as he has a right to live it? But again these are left to the interpretation of the readers. Greene poses at the heart of the text the unanswerable question, 'why does God keep a suffering child alive for forty days and nights in an open boat and then allow him to die?' Orthodoxy is questioned at every step in Greene. He continually casts doubt on the Church's authority in eschatological and moral matters.[131] He creates situations in his fiction, which test the teaching of the Church. When Scobie kills himself he is committing the sin of despair, the only sin, according to the Church, which God refuses to forgive. Greene questions the concept of divine punishment as well as the role of the Church as a mediator between man and God. In particular, Greene questions textbook moral theology which in Unamuno's words has turned religion "into a kind of police-system".[132] Greene goes on to defy this rigid authority. His rcmark is that the storyteller's task is "to act as the devil's advocate, to elicit sympathy and a measure of understanding for those who lie outside the boundaries of state approval".[133] In refusing to judge Scobie on moral grounds by not stating whether he is saved or damned, Greene leaves the end of the novel, open ended and indeterminate.

In his obsession with his point of view, forcing his pity on others, Scobie comes close to being a solipsist. "Inexorably another's point of view rose on the path like a murdered innocent" (p. 181). Religion fails to provide him with refuge and he confesses to feeling "empty" (p. 153). No doubt he is man of religion but unlike believers such as Moses, he does not feel close to the one he loves so much.

Pity takes him to play-acting. His forced attempts at cheerfulness elicit only grimace and sympathy from the readers. "The strained good humour...a scream from a crevasse" (p. 208). Acting to be in pain is very difficult for him. In his dreams he sees himself as his hero Allan Quatermain, but reality soon impinges on him, the identification ceases and contradiction begins, he is alone, without any company. Prayer too becomes a pretension, "An immeasurable distance separated him from these people who knelt and prayed and would presently receive God in peace" (p. 223). He recognizes that he is not a heroic character "Human beings couldn't be heroic all the times: those who surrendered everything—for love or for God—must be allowed sometimes in thought to take back their surrender" (p. 231). The voice within telling him to stop play-acting reveals that he is the one who needs help and pity. Louise perhaps gives the truest opinion about Scobie. He really did "make a mess of things" (p. 271). Scobie despairs of life and, oppressed by guilt and failure, decides to end his miserable existence. In the Church, he hears the voice of Christ speaking to him:

> You say you love me, says Christ to Scobie, and yet you'll do this to me.... I made you with love. I wept your tears. I've saved you from more than you'll ever know. I planted this longing for peace within you...so that one day I could satisfy your longing and watch your happiness. And now you are pushing me away.

His unwilling betrayal into love is made possible by the way in which the totally convincing detail of the fate Greene creates for him taps the deepest levels of his being. That Scobie loves against, as well as with, the grain is revealed by his profound desire for peace and freedom, which in his case takes the form of a special kind of loneliness.

DeVitis[134] quotes from the essay "Felix Culpa", wherein Evelyn Waugh says of Scobie: "we are told that he is actuated throughout by the love of God. A love, it is true, that falls short of trust, but a love, we must suppose, which sacrifices his sins. That is the heart of the matter. Is such a sacrifice feasible..." (p. 190). Waugh insists that such an attitude would mean that one has to be as wicked as Pinkie Brown before he runs into the danger of being damned, and from thereon saved.

Greene understood from Marjorie Bowen's *The Viper of Milan* that human nature was black and gray. "I looked around and saw it so."[135] Greene also saw that it was possible to extract both adventure and romance from the unheroic, the disloyal, the weak and the failed, the post-Victorian. He was also drawn to the Jacobean dramatists because they supplied violence and excitement together with a complex style reposed on a metaphysical foundation. Books which 'really influenced' him were "cloak and dagger" novels, novels of adventure and melodrama. It is the Jacobean influence that makes *The Heart of the Matter*, a melodrama and Henry Scobie an antihero rather than a tragic figure. Paradoxically for Greene, the big terms—the smug, the successful, the invulnerable—expressing their cold virtues were bad, whereas the big terms expressing the warm emotions—revenge, jealousy—passions of a fallible post-Victorian anti-hero were good. Emotional contradictions offered him the grand cosmic backdrop he wanted, the religious sense which would supply ulterior significance and importance to the obscure lives of futility and defeat that he insisted on for his post-Victorian characters.[136]

Discussing the effect of the book, Greene writes: "Goodness has found a perfect incarnation in a human body and never will again, but evil can always find a home there".[137] If Satan can always find a home in the world but God only once, it is no wonder that Scobie is damned. Greene often chooses to portray the weak, the failure; indeed it is perhaps through their very weakness and sense of failure they have a special love for God which makes them the 'heroes' of Greene's books.[138]

Crises and confusion has shaped Greene's sensibility and given him a framework; and perhaps it was the note of "moral desperation" struck in the days of anxiety which has continued to haunt him ever since. But the tone grows mellower, until in the end there is nothing shrill but there is a profound acceptance of life, a tolerance even of those maladies which are not overcome. *The Heart of the Matter* "is the story of every man and more particularly of his own prototype: of the doubts and uncertainties, of the struggles that go unendingly in every human heart".[139]

Greene also exemplifies the phrase *Corropto optimi est Pessima*, very much like the other writers in this study, who continue to prefer the prodigal, the social outcast, and the abnormal character. The phrase *Corropto optimi est Pessima* (The corruption of the best is usually the worst) can be said to be true for Scobie as he is essentially a good man who is led to commit the worst of sins by corruption of his sentiment. These are sins not only in the dogmatic sense of the Church but also in the secular sense as they—adultery, impure communion and suicide—insults the One we deem supreme. Suicide is not only the confirmation of meaninglessness of life and its ensuing despair, but it is flinging God's greatest gift, life, at His Face and denying its importance.

Peguy's remained an important influence—"challenging God in the cause of the dammed". Scobie dies saying: "Dear God, I love...." The rest is silence. Greene was perpetually concerned with the problem of grace, with the shape of God's mercy, and saw Catholicism not as a creed for the triumphant, but rather for the desperate. O'Prey concludes that Greene's conversion was based on an emotional response to Catholicism. The fact that the British were traditionally outsiders of this Church, as well as victims of persecutions may also have had an emotional appeal for him. Thus, Catholicism is an important factor while considering any Greene novel, as it is the frame of reference by which both the characters and their author interpret events.

Graham Greene did not experiment with language, subvert traditional narrative, or choose exotic subjects. For Greene, the artist is in an intermediary role, fulfilling the dual function as a creator, but at the same time also as creature. He wishes to extend a God like compassion over his fictional world but not knowing perfect liberty, he becomes aware of the limitations of his own charity. Greene's seedy, sometimes pathetic characters are often tenuous survivors in a hostile world. What was it that led him to write of those deeply divided creatures that never seem to be rescued except on the wrong side of the grave? The artist becomes conscious of the grimace of his own imperfect image reflected in the creatures he has made, but asserts that he has a right to represent the point of view of the white as well as the black. O'Prey[140] points out that in *The Other Man* (1981), that Greene likens the novelist to a double agent, in a way he "condemns and sustains his characters by turns". Greene insists on being called a writer who happens to be a Catholic rather than a Catholic novelist. He writes as a moralist, as a realist, concerned with the moral complexity and ambiguity at the center of life as well as with the actual experience of life. He believes that he must be free to write as he wishes that he must give doubt, and even denial, self-expression.[141]

Greene's is a bleak vision, as if the only choice is between ignorant, damaging innocence and complicitous but self-aware corruption. Scobie is Catholic who lets down the side and obediently accepts his place in Hell. Greene sees God as the temptation some men finally succumb to. The debate he carries on is the oldest in the world—that between nature and grace. It is the debate of man placed between two worlds: an inaccessible heaven and an earth heavy and rich with the life it bears.

For Scobie, it is, ironically, the best quality in him that leads to his downfall. His wife plays his sense of guilt to her advantage, and bullies him as a failure. To him, Helen is every man and woman, the very type of human spirit mocked by a cruel fate. Pity, Scobie's tragic emotion, drives him out compulsively and causes him to start events which are beyond his control. He is incapable of coping with the situation that ensues. Sierra Leone definitely is no world for the innocent; ideals cannot survive here, yet Scobie is deeply attached to this place. This brings out his active liking for the ugly. Scobie, the contemporary man, reared on the commercial truths of duplicity and evasion knows only emptiness and anxiety. The conflict between his love and his faith, his sin and his inability to expiate it proves too much for Scobie. With Louise's return and her insistence to go to the Holy Communion, Scobie faces defeat. The only escape from mortal sin, as Scobie sees it is suicide. He undergoes the conflict of the soul between an illicit love and a religion that admits no compromise with the world of the flesh.

The ambivalence between what is shown and what the rhetoric urges on the reader has occasioned much confusion. Greene has continually reminded critics that characters do not necessarily express a writer's personal opinion. He states that a novelist's task is strictly confined to creating characters and they must live and seem plausible; but their beliefs and motivations are entirely their own affair and the author is not accountable to them.[142]

Occupying a transitory position between modernism and postmodernism, Greene adds little to the development of the novel as an art form. What distinguishes him from his contemporary society is his Catholic concern with sin and damnation. The theological conflicts of flesh and spirit take on an exciting unexpectedness in the framework of colonial administrators and the gang race. Catholicism allows him full scope to create interesting inner conflicts, to explore the psychological implications of a loss of faith, and to prove the moral conscience on many issues that wouldn't rise in an agonistic world. Catholicism often seems to be an effective device for producing dramatic tension and increasing complexity than a faith profoundly held. Greene's finest characters are the ones who are driven to self-destruction. It is significant that in the end, Greene refuses to judge Scobie and leaves his end ambiguous. Readers are left to deduce their own interpretation, which is further confused by Father Rank's final statement.

The most dangerous crux of the book lies in its projecting on Scobie, a painful sense of separation from other people which is disguised by his steadily maintained life of pitying service. It is faith that is lacking in Scobie and this lack qualifies all his experience. Because he cannot think of his disordered world as one which is actually watched over by a governing power, Scobie dare not place his trust in a supreme benevolent Force. Scobie is perhaps not anybody's idea of a saint. He admits his helplessness and his state of sinfulness, and acknowledges his communality with a fallen race. He is thus able to appreciate the urgent need for the redemptive act. In his deeper perception, he is similar to Pinkie and the Whiskey priest, sharing with them the extra dimension of understanding.[143] He is a post war character challenging a deaf God to help him out of the terrible moral quagmire into which he has sunk. He cannot face the world where right and wrong are far from clear. His sense of isolation and loneliness is accentuated by a strong feeling of remorse of being alienated from the very source of his existence—God.

Scobie is an antihero but is not, as is proved, a man committing evil for the sake of it. Rather, it springs from his compulsive desire to help others. His pity is full of pride but he remains unaware of it. As in a paradox, he rejects God as well as seeks Him. His moral weakness, his indecisiveness, his compulsions and his addiction to sin define him as an antihero. But as a wise fool, he may be the one that Greene alludes to in the novel, "the saint whose name nobody knew".

NOTES

1. Fredrick R. Karl, *A Readers Guide to the Contemporary English Novel*, Octagon Books, 1975, Rev ed., N.Y., p. 6.
2. John Pilling, "The Cultural and Intellectual Background to Samuel Beckett", *Samuel Beckett*, Routledge and Kegan Paul, London, 1976, p. 119.
3. *Ibid.*, p. 115.
4. David. H. Helsa, *The Shape of Chaos: An Interpretation of the Art of Samuel Beckett*, University of Minnesota Press, 1971, p. 8.
5. Brian Finney, "Samuel Beckett", *Encyclopedia of the Novel*, I, ed., Paul Schillinger, Fitzroy Dearborn Publishers, 1998, pp. 94-95.
6. *Ibid.*
7. Gabriel Josipovici, *The New Pelican Guide to English Literature*, ed. Boris Ford, 8, Penguin, 1983, G.B., p. 160.
8. *Ibid.*
9. Samuel Beckett and George Duthiut, "Three Dialogues", (20th Century Views), *Samuel Beckett, A Collection of Critical Essays*, ed. Martin Esslin, Prentice Hall of India, 1980, p. 21.
10. Gabriel Josipovici, *op. cit.*, p. 155.
11. J.A. Cuddon, *The Dictionary of Literary Terms and Literary Theory*, 4th ed., Maya Blackwell, G.B., 1976, 1998, pp. 42-43.

12. Ihab Hassan, *Radical Innocence*, Princeton University Press, Princeton, N.Y., 1961.
13. Ihab Hassan, *The Dismemberment of Orpheus*, Oxford University Press, 1971, p. 217.
14. Germaine Bree, "The Strange World of Beckett's "Grand Articules," trans. Margret Guiton, *Samuel Beckett Now: Critical Approaches to his Poetry, Novels and Plays*, Chicago, ed. Melvin J. Friedman, University of Chicago, 1975, p. 85.
15. Ruby Cohn, *Back to Beckett*, Princeton Univ. Press, 1973, N.Y., p. 83.
16. Karl, *op. cit.*, p. 22.
17. Eric P. Levy, *Beckett and the Voice of Species*, 1980, Gill and Macmillan, p. 64.
18. John Fletcher, "Interpreting Molloy", in Melvin J. Friedman ed., *op. cit.*, p. 161.
19. Karl, *op. cit.*, p. 20.
20. Vico, John Pilling, *op. cit.*, p. 115.
21. Karl, *op. cit.*, p. 26.
22. *Ibid.*, p. 6.
23. David Hayman, "Molloy or the Quest for Meaninglessness: A Global Interpretation", in Melvin J. Friedman ed., p. 129.
24. Levy, *op. cit.*, p. 64.
25. Joseph Campbell, *The Hero with a Thousand Faces*, 1949, World Publishing Company, Meridian Books.
26. Levy, *op. cit.*, p. 67.
27. Pilling, *op. cit.*, p. 121.
28. Northrop Frye, "The Nightmare Life in Death", *20th Century Interpretations of Molloy, Malone Dies and the Unnamable*, ed. J.D. Hara, Prentice Hall, 1970, p. 30.
29. Levy, *op. cit.*, p. 68.
30. Raymond Federman, "Beckettian Paradox; Who is telling the Truth?" in Melvin J. Friedman, ed., p. 109.
31. Paul Davis, "Three Novels and Four Nouvelles: Giving up the Ghost be Born at Last", *The Cambridge Companion to Beckett*, ed. John Pilling, Cambridge Univ. Press, G.B., 1994, p. 45.
32. Hannah C. Copeland, *Art and the Artist in the Novels of Samuel Beckett*, Mouton and Company, Netherlands, 1975, p. 107.
33. Ruby Cohn, *The Comic Gamut*, p. 165, in Copeland, 107.
34. Paul Davis, *op. cit.*, p. 58.
35. *Ibid.*, p. 52.
36. G.C. Barnard, *Samuel Beckett, A New Approach: A Study of Novels and Plays*, 1970, London, J.M. Dent and Sons, p. 5.

37. Barnard, *op. cit.*, pp. 41-42.
38. Hugh Kenner, "The Cartesian Centaur", in Martin Esslin ed. (*20th Century Views*), *Samuel Beckett*, pp. 52-61.
39. Karl, *op. cit.*, p. 33.
40. Davis, *op. cit.*, p. 46.
41. Frye, *op. cit.*, p. 27.
42. Cohn, *The Comic Gamut*, p. 295, in Copeland, p. 77.
43. Frye, "The Nightmare Life in death, in J.D. O' Hara, *op. cit.*, p. 30.
44. Ruby Cohn, *Back to Beckett*, Princeton University Press, N.Y., 1973, p. 82.
45. Ruby Cohn, "Philosophical Fragments in the Works of Samuel Beckett", (*20th Century Views*), *Samuel Beckett: A Collection of Critical Essays*, ed. Martin Esslin, 1980, p. 176.
46. Pilling, *op. cit.*, p. 119.
47. Richard N. Coe, *God and Samuel Beckett*, in O' Hara ed. p. 102.
48. David. H. Helsa, *op. cit.*, p. 100.
49. Maurice Valency, "Beckett", *The End of the World: An Introduction to Contemporary Drama*, OUP, NY, 1980, p. 388.
50. Frye, *op. cit.*, p. 31.
51. Book Review of J.D. O'Hara, ed. *20th Century Interpretations*, by Maratha O'Nan, State University College, of NY at Brockport, Reviews, Recent Books, *MFS*, 316-19, Summer, 1971, 17, 2, pp. 264-68.
52. J.D. Hara, *op. cit.*, p. 22.
53. Nietzsche, *The Birth of Tragedy*, 121, in Copeland, *op. cit.*, p. 40.
54. Edith Kern, "Dionysian Poet", p. 35, in Copeland, *op. cit.*, p. 40.
55. Debra A. Castillo, "Beckett's Metaphorical Towns", *MFS*, Vol. 28, No. 2, Summer, 1982, pp. 195-99.
56. John Fletcher, *The Novels of Samuel Beckett*, Windus and Chatto, London, p. 128.
57. Ihab Hassan, *The Dismemberment of Orpheus*, p. 221.
58. *Ibid.*, p. 233.
59. Willie Sypher, *Loss of the Self*, p. 147, in Copeland, *op. cit.*, p. 87.
60. Copeland, *op. cit.*, p. 87.
61. Jean Jacques Mayous, "Samuel Beckett and Universal Parody", in Martin Esslin ed., p. 82.
62. Edith Kern, "Moran-Molloy: The Hero as Author," in J.D. O'Hara, *op. cit.*, p. 35.
63. Dieter Wellershoff, "Failure of an Attempt at De-Mythologization", in Martin Esslin (ed.).

64. Northrop Frye in David Hayman, "Molloy or the Quest for Meaninglessness", *Samuel Beckett Now: Critical Approaches*, 1975, p. 140.
65. F.J. Hoffmann, *Samuel Beckett*, Southern Illinois Press, 1962, p. 63, Hassan, *op. cit.*, p. 218.
66. Raymond Federman, *op. cit.*, p. 111.
67. Cohn, *op. cit.*, p. 67.
68. Levy, *op. cit.*, p. 71.
69. Germaine Bree, trans. Margaret Guiton "The Strange World of Beckett's 'Grand Articules' *Samuel Beckett Now: Critical Approaches to His Poetry, Novels and Plays*, 1975, p. 83.
70. Beckett, Disjecta, p. 92; Davis, p. 58.
71. Wellershoff, pp. 92-93.
72. Chris Acherley, *Encyclopedia of the Novel. I*, ed. Paul Schillinger, Fitzroy Dearborn Publication, Chicago, 1998, pp. 520-21.
73. Paul O' Prey, *A Reader's Guide to Graham Greene*, Thomas and Hudson, 1988. O' Prey quotes Greene's *Why do I Write?*, 1948, p. 8.
74. A.A. DeVitis, *The Art of Graham Greene*, Twayne Publication, Boston, 1954, p. 9.
75. K.C. Joseph Kurishmmootil, *Graham Greene's The Heart of the Matter, A Study*, Frank Bros and Co., 1979.
76. Kenneth Alcott and Miriam Farris, *The Art of Graham Greene*, 1951, London, p. 214; in A.A. DeVitis, *op. cit.*, p. 19.
77. French text of the epigraph in the novel reads le pécheur est au coeur me^me de chretiente/ Nul n'est aussi competent quele pecheur en/ matiere de chritiente, Nul, si ce n'est le saint (Péguy). Quoted in English by B.P. Lamba, *Graham Greene: His Mind and Art*, 1987, Sterling Publishers, p. 28.
78. Graham Greene quoted by Roger Sharrock, "Saints, Sinners and Comedians," *The Novels of Graham Greene*, Burns and Oats, U.S.A., 1984, p. 152.
79. John Spurling, *Contemporary Writing: Graham Greene*, Methuen, London, 1983, pp. 37-41.
80. Greene, *Ways of Escape* (1980), quoted in Spurling, *op. cit.*, pp. 41-42.
81. O Prey, *op. cit.*, p. 9.
82. *Ibid.*, p. 85.
83. John W. Simon, "Salvation in the Novels", *Commonwealth*, April 9, 1952, p. 75, in B.P. Lamba, *Graham Greene: His Mind and Art*, Sterling Publications, Delhi, 1987, p. 92.
84. J.A. Cuddon, ed. *The Dictionary of Literary Terms and Literary Theory* 4th ed. Maya Blackwell, 1998, G.B., pp. 42-43.

85. Philip Stratford, *Faith and Fiction: Creative Process in Greene and Mauriac*, University of Norte Dame, 1967.
86. Anuradha Banerjee, *Graham Greene: Ways of Salvation*, Ganga Kaveri Publication, 1994, p. 70.
87. Albert Camus, "The Myth of Sisyphus" (1955), trans, Justine O'Brian. *Images of Man: Selected Readings in Arts and Ideas in Western Civilization*, ed. Sydney Thomas, Syracuse University, Holt, Rinehart and Winston Inc., p. 410.
88. Kurishmmootil, *op. cit.*, p. 36.
89. George Orwell, "The Sanctified Sinner", quoted in O' Prey, *op. cit.*, p. 86.
90. Jung, "Aion: Phenomenology of the Self", in *Portable Jung*, ed. Joseph Campbell, N.Y., Viking, 1972, pp. 136-62, Kurishmmootil, p. 44.
91. Judith Adamson, *Graham Greene: The Dangerous Edge: Where Art and Politics Meet*, 1990, Macmillan, London, p. 80.
92. *Ibid.*, p. 82.
93. *Ibid.*
94. Somerset Maugham, "The Lion's Skin", *Stories British and American*, ed. M.G. Narasimha Murthy, Orient Longman, Hyderabad, India, 1974.
95. B.P. Lamba, *op. cit.*, p. 46.
96. Grahame Smith, *The Achievement of Graham Greene*, Harvester Press, 1986, p. 101.
97. Adamson, *op. cit.*, p. 86.
98. Alan Sillitoe, *Saturday Night and Sunday Morning*, The New American Library, Inc., N.Y., Signet Books, 1958.
99. Samuel Beckett, *Molloy, Three Novels*, Grove Press, N.Y., 1955.
100. Ihab Hassan, *Radical Innocence*, Princeton University Press, N.J., 1961, p. 6.
101. Kurishmmootil, *op. cit.*, p. 14.
102. Northrop Frye, *Anatomy of Criticism*, Princeton University Press, 1971, p. 41.
103. Hassan, *Radical Innocence*, p. 28.
104. Judith Adamson's title of the book, *Graham Greene: The Dangerous Edge—Where Art and Politics Meet*, 1990.
105. Fredrick R. Karl, "Graham Greene's Demonical heroes", *A Reader's Guide to Contemporary English Novel*, Rev. ed., 1975, Octagon Books, N.Y., p. 92.
106. *Ibid.*, p. 91.
107. Graham Greene, *Journey Without Maps*, Penguin Books, England, 1936, p. 158.
108. Spurling, *op. cit.*, p. 21.

109. Austin Warren, *Perspectives on Fiction*, N.Y., OUP, 1968, p. 25, in Kurishmmootil, *op. cit.*, p. 16.
110. Greene, *The Ministry of Fear: An Entertainment*, Penguin Books, G.B., 1963, p. 74.
111. Roger Sharrock, *op. cit.*, p. 134.
112. Anuradha Banerjee, *op. cit.*, p. 87.
113. Ngugi wa Thiong'o, *A Grain of Wheat*, Heinemann, London, 1967.
114. Adamson, *op. cit.*, p. 85.
115. Sharrock, *op. cit.*, p. 138.
116. *Ibid.*, 142.
117. Francis Wyndham, *Graham Greene*, published for the B.C. and the National Book League, Longman, G.B., 1955, p. 18.
118. Martin. C. Darcy, "The Anatomy of the Hero", *Transformation Three*, London, pp. 16-19, Quoted in DeVitis, *op. cit.*, p. 91.
119. Karl, *op. cit.*, p. 85.
120. Karl, *Postscript*, 1960-70, *op. cit.*, pp. 335-38.
121. Sharrock, *op. cit.*, p. 146.
122. Adamson, *op. cit.*, p. 89.
123. Sharrock, *op. cit.*, p. 152.
124. Karl, *op. cit.*, p. 88.
125. Stratford, *op. cit.*, p. 235.
126. Kurishmmootil, *op. cit.*, p. 17.
127. *Ibid.*, p. 18.
128. Walter Allen, *The Novels of Graham Greene*, Penguin New Writing, 18, 1943, pp. 148-60; quoted by DeVitis, *op. cit.*, p. 191.
129. F.N. Lees, *Scrutiny*, 19, 1, 1952, p. 39; quoted by Kurishmmootil, *op. cit.*, p. 23.
130. Auden, "The Heresy of Our Lives", Renascence, Spring, 1949, pp. 23-24, quoted by Kurishmmootil, p. 32.
131. O' Prey, *op. cit.*, p. 9.
132. *Ibid.*, p. 83.
133. Graham Greene, *The Other Man*, 1963, p. 73, quoted in A.A. DeVitis, *op. cit.*, p. 10.
134. Evelyn Waugh, "Felix Culpa", Commonwealth, 48, 16 July, 1948, p. 324, quoted in DeVitis, *op. cit.*, p. 190.
135. Graham Greene, "The Lost Childhood", *Collected Essays*, Penguin Books, 1969, p. 17.
136. Spurling, *op. cit.*, p. 29.
137. Graham Greene, *Collected Essays*, *op. cit.*, p. 17.

138. Francis Wyndham, *op. cit.*, p. 5.
139. Kurishmmootil, *op. cit.*, xiv.
140. O' Prey, *op. cit.*, p. 7.
141. DeVitis, *op. cit.*, p. 84.
142. Gene D. Philips's interview of Graham Greene, on the Screen in the Catholic World, *CCIX*, Aug. 1969, pp. 218-21, quoted by Kurishmmootil, p. 48.

5
Conclusion

> A light supper, a good nights' sleep and a fine morning have sometimes made a hero of the same man, who, by indigestion, a restless night and a rainy morning would have proved a coward. Lord Chesterfield.
>
> (*Letters to His Son*, April 26th, 1748)

In the conclusion, an attempt has been made to answer the question relating to the topic *The Archetypal Antihero in Postmodern Fiction*. There will invariably be the question "why an antihero in postmodern fiction?" A study of contemporary fiction will reveal that the two trends of antiheroism and postmodernism have a parallel evolution. However, strains of both can be discerned in literature written as early as the 18th century. But it is in the 20th century with its problematic environment that they have emerged as parallel yet interrelated strains.

This is so because of various reasons, several of which are extraneous to literature specific. Especially in the 19th and the 20th centuries, literature has been strongly influenced by the socio-economic conditions, politics, the fast changing scientific developments, psychology, anthropology, but at the same time there has been a simultaneous loss in traditional values, belief in God, love and even the perfectible nature of human beings. Man, as a social animal, enmeshed in the vortex of these changes, has not been able to keep up with these changes or find satisfactory replacements for these losses. Man has always been the strongest subject for literature, but unfortunately, man in the 20th century is usually seen by artists as an ordinary creature, bogged down by the circumstances, a victim not only of determinism, but paradoxically also of his free will, drives and impulses.

Man is no longer the complete heroic self as represented by the Vitruvian man; rather, he is the fragmented self that one finds in Picasso—fragmented, and antiheroic. For Hassan,[1] it is not the picture of a man less human; it is just another idea of man. One is able to identify with those fragmented selves in the chaotic postmodern literature today because they suggest one's anxiety, alienation, frustration and despair. Man is a product of his upbringing and education resultant of the pressures, forces and influences within and without, to which he has been subjected throughout his life.

With such a subject, passionate but hollow, writers have slowly brought a change in the form and pattern of the novel to incorporate such unheroic characters as main protagonists. Epical forms depicting legends such as Ulysses, Aneas, and Beowulf have transformed slowly to mock epics where even when the pattern is epical, it is so ironical and incongruent that the result is grotesque. Writers have had to adopt stylistic changes in their writing in order to include their moral visions that they saw around them. This is irrevocable because the conventional method of writing is no longer able to include the chaos, Sparagmos, the loss of heroism, the increased consciousness, guilt and shame within its scope. This is one of the reasons of the rise of postmodernism in literature and as such forms the framework within which our antiheroes are studied.

Postmodernism usually speaks of the end of grand narratives of reason, progress and universal emancipation. We cannot establish our activities rationally because there are different, discontinuous and irregular rationalities, and also because any reason we can advance will always be shaped by some pre-rational content of power, belief or interest which can itself never be subjected to rational demonstration. Postmodernism is part of a general attack on Enlightenment truth claims and values, and displays a preoccupation with language as an inadequate vehicle for expressing any sort of reality.

Both postmodernism and antiheroism question the basic tenet of Enlightenment—that man is by nature heroic, reasonable, social and prone to goodness. The texts and characters studied here prove otherwise. The impact of WW I and WW II on writers who tried to interpret the unthinkable in their postwar writing was very deep. They nonetheless responded to a new world order, as it struggled with the question "what role does literature play as a means of understanding the traumatic postwar experience? Is language capable, in its present state, of coping with the trauma that has occurred?"

The proliferation of "Posts" in itself suggests that we live in a period where the multiplication of value system has produced a major crisis in legitimation. Lyotard[2] writes that the postmodern writer is in the position of a philosopher, his texts are not in principle governed by pre-established rules and they cannot be judged according to a determining judgment. Postmodernism either sees the world fragmenting or it sets out to discover modes, which will rupture and dissolve old and supposed verities and unities. The postmodern writer resorts to a number of devices—allusions, intertextuality, pastiche, parody, paradox, metafiction, self-interpretation, minimalism and cross-fertilization between cultures, art forms and disciplines to unveil to others the kind of world the writer beholds in his personal mirror. Postmodern art is apocalyptic, because it is revelatory; it is the apocalyptic, rather than the redemptive, which seems to be the characteristic mood of the postwar period.

Hassan[3] states that literary existentialism proposes a new definition of man; it probes his consciousness and becomes familiar with his terror and horror of life. In showing the terror and cowardice behind the veneer of courage, shame and primitivism under modernity, spiritual failure under worldly success, the novelists discussed here, have depicted the dilemma faced by modern man in their antiheroes. It can be observed that with the gradual diminishing of the capacities of the central characters, writers and their work have revealed doubts about the truth claims of literature. Some gave voice to these doubts by subverting the conventional novelistic forms whereas others push the modernist elements to its extreme boundaries.

Characters are verisimilar, conceptual constructs similar to human beings. Assembled by the authors according to their aesthetic or ideological goals they are realistic because they conform to the author's views of what is possible and probable in the actual world. Uri Margolin[4] writes that the classical hero is one with a clear set of goals, an individual capable of undertaking a series of actions against oppositions and adversity. For centuries, man has turned to God, love, and courage for strength to endure that what is otherwise unendurable. But these options do not seem to possibly exist in the chaotic postmodern times, and so man turns to a new way of dealing with the confusion. This option lacks the dignity, the heroism, the nobility of the other ways because it entails the acceptance of defeat and the loss of heroism, but it temporarily shields man from the void, within and outside him. However, this shield does not offer much protection and man is brought face to face with the stark void.

Beginning with the 19th century and increasingly through the 20th century, the main novelistic character is often an antihero, an individual whose role is primarily passive and whose situation is one of resigned defeat. This reversal of the classical hero lacks the capacity for action and is instead preoccupied with interminable paralysis, which is often accompanied by social isolation, a disillusioned view of life, a lack in the power of language to serve as the basis for interpersonal understanding. The history of the antihero is a record of his recoil, his self-degradation: it is the history of man's changing awareness of himself.

The schism in the protagonist's character seems to be increasing perpetually. Is modern man such a failure and does he really suffer from such extremes of recoil, alienation and nihilism that he has ceased to have qualities that can be deemed heroic? If so, why were they created? Novelists are clearly not neutral observers; they have their own values and prejudices which permeate their work. Whether inventing or interpreting, authors take an approach to their writing that is a reflection of the world of their day. They write in the spirit of their time, of its values, hopes and fears. Objective or subjective, the answer can be found when one studies the perception of the artist, the period in which he lived, the influences and pressures he was open to and then try to understand why he wrote what he wrote. The antihero has to be seen in relation to his creator.

The postmodern writer portrays human activity as largely futile and human nature as inherently given to self-deception and illusory belief. Twentieth century man is embroiled in a new cultural situation, an isolated being confronting existential pain and despair, drifting through life purposelessly. He neither accepts the old religious answers, nor the pseudo-scientific answers of the materialists; he is seeking a new specifically human answer.

The antihero illustrates the concept of *Corrupto Optimi est Pessima*—the corruption of the best is usually the worst. Given different situations, hypothetically, they might have reacted in altogether different ways. Unlike heroes, antiheroes are paradoxical in nature which is exemplified by the protagonists under study here. Heroism entails characteristics, clearly defined in every culture and society. However, antiheroism, like its co-ordinate, postmodernism, is complex, eliciting different responses from different situations, this response is antiheroic as they do not conform to the traditional heroic characteristics. Protagonists here are either interested in saving their own skins or in earning their pound of flesh or trying to escape from this world through suicide. Those who choose to ponder over the spiritual and metaphysical aspects of existence become mental derelicts like Molloy and Scobie. The world of the antiheroes is an exhausted postmodern world which is inhabited by spiritual paupers, bankrupt in the inner man.

Schizophrenic and paranoid, skeptical and solipsistic, selfish, sadistic and cowardly—these are the terms that describe the antiheroes, the unhappy consciousness. They have discovered that the dread and the existential reality are incommunicable, opening up the sensibilities to the possibilities of negative experience. All the six antiheroes discussed here are, in one way or the other, full of self delusion, hypocrisy, and moral laziness. Some treacherous self seekers like Mugo can also be called a false pilgrim because his action is in extreme opposition to his dream of a Moses-like leader.

The antihero reflects contemporary man's condition. Existing in a limbo, he is a figure that lies between the rebellious Prometheus and the stoic—victim Sisyphus. Satan also is the archetypal antihero. As a rebel-victim, he is probably the first existential antihero. He perceives himself as one denied of his rightful position. He too is covered in glory, but because of pride and his attempt to break away from God's scheme of things, God sees him as a mock hero.

In a way, Conrad's Kurtz in *Heart of Darkness* can be taken as the precursor of the modern "hero", the antihero, "diabolic in the concentration of the deviant will and his intellectual gaze, pursuing forbidden experience with the inverted dedication of a questing knight-at-arms, contemptuous of others and of himself, radical and unsatisfied, without outer conventions or inner core, the lonely alien in our midst".[5]

The antiheroes are rebel-victims, rebelling against the conditions they find themselves in. A rebellion is a protest against a prevailing state of things, aiming for a change. However, one needs to differentiate between a heroic and an antiheroic rebellion. Usually a heroic rebellion is one which brings positive changes. Here, the rebel is rarely a victim because he is able to transcend his adversity. Lucifer's rebellion against God can be taken as a supreme example of negative rebellion because it is against a positive order. The result is rarely the desired one, in most cases, the rebel is neither able to change himself nor his circumstances, rather he succumbs either to evil, buffoonery, grotesqueness, or to suicide.

As a rebel-victim, the antihero is at odds, both with the environment and with himself. Having the energy of opposites, his aggressions are either directed against himself (as a victim) or against the world (as a rebel). In either case, he remains a misfit, an outsider, victimized by existential crisis, committing implausible acts, and making choices that not only bring inexplicable suffering but also reveal their antiheroic natures. Hassan's view of the antihero as a rebel-victim is supported by the fact that the contemporary world presents a continued affront to man and thus his response as a rebel or a victim.

The antiheroes, Biswas, Mugo, Jack, Seaton, Scobie and Molloy are all rebels in their own ways. There are similarities in their rebellion, in their resistance to, and questioning of authority, and rejection of the accepted modes of behaviour and conventions. For Naipaul's Biswas, rebellion takes the form of buffoonery, with which he tries to extract himself from his frustrating and harrowing situation. Alan Sillitoe's Seaton protests against the spectacle of the irrational coupled with the unjust. Jack Merridew's is a negative rebellion because it thrives on chaos, negating all that is good and ordered around it. However, they are also a victimized lot. In their own ways, they represent Hassan's assembly of victims—the fool, the freak, the clown, the failure, the outsider and the rebel without a cause. The antihero, rebel-victim, finds his meaning in carrying his rebellion to the point of self-destruction.

There are several characteristics that go on to make an antihero, however, critics such as Chris Baldick and Ihab Hassan have several comments that are germane to our understanding of the antihero. The former asserts that there is a difference between a villain and an antihero.[6] Often characters like Merridew and Mugo may border on villainy, but to brand them as ordinary villains would be to stereotype them wrongly. Supporting this is Hassan's statement that the major difference between the hero and the antihero is one of action, not of passion.[7] Passion-wise, they are equal to the ones deemed heroes, but it is their actions and their reactions to experience, their failure at initiation, that makes them antiheroes. These experiences not only make the schizophrenic, often taking them to the verge of madness, it also leads them to resort to mindless violence, anarchy, evil, and metaphysical prying on the nature of God and their relation to them. In doing so, they reveal themselves to be cowardly, indecisive, bumbling failures, anarchists, buffoons, suffering from the failure of communication, hubris and hamartia. Hamartia in a character brings a shift in his nature from potential heroism to basic antiheroism. One can see how Scobie suffers because of pity and unconscious pride, Mugo from cowardice and indecisiveness, and Merridew from pride, and demonic anarchy inherent in his character.

Heroic characters reach a level of transcendence in a victory over adversity and limitations. Here, the characters studied rarely reveal nobility or heroism. However, the nature of the figure may receive different emphasis in varying cultures and periods. The power of myths weakened with the passage of time, and it became culturally imperative to create new figures representing the age. The postmodern, postindustrial age, while abandoning elements from the earlier period, embraced a new literary figure, a contemporary, less idealized figure. Heroism seems impossible at times, and it certainly seems to be so now. With the type of characters that we come across today, the antiheroic figure may be defiantly proclaimed as a dominant archetype.

The postwar, postmodern novel, worried over the loss of meaning and identity in a modernized society, explores the changing characters and moral standards. In short, it has sought, in many directions, for new characters and new forms.[8] The writers, responding to different situations, write in a world that is subtly different from that of the early modernists, a world, in which art is becoming something other than what it used to be.

As the relation of the hero to the world changes, so does the form of fiction. The fictional form has commensurably changed with the changing, real but unreliable human nature. The innocent hero is a vanishing breed. The alienation of the "hero" defines the shape of the novel. He, who once figured as an Initiate, ends as a rebel or as a victim.[9] This argument gains support from Edith Kern's[10] statement who says that "the hero changes in accordance to a changing society". With time, the proportions of the hero are further shrunken. Societies in ferment produce only antiheroes; with no possibilities of heroic individualism the difficulties of creating an enduring modern hero are obviously great. The unheroic hero can make choices, but has no stirring message with which to lead the people out of the wilderness. He has only a limited, comically qualified control in the midst of the 20th century chaos. Gindin asserts that man's situation and his problems, in addition to his own fallibility, make heroic action unlikely.[11]

For the antiheroes, the world is a sygyzy, for every position there is an opposition, it is characterized by an interplay of opposites—body and mind, self and other, speech and silence, hope and despair, life and death. The antiheroes today are dark figures poised on the brink of the abyss, symbolic of man suffering spiritual and mental agonies. Often the main protagonists are in too great agony or humiliation to gain the privilege of a heroic pose. Heroism, which for Milton consisted of obedience, fidelity and perseverance is absent in the ironic heroes and thus the kind of heroic dignity gained by King Lear in his suffering humanity is denied these antiheroes.

The antihero recoils from nature, reason, language, and society. He strips, sheds, leaving nothing in the shadow of illusion; and comes to the terrible discovery that everything, including himself is *de trop*; hence the total freedom of man and his measureless responsibility. Contradictions in human minds are reflected in the situation of the protagonist who cut across the lines of good and evil; they are neither pure villains nor perfect heroes. The object of our sympathy and the object of our revulsion are often the same person. Lacking full knowledge, he is often a tragic figure in the classic sense. And because his life is so rarely devoid of genuine pain, he is rarely a comic figure of harmless compromise. Neither fully comic, nor completely tragic, the antihero combines in himself elements of the Greek Alazon, imposter, compulsive rebel, or outsider, the eiron, the humble self-deprecating man and the pharmakos, scapegoat and random victim. He is surrounded by confusion that neither resolves itself happily in the end, nor is he able to attain tragic dignity. He is too much of a rebel to be a comic character, too much of a victim to be considered tragic. No longer faced with divinely ordered universe in which he may achieve salvation/damnation through his virtuous adherence to, or sinful rebellion against God's plan he is an existential individualist who must discover his own morality. But can the contemporary protagonist preserve integrity in the face of such confusion? In Ihab Hassan's view, it is this modern predicament, which in forcing the individual to recoil is turning the traditional hero into his descendent—the modern antihero.

Courage ironically becomes the prime virtue because it is the virtue of self-sufficiency conferring small dignity on meaninglessness. The antihero's courage is not the heroic virtue endorsed by Aristotle; rather it is the courage of a simple being. What is here put on trial is the very existence of man. The fear of extinction, uncertainty and insecurity has created severe debacles in all circles of human existence. Literature in the 20th century is thus concerned with the probing of the problem of man's isolation, alienation and thus its ensuing result, antiheroism.

The secular power structure exploded religion as a myth weakening the roots of man's religious sensibility. In the *Myth of Sisyphus*, Camus remarks on the shocks that came with the death of traditional values:

> A world that can be explained even with a bad reason is a familiar world. But, on the other hand, in a universe suddenly divested of illusions and lights, man feels an alien, a stranger. His exile is without remedy since he is deprived of the memory of a lost home or the hope of a promised land. (p. 13)[12]

Such a world has necessarily generated a deep sense of isolation and insecurity in man who is confronted by a total absence of spiritual and moral values. Isolation, a part of human nature, is aggravated by the vicious atmosphere and the destructive economic and political forces prevailing in the 20th century. The system into which man is born and is conditioned is both indifferent and neutral. Eliot's phrase "an immense panorama of futility and anarchy" aptly represents the postmodern situation.[13]

One may ask how does the contemporary hero conforms to the role of an antihero? And why? Does he have a choice? Is he denied a chance through which he might have proved his heroism? For answers, a brief retrospective of the characters in the previous chapters may be helpful.

The first chapter discusses Golding's Jack Merridew and Alan Sillitoe's Arthur Seaton, grouped together because of their anarchistic and rebellious tendencies, but the point of difference consists in their reaction when they come face to face with chaos. Endowed with more than an angelic voice, and the characteristics of the other angel, Lucifer, Jack is Golding's representative of the morally degenerate man, a child with potential satanic characteristics—pride, lust for power, and irrationality. He is the tyrant leader, inscrutable, ruthless, melancholic and with an insatiable will. He is also the defiant antihero, an opposer of society's definition of heroism or goodness. Jack, the demonic hero victim creates meaning by blindly asserting his will.

Jack Merridew as the chief chorister is analogous to Satan as an Archangel. Like Satan, he is a "perfect intelligence operating imperfectly".[14] He insists on his due like Dionysus, coming from an alien tradition; what sets him apart from the other boys in the island is his educational background. He is a prefect, a chapter chorister and probably a scholarship student, he considers himself unique.[15]

Jack's hatred for his dialectical opposite Ralph arises from the fact that the latter possess some innately good qualities, which Jack wants, but cannot possess. However, Jack is simply not an antihero because of his regression to anarchistic primitivism. Jack fails as an actual hero and becomes the antihero because of the choices he makes and because of a failure in moral vision. Evil is one of the aspects of the satanic antihero and Jack's image gives a terrifying insight into the human capacity for evil. As an antihero Jack is situated in the postmodern space revealing the catastrophic tendencies of man in his destruction of the island, which sustains him and the other boys. He has complete disrespect for order. Like Mugo, he also exemplifies the urge to destroy the object which threatens his identity. Jack feels threatened by the other—the total loss of selfhood by being overshadowed by Ralph. His world is a Kurtzian world of primeval power acquisition and gratification. Jack is at once brilliant and depraved, corrupted yet fascinating, charismatic, and like Kurtz, a literary descendent of Satan.

Sillitoe's Seaton is rebellious but this rebellious non-conformity is born out of dissatisfaction with a genuinely disappointing milieu. As Sillitoe's alter ego, he gives a voice to things that obstructs the path to a normal and easy life. He is a teddy boy, a working class man who divides life between mindless work and equally mindless weekend pleasures. Coming from the wrong end of the town, Seaton is a boor, without etiquette or education; when he finds that his way of life is threatened by his neighbor, Mrs. Bull's incessant gossip, he does not have any misgivings about shooting her, and then threatening to beat her husband when he confront Seaton. Nor does he have any guilt in simultaneously two timing the two sisters, Brenda and Winnie. It is not without reason that his brother Fred says that he could be a "real bastard" at times. But Seaton senses the moral and social confusion that he is surrounded by. This is well-illustrated by the Christmas celebration which he spends at Aunt Ada's. Spent in meaningless noise and revelry, it makes Seaton strongly aware of the chaos around and within him, and it also brings the awareness that truth, chivalry and heroism do not have much importance in this world and that the only way to exist is to accept thing as they really are. Seaton is an eiron, a man who makes himself invulnerable and "distrusts the ability of anyone's reason".[16] He has an irresponsible and a *carpe diem* attitude towards life. Uncommitted Seaton wanders through society, searching for some value to which he can attach himself, and seeking to discover who and what he is. As an eiron, Seaton enjoys a limited degree of freedom and makes an uneasy truce with necessity.

Like Seaton, Biswas too is a picaresque eiron and also an alazon. He is both self-derisive and quixotic. An important characteristic of an eiron is that he employs irony to expand consciousnes of his situation, evoking possibilities where only limitations exist. Unlike the scapegoat, he does not derive his being from martyrdom and defeat. Rather, he asserts his humanity by accepting the dissolution of heroism, by maintaining the dialectic between how things are and how they could be.[17]

As a rebel, Biswas at first refuses to accept less than the full share of his life. In the Tulsi household, he is a drifter, an outsider whose presence or absence does not matter. He exists only as an upsetter of routines. Biswas, the dandy, belongs to the "Omphale" archetype, a man bullied or dominated by women.[18] He is the denied antihero whose status and essential otherness makes heroism impossible. As a displaced man, Biswas represents man at the most vulnerable, physically weak and ugly, socially powerless without money, status or family support. His search for security and a concrete identity takes him to extreme lengths even at the end of which, Naipaul does not grant him the pleasure of complete satisfaction. The house that he has bought is overpriced landing him in debt; it is not the romantic house that he had envisioned and he cannot claim total ownership as he has to mortgage it. That Biswas is not a hero can be deduced from a statement quoted in the chapter relating to Biswas. "Mr. Biswas is simply not worth all the details that Mr. Naipaul spins so laboriously around him...he is rather a stupid man...also cowardly and ugly, definitely not the kind of stuff heroes are made of."[19] Finally, the nadir of his disappointments is Anand's desertion, symbolizing the son's refusal to be a part of his failed father's life. It also concretizes Anand's statement as a child when he saw his father as a weakling and as a failure, "I don't want to be like you when I grow up".

Biswas, the antiheroic dandy, is modeled on Naipaul's frustrated father. Seepersad Naipaul existed in three planes—reporter, a reformer and a Hindu; each role making nonsense of the other,[20] a man who "for thirteen years did not have a house of his own" creating a kind of insecurity in him. The grotesque in the novel is the result of collusion, multiple intrusions and shocks, which are psychologically threatening to Biswas. These devices serve to show him as irreverent to the natural order of things.

Both Biswas and Mugo are marginal men, existing between two different worlds. Mental and physical colonization is strongly responsible for creating insecurity in them. Ngugi's Mugo is anomalous in the traditional African society. A complex character, he is a hyper romantic antihero. Various reasons can be put forward for his selfish act of betrayal of Kihika. Mugo, the antihero is the Ngugi weak man standing as a stark contrast to the Christ like, beacon hero, Kihika. Mugo's selfishness obfuscates the need of the community and the nation. Ironically, in his idealized world he dreams of leading the same community to salvation whose interest he has so ruthlessly and cowardly crushed. Both Biswas and Mugo have an idealized image of themselves in their minds which is very far away from their real, puny, and in the case of Mugo, morally runtish self. The novel charts the causes and effects of the betrayal on Mugo. Rather he is a man driven by his irrational and chaotic impulses. He confesses his moral crime in the end, and in doing so rejects the dream of leadership and the messianic role that he had always longed for. He comes across as an unbalanced antihero having both mental and emotional deficiencies. There is a confusing mess in Mugo's head. He is surrounded by the sense of inexplicability of his own action and an absurd non-sensical reality.

If one tries to categorize Mugo, he will, like Biswas and Jack Merridew fit the category of an alazon, belonging to the same dramatic type as Synge's Playboy of the Western World, and Conrad's Kurtz. According to Frye, an alazon, Greek for imposter, is someone who pretends or tries to be something more than he is.[21] Obsession here takes the form of an unconditioned will that drives its victim beyond the normal levels of humanity. The alazon is an imposter in the sense that he is self-deceived/deluded by hubris.[22]

Having misdirected ambition and jealousy, Mugo is motivated into an act of betrayal by envy. Can his act be seen as a parallel to Satan's act over the choosing of the Son? In his imagination, the power, respect and fame that Kihika commands should have been his own. Kihika's complete trust in him was his subconscious opportunity to strike back, to destroy. Like Satan in Eden, glory and renown are foremost in Mugo's and Jack's mind. Like Jack, Mugo is tainted with unbridled ambition, envy, revenge, and a desire for personal aggrandizement. However, Mugo's jealousy, hatred for Kihika, the urge to destroy him and the implacable resolution to succeed are founded on despair.

Biswas, Mugo and Jack, in a way feel isolated from the social group to which they try to belong. It is a study of a isolated mind, broken by a conflict between the inner and the outer world, between imaginative reality and the sort of reality which is established by a social consensus. For them, this is the root idea of misery, leading to buffoonery, dandyism, betrayal and anarchy.

With Beckett's Molloy and Graham Greene's Scobie, we enter the realm of metaphysical rebellion. A similarity between the authors is their ambivalence regarding God, His presumed benevolence, the cruelty of the world and its ensuing absurdity. The difference between the two characters lies in their attitude to suicide, while Scobie resorts to suicide to save others and himself from pain, Molloy decides to live on because for him, death is not an end of suffering. Like Dostoyevsky's alienated antihero in *Notes form Underground* (1864) Scobie and Molloy rage against the optimistic assumptions of rationalist humanism.

Scobie is a plethora of doubt, ennui and boredom. Inhabiting the purgatorial battleground between good and evil, Scobie is an antihero of a different league; he is in a way, a holy gull, affirming and negating the presence of God at the same time. He is a good but a very weak man. Whereas the other antiheroes, apart from Molloy, are assertive to an extreme degree, Scobie exceptionally is unassertive, accepting every tribulation stoically. But his main weakness is his pity, which draws him to the cardinal sin of pride. He remains an inarticulate Prufrockian failure. He is Greene's most complex character, because whereas some see him as a potential saint, others find his heresy demonical. Before his fall, Scobie emerges as a character trapped within his own inevitably and repeatedly fall prone nature. As a man who considers himself hunted by his guilt, Scobie is necessarily an outsider to the Church as he is unable to expiate what he thinks is his sin. His sin, however, is not adultery but pride. In his pity and unconscious pride, he places himself as a superior being, a dispenser of peace, responsible for everybody's happiness and well-being, even God's. He is a rebel who, in the end offers himself as the victim, the hopeless victim of love, pride and pity. He is the modern, postmodern "Christian martyr who can aspire to perdition".[23] Graham Greene's Scobie is a "pharmakos". According to Northrop Frye,[24] the pharmakos is neither innocent nor guilty. As a pharmakos-protagonist, Scobie is a postmodern character because he holds the ambivalent position where one cannot exactly state whether he is saved or damned. Interestingly, in refusing to judge him, Greene has placed him in the postmodern space from whereon he continues to generate much controversy.

In the competitive world of Sierra Leone, Scobie is an isolated being suffering from both mental and spiritual alienation. What he seeks is the concrete human love of God, peace and solitude, not the cold dogmas offered by the church, but is confronted by treachery, doubt and suffering. He tries to evade suffering by trying to make life easier for others but this evasion exposes him more to the fact of social, mental and metaphysical isolation. Scobie is seen as a social failure by his wife because in his inglorious career as a Deputy Commissioner, he fails to get promoted to the coveted post of Commissioner, as a spiritual and mental failure he sees himself responsible for the pain he is causing others including God.

Deprived of all characteristics that would make him seem master of the situation, Beckett's Molloy can be construed as a character only if one follows his continuous monologue. Steeped in existential philosophy, he is what Hassan describes as a metaphysical jester negating everything around him. Molloy is a reverse of the great adventurer Ulysses; he is a tramping wanderer, in search of an elusive destination, which in his case, is his mother whose whereabouts he does not really know. Will-less, impotent and spiritually arid, he can be described as the Cartesian Centaur split between his mind and body. Almost unaware of any standards in life, he is engulfed by the infinite universe, which wears him down, beneath his endless misery. In the novel, Beckett divides Molloy into Molloy and Moran, both of whom are antiheroes trying to fulfill their failed quests which ends so bitterly that in the end they are left with nothing, not even answers to their several hows and whys. In Molloy one can also recognize the familiar figure of the clown and the bum before one sees him as a metaphysical clown and an intellectual bum whose humour tantalizes, and distresses. Recoiling from the external world, Molloy is engrossed with his self and his crippling body. Love means nothing to him, but there is an incestuous streak in his attitude towards his mother. He can be described as an aging antiheroic male with a clown like uniform, infected scalp, which embarrasses him no end, sensory confusion and the failure to communicate. He has a complete lack of heroic qualities, and in some instances, comes across as a merciless, cruel and a blasphemous character.

The impotence that Beckett's deprived, ruined characters sense so keenly and return so consistently is spiritual as well as physical.[25] Molloy's and Moran's journeys are mental explorations of reaching the same state of collapse. Molloy's tale concerns his own misadventures, a crippled, amoral former tramp whose fear-ridden existence has led him finally to shelter, to an ironic rebirth out of the chaos of existence. For the condition towards which he has been unwittingly striving, the estate of his bed-ridden, incontinent and perhaps now dead mother represents both primal innocence and ultimate inanity: the sublimation of the self in a new sort of school. But Molloy is not even ready for or capable of the final surrender.[26]

Subject to imperceptible decay, both Molloy and Moran lack the constraints of a particular identity. Unlike the traditional novelists, Beckett describes his characters' subjective experience as it appears to their disturbed mind. By focusing on men who are in the process of wasting away, Beckett presents an image of the human condition uncluttered by superfluous detail. Fletcher writes, "Man is best seen then, when his passions are largely dead".[27]

The above discussions of the protagonists perhaps would be enough to demonstrate that they are by nature antiheroic. Since they are studied in the postmodern frame, one needs to see the relation that exists between antiheroism and postmodernism. It needs to be mentioned again that though the novels have been, more or less, written in the conventional pattern, yet they have been discussed from the postmodern point of view because of the presence of a number of a postmodernist elements in them. Since the antihero reflects fragmentation, anarchy, chaos, and nihilism, perhaps it is only in the ironic postmodern world that the antihero can be accommodated.

For Hassan, postmodern literature moves, in nihilistic play or mystic transcendence towards a vanishing point, staring at madness. If literature reflects life, then it shows the level of mental and moral degradation into which contemporary society has fallen. Man is obsessed with his search for identity, peace, security and harmony between self and society—elements that seem to elude him eternally. This terror, the pressure, the ambivalence and the meaninglessness of life has created frustration, revulsion and recoil, transforming a potential hero into an antihero.

The problem of the antihero from Merridew to Molloy is essentially one of identity. He seeks existential fulfillment, freedom and self-definition. In its search for identity, the self is led through the dark undersides of experience. It is attended by an acute sense of personal anxiety, a feeling of rage, loss and despair. The ideas of victimization, rebellion, and alienation remain central to western literature since the turn of the century. The self is ineluctably fragile and insecure, and the autonomy and individuality of the self are fictions sustained by the community. Individual identity thus exists in a precarious social frame. Autonomy of the self is undermined because society always impinges on the self. The postmodern world being a Nietzschean world of multiplicity, opposition, and contradiction, man does not feel at home in this chaos and so turns to various methods of adjustment. The individual identity that man creates for himself is constantly in a state of chance contingency with all that surrounds him, and both he and his circumbient world are wholly ungrounded, making for a condition of fundamental absurdity.

For each character, this world is absurd, inexplicable. Sartre declared that human beings seek a rational basis for their lives which they are unable to achieve, so that human life is a "futile passion". For Camus, absurdity means life lived solely in a universe which no longer makes sense, because there is no God to resolve the contradictions. According to Nietzsche, suffering is not man's problem, but the lack of reason for his suffering, to the lack of answer to the question "why do I suffer?" Nietzsche[28] writes:

> Man, the bravest of animals and the one most accustomed to suffering does not repudiate suffering as such, he desires it, he even seeks it out, provided he is shown a meaning for it, a purpose of suffering. The meaninglessness of suffering, not suffering itself, was the curse that lay over mankind....

The absence of God makes man forlorn, because he does not find anything to cling to. Man is condemned to be free. Condemned, because, he did not create himself, yet in other respects is free, because, once thrown into the world, he is responsible for everything he does.

The search for a concrete identity, the spurts of madness, schizophrenia, anarchy, violence, negation of reality are all interconnected. In a world devoid of God or meaning, these antiheroes try to create meaning on their own. Their extreme stances of selfhood bring out the nihilistic and existential elements in them. In many cases, they are anti-institutions and anti-authority. In modernist fiction, the disintegration of a character gets revealed; postmodern fiction generally takes this disintegration to a stage further, often playing with the conventions governing the representation of character in works of fiction so as to expose this to the reader's scrutiny.

Schizophrenia and madness results when 'reality' becomes unendurable. It is easily discernable in Mugo, Biswas, and Molloy. The split in personality occurs because of an inability to mediate between external society and internal truth, between the outer and inner selves. The antiheroes are able to envision an ideal but are unable to achieve it and this result in frustration. It is the bridge between the conflicts of pain and pleasure, between reality and the self, between power and love. Freud's idea of a split personality is that of a self-divided in its own house. Man is as much his own victim as he is a victim of society. The schizoid figures of the antiheroes are a grim reminder of the struggle and the inability to attain a concrete unified identity, an identity that is respected and acknowledged by others. It is to this end that Mugo strives for when he envisions himself as a leader of the community. He wants to gain respect by dint of his hard work. He undergoes periods of extreme turmoil and hallucination before and after the act of betrayal. Biswas too suffers from a bout of madness when he is unable to create a house for himself, an extension of his own personality and identity. Mugo and Biswas, as children feel despised, rejected and wretched. In Mugo's case, pain erupts in violence, and this violence destroys itself again. The inner boredom, frustration and anxiety of the disinherited self are reflected on the external level of existence in different forms of hysterical outbursts. As Mugo's naive desire for a heroic stature grows to an obsession, it threatens to swallow the reality around him. He projects a vision of himself in a messianic role that lacks any basis in reality. Mugo is initiated into moral complexity in his confrontation with conflicting sights. Acting out of egotistic self-interest, he betrays a basic tenet, and this inevitably culminates in self-betrayal, ending in an ambiguous act of self-destruction. Biswas too has an idealistic self-image which does not materialize because he lacks the adequate conditions to create it. They portray and explore the conflicting loyalties and multiple identities of "those who have been denied their cultural birthright".[29]

The antiheroes can be found exhibiting extreme mental stress such as ecstasy, outrage, madness, and mystic trance. In madness, with the terror of complete extinction, one is unable to separate reality from illusion. Instances can be taken from Biswas's period of madness and mental agony, Mugo's paranoia and Jack taking over the leadership from the democratic Ralph, where imagination appears in its negative capacity as a destructive and devouring force rather than one that creates and interprets. Biswas, Jack, Mugo, Molloy, Seaton are existentially isolated, remote from communal and human attachment. There is the division of romantic inclination, the apprehension of the external world with things as exactly as they are, and the pragmatic, practical necessity of dealing as far as possible in one's own terms.

Schizophrenia in postmodernism is a *fin-de-sicle* parody of a dualism inherent in the Western trend of thought where the self is defined as a transcendent rationality, which necessitates splitting of what is considered emotional, irrational. If ego is the product of culture as Freud argued, and if ego may only be defined in terms of separateness, impersonality containment and pure reason, then culture has produced only divided and deformed human beings. One can thus understand why the two main preoccupations of 20th century novelists seem to be culture and consciousness. In modernist and postmodernist literature, the disintegration of the world of man and consequently the disintegration of personality coincides with an ideological intention. Thus, angst, the basic modern experience, has its emotional origin in the experience of a disintegrating society.

Fredrick Jameson in *Postmodernism and Consumer Society*[30] connects schizophrenic tendency in postmodernism with a pervasive nostalgia. Often in Waugh's view, it is the nostalgia, which produces the desire to fragment the impossible yearning for the lost object of desire, which issues in the frustrated and atavistic smashing of the ideal object. Mugo's betrayal and the urge to destroy Kihika and Merridew's similar desire to hurt Ralph can be explained in postmodern terms. This is the fear of being overshadowed by the other, and so there is the desire to destroy that which threatens to annihilate oneself.

The unconscious is like a storehouse, storing experiences, especially inadmissible rational fears and socially unacceptable desires. The recognition by the conscious ego of these unacceptable contents is blocked by the superego, but these contents gain expression in disguised form through compulsive actions and what is of greatest importance for their interpretation, in dreams. This is explanation enough to understand Mugo's betrayal of Kihika, convincing himself that the latter was putting him in danger by involving Mugo in politics, and his obsessive, repetitive dreams where he sees himself as the chosen leader, where voices call out to him and his name 'Mugo' mingles with that of Moses.

Homelessness is a universal feature of the contemporary world, even for those inhabiting the metropolises of the world. The modern temper is characterized by introspection, anxiety and radical doubts about human freedom and dignity. Exile plays an important role in the development of contemporary writers. The insecurity of homelessness and alienation, a powerful influence on exiled writers is often reflected in their characters. Placelessness is a condition of the postmodern. It entails a lack of belonging, or loss of identity, often disorienting, leading to the loss of sense of reality. Rootlessness makes people manufacture identities and rituals and play at relationships. In the Absurd fiction of Beckett, there is alienation, angst, fear, solipsism; man is trapped in a meaningless universe, wandering goal-less, or in circles of habitual action, and it is in this that the postmodern temper is fully realized.

Michael Foucault writes that the "hero" in modern life is the dandy who has perceived the fundamental role of style in the creation of the modern. He is not the man who goes to discover himself, "he is the man who tries to invent himself".[31] Role-playing becomes an important factor in the search for one's identity, but this pushes one to the extreme state where one cannot distinguish between the real and the played identity. Biswas resorts to grotesque dandyism to gain acknowledgement. As a reporter he continually recreates himself and at the Tulsi household he plays the role of the absurd rebel and buffoon. But in spite of playing the role of the run-away husband, the crazy shopkeeper, the reformer, the sensational reporter and finally, the father, Biswas succeeds in gaining the readers' sympathy, not their admiration.

In *Lord of the Flies*, Jack plays the role of chief to the hilt. It is as if only by playing the role of a hunter and later the truant chief he would be able to define for himself a specific identity that is different from Ralph's. But role-playing brings out the latent evil that is in him, revealing him to be an antihero. However, he is pushed to this position. Ralph also plays a role in turning Jack into an antihero. He is given his choice of role, but Ralph regards hunters as inferior and also tries to determine how Jack will play it. Gradually, ineluctably, Ralph turns Jack into an antihero.

In his hallucinatory dreams, Mugo realizes the role of a messianic leader, believing that God has put him in the position of Moses, but in reality, he has none of the virtues of being a leader. He has the desire, but neither the selflessness nor the moral strength to turn it into a reality. When he is given a chance he bumbles and makes the wrong decision.

Similar is the case with Scobie, who carries on the role of the suffering martyr responsible for everyone's well-being at his expense. He tries to juggle his role as the upright, incorruptible policeman, thoughtful husband and the caring lover, but fails miserably. Near the end of the novel, as he sets up an elaborate plan to commit suicide, a small rational voice within him tells him to stop play-acting, but he is so tired, that he rejects life itself.

Existentialism, with its emphasis on individual existence, freedom, and choice, influenced writers in the 19th and 20th centuries. It lays stress on concrete individual existence and, consequently, on subjectivity, individual freedom, and choice, concentrating on the dark and somber aspects of human condition with its three Ds—dread, despair, and death. The action of time is one of ironic and eternal recurrence as it only serves to bring defeat. In existential fiction, the illusion of choice is maintained, though it brings no victory. Necessity becomes an inner compulsion, purposeless and self-destructive.

Choice figures prominently as a theme, largely depicting the reasons why the protagonists turn out to be basically non-heroes or antiheroes and how they came to make these choices. Humanity's primary distinction is the freedom to choose but these choices have not always turned out to be happy ones, and even if one tries one does not succeed in avoiding the chaotic void that lies at the center of all life. Choice is central to human existence, and it is inescapable; even the refusal to choose is a choice. Freedom of choice entails commitment and responsibility. Because individuals are free to choose their own path they must accept the risk and responsibility of following their commitment wherever it leads. After the betrayal, Mugo is unable to face the choice and the horrific result that it has brought. Several times, he tries to reason but gradually comes to accept his responsibility for it and suffers from tremendous guilt.

With such responsibility, one experiences a feeling of general apprehension, an unknown sense of dread. Anxiety leads to the individual's confrontation with nothingness and with the impossibility of finding ultimate justification for the choices she/he must make. Sartre's "nausea" can be used for the individual's recognition of the pure contingency of the universe, and "anguish" for the recognition of the total freedom of choice that confronts the individual at every moment. Angst, as a dominant existential condition, leads to an impoverishment, reduction and distortion of the image of man and of described reality, excluding everything lying beyond its own radius and particularly everything that invests man and his environment with social significance.

Existentialism speaks powerfully to the sense of 20th century as a chaotic and catastrophic era, in which certainties have been lost and man is faced with the abyss of nothingness or of his own capacity for evil. Extremity and existential dread are important in the works of William Golding, Graham Greene, Naipaul, Ngugi, Sillitoe, Beckett, and also of Joseph Conrad, who in this respect anticipates the modern 20th century *Zeitgeist*. The absurdity of the universe and its reality always evades adequate explanation and remains radically contingent and disordered. Existential doctrines have contributed much to the general ethos of postmodernism and affected a number of writers. Thus, the postmodern concern with the nature of fictionality arises in part from the sense that neither individuals nor reality as a whole can be adequately conceptualized.

Philosophers in the middle of the 20th century, especially Sartre, combined Marxism, existentialism, phenomenology, and a bit of Freudian psychoanalysis; these intellectual movements picturized the individual human being or his consciousness as alienated in contemporary society. The source of estrangement was sometimes capitalism (for Marxism), the excessively repressive social mores (for Freud), the scientific naturalism pervading modern western culture (for existentialism), or even religion.[32]

Alienation is a major factor in shaping a person psychologically, be it metaphysical as in Beckett and Greene, cultural as in Naipaul and Sillitoe or psychological as in Ngugi and Golding. Man is assailed by a presiding sense of alienation in the knowledge that he is an entity separate from all that surrounds him, left alone to create his values without any means of justification. The antihero suffers from anguish, he is the man who involves himself and who realizes that he is not only the person he chooses to be, but also a lawmaker who is, at the same time, choosing all mankind as well as himself, cannot help escape the feeling of his total and deep responsibility.[33]

These antiheroes suffer from a lack of solid anchoring. Most of the time, joy comes, as in Jack and Seaton, from always being in contradiction with the other or in total negation of all authority. Alienation creates a sense of stoicism and skepticism in the characters arising from the belief that each man is for himself. This often turns out to be negative and destructive, not only for themselves but also for others, a fact which turns to be fatally true for Scobie and Mugo in particular, and for the other antiheroes in general. The whole process of life for them is a Promethean attempt to change life and a Sisyphus like inability to attain it.

Postmodern fiction communicates a deeper sense of nihilism because it excuses no one from its purview. One has a sense of being overpowered by the agonizing awareness of an unstable universe, both natural and metaphysical, to which is added the relentless domination of man by the industrial world. The technique that expresses this marginalized vision can therefore be only a reductive one; to place man as an object in a world of objects, knowable at the surface or just below.

M.K. Ray[34] writes that the popular conception of morality before Nietzsche was essentially indisputable, anchored by the concept of a God outside the human machine, but later on, it became a necessary and effective human fiction subject to human readjustment, leading to an existential anguish. From the middle of the 19th century, the foundations of the understanding of the nature of humanity, of morality, of Enlightenment, and absolute certainties were so shaken that artists throughout the world developed a future shock, a sense that the old concrete view of the world and the meaning of life and existence had been taken away from them and a replacement had not yet arrived. For replacements, there was a bewildering array contending to be chosen.

With the change in perception, there is a change in the narrative, resulting from different world views, philosophies and ideologies. There is a parallel between the belief in an absolute God who sees everything and the writers' use of omniscient narrators. Loss of such a belief seems to have been paralleled by disenchantment with the possibilities of narrative omniscience.

In most of the novels discussed here, there are no extreme postmodern strategies, but each novel is informed by the mood of the postmodern, using contestory voices, challenging, by using ironic and parodic modes, the dogmatic ideas of what a man should be, and showing what he essentially is, and also expanding the concepts of personal identity. Distributed among the novels are the dislocating anachronological technique of frequent anticipation and flashback, in *A Grain of Wheat*, *Lord of the Flies*, and *Molloy;* the variations in tempo, again in *Molloy*, *Lord of the Flies*, *Saturday Night and Sunday Morning*, the occasional grotesque, in *Molloy* and *A House for Mr. Biswas* and the general atmosphere of dream and hallucination. This can be found in *Molloy*, *A House for Mr. Biswas*, *A Grain of Wheat*, and *The Heart of the Matter*.

A work of art may be unequivocal in content and structure and yet open to differing, even often contradictory interpretations. Though some of the novels may be technically conventional, the contents of these novels reveals them to be essentially postmodern in that they probe, subvert and ask questions. In these novels there is a play of chance and expression of total chaos and fragmentation. However, in doing so they have come to accept the chaos, anarchy and fragmentation that characterizes the contemporary world. Green, Golding and Beckett put forward the metaphysical questions about the existence of God and seek to find a purpose for suffering. Greene questions the right of man to live as well as to end his life, the sanctity of marriage and love. In Naipaul, one comes to a point where Biswas's past is not only falsified but also erased. In the novel, fact continually mocks fiction revealing the fears of the marginal man. Ngugi reveals the gap, the indeterminate relationship that exists between the signifier and the signified. He also combines the factual and folklore with the fictional to create a powerful work on independence and its resultant disillusionment. In Sillitoe, there is the use of postmodern, suspensive irony that allows Seaton to accept the absurd and uncertain world. Beckett is considered as the supreme example of the postmodern artist. His work continually moves towards a void trying to express which is essentially inexpressible.

The term "Postmodern" can be attached to almost any work that refers, directly or by allusion, to other texts; and that makes problematic the idea of "characters" and of a narrative that can lead to a fixed point and convey a fixed meaning. Focus is also shifted from idea to the language in which thinking is expressed. "I" or the unitary human subject is the very cornerstone of Western logic and philosophy. That the novelists see the protagonists not as whole characters but as fragmented beings, the "Blakean divided man", antiheroes who shift their roles frequently to adapt to the changing and the harsh realities of life illustrates the point that they perceive the idea of characters as problematic. The shifts in the roles are almost so sudden and frequent that at times, the protagonist himself does not know who or what he is. Another type of the problematic concept of a character occurs in Beckett's *Molloy*, wherein the reader is left in the dark whether Molloy and Moran are two different characters, or Moran is the split other self of Molloy or Moran turns to Molloy in the end. The situatedness of "I" as a concrete human self, with the ability of being related to, both spatially and temporally, seems to be undermined by these novelists here. The "I" has stood as a connotation of heroism and individualism throughout the centuries but now the very idea of the "I" seems to be questioned by both postmodernism and antiheroism. Both the stances refuse to accept the uniqueness of the human self seeing it more as a mass, not individually but as fragmented split being divided between the self and the other and incapable of any heroic action.

Postmodernism can be used in a wider sense to refer to a general human condition, or a society at large, as much as to art and culture. According to Jeremy Hawthorn,[35] post-modernism takes the subjective idealism of modernism to the point of solipsism, but rejects the tragic and pessimistic elements in modernism to conclude that if one cannot prevent Rome burning, then one might as well enjoy the fiddling that is open to one. Whereas modernists reacted with horror or despair in their perception of these facts, postmodernism reacts in a far more accepting manner, as Alan Wilde remarks in his essay "Modernism and the Crisis of Aesthetics". Post-modernism is a coming to terms with incoherence and alienation, "an indecision about meanings or relation of things is matched by a willingness to live with uncertainty, and to tolerate and in some cases to welcome the world seen as random and multiple, even at times, absurd".[36]

Several critics tend to see postmodernism as post-structuralism or to take the latter as a theory underlying the former. However, although poststructuralism has its effects on contemporary intellectual currents, the motivations behind postmodern literature or postmodern thought cannot be always satisfactorily considered under poststructuralist arguments.

Postmodernism is a response, direct or oblique, to the unimaginable that modernism glimpsed only in its most prophetic moments.[37] One is surrounded by fragmentation and anarchy everywhere. Irony becomes radical, comedy of the absurd, black humour, insane parody. One of the common features of postmodern, spiritual fiction is "recourse to the stylistic mode of the grotesque as a means of expressing the uncertainty of human knowledge and the vertiginous experience of always being suspended between finally unknowable redemptively comic or entropically tragic grand plots".[38] Beckett's tramps are aware that the desire for final explanation will always be a peep into the dark abyss, revelation undistinguishable from fantasy, reason a construction on the back of desperation. Beckett's and Golding's ambiguous and compacted style is an attempt to probe metaphysical truth in an age where language has largely lost its sacramental force.

The most perceptible feature in the works of Beckett, Greene, Golding, and Naipaul from that of other contemporary writers exploring much the same themes is that in the case of the former mentioned writers, the stylistic and formal qualities of their work reinforce the bleakness of the content. Form and content exist in a particular relation to each other, forcing the reader to a degree of experience. These writers offer little or no consideration that a neat and well rounded form can give to an otherwise disturbing material. Invariably such matter has had something unusual, the apocalyptic and even the bizarre. Bhatnagar draws attention to the Marxist critic Terry Eagleton's statement about the unusual perspective brought in by postmodern writers:

> Postmodernism takes something from both modernism and the *avant garde*, and in a sense plays one off against the other. From modernism proper, postmodernism inherits the fragmentary or the schizoid self, but eradicates all critical distance from it, countering this with a poker faced representation of "bizarre"

> experiences which resembles certain *avant garde* gestures.[39]

In postmodernism, there is basically a pronounced shift in the basis of characterization, from concentration on the outward to the inner, from the mode of action to the mode of concealed motivation, reverie, dream and atavism, from the traditional area of chronological time and outward space to the radically new dimensions of psychological time and non-linear and non-logical organization which is evident in the novels discussed here. Moreover, these novels do not move towards a predictable conclusion, and in almost all cases, eschew the traditional novel's sub-plotting. The thrust of the postmodern literary endeavour has been to jolt the reader into a fresh awareness of things free from halos or pre-ordained canonization. Postmodern fiction emerged at a time when the certainties that underpinned realist fiction had in their turn been underpinned.

Not following the conventional pattern, the novels blend the serious with the comic, the sacred with the ludicrous. The techniques of postmodernism are subversive of the established literary practices and these are often combined with "outrageous" subject matter. Beckett's work invariably has tramps and social outcasts as protagonists. Golding uses children to allegorize the fallen human nature, Ngugi has the indecisive and untrustworthy Mugo as an example of independent Kenya's future and the representative of modern British welfare society is the workingclass antihero Arthur Seaton. Postmodernism consciously chooses to dabble in experiences and ways of living which deviate in strong ways from the mainstream, are marginalized, and placed on the cultural, social and moral periphery.

With uncertainty reigning supreme, the most important feature becomes indeterminacy. This is, partly, a result of our sense of fragmentation. With Nietzsche's "Death of God",[40] the sense of fragmentation set in, and this process proves to be an ongoing one. In postmodernism, the traditional values are not only flouted, it has a pleasure principle, insisting on the pleasures of the moment, *monokronos hedonis,* [41] an element that is evident in the hedonistic and *carpe diem* attitude of Seaton and Jack Merridew.

In his essay on Beckett, Maurice Nadeau[42] writes that Beckett's literary production took a course that made him "abandon the conventional fields of literature and penetrate deeper into that zone of darkness, into that border region where language fails, where life and death meet, where existence and consciousness dissolve and the explorer's path leads to the ante-chamber of silence, of pure reality". Summing up, he says, "with Beckett, triumphant nihilism penetrates into the work of art itself; dissolving the thing it creates into a fog of meaninglessness. In the end, the author has not only made plain his intention not to say anything: he has succeeded in not saying anything. The sound of his voice in our ears is our own voice sought for and found at last".

An attenuation of reality underlies Beckett's stream of consciousness, which intensifies where the stream of consciousness is itself the medium through which reality is presented. It is often carried *ad absurdum* when one can rely only on the reliable Molloy. Attenuation of reality and dissolution of personality are interdependent. Underlying both is the lack of a consistent view of human nature. In some cases, man is reduced to a sequence of unrelated empirical fragments; he is as inexplicable to himself as he is to others. Lack of objectivity in the description of the outer world finds its complement in the reduction of reality to a nightmare. Nadeau states that Beckett's *Molloy* is the *ne plus ultra* of this development, containing a nightmarish quality of the same vision twice over.

Ihab Hassan[43] writes that Beckett pursues the vanishing form till it nearly vanishes. He is an apocalyptic and a supreme example of the postmodern artist, turning the malice of language against itself. The sounds and the silences in his work dramatize, in Cartesian parody, the very laws of thought; in bits and pieces, they summon universal man, *quidam*, "somebody; one unknown". For all its obscenity and scatology, Beckett's art is ascetic, achieved by the elimination of nearly all the equipment artists have been at such pains to invent. In his art, he has indeed renounced, despised, and derided all things. Beckett holds a definite transitory position. His modernism is radically made into something else, something postmodern. The modernist sense of apocalypse has returned with Beckett, who gives his art a futuristic dimension, one of openness to the next phase of experience which in part appears to threaten the writer's own place and position.

In his interview with Tom F. Driver, Beckett insisted that art must admit into itself "the mess" or "the confusion". It is not a mess you can make sense of...one can only speak of what is in front of him, and that now is simply the mess."[44] If the relation between form and chaos is the technical problem, which the artist must solve, the chaos itself is his continuing theme. "The chaos", simply means the absurdity of human existence.[45]

The deadpan repetition of meaningless rituals, with hat, crutch or stone, is a parody of all rhythm and order, the conception of the body as a machine is a denial of organic life, and the confusion of erotic and excremental functions is a repudiation of the vital, binding instinct.[46] Beckett's work is eschatological. The peace here is the peace of frozen silence. Beckett laughs at and with alienation and comes to the point of chaos, discontinuity and absurdity.

In his novels, Greene rarely uses any postmodern strategy. Compared to other novels, *Heart of the Matter* is a very conventional novel; there are no holes in the page, no formlessness of matter, yet Greene's treatment of the issues in the novel can be viewed in the postmodern mode. Despite his conversion to Catholicism, Greene shares a problematic relationship with religion and the church, a relationship which is true of his character, Scobie. The novel reveals his unorthodox religious views, as Scobie feels let down by the organized religion which fails to understand God's creatures.

Greene asserts on his right to represent people who usually hold no interest for others, to act as the devil's advocate, and to elicit sympathy for those who lie outside the boundaries of state approval.[47] Scobie, in himself is a postmodern character because of his ambiguous position wherein one cannot definitely judge him to because good or bad, redeemed or damned. The role of the Church is also subtly questioned, asking how far it has succeeded in being a mediator between God and His creation. By offering only cold dogmas, has it, instead taken God far away from the reach of ordinary man? Father Rank's closing statement in the novel makes the situation doubly ambivalent. The institutions of marriage and the sanctity of love are inquired into. Does one have to remain within an unhappy relationship, and be held responsible for the other's happiness, only because the Church does not sanction a separation? Does love only mean providing for others, getting nothing in return except boredom and suffering and further moral and spiritual confusion? If a man has a right to live, does he also have an equal right to end it? If Scobie's character is ambiguous, so is the ending of the novel. By refusing to judge Scobie on a social and a moral scale, Greene leaves a lot unanswered.

In his *Anatomy of Criticism*, Frye[48] makes a statement regarding Greene that can also be applied to *The Heart of the Matter*; he states that in Greene, one finds that there is a kind of intellectualized parody of the melodramatic formulae. This is an ironic comedy addressed to the people who can realize that murderous violence is less an attack on the virtuous society by a malignant individual than a symptom of the society's own viciousness. Greene lived on the dangerous edge of things, on the narrow boundary between illusion and reality where the uncomplicated pleasures of childhood existed side by side with the quick recognition of instability, cruelty and social order. To Greene, man is made up of dialectical contradictions, existing on the narrow boundary between loyalty and disloyalty, between fidelity and infidelity; it is the paradox that one carries within oneself.

Like Molloy, Biswas too views writing as a central act of self-definition. Naipaul also makes a direct connection between Biswas's attempts at freedom and the quality of language he uses ranging from ironic to abusive, to demonstrate that it is only during his carefree tenure as reporter under Mr. Burnett that Biswas achieves that free and heightened quality of life that he had failed to arrive at elsewhere. The ironic situation of the jobless Biswas painting a signboard "No hands wanted" and "No entry" hoping to get a reporter's job point to a colonial world where the outside denotes comedy. But an inner core probes the true reality of the shame, defeat, mental slavery, which stares back at the colonized. In an interview published in the *Sunday Times Magazine*,[49] Naipaul states that while other writers depicted ordered societies, his father's work showed him "that one could write about another kind of society" one that is raw, chaotic and centreless. Like his creator Naipaul, Biswas is aware of the incongruity between his situation and the language available to him for expression. When he sarcastically refers to his wife as Mrs. Samuel Smiles he is registering his own rejection of the appropriateness to the poor-boy-makes-good-myth he himself had once so strenuously adopted. Naipaul views Biswas in the light of opposition relating to tradition/modernity, western/eastern values, history/religion, myth and dependency/freedom resulting either in fragmentation or wholeness of identity. Naipaul seems preoccupied with a sense of "nihilistic disorder" behind the still chaotic surface of life and reality.

Repetition of words or phrases in various circumstances indicates a limited experience of language, intellect or imagination, conjuring the reality of a man unable to transcend his material fragmented existence. Naipaul sees the truth of modern life as an interplay between man's sensibility, situation and language. Structurally, the novel emphasizes the importance of the subjective sensible life as a foundation for identity. They explore the possibilities inherent in man's imagination and linguistic capacity to create a world out of the experience of absurdity. But this attempt also leaves him emptied out, alienated and facing the void experiencing the necessity for a fresh start.

By redeploying his father's story about the birth of Mohun to describe the fictional father's own birth, Naipaul is playing games with the fictional process. When at the end of the book he has created Anand as the child of his father's tradition, he has in essence created himself.[50] In ironic literature there exists an unstable relation between style and subject, between rhetoric and reference, so the style employed is epical whereas its subject is the buffoon Biswas. Without employing any desperately avant-garde technique Naipaul manages to bring out the ambiguities of the Third World. The epical pattern of the novel with Prologue and Epilogue but with a mock epical character can be considered as the post-modern way of mocking traditional novelistic forms. Based on the mock epic style, the novel suggests the different ways of looking at the text, narrated from a shifting point of view. It is also ambiguous, because of its open endedness, and because of its dense multiplicity.

A House for Mr. Biswas is autobiographical in various levels. Seepersad Naipaul was a major influence in Naipaul's life. Naipaul's story is dually autobiographical—one, as a portrait of his father, and two, that of himself developing as a writer/Anand. The lives of the son and the father are inextricably intra-linked and inter-related, with the fictional characters of Biswas and Anand. Born to a jobless, property-less father, who lived with his wife's family, Naipaul as a boy experienced shame and tension of his father's condition, who dangled all his life in half dependence and half esteem. An exact relationship is portrayed in the novel between Biswas and Anand. Naipaul too, as Anand acknowledges the defeated life of his father. Naipaul Sr. too could not bring himself to confront the "material and cultural dereliction" that surrounded him. Writing for him was "a way of concealing personal pain".[51] Biswas, as Seepersad Naipaul is thus the portrait of a man, totally broken down by circumstances and part of the dereliction he wrote about.[52]

The son shares the father's fear of extinction: "...his fear of extinction.... That fear became mine as well. It was linked with the idea of a vocation; the fear could be combated by the exercise of a vocation."[53] It is therefore no surprise that Seepersad Naipaul and Mr. Biswas try to construct and then hold on to their fragile identities through writing. As Anand retelling the story of Mr. Biswas, Naipaul narrates the story of his father's life, the dreams, the failures and the frustrations.

As a colonial who willed himself to become a writer in order to escape the colonial condition, and denying the confinements of nationality and history, Naipaul often speaks of the power of writing as an institution of self-development.[54] Identity, self-discovery, reclaiming of home and the past, return and arrival—all are linked to the art of writing. The first attempt at self-assertion and self-definition are threatened by failure because of the persistence of colonial mentality and the attempts to remain too timid. Writing for Biswas is an attempt to impress form upon the formless experience of his life.

Ngugi wa Thiong'o's *A Grain of Wheat* like Naipaul's *A House for Mr. Biswas*, also reveals a world of the marginalized, the mentally and the socially colonized. David Cook regards the interlocking of different phases of time in *A Grain of Wheat*, as essential to Ngugi's juxtaposition of the various aspects of the characters' lives, since he is concerned to "move out of a period of simple heroics into much more baffling and complex realities of our independence".[55] Construed as a montage of narrative passages, interior monologues, dialogue, recollection and anecdotes, the novel attempts to demonstrate how each character's present state of mind is the result of numerous past events and circumstances. Ngugi also refrains from taking an omniscient narrator's position, so the reader becomes aware of the character's inner lives at the same time that the characters grow to know themselves. The absence of a singular narrative voice also embodies the postmodern trait of foregrounding narrative collapse. Ngugi comes close to pastiche renouncing unity of style, with a montage of folklore, sudden flashbacks, etc.

Critics have noted that Ngugi's technique to temporal oscillation, and of delaying information within the narrative, suggests a profound debt to Conrad's narratives. The novel also marks Ngugi's firm commitment to Marxist thought; projecting a socialist vision that meshes with the religious metaphor alluded to in the novel's title and epigraph. Unlike Ngugi's previous fiction which sought messianic heroes, *A Grain of Wheat*, consciously reveals the weakness and limitations of its characters to be the result of material and social conflict. Simon Girandi[56] writes that the novel is the story of a man's mistaken heroism, and the capacity for betrayal can be read as an allegory for the culture of post colonialism.

In *A Grain of Wheat*, Ngugi presents a world which calls for historical and cultural repositioning, denying what Henry Giroux[57] calls a "comfortable sense of time and place", encouraging us to ask questions which are essential in postmodernism's "redrawing and rewriting how individual and collective experiences might be struggled over, felt and shaped". The position of the primarily white, male, Eurocentric view of both culture and history and its infallibility is questioned. As a work of fiction, Kessler states, Ngugi's multi-layered narrative demonstrates his overriding concerns with the blurring of boundaries, rejecting the idea of unified self, reclaiming individual and national histories, and rethinking the concept of tradition and heroism.

Another writer who projected his view of man as antiheroic and also used children as main protagonists, so far marginalized from the mainstream social and literary world, is Golding. He situates his characters at the intersection of grand and foundationalist but ultimately incommensurable and competing plots which can offer neither the comfort of absolute faith nor a release into a blithe and celebratory nihilism. He does not allow his characters either complete faith or to exult in his despair, placing them in a condition of the grotesque. This is a condition of hesitation where one can neither make a leap of faith toward God and redemption nor yet resign oneself to the materialistic determinism of scientific entropy. In such absurdity and mystery it may be impossible to tell the saint from the fool or the true mystic from the charlatan.[58]

Golding expresses his moral vision through literary but inverted motifs like odyssey, quest, journey to self-knowledge, and characters like castaways and overreachers, incorporating them into a narrative that ends disturbingly. Out of a potentially comic or tragic island literature, Ballantyne had chosen order; Golding chooses chaos. In refusing to coincide with his predecessor, Golding's Jack is hardly the "handsome, good-humoured" lad he was in his Victorian incarnation, and he reveals the natural human proclivity to evil that can subvert harmony and order. The *deux-ex-machina* ending, the gimmick, in the novel, is ironic and parodies the ending of the Coral islands. In *Lord of the Flies*, the story has to be pieced together from the scattered hints in the boys' conversation. In his rewriting of *The Coral Islands*, Golding declares the portrayals of the idealized English boys in their tropical island to be fake.

Lord of the Flies presents the world of nightmare, and the scapegoat, of bondage, pain, confusion, the world of perverted or wasted work. The demonic world is a society held together by a molecular tension of egos, a loyalty to a group or a leader which diminishes the individual, or contrasts his pleasure with his duty.[59]

From Golding's *Lord of the Flies* to Alan Sillitoe is a transition from a world of nightmare to a fast paced industrial world but which too is pervaded by menace and anarchy. And like Greene and Golding, Alan Sillitoe is, in a sense, a realist. Realism is the sum total of effects used by novelists to provide readers with a sense of life, where, the language of realism does not draw the attention to oneself. However, Sillitoe's themes and his treatment of it are radically postmodern. He projects a fast changing reality. Seaton and the other characters in the novel ignore the old, novel and conventional standards of sexual morality. The idea of maximizing pleasure pervades the tone of the whole novel, corresponding to *monokronos hedonis*.[60] But there is also an escapist trend behind this mindless hedonism. Seaton's short affair with Winnie, Brenda's sister, is a negligent attitude;[61] however, it can also because evaluated as an extreme form of defying moral values. Even after deciding to marry Doreen, Seaton's inner conflicts show that he has not solved his blurred anarchic thoughts. Open ended, the novel does not end on a winning post, starting as it does in the middle of things and ending with things much the same when it began.

Each text focused upon here, is a network that recalls many other texts and opens up a horizon of intertextuality, making references to different novels. The texts do not say anything determinate; mostly ending on an ambiguous note. They are full of multiple meanings which can be interpreted variously, depending on the reader's perception and mentality, education, tradition, and most important, culture.

This post-enlightenment world faces the question whether language in its present state can cope with what has occurred? Perhaps this is why the literary form has been moving towards formlessness because the conventional form of literature has not able to accommodate the apocalyptic crisis that our contemporary world faces. And even when the writer compromises the form with the content as with several writers who inhabit the transition territory between modernism and postmodernism, their works are replete with questions and doubts. For instance, for Beckett, chaos cannot be reduced to the shape of form. Rather, the artist has to find a form that accommodates the chaos, the mess. Post war writing argues for literature's value as an instrument for the examination of social values. The language of the novel mimes its way to desperate truths, dangerously veering towards absolute silence. Language in these novels has the echo of communicative despair, which is characteristic of the postmodern art form.

Language is inadequate in conveying ideas and it is impossible for an idea to be the same in different minds. Beckett demonstrates that language is of fundamental deception, as does Golding when he describes the final scene with the boys and the naval officer. When at first, the latter gets the response to his 'hullo' he seems satisfied but the traumatic reality of the island seems as if cannot be linguistically expressed, and its horrific dimensions can only be vaguely felt when Ralph breaks down. Language becomes a system of sounds devoid of meaningful content. Because the word is not the thing it indicates, one can believe one is speaking of something without any understanding of it, however, it is expressed, there remains a gap between the expression and its indication, between the signifier and the signified. These writers, Golding, Beckett, Naipaul, Ngugi, Sillitoe, and Greene, seem to say that art cannot always redeem, language covers as well as exposes the bloodletting of history, the Holocaust, the Great Wars, the racial divide and the steady degeneration of mankind into an abyss; sacrifice becomes suspect and authority corrupt. The artist is engaged in mediating between his fictions and the world about him. Language is both imperfect and arbitrary, but apart from silence, it is the only medium for conveying basic conditions of experience. Even when it lacks obvious sense, it is a gesture towards the significant if intrinsically inexpressible meaning.

Modernism tries to impose aesthetic unity on fragmentation, postmodernism parodies this pretension of order through language. Language does break down even in Sillitoe, when Seaton is beaten up unconscious by the swaddies. While recuperating, he faces a void, a nameless malaise, and is unable to express this unnamable malady through common language and recoils into a state, though temporary, of silence.

Postmodernism extends modernist uncertainty, often by assuming that reality is unknowable, and that language is detached from reality. Postwar and postmodern literature poses a radical crisis in art, language, culture and consciousness. Art, language and consciousness may seek to empty themselves as man recoils into a negative state of silence. Perhaps the best example to illustrate the condition of language can be taken from Golding's *Lord of the Flies* where Percival Madison is unable to recall his name in the end. It is also illustrative of the fact that language has no importance as chaos and anarchy take over the sanity of the world.

In the past, writers conventionally wrote about other people, about knights, nuns and warriors; heroes who loved, ruled and avenged evil, and were capable of sacrifice, about people in the grip of political, economic or social forces, and how they came out of it a stronger person, losing little and gaining all. In this idealized world, the mode of romance—heroes were brave and handsome, heroines, beautiful, and life was, more or less, free from the frustrations, ambiguities and embarrassments of ordinary life. People gained strength from faith in God, in each other and in themselves, and the writer with little imagination created everlasting tales. But things have changed a lot since then. The destructive enormity of the two World Wars led men to wonder and fear, faced as they were by the Holocaust and the threat of annihilation. Literature responds, as it has through the ages, to the threat of apocalypse, responding diversely, encompassing the full range of human possibilities under impossible human stress.

The responses of the protagonists are, no doubt antiheroic, as can be understood from the behaviour of the characters ranging from Merridew to Molloy, but the unheroic, ordinary, plodding apprehension and acceptance of "things exactly as they are" (*Lord Jim*, p. 161) seems undoubtedly necessary for continuing existence.

The present condition is a confused and liminal realm caught between hope and tragic determinism, where grand and heroic spiritual plots are continuously kept alive but simultaneously deflated and exposed as the sublimation of desires arising from the material and physical limitations of human corporeal existence.[62] Frye writes that the figure of the eiron is irony's substitute for the hero, and when he is removed from satire we can see clearly that one of the central themes of the mythos is the disappearance of the heroic.[63] The form gradually moves towards a silence which derealises the world, which fulfills the extreme states of the mind—void, madness, ecstasy, outrage, and mystic trance—when ordinary discourse ceases to carry the burden of meaning.[64]

Postmodern literature uses irony as a primary mode of expression, but is also abuses and subverts conventions. Art and literature have increasingly incorporated a sense of irony and skepticism towards art's traditional pretension to truth, high seriousness, and profundity to meaning.[65] The imagery of fiction is often dominated by cruelty and disorder, sparagmos and suffering. The fictional form tends to be correspondingly ambiguous as there are various points of perception and conflicting levels of meaning. Sparagmos[66] is the archetypal theme of irony. It is the sense that heroism and effective action are absent, disorganized or foredoomed to defeat, and that confusion and anarchy reign over the world. The rejection of the entertainer, whether fool, clown, buffoon, or simpleton can be one of the most terrible ironies of art.[67] Frye shows irony to be the form to which all other forms tend when disintegration takes place. The fictional pattern shows the antihero to be a child of ironies, parodying man's quest for fulfillment and definition, trying to mediate between bipolar claims.

The fictional pattern in the novels discussed is contained and self-reflexive, disordered and acknowledging the nakedness of man by a parody of manners, quests, social and religious absolutes. The 'hero' remains a clownish figure as in Biswas, Arthur, and Molloy or a marginal figure, as in Merridew, Mugo and Scobie, a creature of the underworld.

When the novel deals with a pharmakos, as with Scobie in *The Heart of the Matter*, the ironic mode veers near tragedy. Ruled almost by necessity, he enjoys little or no freedom of action. Hassan writes that the form of fiction is closed to any real change in the life of the hero; there is no chance of self-renewal. When dealing with the eiron, the form of fiction here is suspended and the ironic mode hovers between comedy and tragedy. An alazon enjoys considerable degree of freedom and gives the illusion of escaping from reality. In *A House for Mr. Biswas* and in *Lord of the Flies*, chance, the very form of the book seems to say, is the necessity which controls men.

In *Molloy*, the form is detached from its content by being treated ironically. The division of the pursuit in two parts, the failure of the pursuit, are obviously signs of its ironic treatment. Within each section of the novel, as the formal elements are extended, they tend to weaken and almost to disappear. Those initially realistic situation and concerns blur into nightmare of isolation, decay, panic and violence.[68]

By denying the truth of the first two sentences of his story, Moran confesses that his account is but a tissue of lies. In the pure narrator, comprising only of his words, and his experiences of nothing, Beckett expresses the impasse reached by the great Western Humanism. Even as the narrator-protagonist speaks, each word borrowed from the community of men, compromises the isolation of which he tries to speak.

In the context of a later postmodern awareness, the novels discussed reveal the need to recognize that history has many cunning passages; that the historicist universalism which promised salvation though a world telos where man plays God is precisely what has brought the suffering and the confusion. Human motivation cannot be reduced to rational explanatory schemes. Even if man tries to be courageous and act heroically, the result will be, in spite of his attempts, a failure.

A basic question that rises over the term "postmodernism" is how can something contemporary and hence modern, postdate the modern, being chronologically modern, but critically postmodern?[69] M.K. Ray writes that postmodernity, like modernity, is a matter of sensibility. The concept of reality changes with the developments of knowledge. Similarly, Hassan writes in POSTmodernISM,[70] that modernism does not suddenly cease so that postmodernism may begin; they now co-exist.

The term was used by Arnold Toynbee to mean the post WW I rise of mass society, in which the working class surpasses the capitalist class in importance. Toynbee classifies the postmodern age as the fourth and the final phase of history and as one dominated by irrationalism and helplessness, and nihilism. In this world, the self and the consciousness are discovered to be adrift, increasingly unable to anchor itself to any universal ground of justice, truth and reason, and thus is itself "decentered".[71]

The increase in skepticism concerning religion, history, civilization, human nature is further complicated by religious nostalgia, by the serving modes of faith and by the fast receding humanist hopes. Caught between the past and the present, it is a complex world where one can't deny either the past and conventional beauty, or the present, and the current technical social reality. Beckett insistently refuses to ground the text by continually undermining narrative authority, and it purposely encourages a nostalgic, wistful longing for a once present centre. There is also a full scale questioning of the concept of the heroic self and heroism; what is dismantled is the exterior posturing and its inner basis in the imagination.

Postmodernism is both a continuation and a break from modernism. In fact, one finds that there is nothing much that is novel in postmodernism that cannot we found in modernism, which is to say that the disturbing trends that one can see in modernism are taken to its extremities. Postmodernism despairs of human history, and abandoning the idea of a linear historical development tries to accept the chaotic anarchy and the fragmentation that is life today. This is a recurrent tendency throughout history to oppose and parody the conventional social norms and the dominant forces in a culture. In its literary sense, postmodernism may be defined as the movement within contemporary literature and criticism that calls into question the traditional claims of literature and art to truth and human value. Postmodernist texts relate parodically to traditions and conventions. Polemical, politically oriented criticism influenced heavily by neo Marxism, links postmodern literature and art to the present state of society. Discussion of literature becomes inseparable from an analysis of the existing socio-economic, capitalist, cultural system. In *Homecoming* (1972), Ngugi writes, "literature does not grow in a vacuum. It is given impetus, shape, direction and even area of concern by the social, political, and economic forces in a particular society.[72] Ngugi's statement reflects the basically Marxist proposition that the creative process cannot be free from the conditioning imposed by socio-historical forces.

Factors like the socio-political condition, the cultural stagnation, and spiritual aridity have contributed to this form of character formation. Contemporary fiction appeals to many because it interconnects three important areas of life—psychological, socio-economic and religious. In every age the theories of society and of personality have closely approached each other. If one is placed against/in an indifferent and an irrational world, coupled with his own weak nature and limitations, he would, rarely, be able to transcend over his adversities or circumstances, succumbing to the pressure. The ontological being of the characters cannot be largely distinguished from their social and historical environment. Their specific individuality cannot be easily separated from the context in which they were created. Modernism held that man was by nature, asocial, solitary, unable to enter into relationships with other human beings. In the postmodern context, this trait is extended and it becomes the inescapable, central fact of human existence.

The 20th century is characterized by social, economic, political, racial, civil, national, and international warfare, displacement, by the slow-motion collapse of social, political, and religious institutions, and by the decay of personal and communal morality. Psychologists have stripped the mind of nobility, of natural goodness, and even of competence in dealing with the outside world. Wisdom has been reduced to words and words to arbitrary conventions.[73] In such a condition, ruled by chaos and where language is rendered arbitrary, what is the relevance of the archetype? How does it serve as a common symbol to unify men across the world? As Jung explains, the archetype is a communicable symbol, common to all men because it is not acquired like language but is a pre-conscious, primitive expression that is universal as it derives from the fact that men undergo common and essential experiences.

The fact that the archetype is primarily a communicable symbol largely accounts for the ease with which ballads, folk tales and mimes travel through the world, like so many of their heroes and other archetypal characters. There are some symbols, images of things that are common to all men. They have a communicable power, which is potentially unlimited. Biswas is a Trinidad East Indian; Mugo, a farmer detainee in Kenya; Scobie, a British policeman in Sierra Leone; Molloy, a homeless wanderer in an elusive quest; Seaton, a lower middleclass workingman; and Jack Merridew, a twelve year old English prefect, chapter chorister and later a tribal warlord. If we look at each character, we will see no superficial similarity, but deep within their natures, each of them is in search of an identity, individual and social fulfillment, and pass through phases of role playing in his own failed quests.

Breaking down the barrier of culture, discourse, these characters have glimpsed the void in their own ways. They are all potential heroes who might have become great writers, leaders, religious and secular, had they not been faced with such circumstances in their lives and had they not made the choices they made. But theirs is a paradoxical life in that there is not much choice available to them, as they are propelled by their impulses, and doubts and the world that they find themselves in are so full of chaos, anarchy and meaninglessness. They are socially, mentally, emotionally fragmented characters unable to decide between the several courses of action, none of which will lead them to eternal happiness or salvation.

Hungry, bitterly ironic and introspective, the novels reveal a stark awareness of the paradoxical condition of a man's life and his inability to transcend it. In this postmodern age, one really does not have much choice, man is burdened with the knowledge that there is no meaning in anything especially suffering and that it is inescapable. This knowledge makes the modern protagonist cynical, nihilistic, antiheroic. A tale of a man slowly worn to death by disease, poverty, little cares, pithy pretensions, however piteous and dreadful it might be, would not be tragic or heroic in any sense. The antiheroic characters, from Beckettian tramps to Golding's fallen man, to Greene's hunted heroes and Sillitoe's angry young man—may be subtly different—but the difference is one of degree, each one in his own characteristic style impresses his disillusionment, failure and alienation—mental and spiritual.

The novels as well as the characters offer a concise iconography of contemporary and postmodern corruption and disorder in one way or the other. It also sums up the areas of experience that gained prominence in the light of historical events in the 20th century. They have in their various ways epitomized 20th century problems and mode of exploitation, corruption, and decadence. They invoke a humiliating chronological perspective, jolting the reader to circumspection. The novels in question strive to expose the hidden truths about human nature. The parallel movements of postmodernism and antiheroism seem to ascertain certainly radical changes. They seem to announce the end of rational inquiry into truth, the illusory nature of any unified, holistic self, the impossibility of a clear, unequivocal and absolute truth, the weakness of Western civilization and the oppressive nature of the modern institutions.

Jean Francois Lyotard writes in *The Postmodern Condition: A Report on Knowledge*,[74] that the narrative function, its great hero, its great dangers, its great voyages and its great goals have lost their relevance in the postmodern world. If literature is a mirror of the world, the present condition does not allow one to construct a brave, adventurous hero and to believe in him, except perhaps with the "willing suspension of disbelief". The knowledge that the antihero acquires is a postmodern one which helps him to refine his sensibilities to differences and to reinforce his ability to tolerate the incommensurable. Postmodernism opens with the sense of irrevocable loss and incurable fault. The history of religious thought in the west can be read as a pendular movement between seemingly exclusive and evident opposites. If there was, at one time, God, eternity, permanence, order, meaning, identity, affirmation, certainty, sanity, innocence, honesty, purpose; now there is materialism, change, chaos, absurdity, anarchy, difference, negation, uncertainty, madness, guilt, duplicity, and purposelessness. It is modernism and its extension in postmodernism that reflects its trend and it is the antihero who undergoes these experiences, not only in his external, social world but also within him.

With the use of stylistic polyphony, chronological, sudden shifts, and ideological indeterminacy, the novels seem to ask, 'are civilization and humanity durable'? These works of fiction challenge 19th century modes of perception and literary representation. The novels, *Saturday Night and Sunday Morning*, *A House for Mr. Biswas*, *A Grain of Wheat*, *Heart of the Matter*, *Molloy* and *Lord of the Flies* dissect and reassemble the activities and consciousness of the characters, who in their failings and virtues, appear to be ordinary and one of us. In the novels, the details change, but the tone of helplessness remains from Golding's horror at the human condition, to the desperation in Ngugi's Mugo and Greene's Scobie to the absolute dread and despair at the world of unconstructed reality in Beckett's Molloy. These works portray human activity as largely futile and human nature as indifferent, given to self-deception and illusory belief. Literature has been intensely concerned with the theme of alienation and it results from several events that occurred historically and culturally in western civilization.

In the contemporary postmodern novels, instead of a holistic image of man, the picture that emerges is that of a fragmented man deprived of his sense of identity, one that is not bound by a traditional background and its values but by the loose threads of a derelict civilization. The view of human nature that emerges from these novels is that it is unpredictable and perversely self destructive. Similarly, the world of the antihero is ruled by a variety of fantasies, instantaneous, comical and often dreadful. The alienation deepens the experience of affinities between the characters as well as the fact that they belong to a paradoxical world which is "extensively homogenized yet intensely fragmented".[75]

Each of the antiheroes discussed here in his own way illustrates the postmodern trait of rootlessness, horror, trauma, anxiety, anarchy, antinomianism and chaos. In a way, being an antihero and acknowledging a life of guilt and defeat, is the only way available to him to continue his existence, and some like Scobie choose a way out through suicide. Merridew, Seaton, Biswas, Mugo, Molloy and Scobie are not without qualities or passions but these have been rendered valueless in the chaotic and problematic world that they inhabit. The antihero is thus the subverting *etranger*; Molloy is a man without qualities, in fact, he might be any old beggar that one might chance upon in a street. In Mugo, he has the appalling face of a glimpsed truth—a commingling of hate and desire, the perception of an underlying and ungraspable horror of experience. He represents the unspoken, the buried side of human nature. The sense of compounded guilt and absurdity defines the point at which victimization and rebellion meet. The antihero in Jack Merridew and Seaton pitches himself to the terrible limits of experience, as Lucifer did. In Mugo and Merridew, the heroic yields to the perverted. The antihero

Scobie is a combination of saint and criminal, and Biswas, is a pure combination of rebel and victim. The freedom the antihero achieves is a criminal state of autonomy. These antiheroes seek freedom, but are horrified and repelled by it. They act in the full foreknowledge of their fatality. Recoil and retreat leads the antiheroes' selves in the ways of violence and alienation, augments its sense of guilt and absurdity and offers an objective standard for evaluating the worth of human action. As discussed in the preceding chapters, the antiheroes in the contemporary, postmodern fiction must be viewed in the perspective of estrangement and desire. In these characters, Merridew, Seaton, Biswas, Mugo, Molloy and Scobie, the antihero is both the clown and the scapegoat, is comic and elegiac, revolting and pathetic, and as always, he remains rebel, victim, outsider.[76]

The antihero is thus situated in a paradoxical and postmodern condition, his life is not only one of defiance, but at the same time also of the chaotic and the problematic condition that is life today. An archetypal figure, common to almost all cultures, the antihero represents our present day confusion and anguish of time, space and destiny. The postmodern condition can be defined by a kind of shattering and schizophrenia, which is a fact exhibited by the novels as well as the antiheroes discussed in this study. Though these novels are constructed with a solid base in realism, it does however reveal the acceptance of flux, chaos and anarchism. By presenting the alienated and asocial antihero, the opposite of the hero as its protagonists, they illustrate a defiance of the novelistic content; demonstrate a protest against traditional themes and in doing so shatters the great Monomyth "the myth of the hero".

NOTES

1. Hassan, "Paracriticisms, Postmodern ISM: A Paracritual Bibliography in Choone" (ed.). *From Modernism to postmodernism: An anthology*, 1996, Blackwell, USA, p. 292.
2. François Lyotard, Quoted by Edmund Smyth, *Postmodernism and Contemporary Fiction*, 1990, p. 14.

3. Hassan, *The Dismemberment of Orpheus: Towards a New Postmodern Literature*, 1971, N.Y.: Oxford University Press, p. 177.
4. Uri Margolin, "Characters" in Paul Schillinger (ed.) *Encyclopedia—I*, p. 197-200.
5. Kenneth Graham, "Conrad and Modernism", pp. 210-11, J.H. Stape, (ed.) *The Cambridge Guide to Joseph Conrad*, 1996, Cambridge University Press.
6. Chris Baldick, 1990: *The Concise Oxford Dictionary of Literary Terms*, Oxford: Oxford University Press, p. 11.
7. Hassan, Radical, 1961: *Radical Innocence: Studies in the Contemporary American Novel*, Princeton, N.Y.: Princeton University Press, p. 327.
8. Malcolm Bradbury, "The Novel", p. 321, C.B. Cox and A.E. Dyson, (ed.) *The 20th Century Mind, History, Ideas, and Literature in Britain III: 1945-1965*, London: Oxford University Press, pp. 319-47.
9. Hassan, *Radical Innocence*, p. 1.
10. Edith Kern, "The Modern Hero—Phoenix or Ashes", *Comparative Literature*, 10, 4, Fall 1958, p. 326, Panduranga Rao, p. 134.
11. Gindin, James 1963: *Post War British Fiction: New Accents and Attitudes*, London: Cambridge University Press, p. 235.
12. Albert Camus, 1955: *The Myth of Sisyphus* (trans. Justine O'Brian. 1975), Penguin Books, p. 13.
13. Gerald Graff, p. 236.
14. John Carey, "Milton's Satan", *The Cambridge Companion to Milton*, ed. Dennis Danielson, Cambridge University Press, 1989, p. 165.
15. Bernard F. Dick, *William Golding*. (Twayne English Author's Series) Rev. ed. Massachusetts: Twayne Publishers, 1997, p. 14.
16. Northrop Frye, *Anatomy of Criticism: Four Essays*. N.Y.: Princeton University Press, 1957, p. 40.
17. Hassan, *op. cit.*, p. 178.
18. Frye, *op. cit.*, p. 228.
19. "High Jinks in Trinidad", *TLS*, 29 Sept., 1961, p. 641, quoted by C.B. Joshi, p. 142.
20. Sudha Rai, *Homeless by Choice, Naipaul, Rushdie, Jhabvala and Judia*, Jaipur, Printwell, 1992, p. 32.
21. Frye, *op. cit.*, p. 39.
22. *Ibid.*, p. 217.
23. Hassan, *op. cit.*, *Radical Innocence*, p. 28.
24. Northrop Frye, p. 41.
25. Alvarez., *Beckett*, 1973, Fontana Modern Masters, G.B: Fontana, p. 56.
26. David Hayman, "Molloy or the Quest of Meaninglessness: A Global Interpretation", *Samuel Beckett, Critical Approaches*, 1975, p. 164.

27. John Fletcher, *Samuel Beckett's Art*, 143, Hannah C. Copeland, p. 78.
28. Nietzsche from the *Genealogy of Morals*, trans. Walter Kaufmann and R.J. Hollingdale, quoted Fredrick Cahoone, p. 128.
29. Gene M. Moore, J.H. Stape, p. 223.
30. Fredrick Jameson, in Waugh's *Practising Postmodernism/ Reading Modernism*, G.B., 1992, Arnold, p. 122.
31. Michael Foucault, *The Uses of Pleasure*, *ibid.*, p. 79.
32. Cahoone, *op. cit.*, p. 4.
33. Jean Paul Sartre, "Existentialism", trans. Bernard Fretchman in *Existentialism and Human Emotions*, 1985, quoted in Cahoone, p. 260.
34. M.K. Ray: *Studies in Literary Criticism*. Delhi: Atlantic Publishers and Distributors, 2001.
35. Jeremy Hawthorn, *Studying the Novel, An Introduction*, Edward Arnold, London, 2nd ed., 1985.
36. Alan Wilde, Modernism and the Aesthetics of Crisis in Patrccia Waugh (ed). *Postmodernism: A Reader*, Edward Arnold, London, 1992, p. 14.
37. Hassan, Cahoone, p. 395.
38. Waugh, Harvest, p. 104.
39. Bhatnagar, p. 5.
40. Nietzsche, "The Madman", Cahoone, p. 102.
41. M.K. Ray, *Studies in Literary Criticism*. Delhi: Atlantic Publishers and Distributors, 2001, p. 17.
42. Maurice Nadeau in Lukacs, *The Meaning of Contemporary Realism*, trans. John and Necke Mander, London, 1962, p. 66.
43. Hassan, "Imagination Ending", *The Dismemberment of Orpheus*, p. 210.
44. David H. Helsa, 1971: *The Shape of Chaos: An Interpretation of the Art of Samuel Beckett*, Minneapolis, University of Minnesota Press, p. 6.
45. *Ibid.*, p. 7.
46. Hassan, *Dismemberment of the Orpheus*, p. 227.
47. Greene, *The Other Man*, A.A. DeVitis: *The Art of Graham Greene*. Boston: Twayne Publications, 1954, p. 10.
48. Frye, Northrop: *Anatomy of Criticism: Four Essays*. 1957, N.Y.: Princeton University Press, p. 48.
49. *Sunday Times Magazine*, 26 May 1963, Gamini Salgado, 1995: "V.S. Naipaul and the Politics of Fiction", Ford (ed.) *The New Pelican Guide to English Literature*, 8. (pp. 305-15).
50. Gurr, Andrew, 1991: *Writers in Exile, The Creative Use of Home in Modern Literature,* Sussex, G.B.: Harvester Press, p. 82.
51. Naipaul, Foreword, p. 16, Joshi, p. 31.

52. *Ibid.*, p. 18, Chandra B. Joshi, p. 29.
53. Naipaul, *Finding the Centre*, p. 72, Sudha Rai, p. 33.
54. Renu Juneja, "V.S. Naipaul: Finding a Voice", *Caribbean Transactions: West Indian Culture in Literature*, Warwick University Caribbean Studies: Caribbean Macmillan, p. 149.
55. David Cook, "A New Earth: A Study of Ngugi's *A Grain of Wheat*", *African Literature: A Critical View*, 1977, quoted by Tim S. Woods, "*A Grain of Wheat* by Ngugi wa Thiong'o", *Encyclopedia of the Novel I*, p. 503.
56. Simon Girandi, "Ngugi wa Thiong'o", *Encyclopedia of the Novel II*, pp. 934-35.
57. Henry Giroux in Kathy Kessler, *Ariel*, 25, 2, April 1994, p. 230.
58. Waugh, Harvest, p. 104.
59. Frye, *op. cit.*, p. 147.
60. Ray, *op. cit.*, p. 17.
61. Özüm, Aytül 1995: "The Representation of the Working Class and Masculinity and Alan Sillitoe's *Saturday Night and Sunday Morning*", *JELL: Hacettepe University Journal of English Language and Literature*, No. 3 (pp. 39-50).
62. Waugh, Harvest, p. 103.
63. Frye, *op. cit.*, p. 228.
64. Hassan, *Dismemberment of the Orpheus*, p. 13.
65. Gerald Graff, "The Myth of the Postmodernist Breakthrough", (Triquaterly, 1973). Bradbury (ed.) 1977: *The Novel Today: Contemporary Writers on Modern Fiction*. G.B.: Fontana/Collins, p. 220.
66. Northrop Frye, p. 192.
67. *Ibid.*, p. 45.
68. J.D. O'Hara, *20th Century Interpretations of Molloy*, p. 19.
69. M.K. Ray "Postmodernism, An Introduction", M.K. Bhatnagar, *Postmodernism and English Literature*, 2001, p. 1.
70. Hassan, *Postmodernism A Paracritical Bibliography*, Cahoone, p. 387.
71. Waugh, *Practising Postmodernism/Reading Modernism*, p. 8.
72. Mala Pandurang, *Postcolonial African Fiction: The Crisis of Consciousness: 1997*, Delhi, p. 8.
73. J.D. O'Hara, *A Collection of Critical Essays*, Prentice Hall, Inc., Spectrum Englewood Cliffs, N.Y. 1970, p. 1.
74. Jean Francois Lyotard, *The Postmodern Condition: A Report on Knowledge*, in Cahoone, 482.
75. Hassan, *op. cit.*, p. 328.
76. *Ibid.*, p. 78.

Select Bibliography

Primary Texts

Beckett, Samuel 1955: *Molloy, Three Novels*, N.Y.: Grove Press.

Golding, William 1954: *Lord of the Flies*, London: Faber and Faber.

Greene, Graham 1948: *The Heart of the Matter*, England: Penguin Books with William Heinemann Ltd.

Hassan, Ihab 1961: *Radical Innocence: Studies in the Contemporary American Novel*, Princeton, N.Y.: Princeton University Press.

Naipaul, V.S. 1969: *A House for Mr. Biswas*, Harmondsworth, Penguin Books.

Ngugi wa Thiong'o 1967: *A Grain of Wheat*, London: Heinemann.

Shawcross, J.T., Burrows, D.J. and Lapides, F.R. (ed.) 1973: *Myths and Motifs in Literature*, N.Y.: The Free Press.

Sillitoe, Alan 1958: *Saturday Night and Sunday Morning*, N.Y.: Signet Books, The New American Library, Inc.

——. 1959: *The Loneliness of the Long Distance Runner*, Introduction by David Elloway. Heritage of Literature Series, Singapore: Longman Singapore Pub. Ltd.

Secondary References

Abrams, M.H. 1971: *From Blake to Coleridge: Natural Supernaturalism: Tradition and Revolution in Romantic Literature*, New York: W.W. Norton and Co. Inc.

——. (ed.) 1993: *A Glossary of Literary Terms*, 6th ed. Bangalore: A Prism India Ltd. Holt, Rinehart and Winston, Inc.

Acherley, Chris 1998: "Graham Greene", Schillinger (ed.) *Encyclopedia of the Novel I*, Chicago: Fitzroy Dearborn Publications, pp. 520-21.

Adamson, Judith 1990: *Graham Greene: The Dangerous Edge: Where Art and Politics Meet*, London: Macmillan.

Allsop, Kenneth 1964: *The Angry Decade: A Survey of the Cultural Report of the 1950s*, London: P. Owen.

Alvarez, A. 1973: *Beckett*: Fontana Modern Masters. G.B.: Fontana/Collins.

Anderson, L.R. 1978: "Ideas of Identity and Freedom in V.S. Naipaul and Joseph Conrad", English Studies, *A Journal of English Language and Literature*, Vol. 59, No. 6, pp. 510-17.

Babb, Howard S. 1970: *The Novels of William Golding*, Columbus: Ohio University Press, Faber Publication.

Baldick, Chris 1990: *The Concise Oxford Dictionary of Literary Terms*, Oxford: Oxford University Press.

Banerjee, Anuradha 1994: *Graham Greene: Ways of Salvation*, Varanasi: Gangs Kaveri Publications.

Barnard, G.C. 1970: *Samuel Beckett: A New Approach: A Study of the Novels and Plays*, London: J.M. Dent and Sons.

Baugh, E. (ed.) 1978: *Critics on Caribbean Literature, Readings in Literary Criticism*, London: George Allen and Unwin.

Beckett, Samuel and Duthuit, Georges 1949: "Three Dialogues" from Transition Forty-NiM 5, in Esslin, Martin 1980: *Samuel Beckett: A Collection of Critical Essays*, New Delhi: Prentice Hall of India Pvt. Ltd., pp. 16-22.

Berzongi, Bernard 1970: *The Situation of the Novel*, London: Macmillian.

Bharat, Meenakshi 2003: "Colonial Maladies, Postcolonial Cures? 'Sick' Politics in *A House for Mr. Biswas*",

Panwar, (ed.) 2003: *V.S. Naipaul: An Anthology of Recent Criticism*, Delhi: New Orientations, Pencraft Intl., pp. 67-78.

Bhatnagar, M.K. (ed.) 1999: *Comparative English Literature*, Delhi: Atlantic Publishers and Distributors.

Bhatnagar, M.K. and Rajeshwar (ed.) 2001: *Postmodernism and English Literature*. Delhi: Atlantic Publishers and Distributors.

Blackmur, R.P. 1955: *The Lion and the Honeycomb: Essays in Solitude and Critique*, A Harvest Book: Harcourt, Brace and World, Inc.

Bodkin, Maud 1973: "Archetypal Pattern in Tragic Poetry" *Archetypal Pattern in Poetry*, Oxford University Press. Shawcross (ed.) *Myths and Motifs in Literature*, New York: The Free Press, pp. 5-21.

Boxhill, Anthony 1975: "V.S. Naipaul's Starting Point," *Journal of Commonwealth Literature,* Vol. 10/1, pp. 1-19.

——. 1977: "Mr. Biswas, Mr. Polly and the Problem of V.S. Naipaul's Sources", *Ariel*, 83, pp. 129-41.

Bradbury, Malcolm 1972: "The Novel", C.B. Cox and A.E. Dyson, (ed.) *The 20th Century Mind, History, Ideas and Literature in Britain III: 1945-1965*, London: Oxford University Press, pp. 319-47.

——. (ed.) 1977: *The Novel Today: Contemporary Writers on Modern Fiction*, G.B.: Fontana/Collins.

Bree, Germaine 1975: "The Strange World of Beckett's 'grand articules'" (trans. Margret Guiton), in Friedman, Melvin J. 1975: *Samuel Beckett Now: Critical Approaches to his Poetry, Novels and Plays,* Chicago: University of Chicago Press, pp. 73-87.

Burgress, Anthony 1971: "A Sort of Rebels", *The Novel Now: A Student's Guide to Contemporary Fiction*, G.B: Faber Paperback.

Cahoon, L.E. 1996: *From Modernism to Postmodernism: An Anthology*. Massachusetts, U.S.A.: Blackwell Publishers.

Campbell, Joseph 1949: *The Hero with a Thousand Faces*, Meridian Books. World Publishing Company.

Camus, Albert 1955: *The Myth of Sisyphus* (trans. Justine O'Brian, 1975), G.B.: Penguin Books.

——. 1956: *The Rebel: An Essay on Man in Revolt* (trans. Anthony Bower), N.Y: Vintage.

——. 1962. "Hope and Absurd in the Work of Franz Kafka", Ronald Gray (ed.) *Kafka: A Collection of Critical Essays*, N.J.: Prentice Hall, Inc., Englewood Cliffs.

Camus, Albert 1972: "The Myth of Sisyphus", Sidney Thomas (ed.): *Images of Man: Selected Readings in Art and Ideas in Western Civilization*, Syracuse University: Holt, Rinehart and Winston Inc.

Carl, G. Jung 1974: "Archetypes of the Collective Unconscious", *20th Century Criticism: The Major Statements* ed. W.J. Handy, Max Westbrook, Life and Light Publication, New Delhi.

Castillo, Debra A. 1982: "Beckett's Metaphorical Towns", *MFS*, Vol. 28, No. 2, Summer, pp. 195-99.

Chambers, Ross 1963: "Beckett's Brinkmanship", *AUMLA, Journal of the Australasian Language and Literature Association*, 19: in Esslin, Martin 1980: *Samuel Beckett: A Collection of Critical Essays*, New Delhi: Prentice Hall of India Pvt. Ltd., pp. 152-68.

Christopher, Cooper 1970: *Conrad and the Human Dilemma*, London: Chatto and Windus.

Coe, Richard N. 1965: "God and Samuel Beckett", in O'Hara, J.D. (ed.) 1970: *Twentieth Century Interpretation of Molloy, Malone Dies and The Unnamable: A Collection of Critical Essays*. New York: Prentice Hall, Inc Spectrum: Englewood Cliffs, pp. 91-112.

Cohn, Ruby 1964: "Philosophical Fragments in the Works of Samuel Beckett" in Esslin, Martin (ed.) 1980: *Samuel Beckett: A Collection of Critical Essays*, New Delhi: Prentice Hall of India Pvt. Ltd., pp. 169-77.

——. 1973: *Back to Beckett*, N.Y: Princeton University Press.

Conrad, Joseph 1949: *Lord Jim*, Harmondsworth: Penguin.

——. 1995: *Heart of Darkness*, Delhi: Oxford University Press, with an Introduction by Maria Cauto.

Copeland, Hannah C. 1975: *Art and the Artist in the Work of Samuel Beckett*, Netherlands: Mouton and Company.

Cooper, Christopher, 1970: *Conrad and the Human Dilemma*, London: Chatto and Windus.

Crehan, Steward 1995: "The Politics of the Signifier: Ngugi wa Thiong'o *Petals of Blood*", Parker and Starkey (ed.) *Postcolonial Literature*, New Casebooks. London: Macmillian.

Cuddon, J.A. 1998: *The Dictionary of Literary Terms and Literary Theory*, 4th ed. G.B: Maya Blackwell.

Das, Bijay. Kr. 1984: *Colonial Consciousness in Commonwealth Literature*, (ed.) G.S. Amur and S.K. Desai: Somaiya Pubs. Pvt. Ltd.

——. 1995: "From Slavery to Freedom: A Study of V.S. Naipaul's *A House for Mr. Biswas*", *Aspects of Commonwealth Literature*, New Delhi.

Davidson, G.W., Seaton, M.A., Simpson, J. (ed.) 1986: *Chambers Concise 20th Century Dictionary*, New Delhi: Allied Publishers.

DeVitis, A.A. 1954: *The Art of Graham Greene*. Boston: Twayne Publications.

Dick, Bernard F. 1997: *William Golding*, Twayne English Author's Series. Rev. (ed.) Massachusetts: Twayne Publishers.

Drabble, M. (ed.) 1995: *The Oxford Companion to English Literature*, 2nd Rev/5th ed. Oxford: Clarendon Press.

Dostoevsky, Fyodor 1989: *Notes from Underground*, John Wiley & Sons Inc.

During, Simon 1995: "Postmodernism or Postcolonialism Today" (*Textual Practice*, 1987), Tiffin, Ashcroft, Griffiths (ed.) 1995: *The Postcolonial Studies Reader*, London, N.Y.: Routledge.

Eagleton, M. and Pierce, David 1979: "Attitudes to class in the English Novel" *Walter Scott to David Story*, London: Thames and Hudson.

Elloway, David (ed.) 1959: *Heritage of Literature: Billy Liar and The Loneliness of the Long Distance Runner*, Keith Waterhouse and Alan Sillitoe, Singapore: Longman.

Esslin, Martin 1980: *Samuel Beckett: A Collection of Critical Essays*. New Delhi: Prentice Hall of India Pvt. Ltd.

Finney, Brian 1998: "Samuel Beckett", *Encyclopedia of the Novel 1*, ed., Paul Schillinger, Fitzroy Dearborn Publishers, pp. 94-95.

Federman, Raymond 1975: "Beckettian Paradox: Who is Telling the Truth?" in Friedman, Melvin J. (Ed.) 1975: *Samuel Beckett Now: Critical Approaches to His Poetry, Novels, and Plays*, Chicago: University of Chicago Press, pp. 103-17.

Fiedler, Leslie 1952: "Archetype and Signature—The Relationship between Poet and Poem", *The Sewanee Review*, L X 2, Spring, Shawcross *et al.* (ed.) pp. 22-36.

Flack, Colin 1989: *Myth, Truth and Literature: Towards a New Post-modernism*, Cambridge: Cambridge University Press.

Fletcher, John 1964: *The Novels of Samuel Beckett*, London: Chatto and Windus.

——. 1975: "Interpreting Molloy" in Friedman, Melvin J. 1975: *Samuel Beckett Now: Critical Approaches to His Poetry, Novels, and Plays*, Chicago: University of Chicago Press, pp. 157-70.

Ford, Boris (ed.) 1996: *The New Pelican Guide to English Literature 7: From James to Eliot*, Rev. Ed. London: Penguin Books.

——. 1995: *The New Pelican Guide to English Literature 8: From Orwell to Naipaul*, Rev. Ed. London: Penguin Books.

Forster, E.M. 1941: *Howards End*, Epigraph, G.B.: Penguin Books.

Frazer, Robert 2000: *Lifting the Sentence: A Poetics of Postcolonial Fiction*. G.13: Manchester University Press.

Freud, Sigmund 1996: "Civilization and Its Discontents", Chap VI and VII (trans. James Starchey), N.Y. in Cahoon (ed.) 1996: *From Modernism to Postmodernism: An Anthology*, Massachusetts, U.S.A.: Blackwell Publishers, pp. 212-18.

Friedman, Melvin J. 1975: *Samuel Beckett Now: Critical Approaches to His Poetry, Novels, and Plays*, Chicago: University of Chicago Press.

Fromm, Eric 1973: *The Anatomy of Human Destructiveness*, Connecticut: Fawaeett Publications.

Frye, Northrop 1957: *Anatomy of Criticism: Four Essays*, N.Y.: Princeton University Press.

Frye, Northrop 1960: "The Nightmare of Life in Death" in O'Hara, J.D. (ed.) 1970: *Twentieth Century Interpretation of Molloy, Malone Dies and The Unnamable: A Collection of Critical Essays*. New York: Prentice Halls, Inc. Spectrum: Englewood Cliffs, pp. 26-34.

Garebian, Keith 1975: "V.S. Naipaul's Negative Sense of Place", *Journal of Commonwealth Literature*, Vol. 10/1, pp. 24-35.

——. 1984: "The Grotesque Satire of *A House for Mr. Biswas*", *Modern Fiction Studies*, 30/3, pp. 487-96.

Gasoirek, Andrezej 1995: *Post War British Fiction: Realism and After*, London: Edward Arnold.

Gera, Anjali 2003: "Strange Moves: Girmitya Turns Cosmopolitan", Panwar, (ed.) 2003: *V.S. Naipaul: An Anthology of Recent Criticism*, Delhi: New Orientations, Pencraft Intl., pp. 26-42.

Ghosh, Sishir Kr. 1974: *Modern and Otherwise*, New Delhi: DX Publishing House.

Gindin, James 1963: *Post War British Fiction: New Accents and Attitudes*, London: Cambridge University Press.

Girandi, Simon 1998: "Ngugi wa Thiong'o" in Schillinger, Paul (ed.) 1998: *Encyclopedia of the Novel and 11*. Chicago: Fitzroy Dearborn Publications, pp. 934-35.

Golding, William 1955: *The Inheritors*, London: Faber.

——. 1956: *Pincher Martin*, London: Faber and Faber.

——. 1961: *Free Fall*, London: Faber.

——. 1970: *The Hot Gates and Other Occasional Pieces*, London: Faber and Faber.

——. 1982: *A Moving Target*, London: Faber.

Goodheart, Eugene 1968: *The Cult of the Ego: The Self in Modern Literature*, Chicago: University of Chicago Press.

Graff, Gerald 1977: "The Myth of the Postmodernist Breakthrough", in Bradbury (ed.) 1977: *The Novel Today: Contemporary Writers on Modern Fiction*, G.B: Fontana/ Collins.

Greene, Graham 1936: *Journey Without Maps*, England: Penguin Books.

——. 1963: *The Ministry of Fear: An Entertainment*, G.B: Penguin Books.

——. 1969: "The Lost Childhood", *Collected Essays*, G.B.: Penguin.

Graham, Kenneth 1996: "Conrad and Modernism", in Shape, J.H. (ed.) 1996: *A Cambridge to Joseph Conrad*, London: Cambridge University Press, pp. 210-22.

Griffith, John W. 1995: "Joseph Conrad and the Anthropological Dilemma" *Bewildered Traveler*, Oxford: Clarendon.

Gurr, Andrew 1991: *Writers in Exile: The Creative Use of Home in Modern Literature*, Sussex: Harvester Press.

Halperin, John 1979: "Interview with Alan Sillitoe", *M.F.S.*, 25/2, pp. 175-89.

Harris, Thomas A. 1967: *I'm Ok, You are Ok*, N.Y.: Avon Books.

Hassan, Ihab 1971: *The Dismemberment of Orpheus: Towards a New Postmodern Literature*, N.Y.: Oxford University Press.

——. 1973: *Contemporary American Literature: An Introduction 1945-72*, N.Y. Fredrick Unger Publication.

——. 1975: "POSTmodernISM: A Paracritical Bibliography", (Paracriticisms: Seven Speculations of the Times), in Cahoone (ed.) 1996: *From Modernism to Postmodernism: An Anthology*. Massachusetts: Blackwell Publishers, pp. 382-401.

——. 1975: "From Paracriticisms", *From the New Gnosticism: Speculations on an Aspect of the Postmodern Mind* in Patricia Waugh (ed.) 1992: *Postmodernism: A Reader*, London: Edward Arnold, pp. 60-78.

Hawthorn, Jeremy 1985: *Studying the Novel: An Introduction*, 2nd ed. London: Edward Arnold.

——. 2000: *A Glossary of Contemporary Literary Theory*, 4th ed. London: Arnold.

Hayman, David 1975: "Molloy or the Quest for Meaninglessness: A Global Interpretation", in Friedman, Melvin J.: *Samuel Beckett Now: Critical Approaches to His Poetry, Novels, and Plays*. Chicago: University of Chicago Press, pp. 129-56.

Helsa, David H. 1971: *The Shape of Chaos: An Interpretation of the Art of Samuel Beckett*. Minneapolis, University of Minnesota Press.

Holbroke, David 1974: "Prostitution, Politics and Egotistical Nihilism", *Critical Quarterly*, 16/3, pp. 227-29.

Hughes, Peter 1988: *Contemporary Writers: V.S. Naipaul*, London: N.Y. Routledge.

Janvier, Ludovic 1966: "Molloy" (trans. J.D. O'Hara) in O'Hara, J.D. (ed.) 1970: *Twentieth Century Interpretation of Molloy, Malone Dies and The Unnamable: A Collection of Critical Essays*, New York: Prentice Halls, Inc. Spectrum: Englewood Cliffs, pp. 46-57.

Jencks, Charles 1996: "What is Post-Modernism?" in Cahoone (ed.) 1996: *From Modernism to Postmodernism: An Anthology*, Massachusetts: Blackwell Publishers.

Joshi, Chandra B. 1994: *The Voice of Exile*, New Delhi: Sterling Publications.

——. 2003: "Very Much My Father's Book: Autobiographical Elements in *A House for Mr. Biswas*", Panwar (ed.): *V.S.*

Naipaul: An Anthology of Recent Criticism, Delhi: New Orientations, Pencraft Intl. pp. 79-92.

Jospovici, Gabriel 1995: "Samuel Beckett: The Need to Fail", Ford (ed.): *The New Pelican Guide to English Literature 8: From Orwell to Naipaul,* Rev. Ed. London: Penguin Books, pp. 155-65.

Juneja, O.P. 1995: *Post Colonial Novel: Narratives of Colonial Consciousness*, Delhi: Creative Books.

Juneja. R. 1996: "V.S. Naipaul: Finding a Voice", *Caribbean Transactions: West Indian Culture in Literature*, Warwick University Caribbean Studies: Caribbean Macmillan.

Jung, Carl G. 1974: "Archetypes of the Collective Unconscious", William J. Handy, Max Westbrook (ed.): *20th Century Criticism: The Major Statements*, Delhi: Life and Light Publications.

Kamra, Sashi: "The Novels of V.S. Naipaul: A Study in Theme and Form" *V.S. Naipaul: Profile of a Literary Radical.* New Delhi: Prestige.

Kant, Immanuel 1992: "An Answer to the Question: What is Enlightenment" (trans. H.B. Misbet), in Cahoone 1996 (ed.): *From Modernism to Postmodernism: An Anthology*, Massachusetts: Blackwell Publishers, pp. 54-60.

Karl, F.R. 1975: *A Reader's Guide to Contemporary English Novel*, Rev. Ed. N.Y. Octagon Books.

Kenner, Hugh 1961: "The Cartesian Centaur", in Esslin, Martin (ed.) 1980: *Samuel Beckett: A Collection of Critical Essays*, New Delhi: Prentice Hall of India Pvt. Ltd., pp. 52-61.

Kermode, Frank 1971: *Modern Essays*, Fontana: Collins Books.

Kern, Edith 1959: "Moran-Molloy: The Hero as Author", in O'Hara, J.D. (ed.) 1970: *Twentieth Century Interpretation of Molloy, Malone Dies and the Unnamable: A Collection of Critical Essays*, New York: Prentice Halls, Inc. Spectrum: Englewood Cliffs, pp. 35-45.

——. 1975: "Black Humour: The Pockets of Lemuel Gulliver and Samuel Beckett", in Friedman, Melvin J. (ed.): *Samuel*

Beckett Now: Critical Approaches to His Poetry, Novels, and Plays, Chicago: University of Chicago Press, pp. 89-102.

Kessler, Kathy 1994: "Elements of Postmodernism in Ngugi wa Thiong'o's Later Novels", *Ariel*, 25, 2, April, pp. 75-90.

Lambs, B.P. 1987: *Graham Greene: His Mind and Art*, Delhi: Sterling Publications.

Lee, Alison 1990: *Power and Realism: Postmodern British Fiction*, London: Routledge.

Leventhal, A.J. 1963: "The Beckett Hero", in Esslin, Martin (ed.) 1980: *Samuel Beckett: A Collection of Critical Essays*, New Delhi: Prentice Hall of India Pvt. Ltd., pp. 37-51.

Levy, Eric P. 1980: *Beckett and the Voice of the Species*, Dublin: Gill and Macmillian.

Luckas, Georg 1962: *The Meaning of Contemporary Realism* (trans. from the German by John and Necke Mander), London: Merlin Press.

Lyotard, Jean Francois 1996: "The Postmodern Condition: A Report on Knowledge", in Cahoone (ed.): *From Modernism to Postmodernism: An Anthology*, Massachusetts: Blackwell Publishers.

Maini, D.S. 1984: "The Complex Fate of V.S. Naipaul," G.S. Amir and S.K. Desai (ed.): *Colonial Consciousness in Commonwealth Literature*, Somaiya Publication Pvt. Ltd.

Maugham, Somerset 1974: "The Lion's Skin", in M.G. Narasimha Murthy (ed.): *Stories British and American*, Hyderabad: Orient Longman Pvt. Ltd.

Mayoux, Jean-Jacques 1960: "Samuel Beckett and Universal Parody" (trans. Barbara Bray) in Esslin, Martin (ed.) 1980: *Samuel Beckett: A Collection of Critical Essays*, New Delhi: Prentice Hall of India Pvt. Ltd., pp. 77-91.

Mboukou, J.P. Makouta 1970: *Black African Literature: An Introduction*. Washington D.C. Black Orpheus Press. (trans by Black Orpheus Press, 1973).

McHale, Brian 1987: *Postmodernist Fiction*, London and N.Y.: Methuen.

Moore, G.M. 1996: "Conrad's Influence", Stape, J.H. (ed.): *A Cambridge to Joseph Conrad*, London: Cambridge University Press.

Mustafa, Fauzia 1995: *V.S. Naipaul: Cambridge Studies in African and Caribbean Literature*, Cambridge: Cambridge University Press.

Mutiso, G.C.M. 1974: *Socio-Political thought in African Literature, Weusi?* London: Macmillian.

Naipaul, V.S. 1962: *The Middle Passage: Impressions of Five Societies: British, French and Dutch in the West Indies and South America*, London: Andre Deutsch.

Nandan, Satendra 1996: "The Diasporic Consciousness from Biswas to Biswasghat", Harish Trivedi and Meenakshi Mukherjee (ed.): *Interrogating Post Colonialism: Theory, Text and Context*, Indian Institute of Advanced Study.

Narang, Harish 1995: *Politics as Fiction: The Novels of Ngugi wa Thiong'o*, New Delhi: Creative Books.

Nietzsche, Fredrick 1996: "The Gay Science" (trans. Walter Kaufmann) in Cahoone, L.E. (ed.): *From Modernism to Postmodernism: An Anthology*. Massachusetts: Blackwell Publishers, pp. 102-04.

——. 1996: "The Genealogy of Morals" (trans. Walter Kaufmann and R.J. Hollingdale) in Cahoone, L.E. (ed.): *From Modernism to Postmodernism: An Anthology*, Massachusetts: Blackwell Publishers, pp. 120-29.

O'Hara, J.D. 1970: *Twentieth Century Interpretation of Molloy, Malone Dies and the Unnamable: A Collection of Critical Essays*, New York: Prentice Halls, Inc. Spectrum: Englewood Cliffs.

O'Nan, Maratha 1971: Book Review of J.D. O'Hara, ed. *20 Century Interpretations of Molloy, Malone Dies and the Unnamable* by State University College, of New York at Brockport, Reviews, Recent Books, *MFS*, 316-19, Summer, 1971, 17, 2, pp. 264-68.

O'Prey, Paul 1988: *A Reader's Guide to Graham Greene*, London: Thomas and Hudson.

Ozum, AytUl 1995: "The Representation of the Working Class and Masculinity and Alan Sillitoe's *Saturday Night and Sunday Morning*", *JELL: Hacettepe University Journal of English Language and Literature*, No. 3, pp. 39-50.

Padhi, Bibhu 1984: "Naipaul on Naipaul and the Novel", 30/3, *Modern Fiction Studies*, V.S. Naipaul Special Issue, pp. 455-65.

Page, N. 1985 (ed.): *William Golding's Novels: 1954-1967*. Casebook Series, London: Macmillan Press.

Palmer, William J. 1979: "Book Review of Ronald De Vareka: Commitment as Art, A Marxist Critique of a Selection of Alan Sillitoe's Political Fiction", University of Uppasala, Stockholm, *M.F.S.*, Vol. 25, No. 4.

Palmer, Eustace 1979: "Ngugi's Petals of Blood", Eldred Durosimi Jones (ed.): *African Literature Today, 10, Retrospect and Prospect*, London: Hienemann; New York: Africans Publishing Co.

Pandurang, Mala 1997: *Postcolonial African Fiction: The Crisis of Consciousness*, Delhi: Pencraft Intl.

Panwar, Purabi (ed.) 2003: *V.S. Naipaul: An Anthology of Recent Criticism*, Delhi: New Orientations, Pencraft Intl.

Parker, M. and Starkey, R. (ed.) 1995: *Postcolonial Literature: Achebe, Ngugi, Desai, Walcott*, London: Macmillan.

Parker, Sidney: "The Egoism of Max Stirrer: Some Critical Bibliographical Notes", Mackay Society of New York; Source: The Internet.

Phelps, Gilbert 1995: "The Post War English Novel", Boris Ford (ed.): *The New Pelican Guide to English Literature 8: From Orwell to Naipaul*, pp. 413-21.

Pillai, A.S.D. 1991: *Postmodernism: An Introduction*, Tiruchirapalli, India: Theresa Publications.

Pilling, John 1976: *Samuel Beckett*. London: Routledge and Kegan Paul.

——. 1994: *The Cambridge Guide to Samuel Beckett*, G.B.: Cambridge University Press.

Praz, Mario 1969: *The Hero in Eclipse in Victorian Fiction* (trans. from the Italian by Agnus Davidson), London: Oxford University Press.

Pritchett, V.S. 1985: "Pain and William Golding" in Norman Page (ed.): *William Golding's Novels 1954-67*, Casebook Series, Hampshire and London: Macmillan.

Quinn, Martin 1962: "The Unheroic Hero—William Golding's *Pincher Martin*", *The Critical Quarterly*, 4/3, pp. 247-56.

Ray, M.K. 2001: *Studies in Literary Criticism*, Delhi: Atlantic Publishers and Distributors.

Rai, Sudha 1992: *Homeless by Choice: Naipaul, Jhabwala, Rushdie and India*, Jaipur: Printwell.

Rajan, B. 1973: "The Problem of Satan", A.E. Dyson and Julian Lovelock (ed.) 1947: *Milton's Paradise Lost* (Casebook Series), London: The Macmillian Press, Ltd.

Rao, K.I. Madhusudana 1981: "The Complex Fate: Naipaul's View of Human Development", Avadhesh K. Srivastava (ed.): *Alien Voices: Perspectives on Commonwealth Literature*, India: Print House.

Rao, Panduranga, 1987: "The Resolution of the Hero Identification in Ngugi's *A Grain of Wheat*", Dhawan, R.K., Dhamya, P.U., Shrivasta, A.K. (ed.): *Recent Commonwealth Literature II*, New Delhi: Prestige Books.

Ravenscroft, Arthur 1973: "Novels of Disillusionment" in William Walsh (ed.): *Readings in Commonwealth Literature*, Oxford: Clarendon Press.

Rosenberg, Ingrid Von 1982: "Militancy, Anger and Resignation: Alternative Moods in the Working Class Novel of the 1950s and the early 1960s", H. Gustav Klaus. (ed.): *The Socialist Novel in Britain*, Harvester Press.

Salgado, Gamini 1995: "V.S. Naipaul and the Politics of Fiction", Ford (ed.): *The New Pelican Guide to English Literature 8*, pp. 305-15.

Schillinger, Paul 1998: *Encyclopedia of the Novel I and II*, Chicago: Fitzroy Dearborn Publications.

Shakespeare, William 1969: *King Lear: The Complete Works*, The Complete Pelican Shakespeare, General Editor, Alfred Harbage, New York: The Viking Press.

Sharma, Govind Narain 1979: "Theme and Pattern in *A Grain of Wheat*", Eldred Durosimi Jones (ed.): *African Literature Today*, 10, *Retrospect and Prospect*, London: Hienemann, New York: Africans Publishing Co.

Sharrock, Roger 1984: *Saints, Sinners and Comedians: The Novels of Graham Greene*, U.S.A.: Burns and Oats.

Shipley, J.T. 1972: *Dictionary of World Literary Terms*, U.S.A.: Littlefield Adams and Co.

Singh, M.I. 2001: *V.S. Naipaul, Writers of the Indian Diaspora,* Jasbir Jain (ed.): 2nd edition: Rawat Publications.

Smith, Grahame 1986: *The Achievement of Graham Greene*, Sussex: Totowa; N.J.: Harvester Press: Barnes and Noble.

Smyth, Edmund 1990: *Post modernism and Contemporary Fiction*, London: Batsford.

Spears, Monroe K. 1970: *Dionysus and the City: Modernism in the 20th Century Poetry*, N.Y.: Oxford University Press.

Spurting, John 1983: *Contemporary Writers: Graham Greene*, London: Methuen.

Stape, J.H. (ed.) 1996: *A Cambridge Companion to Joseph Conrad*, London: Cambridge University Press.

——. 1996: "Lord Jim", *A Cambridge Companion to Joseph Conrad*, London: Cambridge University Press, pp. 63-80.

Stratford, Philip 1967: *Faith and Fiction: Creative Process in Greene and Mauriac*, Norte Dame: University of Norte Dame.

Subbarao, V.V. 1987: *William Golding: A Study*, Delhi: Sterling Publications.

Swain, S.P. 1999: "The Crisis of Identity: Naipaul's *A House for Mr. Biswas*", M.K. Bhatnagar (ed.): *Comparative English Literature*, Delhi: Atlantic Publishers and Distributors.

Thieme, John 1975: "V.S. Naipaul's *Third World: A Not So Free State*", *Journal of Commonwealth Literature*, 10/1, pp. 10-22.

Tiffin, Helen 1988: "Postcolonialism, Postmodernism and the Rehabilitation of Postcolonial History", *Journal of Commonwealth Literature*, 23/2, pp. 169-181.

Tiffin, Helen Ashcroft; B. Griffiths, G. (ed.) 1995: *The Postcolonial Studies Reader*, London, N.Y: Routledge.

Tompkins, Joanne and Gilbert, Helen, 1996: *Postcolonial Drama: Theory, Practice, Politics*, Routledge.

Valency, Maurice 1980: *The End of the World: An Introduction to Contemporary Drama*, N.Y: Oxford University Press.

Wagoner, David 1958: "The Hero with One Face", *A Place to Stand*, Indiana University Press. Shawcross et al. (ed.) New York: The Free Press, pp. 113-14.

Walcutt, C.C. 1966: *The Diminished Self: Man's Changing Mask—Modes and Methods of Characterization.* Minneapolis: University of Minnesota Press.

Walsh, William 1973: *Commonwealth Literature*, London: Oxford University Press.

Ward, A.C. (ed.) 1970: *Longman Companion to 20th Century Literature*, Hong Kong: Oxford University Press.

Watts, Cedric 1996: "Heart of Darkness", in Stape, J.H. (ed.): *A Cambridge Companion to Joseph Conrad*, London: Cambridge University Press, pp. 45-62.

Waugh, Patricia 1992: *Practising Postmodernism/Reading Modernism*, G.B.: Arnold.

——. 1992: "Modernism, Postmodernism, Feminism: Gender and Autonomy Theory" in Waugh (ed.): *Postmodernism: A Reader*, London: Edward Arnold, pp. 189-204.

——. 1995: *Harvest of the 60s: English Literature and Its Background, 1960-1990*, Oxford: Oxford University Press.

Weekes, Mark Kinkaid and Gregor, Ian 1967: *William Golding: A Critical Study*, London: Faber and Faber.

Weekes, Mark Kinkaid 1982: "Bone Flute? Or House of Fiction: The Contrary Imaginations of Wilson, Harris and V.S. Naipaul" in Douglas Jefferson and Graham Martin (ed.): *The Uses of Fiction*, Open University Press.

Werblowsky, R.J. Zwi 1973: "Antagonist of Heaven's Almighty King" A.E. Dyson and Julian Lovelock (ed.) (1952): *Milton's Paradise Lost,* (Casebook Series), London: The Macmillian Press, Ltd.

Wellershoff, Dieter 1963: "Failure of an Attempt at De-Mythlogization: Samuel Beckett's Novels" (trans. Martin Esslin), in Esslin, Martin (ed.) 1980: *Samuel Beckett: A Collection of Critical Essays*, New Delhi: Prentice Hall of India Pvt. Ltd., pp. 92-107.

White, Landeg 1975: *V.S. Naipaul: A Critical Introduction*, London: Macmillian.

Wilde, Alan 1987: "From Modernism and the Aesthetics of Crisis" in Waugh, 1992: *Postmodernism: A Reader*, London: Edward Arnold, pp. 14-21.

Woods, Tim S. 1998: "*A Grain of Wheat* by Ngugi wa Thoing'o" in Schillinger, Paul (ed.): *Encyclopedia of the Novel II*, Chicago: Fitzroy Dearborn Publications, pp. 934-35.

Worth, Katherine J. 1968: "The Angry Young Man", John Russell (ed.) 1963: *Look Back in Anger* (Casebook Series), London: Macmillian and Co.